Abide

JoAnn Durgin

Author's Note

~~♥~~

Dear Readers,

This seventh installment of The Lewis Legacy Series belongs to Catherine "Caty" Lewis, the youngest daughter of the Lewis family headed by Samuel J. Lewis, Sr. and Sarah Jordan Lewis, whose love story was told in *Prelude*, the prequel to the series. Caty was briefly introduced in *Awakening*, and she's very close to her oldest brother, Sam Lewis, Jr., the "Papa Bear" of my TeamWork Missions volunteer crew throughout this series.

Abide takes the series in a fresh and exciting new direction featuring the three youngest siblings in the Lewis family. In this book, you'll also be introduced to NASA shuttle commander, Will (*Pursuit*, Book 8, releases in the fall of 2016), as well as the youngest Lewis sibling, Carson, a seminary student (his story is told in *Assurance*, Book 11, the final book of the series). The Houston-based TeamWork members are featured in small roles in *Abide*, particularly Marta and Eliot Marchand, and you'll be brought up-to-date with familiar characters from the previous books.

When you reach the end of *Abide*, I hope you'll hold these characters close to your heart. Through the events in their lives, I like to show how a personal relationship with Jesus Christ can bring an inner peace and hope for the future that nothing, or no one else, can provide. As you read any one of my books, I pray you'll be challenged in your personal journey with our great and merciful God. And then continue to write the story of *your* life. After all, no one can write that story better than you!

Thank you for joining me in this latest adventure in The Lewis Legacy Series. And now, it's my honor and privilege to present *Abide*.

Blessings,

JoAnn Durgin
Matthew 5:16

Dedication
~❤~

In late May of this year, heaven gained a beautiful woman named Aubrey. She was a daughter, sister, grandchild, aunt, cousin, and faithful friend to many. Aubrey worked as a Neonatal Intensive Care Nurse in Texas for nineteen years, and she was beloved.

I did not know Aubrey personally. She was my acquaintance and friend on Facebook. I know she had several of my books, but I don't know if she ever had the opportunity to read them. That's not what's important.

When I heard the shocking news of her passing from cancer at a young age, one of the things that impressed me most was what a strong impact Aubrey made in her community. She was a shining light and witness for Jesus Christ, and her life truly epitomized the theme verse for my life and writing ministry:

> **Let your light shine before men in such a way**
> **that they may see your good works,**
> **and glorify your Father who is in heaven.**
> ~Matthew 5:16 (NASB)

The characters in **Abide** are impacted by the death of someone they lost to cancer at a young age. In the book, Caty and Caleb visit a field of bluebonnets in Brenham, Texas. I was writing that chapter when I learned of Aubrey's death. When I read through the many personal testimonies on her Facebook page, and when I noticed a group of her dear friends were gathering to celebrate Aubrey's life in Brenham, I wept. Tears of sadness but also tears of sweet joy. God used her mightily during her time on this Earth.

This book is dedicated to Aubrey and all those like her who fight the battle against cancer. Who is *your* Aubrey? Hug that person a little tighter, hold them a little closer. Cherish your time together, and thank the Lord for the *blessing* of having them in your life.

Books currently available in
The Lewis Legacy Series:
~~♥~~
Available exclusively on Amazon

More adventures to come!

Abide
Book Description
~~♥~~

Catherine "Caty" Lewis is thrilled to be home again with her family and friends. After working as a chief accountant for a multinational oil corporation in Dallas and then Lubbock the past five years, she's been transferred to their new world headquarters in downtown Houston. Before she can even inhabit her new office, she schedules a private meeting with the reclusive founder and CEO. Someone in her division appears to be embezzling funds, and Caty prays she's not the prime suspect.

After suffering a deeply personal loss, Caleb Reid is struggling to raise his precocious twelve-year-old daughter, Lauren, on his own. He moved to Houston for a fresh start and to escape the threats that have plagued him the past few years. Then quickly discovers he can't outrun them.

When these two meet, romantic sparks fly. Caty stares down fear with the kind of strong faith Caleb has neglected along the way. Can he risk endangering Caty in his fight against an unseen threat? Have the walls he's built around him and his daughter served to protect them or to keep others from getting too close to his heart?

Abide
An enduring love story
between a man and a woman.
A story of standing firmly on God's promises,
never giving into fear, and
placing our trust in the One
who is infinitely more capable.

Theme Scripture Verse

~~♥~~

John 15:4

Abide in Me, and I in you.
As the branch cannot bear fruit of itself
unless it abides in the vine,
so neither can you
unless you abide in Me.

Chapter 1

Early April 2007

This had to be one of the dumbest things Caty Lewis had ever done.

No, make that *the* dumbest.

She might as well sign her own pink slip and be finished with this phase of her life. If the worst case scenario happened, she could chalk it up to experience and move on to the next challenge. Unease rumbled in Caty's stomach, her nerves so tight she felt they might snap. Her professional reputation for remaining calm and unflappable under pressure could be in serious jeopardy.

Should she call and cancel her four o'clock appointment? No, no. Nerves were one thing, but she'd never been accused of being indecisive. Her accounting position for Belac, Inc. was her livelihood. Her *life*, actually. Maybe she should rethink her priorities, but she was a valued five-year employee with awards, stock options, and bonuses. After coming this far, she couldn't chicken out now. She'd requested this meeting with the corporation's reclusive CEO and founder for a specific purpose, and it was important. *That* needed to be her focus.

Shivering for reasons that had nothing to do with the temperature, Caty glanced at the high-rise building across the street. One entire floor of the building housed the newer, bigger Houston office of Belac, Inc., also now the corporation's *world* headquarters.

Think positive. You can do this.

As she tightened her grip on the handle of her briefcase, Caty's features settled into grim determination as she entered the downtown Houston crosswalk with a dozen other pedestrians. Head held high, she walked with renewed purpose. When she reached the opposite sidewalk, her steps slowed as she surveyed the office building. Narrowing her gaze, she silently counted the floors until they disappeared into the low-hanging clouds.

Whomp! Someone plowed into her from behind with the force of a linebacker, pitching her forward. Her briefcase flew out of her hands. With a small cry, Caty landed with most of her weight balanced on her right hand, fingers splayed on the sidewalk. *Ouch.* Her back would likely feel the aftereffects tomorrow. When she heard a ripping sound, she bit her lower lip to keep from groaning.

"Sorry, lady." A stocky man appeared by Caty's side and planted a beefy hand beneath her elbow. "You okay?" He helped her to her feet and then released his hold.

"I'm fine, thanks. My fault for stopping in the middle of the sidewalk." Saying she was *fine*, even when she wasn't, was her usual response. She also routinely apologized for things beyond her control, but this pratfall? Completely and totally her own fault. She hadn't been paying attention and could only blame it on a bad case of nerves.

A city bus rumbled by, spewing a cloud of black exhaust. Sputtering, Caty waved her hand and coughed. The man bent to retrieve her medium brown leather briefcase. To her horror, the case fell open and scattered the evidence of her innocence, so to speak, all over the sidewalk.

"Oh, no! Can you please help me? I can't lose those papers." Today, of all days, she'd neglected to lock the case? No doubt about it, she'd lost her mind. Spilling confidential Belac accounting records on the city streets? That'd do more than get her fired. Why, it'd probably be grounds for criminal prosecution.

Get those papers now! Bypassing embarrassment, she went straight into *preserving the job* mode.

Darting here and there, with the man working beside her and the aid of a few kindhearted passersby, Caty snatched up the papers as fast as she could before a gust of wind could carry them away. The saving grace was that the streets had dried from the earlier heavy rain.

"Thank you so much." Caty stuffed the last of the documents and spreadsheets back in her briefcase. After the man handed her a red folder with the most important data, she perused it quickly and blew out a sigh of relief. Everything appeared in order.

"You should be more careful," he cautioned. "You can't just stop walking in the middle of the sidewalk."

Caty nodded. "Trust me, I learned that lesson. I appreciate your help."

"Welcome." He gave her a gap-toothed grin. "You have a good day."

"You, too." Tucking the folder back in the briefcase, she clicked the locks in place. And checked them again. Then grimaced when she spied a dark scuff mark that hadn't been there when she'd left for the meeting an hour ago. It wouldn't matter so much if she hadn't bought the briefcase only two weeks ago in anticipation of her new downtown office.

Just a material thing. Not a big deal.

Lord, can you please rewind the clock and start this day over? The last five minutes would be good. Stopping in the middle of a busy sidewalk? Okay, *that* had to be the dumbest thing she'd done so far today, and perhaps in the entire past year. Hearing her cell phone, Caty stepped out of the path of oncoming pedestrians and quickly retrieved it from the pocket of her skirt.

She checked the display. *Sam Lewis.* Maybe her older brother would be the voice of sanity amidst the madness.

"Hey, Sam. Make it quick. I'm standing outside the building, trying to psych myself up for this meeting." Goodness, she was still shaking.

"You'll be fine," he said. "I'll be in the TeamWork office until five if you need to talk."

"I'll keep you posted." A sleek black Porsche 911 Carrera zoomed her way. Caty's eyes widened when she spied the standing water along the curb. The storm drain must be clogged, but the speed demon apparently didn't notice or care.

"Ohhh!" She jumped out of the way seconds before the car pulled to a stop at the curb and a spray of water splashed in a high arc over the pavement. Whew! That was close. She seemed to be tempting fate this afternoon. Not a good sign.

Feeling wobbly and off-balance, Caty glanced down at her feet. Wonderful. The heel of her right pump was loose and cockeyed. At nearly five foot ten, she rarely wore heels, but she'd splurged and bought expensive navy slingbacks especially for this meeting. Go figure.

"This is soooo not happening," she muttered under her breath.

"Should I ask?" Sam sounded slightly alarmed. "Caty? Everything okay?"

"I'm honestly not sure how to answer that." She moved one hand over her stomach and deep breathed a few times. "You wouldn't believe how many things have happened in the last five minutes alone. I hope it's not some kind of sign I should cut my losses, go back home, and wait to be summoned to the great throne room." As it was, if the current trend continued with the Reidco Oil account she managed for Belac, this meeting would be inevitable sooner than later.

Her oldest brother had the nerve to chuckle. "The CEO had the good sense to hire you, so I'm sure he'll listen to your concerns."

"Remember, *he* didn't hire me," Caty said. "I've never personally met the man. Matter of fact, I've never even seen a photo of him, although we're exchanged a few emails, and his tiny, illegible signature is stamped on all of the important corporate documents."

"Including your paychecks."

"Yes, that too, smart man." Timely reminder. "My point being that he's like a modern day Howard Hughes. Powerful and reclusive."

"I'm sure he works closely with his associates," Sam said. "I doubt they do anything without his direction. You might as well check out your new office while you're there in the building. Maybe it'll be ready earlier than expected."

Caty drew in a quick breath. "We'll see how the meeting goes first. That'll determine whether I'm feeling optimistic. Just pray I survive this day."

"Will do. Listen, I talked to Mom and Dad a few minutes ago, and they said to tell you they're thinking of you. Even though we know you can't tell us what's going on, we understand how important this meeting is, Caty Bug. It's not every day you request a personal meeting with the CEO and founder of the corporation."

"Try *never* before, but thanks." Did Sam have to use her nickname *now*? She already felt like a kid this afternoon. "I'd better keep moving. Hopefully, I'll call you later to let you know that I haven't been swallowed whole. If you don't hear from me—"

"Remember this: 'For God has not given us a spirit of timidity. But of power and love and discipline,'" Sam said. "It takes guts to bring your concerns to the top man in the corporation. You're following your instincts, and I admire your initiative."

Tears stung her eyes, and Caty breathed out slowly. "Sam, you are my anchor." Her older brother's tendency to be right a majority of the time, and his ability to spout Scripture at any given moment, could be annoying at times. But, of all her siblings, Sam was the one who'd always been there for her without fail.

"If I don't talk with you before Saturday morning, we'll be there to help move you into the townhome at seven."

"Thanks. See you then. Give my love to Lexa and the kids. I'd better go." After signing off, Caty tucked her phone back in her skirt pocket. Her right palm was lightly scraped and dotted with pinpricks of blood. *Yikes.* Quickly digging a tissue from her purse, she pressed it against the affected area.

What felt weird? She moved her right arm back and forth a couple of times. The ripping sound... A sinking feeling settled in her stomach. Reaching beneath the right arm of her jacket, Caty ran her fingers along the seam and let out a small groan of frustration when she felt a hole. Not gaping, but a rip about an inch long.

Oh, joy in the afternoon. What more could possibly happen? Never in her professional life had she felt so out-of-sorts.

Caty lowered her arm, feeling silly for touching her underarm on the busy city street. As it was, she'd been graced by some interesting glances from office workers and tourists.

"Miss, are you all right?"

Startled by the deep male drawl, Caty spun around a bit too fast, making her teeter on the loose heel. Wasn't one stumble enough for the afternoon?

Reaching for her, he steadied Caty with a hand on her arm. "Careful now." He waited a few seconds. "Okay to let go?"

"I think so, thanks. Just call me Grace." She smoothed her free hand over her hair.

"Bad day?"

Caty stared at him for a long moment as he released his hold. Where had he come from? A momentary panic hit her as she wondered how much he'd witnessed. Oh well, what did it matter now?

"I'm, um, a little embarrassed by being plowed down, nearly falling face-first on the sidewalk, and being fumigated by a city bus. Not to mention narrowly avoiding being drenched by a flashy car driven by a maniac with no apparent regard for pedestrians. And that's just for starters." She stopped and laughed under her breath.

"I'm sorry. You didn't need to hear all that. Suffering from a need to blabber apparently ranks right up there, too."

A few inches taller than her, Caty estimated the man to be in his mid-to-late thirties. He certainly fit the urban cowboy image—jeans, a tucked-in white dress shirt, and a well-worn brown leather jacket. His skin was sun-kissed with natural-looking color, his eyes shaded by dark sunglasses although the sky was overcast. Likewise, his jaw sported about a day's worth of new stubble. A tan Stetson sat pushed back on his forehead, revealing a few strands of thick, medium-length, dark brown hair. Most younger men didn't wear Stetsons in the city anymore unless they'd come in from the ranch, but she'd always liked the tradition.

Three boxes of Chinese takeout dangled from his hand. Now *that* was unexpected. Caty's gaze traveled to his boot-covered feet. He'd walked more than a mile in those boots. Another plus. If she thought she could get away with wearing her red cowgirl boots with her business suit, she'd have them on this second.

The corners of the man's mouth hitched. "Sounds like you've had quite a day, but I was referring to your hand."

"Oh, that." She held up her mummified right hand. The tissue stuck to the blood on her palm and fluttered in the wind. "This would be another result of my fall from grace. I'm not usually a complainer or so…seriously inept."

Resisting the urge to chew on her lower lip, Caty set her briefcase on the pavement. She yanked the tissue from her hand and stuffed it in the pocket of her skirt. Based on the warmth in her cheeks, they must be positively flaming.

"They have antibiotic cream and bandages at the front desk in the building straight ahead of you." He glanced down at her feet. "They might also have glue as a quick fix for that broken heel."

He'd noticed *that*, too? "I would not, could not, ask for glue. For my shoe." Shaking her head, Caty twisted her lips not to burst out laughing. The only other option was to cry.

"Dr. Seuss fan?" Oh my, he had a nice smile. A *kind* smile. Awareness rippled through her. *Lord, are you serious? You plant a nice guy in front of me now?* How was that fair?

"I suppose so. In spite of what you're probably thinking, I didn't have cocktails with lunch."

"That's not what I was thinking." He lowered his sunglasses. His eyes were a rich, medium brown fringed by long, dark lashes. The tiniest little lines feathered away from the corners of those eyes. Her heart thudded when her gaze rested on a platinum ring that occupied a significant finger on his left hand. Perfect. This day kept getting better with each passing minute. Of course, the ruggedly attractive cowboy was a married man. A guy like this was too great *not* to be married.

"If you have time before your meeting, my assistant is the master seamstress of the 35th floor, and she's helped me out a few times." He angled his head once more to the building ahead of them before returning his gaze to hers.

Her jaw dropped. Well, if that comment didn't make her even more self-conscious. Caty resisted the strong urge to touch her underarm seam again. "I appreciate your concern, but I'll take my chances." She looked the other way and blew out a sigh. "I have an important meeting in a few minutes, and I don't mind admitting I'm nervous. I appreciate your concern for a stranger, and your...powers of observation. Consider yourself duly thanked."

She might as well call it a day, drive straight home, and bury her head under her pillow. Pray for the blessed relief of sleep and hope she wouldn't be plagued by nightmares. Drowning her inadequacies with a pint of chocolate chip cookie dough ice cream sounded about right.

"Good enough, Grace." Turning to leave, he tipped his Stetson, causing her knees to inexplicably go weak. The gesture was a forgotten art with most men, symbolic of throwback chivalry from days long gone.

"It's Catherine. Caty, actually. That's what...most people call me." Why she felt the need to tell him that, she didn't know. Perhaps because he'd been kind enough to offer assistance. She wouldn't mention that her middle name was, in fact, Grace. At the moment, the name seemed not only inaccurate but sadly comical.

She didn't think it was her imagination that the cowboy's shoulders visibly stiffened as he faced her once more. He settled the shades back in place, masking his eyes.

"It's very nice to meet you, Caty. I'm...Abe." Instead of offering his hand, he tipped his Stetson once more. She tamped down disappointment he hadn't offered his hand, but it was for the best. The man seemed dangerous enough without actual physical contact.

"As in Honest Abe?" How silly. Her lack of conversational skills would surely be the end of her. Funny, she'd always considered her brother Will to be the inarticulate one. Guess again.

"It's Abernathy. An old family name."

She swallowed her inclination to smile. "Abernathy is distinctive. Memorable, although you don't really look like an Abernathy." She wondered why he hadn't offered his full name, but neither had she offered hers.

"I'm not sure *anyone* looks like an Abernathy," he said. "The name doesn't exactly roll off the tongue. It took me forever to learn it, much less spell it, when I was a kid." He hesitated a moment. "I have a confession to make."

What on earth? Kind and helpful or not, she was *not* looking for a married man who flirted with women on the Houston city streets. *If that's what he was doing.* Her confusion only added to the strangeness of the last few minutes. Maybe this was all a crazy dream.

Needing something to do, Caty retrieved her briefcase. "Don't tell me. You're my fairy…cowboy, come to save me from myself?" Her cheeks flooded with warmth. "Okay, that didn't come out at all the way I meant it."

"Calling you Grace was my underhanded way to get your real name." She appreciated the fact that he chose not to dwell on her last ridiculous statement.

Uncertain how to answer, Caty focused on a passing taxi. "Well, I'm clearly more comfortable with numbers than social graces. Thank you again. Not many people would have stopped to make sure I was all right."

"I try not to be like most people. It was very nice to meet you, Catherine Caty." *No, you're not like most people.*

"You too, Cowboy Abe. Enjoy your"—she motioned to the boxes in his hand—"Chinese."

"I trust your day will improve." With another respectful tip of his Stetson, he departed.

Caty stared after him as Abe walked toward the building. He didn't strut, didn't swagger. Somewhere in Houston was a mighty blessed woman. Then again, maybe not. Was he a smooth operator or a genuinely nice guy? A very thin line existed between flirting when a married man tried to help a single woman. The boundaries could become so easily blurred.

This is why you don't date much.

Caty shook her head, muttering to herself like a deranged person. She didn't have time to think about the cowboy. She had a mission to fulfill. They'd shared a nice moment, but it was time to move on. Right.

Squaring her shoulders, she lifted her chin. "All right now. Let's try this again."

Chapter 2

Caty started in the direction of the revolving glass doors. Her ankle wobbled, reminding her to be careful with the broken heel. Cowboy Abe had a great idea about the glue, but she might be late if she stopped at the front desk. For now, she'd have to make do and pray for the best.

She motioned for a young woman with a little girl to enter the revolving doors first. Although she was quaking inside, she could try to present the image of self-confidence. Once inside the massive lobby, Caty followed the woman and child toward the bank of elevators.

Stepping into the already crowded compartment, she punched the round BELAC button, and then squeezed in between two large gentlemen. When they stepped aside to give her more room, she caught the scent of competing masculine colognes. She prayed she wouldn't sneeze. Unlike most women, she was not a pretty sneezer. Or even a quiet one. Once the men exited the elevator—hopefully on the lower floors—she would breathe normally again.

Pinching her lips together, Caty ignored a man across the elevator car smiling at her with more than passing interest. *Look the other way, buddy.* Why couldn't he be a single, compassionate, Chinese takeout-carrying, handsome cowboy? She focused on the elevator control panel with the lit BELAC button with 35 listed beside it.

Wait a second. The cowboy mentioned the 35th floor. *Whoa.* Cowboy Abe worked for Belac? Why hadn't that computed until now? Her brain cells must have been momentarily frozen.

Could he possibly be... Did the *A* in A.C. Reid stand for Abernathy? That couldn't be possible. Abernathy couldn't be any older than his early forties, and that seemed a stretch. With the companies A.C. Reid had amassed, he had to be in his late fifties if not much older, although that was an assumption. As intensely private as A.C. Reid was, she doubted he'd be offering assistance to clumsy, inarticulate accountants on the street.

She had no idea what A.C. Reid looked like and no clue about his personal life. No photos of the man could be found in the corporate literature, only pictures of oil rigs and the Texas landscape.

The rumors swirling around Mr. Reid—from those who'd never met him—ran from speculation that he'd survived a horrible disfigurement while serving in the military to a theory he suffered from a debilitating social phobia necessitating that he conduct business behind closed doors in heavily secured areas. What prompted the move to Houston had likewise been the subject of rumors for which no one had a definitive answer.

Those who'd worked for him a long time kept their lips firmly closed. Whether out of respect or because they'd been paid off, she couldn't know.

Be nice, Caty. Her sarcasm was running especially high today.

After the cologne-doused men exited the elevator together, the little girl moved closer to Caty and then handed an empty candy wrapper to the woman. *No, no, no.* Sure enough, those little fingers were smeared with half-melted chocolate.

Hoping to avoid another disaster, Caty inched closer to a woman standing on the other side of her who lifted a brow, clearly irritated by the unwelcome invasion of her personal space.

Trying to maintain a respectable distance from the child, Caty scooted back in the other direction. Would this elevator ride never end? She noted the woman had given the little chocolate lover a tissue to wipe her hands. Small comfort.

The little girl pointed to the BELAC button. "Look, Mommy! It's a belly button. Get it?" Then she examined it closer. "What does it say? Bellyache?"

"It's the name of my company. *Bell-ack*," Caty said. "I've just transferred here from the Lubbock office."

The woman smiled. "Welcome to the building. My husband works for Wells Fargo here on 25."

"We're taking Daddy to dinner. We come here every Wednesday." When the elevator doors opened, the girl pushed past Caty and then jumped with both feet onto the carpeted lobby.

The child's mother tossed Caty an apologetic glance as she followed her daughter off the elevator. "I'm sorry about your skirt. I'm sure the dry cleaners can get it out. Good luck in your new office." She mentioned her husband's name and told Caty to contact him so they could reimburse her.

"Enjoy your dinner." Caty pasted on a smile as the doors closed but refused to look at her skirt. Chocolate dried fairly quickly, right? The best she could hope for was to discreetly scrape it off with a fingernail before her meeting. And no way would she contact the woman's husband and ask him to pay her bill.

Always find the blessing in what you're given. No matter the circumstances, her mother had ingrained that sentiment in her. The best thing about *this* situation was that she'd worn her navy blue suit instead of the pale gray.

By the time the elevator stopped on the 35th floor, Caty was alone. The doors slid open, and she stepped onto a gray tiled floor. The entrance was impressive without being overly opulent.

A platinum-plated sign mounted on the opposite wall greeted her: WELCOME TO BELAC, INC. And then beneath it, FOR BY YOUR STANDARD OF MEASURE IT WILL BE MEASURED TO YOU IN RETURN. ~LUKE 6:38.

The corporate logo of an oil rig in the setting sun was etched into the frosted, double glass doors along with the six cities boasting Belac, Inc. offices: Austin, Dallas, Houston, Laredo, Lubbock, and San Antonio.

Lovely paintings of the Texas landscape adorned the walls— vibrant pieces of art featuring bluebonnets, one of her favorite flowers and also the state flower of Texas. The artwork provided a warm contrast to the more austere gray flooring and platinum fixtures.

When her phone rang again, Caty debated whether or not to answer, thankful for the reminder to set her phone to SILENT. Pulling it from her pocket, she glanced at the screen. *Marta Marchand.* Her good friend could always make her smile. Talking with her for a couple of minutes might help to calm her nerves.

She clicked on the phone. "Hi, Marta."

"Hey, Caty. Just wanted to check on you. Where are you now?"

Lowering her voice, Caty spoke in hushed tones like an announcer during a televised golf tournament. "Well, Marta, I'm currently standing in the elevator lobby outside the Belac, Inc. world headquarters."

Marta laughed. "Has anyone told you lately that you're a nut?"

"Today? Only me, but I'm sure a few pedestrians outside this office building would agree." Caty stepped closer to one of the paintings. "The lobby has gorgeous paintings. I wonder if they're bolted to the wall."

"And that matters…why?"

Stepping to the side of one of the paintings, Caty peeked behind it. "For one thing, it could reveal Mr. Reid's level of trust in his fellow man. Or *dis*trust, as the case may be."

"Interesting theory. And the verdict is…?" Marta's amusement was obvious in her tone.

"I can't see that they're bolted down, but I'm sure there must be surveillance cameras," Caty answered. "The way my day is going, if I touch one of these babies, loud alarms will sound and security will come running. Meeting my boss for the first time while cuffed and shackled would be memorable but regrettable. Not exactly the first impression I'm trying to make."

"Then keep your hands off the paintings. Listen, crazy girl. I'm praying for your meeting."

"You can't even know how much I appreciate those prayers." Caty's voice filled with emotion. "It's been quite the adventure so far."

"You're not getting weepy on me, are you? Dry those tears and be strong."

"I'm not crying. I'm just feeling…grateful. I appreciate your sense of humor. I need that in my life, especially now." She loved how Sam and Marta's prayer warrior instincts had kicked in when she needed them most although they didn't even know the reasons for this meeting. More like they *couldn't* know the reasons. The confidentiality clause she'd signed when she'd joined Belac prevented her from saying anything to anyone outside the corporation. She was nothing if not loyal.

"Give me the short version of what's happened so far," Marta prompted. "If you have time."

"The good news is that I'm still standing." Caty rotated her shoulders in an attempt to loosen her tight muscles. "Let's see. It involved a burly man, a fall, a scraped hand, a maniac Porsche driver, a broken heel, a handsome, helpful cowboy…"

Marta didn't need to hear the entire rundown of her mishaps, but a little sympathy sometimes helped. That was her only valid excuse.

"And to think some people think *my* life as the weekend weather girl is exciting," Marta said. "They obviously haven't met Caty Lewis yet."

"Believe you me, I much prefer my normal life as a boring accountant. I've never been so out of sorts, but does it have to be on the day I'm finally meeting face-to-face with my reclusive boss?"

"You're never boring, Caty. Now, go back to that helpful cowboy for just a sec—"

Caty sighed. "Apparently, he works for Belac, but he's also married. If you've got matchmaking on the brain, you can give up that idea."

"You never know. Maybe the cowboy has a handsome, helpful brother. Want to meet for dinner after your meeting? Eliot's out on a job, and I don't expect him home until late. I've spent too much time in the office lately, and I'm craving some serious girl talk. Have I mentioned how happy I am that you've moved back to Houston?"

"You and me both." Relief rushed through Caty. "Dinner sounds great, but I don't know how long this meeting will last. I'll call you when I'm done, but be forewarned in case I need a shoulder to lean on. Not cry on, mind you. Lean on."

"You've got it. Whatever you need, Caty, I'm your girl. As long as I'm in the studio by nine tonight, I should be fine."

That was a surprise. "Hold up a second. You're on *tonight's* broadcast?"

"I am. Brandy called in sick again—third day in the last two weeks. As far as I know, she's not pregnant, but I'm sure the producers have to wonder what's going on with her. I find it hard to believe she'd put such a great job in jeopardy."

"It sounds like you might be moving to the week*night* weather spot sooner than later."

"Could be. I should give Brandy a call. Maybe she needs a listening ear or a friend."

"I'm sure she'd appreciate it." A bell dinged and a young woman stepped off the elevator—every blonde hair in place, impossibly thin, impeccably dressed. With a polite nod for Caty, she walked toward an unmarked door at the opposite end of the hallway. After pulling a card from a pocket in her skirt and swiping it on the keypad, she disappeared inside.

Caty checked her watch. Five minutes to spare before her scheduled appointment. Her heart was pounding like crazy. Trying to slow it down was probably a lost cause now.

"I'd better get moving, Marta. I'll talk with you later."

"Sounds like a plan. Everything according to *His* purpose."

"Amen." Caty smiled at her friend's catchphrase—the same one Marta's husband, Eliot used—usually accompanied by a fist bump between Eliot and the male members of her brother's TeamWork Missions volunteer crew.

Disconnecting the call and pocketing her phone, Caty surveyed her reflection in the shiny elevator doors. Not bad, although by comparison to the blonde, she personified walking dishevelment. Before leaving her apartment, she'd taken great pains to ensure her hair and understated makeup were professional. Remnants of the tissue were still stuck to her hand. Ugh. At least her hair's long layers, framing her face and falling around her shoulders, still looked presentable.

Caty quickly ran her fingers over the buttons on her blouse. The way her day was going, it couldn't hurt to make sure they were intact. "Nice to meet you, Mr. Reid," followed by her blouse popping open, would be the ultimate humiliation. Next, she ran her hand down the side of her pencil skirt. The chocolate seemed to be drying, but she'd give it a few extra minutes for good measure.

Wetting her finger with her tongue, she scrubbed her palm. "Real hygienic, Caty Bug." After dropping the residue in her pocket, she glanced about the perimeter of the rectangular-shaped elevator lobby. In spite of what she'd told Marta, she hoped building security officers *weren't* watching her antics on surveillance cameras. If so, they were probably getting a good laugh.

"You are such a mess." Not much she could do about it now. She tossed a bright smile over her shoulder in case those cameras *were* in place. "Got all that?"

A.C. Reid, here I come. Ready or not.

Caty grabbed hold of the gleaming silver handle on the right door. Resistance. *Push, not pull.* So much for sophistication and making an entrance.

After pushing the door open, Caty stepped inside the spacious lobby. Her heels immediately sank into the beautiful Persian carpet while gleaming hardwood floors peeked out from underneath.

A dark-haired, exotic-looking Asian woman wearing bright red lipstick and a sophisticated headset sat behind a large circular desk. Speaking in low tones, she gave Caty a precursory nod of acknowledgment.

"I'll be happy to direct your call to Mr. Reid's voice mail." The receptionist listened and then nodded. "Very well. Thank you for calling Belac."

"Good afternoon." The woman eyed Caty with a practiced smile. "How may I help you?"

"Hi there. I'm Catherine Lewis, and—" When Caty took a step forward, her two-inch, cockeyed heel caught in all the plushness of that Persian carpet.

Here we go again. Lord, please let my fall be graceful.

Chapter 3

Caty managed to steady herself before she sprawled flat on the carpet at the foot of the Belac altar.

Not an altar, Caty.

Seemed her cynicism had likewise reached a new high today. She silently thanked her mother for insisting she take six years of dance lessons. Grace *could* be learned if only to save herself from her own awkwardness nearly twenty years later.

The receptionist leaned over the edge of the desk, her long, straight hair falling forward over her delicate features. "Miss Lewis? Are you all right?" The woman showed no emotion. Nothing whatsoever. Even amusement would go a long way toward making Caty feel somewhat better about her clumsiness.

Should have stopped to ask about that glue.

Clearing her suddenly dry throat, Caty nodded with as much dignity as she could muster. She needn't have bothered applying blush today. "I'm fine. Nothing a little afternoon do-over wouldn't cure. Please call me Caty."

"If you're here to see your new office, it's not quite ready yet."

"I'm working from home until next week. I have an appointment with Mr. Reid at four today." Snatching the offending navy blue slingback from the carpet, Caty slipped off the other shoe. She tucked both shoes beneath her arm and approached the desk in her stocking feet. "It's nice to meet you"—she checked the nameplate—"Suma."

"Likewise." The woman extended her hand. She must pay a fortune for that perfect manicure on her long, slender fingers. Her nails were painted bright red to match her lips.

Caty shook her hand briefly. "Your name is very pretty. I don't believe I've ever heard it before. What does it mean?"

"Ask." The girl raised one finger in the air. "Just a moment." She answered another call in her velvety-smooth, cultured voice.

Ask? *I just did.* Could this day get any more strange? In that moment, Caty missed the ladies who manned the Belac reception desks—Portia in Dallas and Lisanne in Lubbock.

Suma finished the call. "Suma means *to ask*. It's Japanese. I'll ring for Mr. Reid's personal assistant to come and escort you to his office."

"Thank you." Caty wandered across the lobby to the floor-to-ceiling windows that offered a panoramic view of the Houston skyline, the tops of the buildings still swathed in thick, low-hanging storm clouds. She should also be grateful the skies hadn't opened and drenched her during her festival of chaos outside the building. What a day.

Turning in a slow circle, Caty scanned the walls. Why couldn't A.C. Reid have a nice portrait of himself in his offices like most insanely wealthy heads of multinational corporations?

He wouldn't be the first eccentric, wealthy tycoon to be reclusive, so she respected him although she considered his methods and ways rather odd. He paid her a good salary, a generous cost-of-living raise each year, a solid vacation and benefits package, and an annual bonus. And now she was back in her hometown after paying her dues in Dallas and Lubbock. Those were her primary concerns, and the rest was none of her business.

After slipping on her shoes again, Caty stepped closer to a large sculpture which stood on a pedestal to the right of the windows. Made from pale gray stone, the exquisite piece depicted a barefoot woman in a loose flowing gown. Long, wavy tresses were draped over one shoulder and trailed halfway down her back. Her right forearm rested across her chest as if shielding her breasts, her fist curled over her heart. The woman's head was turned to the side, facing the window. In spite of her battle-like stance, sadness radiated in her faraway expression and the firm set of her lips.

Caty leaned close to read the silver plate mounted on the bottom of the sculpture. *Helena, my valiant warrior.* Beneath that were the words *Commissioned by A.C. Reid, October 2002*, and the scrawled signature of the artist.

"She's quite spectacular, isn't she?" A middle-aged woman appeared beside her. Petite and thin, dressed in a prim dark suit, the woman's shiny silver hair framed her face and flipped at the ends. Her haircut probably wasn't retro so much as simply the way she'd worn it for decades.

"Yes, she is," Caty said. "It takes great skill to convey such deep emotion out of stone."

"Mr. Reid was very pleased with the results." The older woman's eyes were a soft blue, her smile kind, her expression welcoming as she offered her hand. "I'm Cordelia Bonner, Mr. Reid's personal assistant. It's nice to finally meet you, Miss Lewis. I've heard wonderful reports about your work for Reidco. We're looking forward to having you here with us in the Houston office."

The other woman's words unexpectedly soothed her. "Thank you." Caty blinked away the sudden moisture in her eyes. If she cried now, she might as well turn and run.

Cordelia's glance was curious and she arched her brows. "Is everything all right, dear?"

The word *dear* was nearly Caty's undoing. "Yes. I'm just glad to be here. It's been quite an afternoon. If it's not against the rules, I hope you'll call me Caty." Although Cordelia looked nothing like her tall, blonde, brown-eyed mother, Sarah, something about this woman's inherent kindness gave her comfort.

"There's no rule against using first names. Feel free to call me Cordelia. Now, if you'll follow me, Mr. Reid is on an international conference call in another office, but he'll be joining you in a few minutes."

Being mindful of her broken shoe heel, Caty followed the older woman around the reception desk and then down a long hallway on the left perimeter of the building. If she angled her right foot a certain way as she walked, it helped to maintain her balance. She kept pace as best she could, but becoming overconfident might cause another mishap. She couldn't take the risk.

"If I remember correctly, Cordelia was the name of King Lear's youngest daughter. His *favorite* daughter," Caty said.

"That's correct." Cordelia seemed pleased by the observation. "You must be well-versed in Shakespeare."

Caty smiled. "Not really. King Lear was required reading in high school. I think I remember Cordelia because I appreciated how forgiving she was. Even after she was unfairly banished from the kingdom, she still came back and forgave her father."

"Yes, forgiveness is an admirable quality." Stopping abruptly in the middle of a long, wood-paneled hallway, Cordelia used a key card to open an unmarked door.

Caty swallowed her surprise. A hidden entrance? That seemed both awesome yet odd at the same time. Ultimately, it raised more questions in her mind about the CEO and founder of Belac.

"After you." The other woman stood aside and motioned for her to enter the office.

As expected, A.C. Reid's office was massive. He was obviously a professional baseball fan. Lots of sports memorabilia lived here. A signed bat was framed in a shadowbox on one wall. Another shadowbox held a collection of signed baseballs, photos, and other mementos. Sam and her dad would have a field day in this office. For some unknown reason, Caty had expected the man to be a big game hunter, but no mounted deer heads or fishing conquests decorated the walls.

Judging by the classic furnishings, elegant fixtures, and hardwood floors—covered with another large Persian rug—Mr. Reid preferred function and handcrafted beauty to sleek and modern. Given the dimensions of the office, Caty guessed the width must extend from one side of the office tower to the other. She imagined Cordelia's office, as well as those of Mr. Reid's other assistants, must be somewhere nearby.

"Please have a seat." Cordelia gestured to a tall wingback chair, covered in a maroon brocade fabric that faced a large desk made from highly polished mahogany. "Would you like something to drink? A soothing cup of afternoon tea, perhaps?"

Caty set her briefcase on the floor and then took a seat on the chair. "That would be lovely. Anything is fine, thanks. I'm not particular."

"Cream and sugar?"

"A little cream if it's no trouble."

"Not at all. I'll return shortly." Something about the rigid set of Cordelia's shoulders and the purposeful way she moved reminded Caty of her brother, Will, and her father, Sam Sr. They'd both served as Air Force pilots. Could this woman be a military veteran? Caty watched as Cordelia disappeared behind an interior door on the opposite wall from where they'd entered the office.

A large painting of an oil rig in the setting sun—the same design as the Belac, Inc. logo but in full color—hung behind the desk. Everything appeared to have its place, no doubt courtesy of Cordelia's dutiful attention. Colorful folders—one for each of the entities Mr. Reid controlled, perhaps?—sat neatly stacked to one side of the desk blotter, a gold fountain pen beside it.

Reidco was the largest and most profitable division of Belac, Inc., but considering he also owned interest in several international oil corporations, the man's personal financial portfolio must be staggering.

What does a man do with all that money? Own homes across the globe with staff on stand-by? A private jet? She couldn't begin to imagine that kind of wealth.

Twisting in the chair, Caty swept another appraising glance around the office. A few western-themed sculptures, framed documents, and a massive wall clock completed the look of professional sophistication. A fireplace was built into the wall opposite Mr. Reid's desk with a cozy conversational grouping in front of it. A conference table with eight executive chairs sat in one corner. Although a bit dark, the CEO's office was exactly what she'd expect for the head of the corporation.

Caty drew in a deep, cleansing breath, trying to control her racing pulse.

"Everything according to His purpose," she murmured under her breath.

Cordelia returned with a silver teapot and a delicate cup and saucer—hand-painted, bone china—on a silver tray with a matching small pitcher of cream. When she set the tray on the desk, Caty spied a folded, damp paper towel in the woman's hand.

"For your skirt." Cordelia handed her the paper towel.

Caty suppressed her sigh. She'd momentarily forgotten about the chocolate. No wonder this observant woman held the high-ranking position as Mr. Reid's trusted assistant. She ran her finger over the spot, relieved it had finally dried. Using her fingernail, she quickly flicked off the chocolate, brushed the remaining traces into her palm, and then lightly ran the towel over the spot. Good as new. Within seconds, model-of-efficiency Cordelia took the paper towel and pocketed it.

"Thank you," Caty murmured. "As long as we're on my road tour of humiliation, you don't happen to have a quick fix for a ripped underarm seam, do you?"

"No need for humiliation." Cordelia gave her a smile that Caty interpreted as more motherly than patronizing. "I'll attend to your jacket if you'll slip it off and allow me to take it for a few minutes."

"That would be great. Cowboy Abe was right. The ladies of the 35th floor *are* indispensable." She could tell she'd intrigued Cordelia with that statement although she remained silent while Caty unfastened the buttons and handed over her jacket.

After draping it across another wingback chair, Cordelia set about preparing and pouring Caty's tea. "This is Darjeeling tea. It's grown on steep and dangerous slopes in India, Nepal, and the Bhutan border, anywhere from 5,000 to 8,000 feet above sea level."

"In other words, a very expensive tea."

Cordelia carefully set the cup and saucer on the desk beside her. "Spoken like a true accountant."

Caty shrugged. "I can't seem to help myself. It's how my mind works. So, is Mr. Reid more a tea or a coffee connoisseur?"

"That depends on where he is in the world, but he's traditionally more of a coffee drinker. Why don't you try your tea, dear? See if it's brewed to your liking."

"I'm sure it's perfect." She'd rather have Cordelia work on her jacket, but to humor her, Caty took a dainty sip, hoping the other woman didn't notice how her hand trembled slightly. "It's delicious. And is Mr. Reid's favorite coffee made from rare, exotic beans?"

Goodness. She should stop with the *Mr. Reid this, Mr. Reid that* nonsense. Normally, she wouldn't ask so many questions, but when she was nervous, she had the unfortunate habit of saying whatever popped into her mind. Like the fairy cowboy thing. *That* had been a personal low.

"Mr. Reid's coffee preferences aren't exotic. The most expensive coffee would be the Kopi Luwak in Indonesia. Are you familiar with it?"

Cordelia's words interrupted Caty's musing. "No, I can't say that I am." Caty took another quick sip of the tea.

"It's quite fascinating," Cordelia continued. "The coffee is made from beans that have been eaten by a weasel-like animal, partly digested, and then excreted."

Caty slapped a hand over her mouth. "You don't say," she managed, thankful she hadn't spewed tea all over the desk. The way her day was going, the hot liquid would have landed all over that precise stack of multicolored folders. She wiped the corners of her lips with her fingers. "What a lovely story."

Cordelia handed her a napkin. "Supposedly the internal digestion adds a unique flavor to the beans by removing the bitterness."

"I have to say, this has been the most educational tea drinking experience I've ever had." Caty dabbed the corners of her mouth with the napkin. "I think I'll pass on sampling the Copy Loowack in my lifetime."

The older woman appeared amused by her obvious mispronunciation. "You might be relieved to know that Mr. Reid prefers the mountain grown variety."

"Smart man." Caty lifted her cup. "The best part of waking up."

"I'll leave you to drink your tea," Cordelia said. "I'll be back in seven minutes with your jacket, most likely before Mr. Reid joins you."

"Thank you again." Seven minutes? Surely she was ex-military to be *that* exact. If she timed Cordelia, Caty felt sure the helpful woman would return with her jacket precisely when predicted. While she was at it, she should have asked for fixative for her shoe.

Taking another sip, she savored the robust, hot brew. It *was* helping to alleviate her frayed nerves. What an odd afternoon. First the enigmatic but compassionate cowboy, and now the assistant who spouted random and sometimes disgusting facts. What type of person *knew* those kinds of things? Cordelia must be fun at company parties. Get a little alcohol in her, and she must be off-the-wall wacky.

Be charitable, Caty. Not that Belac served alcohol at parties. Not that Belac even *had* parties. Not since she'd worked for them, anyway. With a reclusive owner, parties weren't exactly encouraged.

Restless and needing something to do, Caty walked across the office to the large display case set into the back wall. It reminded her of a museum. The crowning glory was a signed baseball glove illuminated by a soft spotlight. Caty felt like a kid peering in a shop window with her nose pressed so close to the case that she fogged the glass. With a frown, she used the sleeve of her blouse to wipe it off but still couldn't decipher the signature.

Cordelia returned with her jacket in short order. "The temporary stitches should hold until a professional tailor can repair it." Gesturing for Caty to turn, she helped Caty into the jacket. In the process Caty caught a whiff of…Chinese food? A mental image of Abernathy with the carry-out boxes popped into her mind. He'd mentioned *his* assistant. Maybe he also worked closely with Mr. Reid and Cordelia? No matter where he worked, it'd be for the best if she didn't meet up with him for a few days to let the dust settle. By then she'd hope to appear more competent.

"You're the best, Cordelia. I'm sure Mr. Reid must adore you. Have you worked for him a long time?"

"I've been his assistant since he started the corporation almost eighteen years ago. I'd served overseas in the Army and was a widow with two boys in college at the time. Mr. Reid's almost done with his conference call. He's negotiating new contracts with investors, so it's taking a bit longer than expected."

"Perfectly understandable," Caty said. Those contracts helped pay her salary, after all. "I'm in no hurry. I'll be here whenever he's done." She wondered if Cordelia called Mr. Reid by his first name in private. After eighteen years? Surely they were on a first name basis by now. In any case, her loyalty was inspiring.

"I'm going to pick up your parking card at the building office in a few minutes, and I have your Belac ID badge," Cordelia told her. "I'll leave them both for you at the front desk. Be sure and get them from Suma before you leave today."

"I'll do that. Thanks again for all your help."

"You're welcome, Caty. I'll see you again soon."

Caty smiled and nodded. "I'll look forward to it."

After Cordelia departed, Caty investigated the wall-mounted shadowbox which showcased the Louisville slugger with Nolan Ryan's signature. Did A.C. Reid know Nolan personally? That was a strong possibility and would make sense since they might be contemporaries—both native Texans in the same age group.

The interior door opened after a few minutes and Caty heard a man's voice. He paused in the doorway just beyond her range of vision.

Caty inhaled a quick breath and then released it slowly.

Here I go. Lord, please be with me.

Chapter 4

At first glance, A.C. Reid was what Caty expected—early to mid-sixties, tall and lean, glasses, slightly balding on top. He wore a well-tailored navy suit, yellow silk tie, and dark leather shoes. His expression was serious, almost somber, and he gave her a courteous nod as he entered the office.

"Miss Lewis, we finally meet one-on-one."

No *nice to meet you*. No *thanks for your hard work*. Why should she have expected compliments? The first few words of her rehearsed speech flew right out of her mind. Completely gone. *Poof!* She'd have to wing it. She'd done it before.

"Mr. Reid, it's nice to meet you in person. It's been a pleasure working for Belac the past five years." Caty strode forward, praying the broken heel of her shoe stayed in place. She didn't know if she could survive another stumble. Surely, she'd used up her annual quota this afternoon alone.

Meeting him in the middle of the office, Caty offered her hand. "I was admiring your Louisville Slugger signed by Nolan Ryan. Looks like you have an extensive collection of wonderful memorabilia."

"Yes, well, I like baseball." That much was obvious although his less than enthusiastic remark struck her as odd. Didn't most baseball aficionados love to spout a fact or two to substantiate their knowledge of the sport?

"Let's talk." He motioned to the same chair she'd vacated. The man seemed to be all-business and not inclined for small talk. Taking a seat in the other wingback chair facing her, Mr. Reid crossed one elegantly clad trouser leg over the other. "Your email indicated you have a matter of great importance to discuss. Considering this is the first time you've insisted on a private meeting, I'm curious. Tell me what's on your mind."

"That's correct." Caty swallowed. The man's time was valuable, and she needed to state her case before she lost her nerve. She'd worked hard for Reidco to establish a reputation for excellence and proficiency. That alone had earned her an audience with the man today, but she was also here to protect her reputation and integrity *if* it was in question.

"Mr. Reid, based on the last two monthly profit and loss reports for Reidco, I've noticed discrepancies. To be blunt, I strongly suspect someone within our division is testing the waters and"—she hesitated to use the word *embezzling*—"diverting funds, a little at a time. I've found four separate instances of this happening. In the first three cases, the amount increased by a negligible amount, and within a few hundred dollars of the previous amount. This seems to be occurring at random times, different days of the week, and varying times of the month."

Mr. Reid's forehead creased. Shifting his position, he leaned forward and lowered his voice. "I assume you've brought evidence to back up your assertions?"

"I have." No matter that those assertions had been scattered all over the Houston city sidewalk a half hour ago. Pulling the briefcase onto her lap, Caty retrieved the red folder containing the most crucial summary report. She placed the file on the desk and began to run down the line items, pointing out the ones in question.

"You'll see that each of these first three amounts I've highlighted are for losses in the Reidco gas station convenience stores in two locations—Lubbock for the first and Laredo for the other two. Added together, all three amount to $856.93. The first two were recorded as losses due to theft. The last, also the largest individual charge, totaled almost $470, and it was counted as a damaged item. Until last week, there hadn't been a single entry over $1,000 withdrawn that wasn't allocated elsewhere. But take a look at this fourth and final entry. You'll see it's a much larger amount, and it's the main reason for my coming to you directly."

Mr. Reid listened as she showed him a payment of $8,000 to an oil supplier in West Texas. "That payment was the one that clued me in to the sloppiness of the person behind these withdrawals," she told him. "I believe they're getting bolder and overconfident if they believe they're getting away with it."

The man's frown deepened and the crease between his brows grew more prominent. "The payments to oil suppliers are always higher, and the amount seems to have been properly allocated, Miss Lewis."

Stunned speechless, Caty tried not to stare at him in disbelief. Surely he understood the implications. Was A.C. Reid nothing more than a figurehead, a man clueless as to the inner workings of his own multibillion dollar corporation? She'd studied the history of the corporation, enough to understand the brilliant mind behind Belac. Based on the borderline nonchalant reaction of the man sitting across from her now, she had to wonder. More like she wanted to shake him and ask him what he'd done with the real A.C. Reid.

This makes no sense!

Caty drew in a quick breath. At the same time, she tried to tamp down the initial stirrings of suspicion. "With all due respect, sir, Belac stopped accepting shipments from that oil supplier six months ago. As I recall, the internal memorandum issued seven months and six days ago stated that all business ties with that particular supplier were severed, effective immediately." She hesitated and made sure she had his full attention. "A memorandum issued under *your* signature. I have a copy here if you'll give me just a minute."

"That won't be necessary." His tone was almost too calm, his words succinct and measured.

Several seconds passed without either of them speaking. Long enough for Caty's suspicions to grow. *Could it be?* The theory was inconceivable but perhaps no more ludicrous than current circumstances.

Sitting back in her chair, Caty tried to maintain control although her mind was spinning. She nodded to the shadowbox containing the Nolan Ryan signed baseball bat. "What is Nolan Ryan's nickname?" She snapped her fingers as if trying to remember. "It escapes me at the moment."

Lord, forgive that lie. In this case, Caty considered it justified. Something weird was going on here, and she needed to uncover the truth. *Now.*

"I don't recall. Nolan played for the Astros, and that's when he caught my attention." Behind his glasses, the man's eyes avoided hers. If he cared enough to have a Nolan Ryan-signed bat, how could he not be aware of the basic facts most ten-year-old boys in Texas would know?

"He made his major league debut and played for the New York Mets in 1966," Caty said. "Then he went to the California Angels for seven years before coming to the Astros."

Mr. Reid continued to avoid her gaze and drummed his fingers on the desk.

"Do you know where Nolan Ryan ended his major league baseball career...Mr. Reid?"

He rose to his feet and began to pace. "No, but I'm sure you do, Miss Lewis." The man was agitated. Good. She wanted him agitated.

I can't believe this! "Nolan was with the Texas Rangers from 1989 through 1993."

Shoving his hands into the pockets of his slacks, the man stared at her. "Did you work for the MLB at one time, young lady? You seem to have an uncommonly good handle on random baseball facts."

She was surprised he hadn't tacked *for a woman* to the end of that sentence although his expression implied as much. Her respect for the head of the corporation plummeted to the ground and was about to crash and burn. *If* he was the founder and CEO. More than ever, Caty was convinced this man was not A.C. Reid.

Lord, what's happening here?

"I grew up with a dad and three brothers who love Texas baseball. I also happen to like the game very much." Rising to her feet, Caty closed the folder. "Those facts aren't really so random if you're a true Nolan Ryan fan." She hesitated. "Are they?"

Silence reigned in the room, the only sound the ticking from a clock on the wall.

Tick tock.

Caty lifted her chin. "I have one more question."

Tick tock.

"What's that?" He didn't flinch. Neither did she. Adrenaline raced through Caty as curiosity tempered with incredulity—and maybe a tiny bit of outrage—claimed possession of her nerves.

Say it.

"I specifically requested a private meeting with A.C. Reid." Caty spoke slowly and with purpose. "Would you please ask him to come into the office now so that I may speak with him directly?"

Chapter 5

The man's eyes narrowed and he inclined his head. Without another word, he turned and departed out the same side door. Watching him, Caty seethed. How *dare* the man? Was he playing her for a fool? Should she be more peeved with this obvious imposter or with A.C. Reid?

Tick tock.

"Oh, be quiet." Great. Now she was chastising inanimate objects?

When Caty overheard muffled male voices from behind the door, she closed her eyes.

Lord, give me strength.

"The date was September 22, 1993. Nolan's last major league appearance. With the Texas Rangers. His full name is Lynn Nolan Ryan, Jr., and his nickname is The Ryan Express."

She hadn't heard a door open or close. That deep voice, that drawl. It *was* him minus the Stetson and the leather jacket. Abernathy. Cowboy Abe. Also known as A.C. Reid, apparently. The man had a very nice head of wavy, chestnut-colored hair, but that was beside the point.

"Nice to see you again, Miss Lewis."

Caty's eyes flew open, and she locked gazes with him. Now it was Miss Lewis, was it? Suddenly light-headed, she fought to retain her shaky composure. "You were there, I suppose? In the stadium that day in 1993?"

He nodded. "I was. Should I be uncomfortable you seem to know me so well?"

"I don't really know you at all, Mr. Reid. I only know that you're from Dallas, so it was more an educated guess that you might have been in attendance." She nodded over her shoulder. "Am I to assume the glove in your case, the one in the spotlight, is also signed by The Ryan Express?"

"No. In fact, that particular glove was signed by The Great Bambino."

Caty stared. Babe Ruth? *Wow.* She wanted to run over and take another look but stayed rooted to his expensive Persian carpet. "The Sultan of Swat?"

Running a hand over his chin, he smiled. She'd obviously surprised him with her question, but he shouldn't do that. His smile was much too disarming. "Yes, also known as The Big Barn."

Was this all a game to him? Okay, then. She'd play along. "Jack Dunn's baby." She could tell she had him on that nickname. "You just can't beat the person who never gives up," she quoted. "*Can you?*" How on earth she remembered a quote from a long-dead baseball player, legend or not, she'd never know. Especially after the afternoon she'd had.

You're weird, that's how. Living in a house overflowing with testosterone—especially after her much older sisters left home—had made an impact on a tomboyish girl with a brain for numbers.

"I get the feeling you have dogged persistence. That's an admirable quality, especially in my chief accountant for the Reidco division." He paused a moment. Dare she hope he wouldn't be able to come up with another quote? "Every strike brings me closer to the next home run."

Caty avoided those brown eyes while she searched her mind to pull out one last quote. "Never let the fear of striking out get in your way." *Ah, thank you Jesus!* She might be nervous, but it was a good sign that her brain was still functioning.

"I think I've met my match." His statement was accompanied by a deferential nod.

How should she respond to that? "I trust your wife shares your love of the sport." Maybe that was out of line, but she needed to say *something.* Make him aware she honored the vows of marriage even if he didn't. Then again, he probably only meant those words in terms of baseball trivia.

Mr. Reid remained silent but the muscles in his cheeks visibly tightened.

Caty crossed her arms but then lowered them to her sides. "Is your first name really Abernathy?"

"Yes, but I prefer to be called by my middle name—Caleb. You obviously know your baseball, and you have an eagle eye over the Reidco accounts. I'm impressed."

"It's my job to pay attention. Your trusted associate is either thorough or else you were somehow privy to our earlier conversation." Had the other man told him of their discussion? Or were cameras or recorders installed in the office? Talk about invasion of privacy.

His eyes narrowed. "I don't spy, but I do have faithful, loyal employees."

"I'd say so. So loyal that one of them was willing to impersonate you?" Caty bristled and tried to tamp down her increasing irritation. It wasn't working. "With all due respect, what was the point of that exercise in futility? Was it some kind of test?" She tried to keep her tone from sounding accusatory but failed miserably. If she was going to be fired, she might as well go out in style.

This is your boss. Act respectful.

"Caty, it wasn't my doing, I assure you."

"As the CEO and founder of Belac, I should think others do *your* bidding, not the other way around." She lowered her gaze. "Not that it's any of my concern."

"I have a security team. They make recommendations and advise when there are potential risks. I wasn't testing you, and it was never my intention to deceive you."

Caleb's lips thinned, and he either couldn't—or wouldn't—tell her more.

Still, his words mollified her somewhat. "Should *I* be uncomfortable that you had the unfair advantage and knew who I was when we met outside?"

Don't make premature judgments.

"I didn't know you were...well, *you*...until you said your name was Catherine, and then you mentioned the Caty nickname. I'm also aware your middle name is Grace. I checked when I came back to the office."

Caty's breath caught. "Why would you do that?"

"Because you intrigue me, Catherine Grace Lewis. It's as simple—or as complicated—as that. I've appreciated your work for Reidco. Your activities in Dallas and then in the Lubbock community the past two years have only enhanced that opinion."

"Excuse me?" Had he investigated her? How could invading her privacy be allowed? She'd heard how some employers checked into their employees' after-hours activities but never would she have believed anyone at Belac or Reidco would actually *do* such a thing.

"I read a newspaper article about your work with the wives and girlfriends of the prisoners incarcerated at the John Montford Unit," he said. "How you've helped clothe them, find them employment and childcare, and provided them with Bibles. The Montford Mission, isn't that what you call it?"

"That's right, Mr. Reid. I'm a firm believer in following the Lord's nudge when a need in the community is made known." In her family, helping others was practically in her DNA. Caty's initial anger faded after it finally sunk into her muddled brain that he'd actually paid her a compliment.

"It's Caleb." His eyes glimmered with appreciation. "I'm aware a large majority of the men at Montford will never be released because of medical conditions or mental illness. You're providing a vital ministry, and I'm sure you're giving those women the kind of comfort and assistance that only another woman can."

Based on those statements, he must be aware that she planned on continuing the ministry she'd started in Lubbock. Before leaving that city, one of the most important things she'd done was find others to continue the work. She'd return a few times each year to oversee the program and visit the women she'd befriended.

He smiled. "You're the type of person who gets involved in the community and blooms where she's planted, if you'll pardon the cliché. In other words, you're a model employee for Belac."

Tick tock. For some unknown reason, that clock now gave her an odd sense of security.

Although reassuring, those statements—especially the last one—reminded her that he was her boss and she was in his employ. "Were you advised of my suspicions as I explained them to the Mr. Reid imposter?" She cleared her throat. "For lack of knowing his real name."

"Steve Robison. He's my second in command and a longtime employee of Belac. The discrepancies were brought to my attention a few weeks ago, and I'm aware that's why you're here today. Please have a seat so we can talk more about it."

Moving around his desk, Caleb settled in the black leather executive chair. Leaning one elbow on the arm of his chair, he appeared relaxed.

Caty returned to her chair. She'd heard of Mr. Robison but never had any personal dealings with him. Needing something to do with her antsy fingers, she tugged on the hem of her skirt, out of his range of sight. The scenario of pretense still didn't sit well with her. On the other hand, making decisions for such a large corporation must be difficult. No doubt there were matters of which she knew nothing. At least he hadn't said *trust me*. In circumstances such as this, those two words sometimes struck her as insincere. For what it was worth, she sensed he'd been upfront with her.

A thought struck her. *C-a-l-e-b*. She mouthed the letters. Of course! She almost slapped her forehead but tucked her hand beneath her instead.

Caleb leaned forward with a curious expression. "Is everything all right?"

"Belac? The name of your corporation is your middle name spelled *backwards*?" She shook her head and crossed her arms. "You sure pulled one over on us."

"I didn't intend to *pull one over* on anyone." His brow furrowed and his tone took on a defensive tone.

"I'm sorry, but you have to know your employees have speculated on its meaning. Some of the theories have been very creative." The name *was* different, but now that she understood the reasoning, it made perfect sense.

"I was nineteen years old when I started Belac." Caleb's voice was low. "I had no idea if my upstart corporation would last six days or sixty years."

Caty did the mental calculation. At least she knew when the corporation was founded, so that made him thirty-six. *Only* thirty-six. For such a young man, he'd accomplished so much.

"I just turned thirty-seven." The man was uncanny if not a bit scary in being able to read her mind.

"Mr. Reid, you have to know your employees hold you in the highest esteem. Founding such a globally successful corporation at such a young age—upstart or not—is nothing short of astounding. After we first met, I wondered if Abernathy might represent the 'A' in your name, but then I quickly discounted that thought. I thought you had to be a much older man." She hadn't meant it to sound like she was paying him idle flattery, and hoped he wouldn't consider her words insincere.

"Thank you. Again, it's Caleb. Like most things that endure, Belac didn't happen overnight. It took a lot of nurturing and experienced its share of failures along the way." Caleb straightened in his chair. Pulling something out of the middle drawer, he reached across the desk and offered it to her. "Here. Try this for your shoe."

Taking it from him, Caty glanced at what she held in her palm. Glue. "Right here? Now?"

"Why not? Would you like me to fix it for you? Hand it over."

"I would not, could not…" She returned his smile although she knew she'd run the course with the Dr. Seuss analogy. "I think I'm capable." Slipping off her right shoe, Caty balanced it on her lap. Within seconds, she'd applied the glue. Then she capped the tube and handed it back to him. "All done now, thanks."

"You might want to apply pressure on that heel for a minute. It'll help to cement the seal."

"Right," she murmured. "You really are an observant and helpful—"

"Cowboy? Isn't that what you called me?" His lips curved.

"Yes." Caty lowered her gaze. "However, knowing you're my boss changes things."

"No reason anything has to change." He waited until she looked at him again. "We're Caleb and Caty sharing a conversation about our mutual interest in Belac."

"As you wish." If only it could really be that simple. *As you wish?* She'd never said that before, as if he were royalty, and she were his servant. And maybe her imagination was a little too fanciful.

Caleb returned the tube of glue to the drawer and then zeroed his gaze on her, his expression more serious. "Caty, I want you to continue to monitor the withdrawals. If there are more—no matter how big or small—I want you to notify me immediately with the exact amount, the location, any information you have. Even if you think it might be nothing, I want to be informed."

"Of course." Caty tested the heel before applying continued pressure.

"If the withdrawals continue, we'll find the root source so they can be stopped. I agree with your theory that they're testing the waters before they try something larger. It's an age-old scheme, and if needed, I won't hesitate to bring in the authorities."

Caty nodded. "Since they were sloppy on the last withdrawal, I'm thinking it will happen again. Based on the pattern of withdrawals, such as it is, it's my theory we can expect another one within the next month, two tops."

"I agree, and we need to be ready." Twisting the wedding ring on his finger in an absent way, Caleb studied her for a long moment. "What exactly are you afraid of, Caty?"

His question surprised her. "I'm not sure I know what you mean. Right now? In life?"

"You had quite a run of…misadventures…before arriving in the office today. You even mentioned being nervous about this meeting. From what I know of Catherine Lewis, I wouldn't have pegged you as the nervous type."

"I'm not under normal circumstances, but this afternoon has nothing to do with my definition of normal, Mr.—Caleb." She interpreted his comment not as a criticism but an observation. Based on her earlier behavior, she couldn't blame him. She only hoped he wasn't aware of her latest near-disaster on the way to the reception desk.

She shifted in the chair. "In truth, lurking in the back of my mind was the fear you might believe that *I* had something to do with these accounting discrepancies."

"I think we can agree they're not discrepancies so much as intentional errors that someone hoped wouldn't be caught," he observed.

Suddenly it made more sense. "The Mr. Reid imposter—Mr. Robison—was trying to determine whether *I* was a risk, wasn't he? That's what that was all about?" Then another thought slammed into mind. *Oh, no.* "I thought I was being transferred to Houston because the work I'd done in Lubbock warranted an upward move."

Caty shook her head, feeling duped and foolish. "That wasn't the case at all, was it? Mr. Robison wanted to keep an eye on me. Perhaps you share that suspicion?"

So much for not making judgments.

Caleb appeared more conflicted than angry. "I'll admit there was a suspicion you might be personally involved. But one of the things I most admire about you, Caty, is how forthright and almost impossibly honest you are."

"*Impossibly* honest?" Caty swallowed her misgivings. What could that mean?

"Not to mention compassionate. Based on your work record with Belac, combined with what I've personally witnessed today, I think you'd probably apologize to a fly if you'd thought you'd hurt it."

"Well, there goes my tough accountant image." She tried not to squirm in her chair. "I've been known to kill a few flies." What a conversation.

"If it makes you feel any better, at least in *my* mind, I've ruled out the possibility that you have anything whatsoever to do with the accounting discrepancies," Caleb told her. "I can assure you, your job is not in jeopardy."

"Thank you." Drawing in another deep breath, Caty rose from the chair. "Now that I've stated my case, I should leave so you can get back to your business."

"*This* is my most important business at the moment. Caty, can you give me the names of the person or persons you suspect *are* behind these accounting errors?"

Caleb's gaze pinned her down and she lowered back into the chair. She should have known he'd get around to that question, but she wasn't about to answer. "I don't have any names to give you."

He frowned. "Surely you have suspicions."

Caty met those brown eyes. "I really can't say." She wasn't willing to implicate anyone at this early juncture. That would be rash and premature.

"I see." His jaw tightened. "Is your loyalty to others or to me?" The tough, hard-nosed A.C. Reid had emerged.

She gasped. "That's hardly a fair question. It has nothing to do with my loyalty to Belac. It has everything to do with not accusing someone unfairly, especially a fellow Belac employee. That wouldn't be right without proper substantiation. Besides, they're only vague suspicions."

Caleb sat back in his chair and blew out a breath. "You're right. I apologize, although I think it's most likely employees in Lubbock and Laredo since those are the locations with discrepancies. Or at least they *were* in the Lubbock or Laredo offices."

Time to give him more evidence to back up her theory. "I visited the Lubbock Reidco gas station and did a little investigation on my own."

That caught his immediate attention. "I'm listening."

"I spoke with a trusted, long-time employee. She knew nothing of the so-called theft there. Regarding the damaged item in the Lubbock station, in the records, it was listed as a faulty automated coffee machine. It's the one that makes cappuccino, the only machine that makes cappuccino in that particular station. According to my review of the records as recently as yesterday, no replacement machine has been ordered. I called a friend in Lubbock who gets her morning cup of cappuccino at that Reidco station."

"And?" Caleb sat up straighter.

"She told me it's the same cappuccino machine she'd been using for months," Caty said.

"How does she know it's the same one?"

"She knew because it has a mark on the left side…like a rust stain."

He pushed a button on his phone. "Cordelia, please print a list of the employees who've transferred to Houston from the Lubbock and Laredo offices and bring it to me."

"Right away, Mr. Reid."

The man listened well. He missed nothing. She wouldn't mind seeing that list herself. "May I ask why you moved the Belac headquarters from Dallas to Houston?"

"Personal reasons. I'm not at liberty to say more."

Guilt shot through her. "I didn't intend to pry into your personal life, and I meant no disrespect. If there's nothing else, I've taken enough of your time. As you suggested, I'll continue to monitor the withdrawals, and I'll let you know at the first sign of anything suspicious."

"Fair enough." Lifting out of his chair, Caleb walked around the desk. "How's the shoe?"

While he watched, Caty slipped on the shoe. Then she lifted and rotated her foot. "See? All fixed, thanks to you."

"Good." When he offered his hand to assist her from the chair, Caty hesitated. How could she refuse? She tried her best to ignore the strong rush of attraction as their hands touched. How silly, but it couldn't be denied. In all her life, she couldn't recall having such an immediate, strong physical reaction to a man. Somehow, she'd known his touch would be dangerous in its own way.

Lord, Caleb is married and he's my boss. Please take these feelings away from me. For all she knew, he had a mansion in the Houston suburbs, a beautiful wife, and a whole passel of adorable kids. She needed to seriously ramp up her prayer time tonight.

"Earlier this morning, I asked the interior decorator to put a push on finishing your office." Caleb walked with her and stopped beside the door leading into the main hallway. "It should be ready by the end of the week. I'd like to see you in place by next Monday. Cordelia is scheduling the professional movers as we speak."

"Thank you," she said. "I'll look forward to it."

"If you need additional assistance with anything, let her know and she'll take care of it. I understand you've made other arrangements for moving into your personal residence."

"I'm all set. The Lewis Brothers Moving Company is helping me."

"As far as the office, it's a liability thing," he said, either ignoring or not catching her reference to her brothers helping to move her into the townhome. "We have to use the insured movers."

"I completely understand. If you ever allow outsiders to see your office, I'm sure my dad and brothers would drool over your baseball memorabilia." Her cheeks flushed with warmth. "Not that I'm hinting for an invitation. And not that they'd actually slobber over anything."

She needed to stop talking. At least her job was secure, but she'd suddenly turned into a motormouth around her boss. Again. The man was notoriously private. It's not like he'd host tours of his prized baseball collectibles, no matter how much he loved baseball.

"That might be arranged," he said. *Shocker.* "In answer to your earlier question, part of the reason I moved to Houston was for a fresh start. I'd like to be more than a figurehead to my employees. I've been inaccessible too long." When he turned his gaze on her, warmth simmered in their depths. "I have the feeling you might also be able to help me with that mission, Caty."

Wow. Another shock.

"Just be yourself and be accessible, Caleb." Addressing her boss in an informal manner suddenly didn't seem as awkward as she might have thought.

He opened the door. "Thank you for coming to me with your concerns. I appreciate your diligence. We'll figure out what's going on and make sure it doesn't happen again. Together."

She gave his hand a brief shake. Even so, his hand—large and warm as it wrapped around hers—was enough to unnerve her all over again.

"Thank you for your time." Turning, Caty escaped into the hallway, sensing that brown-eyed gaze on her as she walked down the long corridor.

Chapter 6

Since the restaurant was close to where her parents lived—her temporary home for the past two weeks—Caty darted back to the house to refresh her makeup and to change her clothes. Her parents weren't home, but she called Sam to tell him she still counted among the living.

"Glad to hear it," Sam said, chuckling. "Want to come over to the house for dinner? I'm not sure what Lexa has planned, but there's always a place for you at the table."

"Thanks, but I'm all set. I'm meeting Marta at The Back Door Café."

"Sounds like fun, and that's a great place. Tell Marta we've enjoyed watching her weather reports. I think she's found her professional niche."

"I agree. Her warmth and humor shine through even if she's predicting a storm." She chatted with Sam for another minute and then quickly sorted through her sparse wardrobe. For now, she was limited on her choices since most of her clothing was on the moving truck arriving late Friday night.

She tugged on her best dark dress jeans and then selected a light blue silk blouse. While buttoning the blouse, she slipped her feet into black high heels. Fully dressed, she gave her reflection the once-over in the full-length mirror of her old bedroom. *Hmm.* She hoped she wasn't tempting anything by wearing silk but the heels had to go. Why tempt anything by wearing heels twice in one day? She wasn't out to impress anyone, and it wasn't like she wore the heels to make her taller. Tonight was all about fun and catching up with her friend.

After kicking off the shoes, Caty padded across the carpet to the closet and grabbed her red cowgirl boots. Sitting on the bed, she pulled them on. This was at least the third pair of red boots she'd owned in her life. She'd always been partial to the color. *Ahhh.* Nothing felt as right, or as comfortable. She breathed out a sigh of pure satisfaction. "Hello, old friends."

Thirty minutes later, Caty sat across the dinner table from Marta.

After refilling their water, the female server quietly departed the room.

"What's with the private room?" Caty grinned. "Don't tell me. You have fans pestering you for autographs, don't you? The celebrity needs her privacy."

"I'm no celebrity. Nothing like that." Marta waved her hand to dismiss the comment. "Eliot is joining us, after all, and he asked me to reserve a private room. I didn't think you'd mind although I'm sorry we can't have the serious girl talk over dinner like we'd planned."

"It's always a pleasure to spend time with Eliot. We can always talk on the phone tomorrow." Still, the slightest twinge of disappointment pinched Caty. And it still didn't explain the need for a private room.

"This is one of our new favorite restaurants," Marta said. "I would have asked for patio seating, but it's too chilly tonight. They play soft jazz in the courtyard, and it has a distinct New Orleans vibe. You can dance under the stars. It's very romantic."

"I can imagine. Sounds fabulous." Caty sipped her water, ignoring another twinge. Not that she was jealous. Not really. Other than a somewhat serious relationship that lasted from her sophomore to junior year at Wheaton College, she'd been so focused on building her career that she hadn't taken the time to think about romance. She'd had plenty of invitations for dates, but she'd turned down the majority of them. Why start something she knew wouldn't last?

"So, tell me about this mysterious boss of yours," Marta said. "Is he old or young? Nice or cranky? Any weird quirks? Married?" Slicing a piece of warm sourdough bread, Marta popped it in her mouth and offered one to Caty.

Since she'd moved back to Houston, Marta had made it her mission to find a guy for Caty who was as great as Eliot. Not that the he-man, military man was *her* type, exactly. Caty gravitated more to urban cowboys. Professional men with Texas roots. Men as comfortable in a Stetson and jeans as a business suit.

An image of Caleb Reid popped into her mind as Caty chewed the bread.

Go away.

From the time she'd left Caleb's office, Caty had tried to push aside thoughts of her handsome boss. What was it about him that seemed to have such a hold on her? Now that she was back in Houston, she should pray she'd meet a nice high school math teacher or college professor. Someone financially stable who loved the Lord, excelled in his job, and had a heart for kids. Yes, that's what she needed. Someone uncomplicated and...safe.

What am I thinking? For now, she needed to focus on her work, not finding a man to love. She'd never dated simply for the sake of dating. So now here she sat, alone. To the outside world, she was content in her singledom. She *was* content, but increasingly, she'd become all too aware that time was marching on. In her heart, she longed for the kind of lifetime love shared between her parents. Sam and Lexa. Marta and Eliot. The list could go on, but she refused to feel sorry for herself.

If nothing else, she'd learned that everything happened in God's time, not *Caty's* time. Her mother always told her that when the right man of God's choosing walked into her life, everything else would fall into place. Dear Mom and her optimism. She loved how she focused on *when* and not *if.*

"Caty? You still with me?" Pushing shoulder-length blonde curls away from her cheek, Marta fixed her with those unique lavender eyes.

"Sorry." She needed to focus. "He's nice but tough when he needs to be. He's much younger than I expected, and I think he's married." He was also too ruggedly attractive. Too nice, too compassionate, too...everything.

"You *think?* Does he wear a wedding band?"

"Yes. Call me crazy, but I think there might be trouble in paradise. Something's not quite right there. I could be completely off-base, and it certainly wouldn't be the first time. No matter what his situation is, I need to pray for him."

"You are so adorable." Marta squeezed a lemon over her iced tea and then took a quick sip. "Of course, you're right in terms of praying for him. You know, some guys in a position like that— young, wealthy, reclusive—wear a fake wedding band on purpose. Is he good looking?"

Caty distracted herself by cutting another piece of the delicious bread. "I suppose some would call him attractive." The color in her cheeks must belie that statement, and Marta was usually adept at picking up on her nonverbal cues.

"Say the word, and I'll ask Eliot to check him out. Find out his status."

"No, no," Caty protested, chewing her bread. "I repeat, the man is my *boss*. That's an important, four-letter word right there—b-o-s-s. By virtue of that fact alone, he's completely off-limits in the dating department. His life is as tightly guarded as Fort Knox, but I figure everyone's entitled to their secrets and privacy." Although he said he wanted to become more visible. "If he found out Eliot was snooping into his personal life, I can say with a reasonable degree of certainty that he wouldn't take kindly to it. No question in my mind I'd be fired under those circumstances, and I couldn't blame him."

"No problem. We'll just scratch that idea then. Let me know if you change your mind."

Caty drew in a quick breath. "Believe it or not, my boss is the cowboy I mentioned. The one I met on the sidewalk outside the office building." Surely it was all right to mention that much.

"No kidding?" Marta grinned. "You've got to love it. At least he's helpful when he's out and about on the city streets. That's a definite plus, right? If I'm not mistaken, you also called the cowboy handsome."

"All right. Yes, he's very attractive," Caty admitted. "He's also gentlemanly and…authoritative."

"Do you think he knew who you were when you first met?"

"Not at first, but then he figured it out. At least he believed what I had to tell him. That was my primary concern since I wasn't sure whether I'd have a job when I walked out of that meeting. He's ordered a push to get my office done and wants me to report to work on Monday morning."

"Bravo! That means you impressed him." Marta lifted her water glass. "Here's a toast to Catherine Lewis, future CFO!" They gently clinked their glasses together.

Caty spied Eliot approaching their table. "Here comes Mr. Marchand now."

"Hey, babe." Eliot leaned down to drop a light kiss on Marta's waiting lips.

"Hi there, handsome. Glad you could join us."

"Me, too. Caty, always great to spend time with one of my favorite Lewis family members."

"That's diplomatic." Caty smiled after he came around the table and gave her a kiss on the cheek. "Ever think about going into politics?"

"No, thanks. I'll leave the political ambitions to Josh Grant."

"Oh? Is this breaking news?" Something was always happening with Sam's lively TeamWork members. Suave Mr. Grant would make a terrific political candidate. Good looks, wonderful family, law degree from LSU, and solid experience as the primary legal counsel for TeamWork would all work in his favor.

"Perhaps, but I'll let Sam or Josh tell you."

"Thanks. You dangle that tidbit and then have the nerve *not* to tell me?" Caty mock frowned. "I know you must have kept some whopper secrets in your past life, International Man of Mystery."

"Forgive me, but I'll never tell."

After removing his sport coat, Eliot draped it around his chair. Dropping into the seat next to Marta, he moved his arm around her with an air of familiarity that hinted of sweet intimacy. No wonder Marta loved this guy. Hard *not* to love a man who was all brawn and bravado on the outside but turned to mush around his wife. What more could a woman want?

Eliot's military experience was with some elite, specialized unit, but that's all Caty knew. He certainly looked the part—tall, broad-shouldered, muscled. Intelligent and well-spoken, he had a heart for the Lord. Originally from France, if Marta hadn't told her, she'd never have known except for little inflections that crept into his speech on occasion.

Sam had told her enough to know that Eliot's expertise had been invaluable for TeamWork. He'd even saved the life of one of the guys, Mitch Jacobsen, in New Orleans during their post-Katrina mission. In the last year, Eliot had retired from active military duty and started a private security company that also offered Christian-based counseling to individuals traumatized by criminal acts such as bank robberies, home invasions, random shootings, even murders.

Caty pushed the bread tray toward him. "Eat some of this so I don't eat it all. So, how's business?"

"The world's still crazy, so business is good," Eliot said. "Demanding."

Marta put her hand on Eliot's arm. "What a sad commentary but your clients are better off having a man like you to help them, that's for sure. By the way, where's your friend?"

Caty frowned. "Oh no, don't tell me this is a setup. I like you two. Please don't make me revisit that opinion."

"Relax." Eliot chuckled. "This is an old acquaintance from Princeton."

"Exactly how old are we talking?" Marta winked at Caty.

"A few years older than me. He just moved to Houston from Dallas and called me earlier today. Oil man. I figured why not invite him to dinner and welcome him to the area? He seems like a quiet kind of guy, and he's the one who asked for the private room." Eliot glanced at his watch. "I'm sure he'll be here any minute."

Caty's mind swirled. *No way.* Couldn't be. Could it? Old friend from Princeton? She wasn't about to ask Eliot the man's name. Caleb was a few years older than Eliot. She searched her memory but couldn't recall anything in the company literature about where he'd achieved his degrees although it might be there somewhere. As reclusive as he was, who knew? She'd noticed the framed diplomas and certificates on the walls in Caleb's office, but at the time, she'd been more interested in his sports memorabilia than checking out his educational credentials. She could blame that on all the sports nuts in her family, especially the two named Sam.

Perhaps it was more Eliot's statement about the man being private that made her wonder. She remained silent while her friends across the table chatted for a few moments.

Taking a drink of water, Caty sputtered into her fist when she looked up and spied Caleb approaching the room.

Chapter 7

Caty's traitorous pulse took a flying leap. She'd seen Caleb first since Marta and Eliot sat with their backs to the room's entrance.

Lord, your sense of humor is in overdrive today. She couldn't very well tell the Almighty to knock it off.

The man was still wearing his tan Stetson, jeans, and brown leather boots. He'd changed into a blue and white striped dress shirt, tucked in as before, and a silver belt buckle peeked out from his trim waist beneath the leather jacket. The man was too handsome for his own good. Or hers.

Still your boss, Caty. Still married. Had the Lord not heard her short but impassioned prayer to remove the inappropriate thoughts about Caleb from her mind?

In spite of her best efforts, Caty found herself staring at him. In place of his earlier scruff, his face was now clean-shaven. That strong jawline was now smooth as a baby's behind. And would you look at that? He had an appealing cleft in his chin—not too deep but a perfect, small indentation that made him even more attractive if such a thing were possible. Apparently, it was.

A drought of years with only a few decent dates and now…this?

Removing his Stetson, Caleb greeted Marta as Eliot introduced them. Although he kept his gaze carefully trained on Marta, Caty felt sure he'd seen her. How could he not?

"Caleb, I'd like to introduce you to our good friend, Caty Lewis. Caty, this is Caleb Reid." Based on Marta's smile, her friend clearly held high hopes for this little get-together. She was thankful she hadn't mentioned the name A.C. Reid in her conversations with Marta. That old confidentiality clause again.

"Miss Lewis, it's an honor to share dinner with you tonight."

Caty wanted to crawl under the table.

He certainly sounded sincere, but what now? Was she supposed to act as though he wasn't her boss and they'd never met? Straightening in her chair, Caty pasted on a warm, welcoming smile.

She'd follow Caleb's lead and take her cues from him. She'd never pretended to be an actress and wasn't sure she could pull it off if she tried. Loyalty to Caleb and Belac trumped all, she supposed.

Still, Marta and Eliot were her trusted friends. How could she keep this secret from them? What did it hurt for them to know the truth?

This is too weird. This day would go down as one of the most absurd in her life.

"Likewise, Mr. Reader is it?" She might as well have fun. He might be her boss, but if he expected her to play along, surely he'd understand. Loyalty was one thing, but so was teasing him under the guise of pretense.

He cleared his throat. "It's Reid."

"I see. I'm sorry, but I didn't catch your first name." Oh, she was being bad.

"I prefer to be called by my middle name. It's Caleb." Those brown eyes settled on her. "And do you prefer Caty or…"

"You can call me Catherine." She ignored Marta's stare.

"Do you mind if I sit beside you, Catherine?"

"Not at all." She patted the back of the adjacent chair. "Sit a spell. Let's chat." She caught the amused glance exchanged between Marta and Eliot.

After hanging his Stetson on the back of another chair, Caleb took his seat. He smelled soap and water clean. That cleft had a life of its own and practically begged her to trace her finger over it.

Not a good idea, Caty. She dropped her hands to her lap. How long *had* it been since she'd had a date? Too long, obviously. Playacting was one thing, but she didn't want to act completely out of character. Not that Marta wasn't already questioning this charade.

She addressed Caleb. "So, tell me. How do you know Eliot?"

"We met at a Princeton recruiting function a number of years ago," Caleb said. "How about you? How do you know the Marchands, Catherine?" When he stressed her name, Caty repressed the inclination to laugh.

"Marta used to work for my sister-in-law's catering business, and that's how we first met. Eliot and Marta are also both volunteers for a Christian missions organization my oldest brother, Sam, heads called TeamWork." Caty smiled at her friends across the table.

"These two surprised me by marrying at the end of one of Sam's TeamWork missions in Albuquerque. How long has it been now?"

"Eighteen months," Eliot said.

"Caty's brother, Sam, officiated at our wedding along with a Native American pastor," Marta told Caleb. "Eliot and I had known each other a few years through TeamWork, but he was never in one place long enough to date."

Eliot grinned. "So we got married instead. I finally came to my senses is more like it."

"The TeamWork office is also downtown." Caty stopped herself before she said it was five blocks from the Belac headquarters. "Not, um, far from my new office."

"That's convenient for you, I imagine. I've heard of TeamWork." That surprised her although Caleb didn't elaborate.

"I'm sure I'll be working some of their projects. Of course, my time is limited these days." Caty made her sigh as dramatic as possible. "My boss is very demanding, and I rarely have time to myself."

"I thought you said your boss was generous…" Marta clamped her lips closed when Caty shot her a look across the table.

Caleb's forehead creased. "Faithful employees should be allowed free time. I think that's vital to keeping them happy and content. Not to mention loyal."

"You'd think so, wouldn't you? Tell me, do *you* have an understanding boss, Caleb?"

"Caleb *is* the boss. Isn't that right?" Eliot said.

"Yes." Again, Caleb didn't elaborate. The man could certainly be tight-lipped when he wanted.

"Good for you." Twisting in her seat, Caty gave him her full attention. "Tell me, do you find it difficult to keep good employees?"

His lips upturned. "It can be, yes, but it begins with surrounding yourself with solid people and making wise decisions. At least that's been my experience."

Caty nodded. "Well, I'm sure you're the atypical boss. I think most heads of big conglomerates expect everyone else to work as hard as they do. That's all good and well, but I think they sometimes forget that a person's overall health is dependent on carving out time for relaxation and fun pursuits. Like you just mentioned. Take you for instance, Mr. Reid."

"Caleb," he reminded her.

"Right. Tell me, what things do *you* do for fun? Skydive? Climb mountains? Collect expensive sports cars? Stamps? Travel to exotic islands? Watch birds?"

The server came to take their orders, and Caty almost laughed at Caleb's obvious relief. For a man who struck her as unflappable, it seemed she'd managed to fluster him. Good, he deserved it.

As Marta and Eliot discussed their options with the server, Caleb positioned his menu in front of him and leaned close. Opening her menu, Caty followed suit, pretending to study the selections.

"What are you doing?" Caleb's voice was low and controlled. Caty couldn't tell if he was more irritated or amused but guessed it was a little of both.

"Playing along. I thought that's what you wanted me to do. How am I doing so far?" Caty stopped just short of batting her eyelashes.

"If I didn't want you at Belac, I'd say you should move to Hollywood. I had no idea you'd be here tonight, and your presence threw me off at first. Then you started in with your whole *all bosses are evil* routine. In any case, you can expect something extra in your next paycheck."

"Please don't offend me." That came out more of a hiss. "I'm loyal to a fault, and I never take bribes. Maybe *you* make a habit of lying, but I'm not happy lying to my friends."

"It's not a bribe, Caty. I'll make sure Eliot knows tonight. Promise."

"Thank you." Lowering her menu, Caty pointed to the first entrée without looking at it in giving her order to the server. As long as it wasn't seafood that crawled around on her plate, she'd be okay.

Beside her, Caleb nudged her arm. "You're a fan of liver?"

Caty blanched. "Please don't tell me that's what I ordered. Why would a restaurant even have liver on its menu?"

"Some people like it. Not me, but some do. And I think I make you nervous." Caleb smoothed his napkin on his lap.

Did the man have to be so maddeningly perceptive? "Don't flatter yourself, and liver is an equal opportunity meat. Or whatever it is. I'm surprised you're hungry since you had your Chinese meal break so late this afternoon."

"The food wasn't for me," he said, his voice so low she almost didn't hear. "Cordelia worked through lunch. I had another errand to run and offered to pick up something for her."

"How considerate. I understand she's worked with you since you were a baby mogul. Cordelia was extremely helpful to me, and I can see how loyal she is to you. You're blessed."

"Yes, I am."

"If you two can take a break before our salads arrive, I'd like to say a prayer." When Eliot bowed his head to ask the blessing, Caleb rested his left hand on the table, palm up.

Placing her hand lightly in his, Caty tried to ignore the sensations racing through her.

He's your boss. Your married *boss.* This needed to stop. *Lord, forgive me.*

As Eliot began his prayer, Marta waved her hand at Caty like a wild woman before placing her hand over her husband's. Angling her head toward Caleb, Marta winked.

What on earth did *that* mean? Caty was beginning to wish this day would end so she could get back to some semblance of reality.

"...and we thank you for the opportunity to catch up with Caleb and to spend time with Caty," Eliot prayed. "We ask your blessing on their lives as they both begin their work here in Houston. I'd ask that this move be positive for Caty, and that her boss might see that having free time is important to maintaining loyalty to the corporation. If her boss is not a Christian, we pray he might come to know the saving grace of Jesus Christ. Now, Father, we thank you for our food and ask that you bless the hands that have prepared it. We ask all these things in the name of your Son, Jesus. Amen."

"Amen," Caty and Caleb murmured at the same time. Withdrawing her hand from Caleb's, she noted Marta's curious expression. Giving her a reassuring nod, Caty added a bright smile for good measure.

After small talk over their salads, Caty was grateful to discover pecan-crusted chicken when her dinner plate was set on the table. Beside her, Caleb's steak sizzled on his plate, medium rare from the looks of it. More power to him.

"You go for blood, I see." She glanced across the table, thankful to see Marta and Eliot once again engrossed in their own conversation.

"Sometimes I do. On *rare* occasions." When she groaned at his pun, Caleb chuckled. She shouldn't make him laugh. Those tiny little lines surfaced around his eyes and mouth that only made him more attractive. She needed to avoid that cleft in his chin at all costs.

"You lied to me about what I ordered, and you're corny about your seriously undercooked meat. You obviously can't be trusted."

Caleb gripped his chest. "Ah, now you wound me. You have such little faith? In my defense, I flagged down the server when she refilled your water glass and asked her to switch out liver for chicken." He crisscrossed his index fingers. "Liver for chicken. I figured chicken should be safe."

"Again, your powers of observation have served you well, but how can I be certain that's what really happened?"

Caleb leaned close, his lips warming her skin. "The evidence is right in front of you. If you require further proof, I'll ask for the menu again."

"That's not necessary." Caty focused on her food for the next few minutes. She joined in the conversation occasionally and sensed Caleb's gaze on her more than once. He didn't challenge her, didn't mock, didn't tease. Then he asked her about her job and *listened* as evidenced by some of his insightful questions. He appeared genuinely interested in hearing more about her work—imagine that—and she gave him the same basic facts about her job that she'd tell anyone without revealing anything she shouldn't.

Was it possible he honestly didn't know what she did on a daily basis? Why was the man so private? *That* was the question Caty would love to ask him.

"To sum up, accounting's pretty boring as a general rule," she said. "Call me weird, but I love it."

"From what I can tell, you're not boring. Or weird. In fact, I find you fascinating." Caleb didn't look at her but focused on cutting another generous bite of his steak.

"Note I didn't say *I* was boring," she stipulated. "For example, today was a prime example where I couldn't seem to make it to my afternoon meeting without a few mishaps. Keeps life interesting, anyway."

"I'm sure." Caleb's lips twitched as he finished his bite of steak. "Are you glad to be back in Houston?" She gave him a look that implied *you're not supposed to know that since I didn't say anything other than I have family here.*

Ducking his head, Caleb stabbed a baby carrot and plopped it in his mouth. Caty prayed her friends hadn't picked up on anything amiss. Who was she kidding? In spite of his Hollywood comment, she and Caleb were horrible at playacting.

"I'm thrilled to be back," she said. "The work experience in Lubbock was good, but I traveled quite a bit. I'm hoping I'll be able to stay more rooted in Houston now."

"Maybe you should have a chat with your boss about it. See if he's agreeable." With a grin, Caleb shrugged. "You never know." A second carrot found its way into his mouth.

"I'll have to do that." Caty lifted her gaze to meet Caleb's. "So, has your wife adapted well to the move to Houston?"

The pointy toe of Marta's shoe connected with her right shin beneath the table. Not enough to hurt, but she might have a small bruise in the morning. Caty arched her brows and shot Marta a questioning *what was that for?* look. Just when she thought the day was going to end on a high note.

"She hasn't." Caleb's smile had sobered. *Oh, oh.* Had she said something wrong?

"I beg your pardon?" Was the man separated or divorced? That would explain a few things and make her feel slightly less guilty about her attraction to the man, although not much.

Caleb wiped his mouth with his napkin and avoided looking at her directly. "Unfortunately, my wife died five years ago."

Chapter 8

Caty planted her hands on either side of the marble sink in the ladies lounge. "You couldn't have warned me the man's wife *died?*"

"That's what I was trying to tell you with the whole waving and winking routine. Well, not that she'd died, but that he wasn't off-limits." Marta finished washing her hands and dried them with a linen finger towel. "That didn't come out right. I didn't know it at first, so you have to cut me some slack. Seriously, Caty, how was I supposed to know? I've never met Caleb before. Eliot whispered it to me about the same time you two started flirting."

"Flirting?" Caty's nerves made her stomach churn.

"Short of passing you a note—which never works, by the way— I didn't know what to do. I've got your back, girlfriend. Trust me, if Eliot hadn't told me that Caleb was widowed, I would have hauled you in here a long time ago."

"It's not supposed to be this difficult. Why can't a woman talk to a man without it being construed as flirting? Where do you draw the line between being friendly and flirting when your personalities seem to...click?" Caty tapped her fist on her forehead, *thump thump thump*. She let out a small groan. "Oh, Marta. I didn't mean to flirt. I am such a bad person."

Marta's lips curled. "You are not a bad person, Caty. And why does that *why can't a woman* spiel remind me of that song in *My Fair Lady* where Rex Harrison asks and sings, 'Why can't a woman be more like a man?'"

"Because you and my mother love musicals," Caty muttered. "Focus, please."

"In terms of the whole male-female thing, the dynamics can be tricky," Marta said. "You're both very attractive people. Educated. Witty. You obviously share common corporate interests since you both work in the oil industry. That's a big draw right there."

Marta had no idea how close to the truth she came with that statement.

"You were having fun," Marta continued. "It's okay to be attracted to someone. It's what you do, or *don't* do, with that attraction that matters. Look, it's not like you slid your arms around him and tried to sit on his lap. You didn't try to kiss him or offer him anything you shouldn't. But the whole banter thing? That was some of the most *for keeps* serious flirting I've seen since New Mexico between Eliot and me. And would you look how that turned out?"

Caty frowned. "Not helping, my friend."

"Hey, I call them as I see them," Marta protested after Caty shot her a glare. "I *was* surprised to see he wore a wedding ring and was…responding to you, for lack of knowing how else to describe it. It's probably what I mentioned earlier. The ring makes a statement, and it's my guess Caleb wears the ring to discourage unwanted attention."

"Maybe," Caty murmured. She'd met men on business trips, especially in airports or in hotels, who didn't wear a ring because they *wanted* female attention. Either way, she needed to steer clear of this particular man.

"Caty, think about what a conversation starter it would have been if Caleb had announced right off the bat, 'By the way, my wife died, so it's okay to flirt.'"

"It might have spared me some guilt, but you're right," Caty said. A wealthy, handsome man? Women would flock around Caleb, especially if he wore his helpful cowboy persona. What woman in her right mind could resist that? Huh. That thought didn't help.

Marta glanced at her mirrored reflection. "Now that we're here, I might as well refresh my lipstick." She pulled a slim gold tube from her small handbag.

"You never cared much about makeup before."

Marta stopped applying her lipstick and their gazes met in the mirror. "Don't change the subject, but is that a problem?"

"Only an observation. I imagine you've changed a number of things since taking the television job. You have an image to uphold for the station now." Caty shook her head. "You know what I mean. I'm not in my right mind tonight. I'm…flummoxed."

"Well, that's quite a word. Not one you hear every day." Marta smiled. "As far as makeup, I wear as little as possible. Only one coat of mascara and light foundation. And I haven't changed the way I dress when I'm not on-air. This girl still wears her sweatpants and T-shirts to the market. Still dresses nice to go to church."

Marta dropped the lipstick back in her purse. "I'll tell you a secret. The red lipstick has nothing to do with my image or the television station. It has everything to do with wanting to please my husband. Eliot loves to see me wear it. He thinks it's exotic and sexy."

Thankfully Marta had lowered her voice since others had come into the lounge. Rubbing her lips together, she smiled at her reflection and then slicked her tongue over her teeth.

"Okay, you told me a secret," Caty said. "Now it's time to tell you one of mine."

Marta turned to her, eyes wide. "I didn't know the Lewis family had secrets. I can hardly wait."

"Caleb is the helpful cowboy." Caty blew out a breath. "He's also my boss. As in the head of the corporation. As in he *owns* it."

"Whoa!" With a wide grin, Marta shook her head. "Wait a minute. So all that stuff you said about your boss working you too hard and not giving you time off—that whole spiel was teasing?" She laughed. "Oh, you were good, my friend. And Caleb dished it right back. Even better. It was very entertaining, I have to say."

"Of course, I'm sad that Caleb lost his wife." Caty kept her voice purposely low. "On the other hand, I'm glad he's not married. Because of the flirting. *Not* flirting! You know what I mean."

"Caleb and Caty. That has a very nice ring to it. Like the names just go together."

"Stop that," Caty snapped. "And stop saying the word *ring*. Are you forgetting the important fact that he's my boss which means this attraction can't go anywhere? End of story. Finished."

Marta waved her hand. "That's an old-fashioned concept if ever I've heard one, especially if he's the boss and sets the rules for the corporation. Do you know if he's a Christian?"

"I feel safe in saying he is although I don't know for sure. He founded his corporation on Christian principles, and I've only known the man to be fair in his corporate dealings."

"Eliot might know although *he* wasn't a Christian when he was at Princeton."

When another woman approached, Marta guided Caty to a loveseat in the more private sitting area. "Let's talk over here."

"We shouldn't be too long, though. The men will think we're never coming back out again," Caty said. "Or that we're having digestive issues."

Marta smiled. "Men know what women do in the ladies room. I feel safe in saying that Eliot and Caleb are probably having a similar discussion of their own right about now."

"It must be nice to be married and know all the inner sanctum secrets of how a man's mind works."

"Inner sanctum. You really are too cute."

Caty frowned. "That's just it, Marta. I don't want to be *cute*. Or adorable. I want to be putting on red lipstick for my husband because he thinks it's sexy on me. Because he thinks *I'm* sexy. Are single, Christian women not supposed to think about that?" She blew out a sigh. "Sexy is not a fruit of the Spirit, after all."

Marta's gentle smile helped to calm her unsettled emotions. "For now, focus on those qualities that make you special the way you are in God's eyes. Let me see if I can explain it. Being sexy to a Christian man like Eliot or Caleb is different than with most guys. To the rest of the world, it's about wearing provocative clothing and showing off your body. Flaunting yourself before a man. Not that Christian men don't struggle with their thought life. That's how God made them, and men are visual creatures. But with a Christian man, it's about much more than that. It's about a woman being intelligent, funny, and how she has confidence in herself. As Christian women, we have a joy and an inner peace that radiates from the inside out. Men respond to that."

"I guess I never thought about it like that," Caty said. "In a roundabout way, are you saying that *faith* is sexy?"

Marta patted her arm. "All in good time. Guaranteed, the right man for you will find everything about you sexy, but for now, forget about being sexy and be yourself. Based on what I saw tonight, Caleb admires and likes you. As more than his employee. You didn't see the looks he gave you when you were cutting chicken. When you were drinking water. Laughing. When you were blinking, eating, pretty much everything you did. You could have spit a gross, half-chewed piece of food on him, and the man would have been totally enthralled."

"After the inauspicious way we met, I'm almost surprised I didn't."

"He's probably trying to figure out what he's feeling." Marta shrugged. "You know how guys are too logical for their own good sometimes. An intelligent man like Caleb, especially since he's loved and lost, is either more inclined to embrace another relationship when the time is right or else he's afraid to take the risk of getting hurt again." She patted her arm. "For your sake, I hope it's the first of those two options."

"I know Caleb has taken certain risks in his business, but he studies and makes wise decisions based on the facts," Caty said. "Not that I'm saying I want him to take the risk with *me*."

A frown briefly crossed Marta's face before it disappeared. "Try not to overthink it, Caty. I'm thinking Caleb being here tonight is a God thing. For now, be your charming self and enjoy the evening."

"How do you figure it's a God thing?"

"Think about it. Of all the guys in the world who could have called Eliot today and walked into this restaurant tonight, the man happens to be your boss. Who, as it turns out, happens to be single, and seems to be somewhere near your age, maybe a little older. You might as well give up denying you're both attracted to each other."

Caty remained silent.

Marta tucked her blonde curls behind one ear. "I know you probably don't want to hear this, but it's true that if a relationship is meant to develop between the two of you, it *will* happen. In God's timing. That's the best advice I can give you."

A vision of the statue in the Belac lobby came to mind. "Helena," Caty whispered.

"Who's Helena?" Marta whispered back.

"There's a statue of a woman in the Belac main lobby. She looks like a Greek goddess, and it says *Helena, my valiant warrior* with A.C. Reid's name and 2002 beneath it." Slapping her hands on her knees, Caty rose to her feet. "That settles it. I can't deal with a man who's still grieving his beloved, valiant wife who died tragically young."

"Why? Because he had a statue made in her honor?" Marta stood beside her. "That's actually very sweet when you think about it. You don't know what happened other than the fact that she died five years ago. I know nothing about his marriage, but a man widowed for five years has had time to grieve. You've got a lot of love to give the right man, Caty. How do you know it's not Caleb Reid? Men are attracted to you, but you haven't taken the time to be caught...yet.

That's the distinction here. Maybe Caleb's been waiting for a woman like you to come along. And maybe—just maybe—you'll hear God's whisper if you stop long enough to listen."

Caty laughed. "Now you sound like Mom."

"Knowing your relationship with your mom, I know that's not a bad thing."

"It's a very good thing," Caty said. "However, I'm not planning on telling Mom about Caleb Reid unless..." How to finish that sentence?

"Until something develops between you and Caleb."

"*If* something develops."

Marta nudged her arm. "My weather predictions have been more than ninety-four percent accurate so far. Between you and Caleb? Oh yes, my friend. It's definitely in the forecast."

Chapter 9

Caleb had enjoyed Caty's company more than he expected. Or wanted. From what he could tell, she'd been genuinely surprised when he'd walked into the room. He didn't believe in coincidence, but neither was he altogether sold on the idea of a "God thing," as his live-in housekeeper, Lettie, termed such unexpected occurrences.

At first, he'd been glad Eliot and Marta had been there to facilitate the conversation. Turned out, talking with Caty hadn't been a chore but a lot of fun. It'd been far too long since he'd shared dinner in the company of a woman who made him laugh.

His motivation in calling Eliot had been to gauge whether he might be a potential ally for a personal matter involving his daughter. He'd heard through the strong Princeton pipeline of alumni that Eliot's background and training were outstanding and above reproach—a man of uncommon intelligence with demonstrated loyalty, physical strength, a natural leader.

Lauren's well-being was the most important thing in the world. His daughter's safety trumped someone pilfering money from his corporation. Or his growing attraction to Catherine Lewis.

Everything paled in comparison to protecting Lauren.

He couldn't afford distractions. Not even a lovely and tempting one.

"Caleb, I'm sorry we didn't have time to talk privately tonight. If you need my help professionally, give me a call." Eliot handed him a business card.

"Thanks." Caleb stopped himself before he said too much. Not yet. It wasn't the time although he'd probably call Eliot in the future. Digging out one of his cards, he gave it to the other man.

Eliot pushed aside his empty plate. "Tell me if I'm out of line, but I sense a strong mutual attraction between you and Caty."

"She's a lovely, intriguing woman, but there's a whole laundry list of reasons why *not* to pursue a relationship." Caleb rubbed a hand over his chin, glad he'd shaved off the scruff before coming to the restaurant. "For starters, I'm a few years older." When he'd checked her personnel file, he'd noted her age—twenty-nine.

"That's irrelevant. The age difference isn't all that much, and you don't look your age."

Caleb didn't wish to engage in a debate about the subject. "I'm also her employer, Eliot. In my estimation, that's a substantial enough reason not to get involved."

"Ah," Eliot said. "I can see where that could complicate things, but it doesn't have to be a deal-breaker. You're the boss and make the rules, correct?" With a small smile, he took a drink of his water.

Caleb fiddled with the stem of his water glass. "Yes, but are rules meant to confine or are they intended to challenge a person to be the best he or she can be?"

"Depends on your motivation and goals," Eliot said. "I'm the first to admit I haven't always played by the rules. I lived fast and free for a long time. I'm a prime example of how God can transform a man's life. Breathe new life into him through the shed blood of Christ."

"How did you first come to faith?" Crossing his arms, Caleb sat back in his chair. He hadn't had a discussion like this with another man in years. At the end of the day, faith is what mattered—not how much money or property he could amass in a lifetime. Not how many friends he'd accumulated. Family was a natural extension of that faith. Raising godly kids and instilling the love of Christ in them. Creating a legacy of faith.

He'd failed miserably in that regard. Could there still be hope with Lauren or was it too late? He'd pushed aside the thought of remarriage…until now. Did he even *want* to start over again at almost forty?

"A man named Juan gave me a Bible at a church in Santiago a number of years ago," Eliot said. "I'd lost a comrade and was messed up with grief. Juan stuck with me for a long time, listening to me cry and talk about my friend. Caleb, I know God put him there on that day, in that moment, to speak to me. Juan spoke faltering English mixed with Chilean Spanish. I knew enough Spanish, and he knew just enough English, to impress upon me that a man named Jesus loved me enough to die on a cross. He gave me an English version Bible and prayed with me. The guy was in rags, and I don't know how he came to have that Bible, but God provided the way and the means."

Eliot's eyes were bright as he continued his story. "Juan's faith was simple, raw, and honest. It was one of the most beautiful things I've ever witnessed. You know what it was? I saw *Jesus* reflected in the radiant face of another man who cared about my eternal destiny. That's something a man doesn't forget. I still carry that Bible today. It's tattered, and the pages are falling out, but that book represents my healing, redemption, and hope. It's one of my most treasured possessions, and it always will be."

"That's an amazing story," Caleb said. "Thanks for sharing. I placed my trust in Christ when I was ten—my mom led me to faith—but that faith has been severely tested in the last few years. Now, I'm afraid it's wobbly at best. I know that's not the right heart attitude, and those are excuses for my weaknesses, but for better or worse, it's where I'm at right now."

"We all have our trials, brother. God has a way of bringing each one of us around to the truths He needs us to discover. Each person's journey is unique."

Drumming his fingers on the tablecloth, Caleb considered the other man's words. "I'm trying to find my way back, Eliot. I've got to find my way past some major stumbling blocks first."

"I'd be honored to pray for you." Eliot's voice held the kind of compassion from another man he hadn't heard in years. "No wonder what's happening in my life, I've also found that nothing's too big for God. I never expected to meet someone fantastic like Marta and then stay in one place long enough to fall in love. We'd skirted around each other for a few years with TeamWork events, but when we finally had a few weeks together on the mission in New Mexico, that's all it took to solidify our relationship. Then I was knifed—"

"You were knifed on a TeamWork mission?" Incredulous, Caleb stared at the other man.

"Yes, but those were extenuating circumstances. We had some trouble from a local group, and they tried to burn down the Native American church we were building in New Mexico."

Eliot dismissed being stabbed as though it wasn't a major trauma. Compared to what Eliot must have faced in his military life, and the way he'd probably put his life on the line on a daily basis for years, Caleb supposed it would pale in significance.

"So, there I was, lying wounded in a hospital bed outside Albuquerque, and the Lord convicted me that I needed to marry Marta even though the only real date we'd had was to the hot air balloon fiesta." With a smile, Eliot drained his glass of iced tea. "Crazy, I know. We'd had lots of conversations through the years, enough for me to know if I ever settled down, Marta Holcomb was the woman I'd want walking beside me into an eternity in heaven."

"I'm happy for you, Eliot. Marta seems great, and I can tell she's a good friend to Caty. Thank you for sharing your story, and I welcome your prayers." Prayer definitely couldn't hurt, and it was the *best* thing anyone could do for another.

Eliot's look was understanding. "Like I said, call me if you need me otherwise."

Caleb nodded. "Will do."

The ladies returned to their table, and they all declined dessert. Eliot paid the bill, but he accepted Caleb's offer to leave the tip. Usually Caleb was the one who picked up the tab for everyone, and it was a pleasant change to be treated.

As they prepared to leave the restaurant, Marta gave Caty a quick hug before turning to him. "Caleb, it was a pleasure to meet you. I hope we'll see you again."

"Most definitely. We should all have dinner soon, and I'll return the favor." Until the words escaped, Caleb didn't consider the implications of that statement in terms of Caty.

After bidding their friends good night, Caleb grabbed his Stetson. Pressing his hand lightly on Caty's back, they exited the room together. He caught the scent of her, a subtle floral. The same scent that lingered after she'd left his office. The same scent he'd noticed with her sitting so close during dinner.

"May I walk you to your car?" he said.

She gave him a smile that seemed almost shy. He needed to remind himself he wasn't on a date.

"That would be nice, but I need to retrieve my coat first."

"Do you have your claim ticket? I'll get it for you."

"Let's both go." Caty walked beside him to the coat check. Not sure what to say for once in his life, Caleb shoved his hands in the pockets of his jeans and resisted the urge to whistle. Why did he feel like a kid on a first date? In an odd way, he enjoyed it. The newness of it all, the wonder of discovering mutual attraction.

How long had it been since he'd even *had* a date? The clumsy attempts he'd made to take a woman to dinner since Helena's death had failed miserably, leaving him more alone at the end of the evening. He'd finally decided it wasn't worth the effort. The women were nice enough—attractive, fun, intelligent—but something had been missing in each case. Whatever it was the other women lacked, Caty possessed in abundance.

If only he could figure what *it* was. Could be a combination of qualities.

He'd seen Caty's photos before, but not a one of them had done her adequate justice. In person, she was stunning, a woman who'd captivated his attention from the second he'd noticed her on the sidewalk. After her mishaps outside, he'd wanted to sweep her into his arms and carry her into the building before she could hurt herself. Not that he considered himself some kind of romantic hero. That almost made him laugh.

Glancing his way, Caty caught him red-handed in his staring. For once, he didn't care, and he was pleased when she held his gaze. They understood one another, acknowledged the strong undercurrents of attraction simmering between them. He was a man, she was a woman. Couldn't get much more basic than that although he needed to be careful since he hadn't had much contact with the opposite sex—other than in a professional way—in a long time. Not that he'd act on this attraction, but for now, he could appreciate and enjoy it.

He liked her smile and those gorgeous blue eyes. Her lush, dark hair that fell in soft waves around her face and cascaded around her shoulders. Catherine Lewis radiated a girl-next-door type of natural beauty he preferred. Fresh, approachable, and…effervescent. So tall she was nearly his height in heels.

Neither one of them were kids. He couldn't know if she'd had any long-term relationships, but if he had to guess, he'd say no. From what he knew of her, she'd never been married, had no children. If he didn't still cling to a semblance of his once much stronger faith, and if Caty weren't a morally principled woman, their evening would probably end in a much different way. He'd seen too many acquaintances fall into casual physical intimacy in an attempt to validate their worth as a desirable human being. That kind of thinking, and those types of encounters, only led to eventual hurt and possible heartache.

More than that, there was a purity about Caty that called to something inside him. He respected her strength, her honesty, and in truth, everything he knew about the woman. Caty was a true lady in every sense of the word.

His gaze dropped to her feet. She wore cowgirl boots—not only that, they were red, one of his favorite colors. Another surprise from this intriguing woman, and one he liked.

"Nice boots. Not that I normally comment on a woman's footwear," he said, clearing his throat. "Just so we're clear."

"No worries. Don't be surprised if I show up in them at the office one day. They're my footwear of choice."

"Feel free."

"Caleb, I hope you know I was just being silly earlier tonight," she said before the silence between them grew noticeably long.

"I can't remember the last time I had such fun at dinner. Catherine is a beautiful name. Have you always been called Caty?"

"As long as I can remember. I'm named for my grandmother on my dad's side although I don't believe she went by a name other than Catherine. This might sound crazy…" Her voice trailed and she ducked her head.

"What?" He tried to catch her eye. "Tell me."

"When we first met earlier today? On the sidewalk outside the office building? That was a Caty moment."

"And now?" He knew the answer but wanted to hear it from her.

"Now…is *definitely* a Catherine moment." Her voice had grown soft, sweet. Infinitely appealing.

He smiled. "I hope you'll clue me in at the office which kind of day you're having so I'll know which name to call you. And feel free to wear your red boots anytime you'd like." He restrained himself before he winked. For all he knew, he'd already crossed that line unconsciously.

She seemed surprised. "You can call me Caty, but I assumed we wouldn't see each other often."

She was right. Normally they *wouldn't* cross paths. When Caleb opened his mouth to respond, what emerged was, "I might want to drop by sometime." He wasn't sure *why* he'd said it, but for once he'd allowed his emotions to control his words.

Her cheeks flushed, and they stepped closer to the coat check counter, one person away from the front of the line. "Do you travel a lot?"

"I used to travel quite a bit, but in the past year I've been sending other Belac officers in my place," he said. "They're more than capable, and I'm always a phone call or teleconference away."

She nodded. "I'm sure you've earned the right, and I don't blame you."

"It's not so much about the right. There are other factors to consider."

"Do you have children?" She'd read straight through his last statement, but Lauren was so much more than a *factor*. Semantics, but it'd had been a poor choice of words. He was thankful Caty felt comfortable enough to ask him questions, but he hoped she wouldn't ask him about Helena. That was complicated and would take more time than they had while waiting in the coat check queue.

"One daughter—Lauren. She's twelve going on forty-five. Typical, I understand, for that age."

"I'm sure she's a lovely girl."

He swallowed. "She is, actually." He was also losing Lauren, and he needed to do something to rectify the emotional distance between them. She hated that he'd uprooted her, and they'd left Dallas. She hadn't said as much, but she'd become more withdrawn and refused to eat dinner with him lately, opting to take her meal in her bedroom instead. He supposed he should stop allowing that kind of behavior. Finding the right balance and knowing where to draw the lines was one of the most difficult challenges he'd faced.

Since Helena's death, he'd given his daughter everything in order to try and make up for the fact that her mother was gone. As if it was somehow *his* fault. As though material gifts could fill the void. And as a result, Lauren acted alternately spoiled and petulant. But not always. Maybe it was part of the preteen thing, a rite of passage. At times, he glimpsed her inherent sweetness, enough to give him renewed hope.

"Caleb. We're up."

He handed the claim ticket to the waiting clerk, and the woman returned within seconds with Caty's lightweight raincoat. "Thank you." He placed a generous tip in the jar on the counter.

Stepping to the side, Caleb opened the coat and held it for Caty as she slid her arms into the sleeves. The softness in her eyes as she thanked him told him she appreciated his actions. And yes, he'd *missed* doing these kinds of things—the courtesies, the gentlemanly gestures, that could mean a lot to a woman. To a lady like Catherine Lewis.

"Cordelia called to tell me that you hadn't picked up your parking card and Belac badge before leaving the offices today." He reached inside the interior pocket of his jacket. Taking her hand, he placed his personal parking card inside her palm before curling her fingers around it. "You'll need this on Monday morning."

Caty nodded without looking at him. "Thank you. She told me to pick up my parking pass and badge from the front desk, but I obviously didn't remember. One question: where will you park if I have your card?"

"I'll figure out something. I can always get a duplicate made."

Caty handed the card back to him. "You're very kind, but I can't take this."

"Then I'll have Cordelia arrange for your parking card and ID badge to be delivered to the townhome. What day will you be there?"

"I'm moving in on Saturday. I'm at my parents' house until then. It was my fault for leaving the Belac office without them, and I hate for you to go to the expense of having—"

"Let me do this." He found it endearing how she didn't want him to spend money. He gave her hand a slight squeeze before releasing her.

"Thank you, Caleb." Caty pointed to the left side of the lot as they walked outside. "My car's over here." The night air was breezy and chilly. She'd been smart to bring a lightweight coat. "Where are you parked?"

"That's a good question. I'm not sure since the valet parked the Porsche."

Caty's eyes widened. "Is it black? A 911 Carrera?"

"Yes, as a matter of fact." He tilted his head. "Why do you ask?"

Glancing into the distance, Caty blew out a sigh and didn't appear especially pleased. "I was nearly drenched by a speeding 911 today when I was standing by the curb outside the building. Now that I think about it, you suddenly appeared on the sidewalk a few seconds later." She frowned. "Carrying boxes of Chinese take-out."

"I'm sorry. I wasn't aware of the water at the curb."

"How can you park your car in front of the office building? Surely you'll get towed…" Caty's voice trailed. "Forgive me. That was a silly question. You're a major new tenant of the office tower, and I'm sure that comes with certain privileges. And it was very kind of you to get food for Cordelia. I only hope you don't drive like a maniac on a regular basis."

Caleb pinched his lips together. "I try not to make a habit of it."

"You weren't aware of the heavy rains earlier this afternoon?"

"The short answer is no." They'd had a nice evening together, and he didn't want it spoiled by a conversation centering on his ignorance of standing water or his gross negligence. "I knew it had rained before I left the building, but not when or how much. If I'd drenched you, you can rest assured I would have made amends."

"That's not my point. How…" Caty faltered, obviously conflicted.

His jaws tightened. "As you're aware, I've lived a rather isolated existence the past few years. By choice."

"Yes, and that's why no one at Belac knows anything about you." Thankfully, she kept her voice quiet.

"If you'd lost a spouse and had a child to protect, you'd better understand." Her questions didn't irritate him. They were understandable, but he couldn't give her any explanations tonight. Like standing in that coat check queue, he didn't wish to discuss his personal life in a public parking lot.

Caty held his gaze. "I realize it's none of my business that you've apparently chosen to live your life in a cocoon. And you're right. I can't begin to understand what losing a spouse must be like. Caleb, I'm sorry if I offended you by asking about Helena, but you have to know my question was innocent. I had no idea she'd passed away, especially since you wear a wedding ring."

She had him there. He hadn't even thought about removing the ring. The fact it was still on his finger was more an oversight than the idea that it represented the last vestiges of his marriage. Perhaps subconsciously, the ring kept him safe and mirrored the steep walls he'd erected around his heart. In this case, walls meant to protect him as much as to keep others on the outside.

He swallowed hard. "How did you know her name?" Not that it mattered, but he needed time to process this latest self-revelation. Why was it after only a few hours in the presence of this woman, his life seemed altered in a good way? Caty was a fresh breath of spring air bringing a much-needed positive spirit to revive his soured outlook.

"I saw the statue in the lobby," she said. "And the inscription."

"I see." His gaze rested on her lovely face. "I value your honesty and can appreciate that you spoke your mind, Caty. If you want the truth, your observations hit close to home. Not that it's a bad thing." He should apologize for his unkind remark, but he couldn't. Not tonight. "Let me escort you to your car."

"I'll be fine. As expected, I'll report for duty at Belac first thing on Monday morning." She nodded. "Good night."

That one hit a little below the belt. "Report for duty?" By the time he could formulate a follow-up response, she'd left his side. As she walked quickly across the parking lot, he stayed rooted on the sidewalk, staring after her, surprised by her abrupt departure.

Chapter 10

Within the minute, a car started somewhere in the lot, and then a black Volvo sports coupe slowly approached. In the dimly lit lot, and because the car had tinted windows, he couldn't tell if it was Caty until she lowered the window and pulled alongside him.

Prompted by the need to say something, Caleb stepped closer to the curb. "Caty, I hadn't planned on stopping my car in front of the building this afternoon. And since you seem concerned with details, Cordelia sent someone out to park the car for me."

He caught the beginnings of her smile. "Then why did you stop?"

"Because you looked like you might need some help." If he were completely honest, he'd stopped because she was a beautiful woman, although she *had* appeared to be in need of assistance. He was smart enough to keep that thought to himself.

Caty was quiet for a long moment before speaking again. "You continue to surprise me. About that baseball glove signed by The Babe...?"

"Yes?" She'd definitely piqued his attention with that question. Talking baseball with this woman had been energizing. In all his days, he'd never met a woman who knew so much about baseball.

"Was it signed during the time Babe Ruth played with the Boston Red Sox or the New York Yankees?"

"Does it matter?"

"It does to me, yes." Her smile emerged.

"You're sneaky." Tempted to cross his arms and lean on the edge of the window, Caleb remained upright. "You want to know where my loyalties lie."

"I'm sure you're well aware there are fundamental differences in the teams, both then and now," she said. "Take the 2004 Red Sox, for example. From my perspective, in that particular matchup, it all boils down to whether you prefer scrappy team players or overpriced talent."

Abide

"Will you still come to work for me if I give you the wrong answer?"

Caty tilted her head as if considering his question. "Yes, but I'd still like to know."

"The glove was signed in 1916 during the time Babe Ruth played for Boston." Although he admired both teams and enjoyed their age-old rivalry, Boston was clearly the answer she sought.

"And Boston won the World Series that year." A lovely smile curved Caty's lips, although this was more a Catherine moment. "In that case, I'm sure that glove is even more valuable."

"Good night." Caleb lifted one hand in farewell as Caty raised the window and drove out of sight.

After his earlier thoughtless remark, Helena would have stomped off in a huff and not spoken to him for a week. Withheld her physical affections even longer. She'd been the type of person to bear a grudge. Caty, apparently, was not. He could use Caty's sweet optimism in his life.

After only a few hours, she'd somehow managed to work her way past his defenses and into his affections. He wasn't sure how it'd happened. He suspected Miss Lewis could be dangerous for his heart. On the flip side, she might be the answer to his loneliness, something he hadn't wanted to admit even to himself.

"Sir, do you have a valet ticket?"

Startled from his musing, Caleb dug out the ticket and handed it to the kid. "Thanks. Be careful with the car."

"Yes, sir."

The comparisons between Caty and Helena weren't healthy. He shouldn't go there, although perhaps it was inevitable. Caty was a completely different woman from Helena. Likewise, he was a different man today than the self-absorbed, ego-driven kid he'd been when he'd married the beautiful blonde daughter of one of the richest men in Texas. He'd been all of twenty-four and Helena only twenty-two. Babies, really.

Bolstered by early success, he'd been full of himself, arrogant, pretentious, and eager to take on the world. Some would say he'd been young and stupid, but he'd taken on the oil and mineral industry at the "right" time. In countless interviews, he'd been called "lucky." Not that he'd ever termed it that way. What he'd done was surround himself with the right people. As a result, he'd accumulated wealth beyond his wildest imaginings. Not for one minute had he entered the oil industry to get rich, but it'd been a nice by-product. He'd remained honest, principled, and built a solid reputation through the years. When it came to business, he'd never compromised. But at what cost? His family? His marriage?

You've been blessed, Caleb. Call it like it is.

Caleb checked his watch as the valet stopped the Porsche beside the curb. Nine o'clock. Still early enough to spend a little time with Lauren. Not that she'd be receptive, but he needed to try. Things had to change, and it started with trying to repair his relationship with his daughter. He wished he could pinpoint when things had gone so wrong. Was it only the move to Houston or was there more to it? For all he'd accomplished in the business world, his biggest challenge had been to be a good husband and father.

In many ways, perhaps in the ways that counted most, he'd failed both Helena and Lauren.

Handing a generous tip to the teenager, lost in thought, Caleb slid behind the wheel. Now he needed to focus on the most precious reminder of his fateful union with his wife—his daughter. Lauren used to look at him with adoring eyes and make him feel like the best father in the world. Now she admired grungy rock stars and athletes whose bodies were covered in tattoos. At least she had to wear a uniform to school. He shuddered to think what she'd wear if that weren't a mandatory restriction.

Sure, her behavior and the way she dressed was probably considered typical for most kids on the cusp of adolescence, but Lauren wasn't a typical kind of kid. He didn't *want* her to be typical in any sense of the word. He wanted her to stand out among the crowd for the *best* reasons. The right reasons. He needed to set the example. Lord knows, he'd tried.

Exiting the parking lot and pulling onto the street, Caleb's thoughts again strayed to Caty. Now, there was an enigma of a woman who spoke her mind. A gutsy, intelligent, lovely woman with a mind for details who could spout facts about baseball in a bygone era.

For the first time in five years, a woman made him feel like a man again. Awakened deep, personal emotions in him and stirred physical desires he'd buried deep for the past few years. Could he be worthy of a woman like her? Those blue eyes were untainted by the ugliness of sin. From all appearances, she came from an upstanding and godly family who depended on the things of the Lord much more than worldly possessions.

A sad truth, a sobering truth, slammed into Caleb's muddled mind. Once she got to know him better and discovered the heavy personal baggage he carried in his heart, Caty wouldn't want to stick around as anything more than his chief accountant for Belac.

"Welcome to my world, Miss Lewis."

Hitting the open highway with a heavy heart, Caleb headed for home.

Chapter 11

Saturday Morning

"Caty, the upper cabinets are done. I'll start on the lower cabinets next." Wiping her brow with the back of her hand, Sarah Lewis stood aside as Caty joined her in the kitchen.

"They look great, Mom. You spoil me too much."

"Not possible." Sarah gave her a hug, at least the tenth one since they'd started working earlier that morning. "Have I told you how happy your Dad and I are to have you back home in Houston?"

"Not in the last hour. You can't be any happier than I am." Caty kissed her mother's cheek. Through the pass-through window leading into the dining room, she spied her father. Sam Sr. ducked his head and stepped inside the front door with a bulky box in his arms.

"Caty, where do you want this box of"—he darted a glance at the label—"miscellaneous items?"

"Sounds like a corner of the living room box to me. I marked all the essentials, so that one can wait until later." Caty grinned. "You two might as well admit you're glad I won't be camped out at the house after tonight."

"Nothing could be further from the truth," Sarah protested. "We've loved catching up with you. I'll miss the girl talk and popcorn movie nights we've had the last couple of weeks."

"We'll talk and email, Mom. You know keeping in touch won't be an issue." Her mother hated cell phones although her father used one.

"I know, but feel free to stop by anytime." Her mother grabbed the ruler and shelf liner paper before settling on the floor beside the lower cabinets. "You still haven't said anything about your meeting with your boss earlier this week. Not to pry, but did it go all right?"

Where to begin? "Well, I finally have a face to put to his name. After five years, I consider that a significant step forward." Something held her back from saying more. Caleb wanted to remain anonymous, and she needed to respect his wishes although she knew her family wouldn't breathe his secrets to anyone. She was dying to tell Sam about Eliot and Caleb's Princeton connection. God's world grew smaller every day.

"What's he like?" Sarah said as her father called to tell her that he was heading outside for another load.

"He was very nice, actually. Younger than I expected. Huge baseball fan. He's noticed my work with the Montford Mission, which surprised me in a good way." *Strong in character. Intriguing. Handsome. Business mogul. Widower. Father.*

Her mother peeked out from halfway inside the bottom cabinet. "Now I'm more interested in what you're *not* telling me."

How did Mom always know? Needing something to do, Caty pulled out her phone and snapped a photo. "You are so great to do this for me."

"I'm in my oldest work clothes, and my hair's a mess. I hope you don't plan on using that photo to bribe me." Sarah gave her a wry grin. "Don't think I'm not aware you changed the subject."

"You're too smart for me." Trained as a nurse, Sarah had worked hospital shifts around the family's schedule early on and then taken a position as a traveling school nurse in the Houston public school system. Mom had always been home when she came in the door every afternoon.

Caty couldn't help but wonder about Caleb and his daughter. Did Lauren have a female presence in her life? A grandmother or other relative? On the cusp of her teens, she was at a pivotal age. Caty couldn't imagine what she would have done without her mother or older sisters when she'd been twelve. Caleb must work long hours in his office, so surely he had someone to help him. A man with his resources might have several staff members.

"I get the point about your boss," Sarah continued. "You either don't want to talk about him or feel like you can't. I know how curious you've been to meet him, so I'm happy that's been rectified."

"Caty, can you come and give us the layout for the living room furniture?" At Sam's call, Caty smiled to know her brothers had arrived. Although she'd told Sam that Belac would pay for professional movers, he'd insisted. Her brother could be stubborn that way, but she loved his protectiveness.

"Coming! Mom, do you have everything you need for the moment?"

"Everything's all good," Sarah called from inside the cabinet. "Go out there and boss those guys around. You don't get many opportunities to do that."

"Yes, ma'am." Laughing, Caty scurried out to the other room where Sam held one end of her sofa and Josh Grant the other. "Hey, Josh! I didn't know you were coming to help."

"Anything for you, Caty. Not to mention your brother is a master recruiter." Josh flashed one of his trademark grins.

After she instructed them where to position the sofa, Caty smiled when she spied Kevin Moore negotiating the front door with an oversized side chair.

"Welcome home, Caty. Where do you want this chair?"

"Thanks, Kevin. It's great to be back. Thanks for helping. You can put the chair across from the sofa for now. There's one more matching chair, and the coffee table will go between them." Sliding her hands to her hips, Caty grinned. "So, to what do I owe the honor of the TeamWork crew showing up this morning?" All three men were dressed in matching green TeamWork T-shirts, jeans, and baseball caps—UT for Sam, LSU for Josh, and A&M for Kevin.

"Will jetted off to an aeronautical convention in Seattle this weekend, and Carson's studying for finals," Sam said. "I scraped the bottom of the barrel and came up with these guys."

Josh playfully punched Sam in the arm. "Love you, too, Love Master."

"Truce." Laughing, Sam raised his arms in surrender and lifted Josh's baseball cap before plopping it backwards on his friend's blond head. "You must have gotten that one from Marc."

"You know it," Josh said.

Caty figured the Love Master nickname had something to do with Sam's successful marriage and family books. She hadn't met Marc Thompson, but he and his wife, Natalie, lived in Boston and were faithful TeamWork volunteers. They had three little girls: Gracie—close in age to Sam and Lexa's son, Joe—Faith, adopted from China, and another daughter, Joyanne they called Joy.

"I hope you know how much I appreciate you for doing this. Mom's preparing *Caty's Moving Feast* for everyone back at the house when we're done here," Caty said. "I hope you can join us, and feel

free to invite your wives and children. Peach pie included, of course."
She directed that last comment to Sam. Like their father, her oldest
brother would do almost anything for a slice of homemade peach pie.

When her cell phone rang, Caty tugged it from the pocket of her
jeans. *Caleb Reid.* Why was Caleb calling her today? Her pulse did a
little flip.

"Excuse me a minute. I should take this." Heading for the back
patio, she closed the sliding door behind her.

"Caty Lewis."

"So today is a Caty day."

"For now. Stay tuned. You'll be happy to know I haven't had
any mishaps today although circumstances are always subject to
change. Don't tell me you've changed your baseball affiliation."

"Not quite." Caleb's chuckle was warm. "I wanted to check and
see if you're getting settled."

"I am. Sam showed up with some of the TeamWork guys since
the astronaut brother and seminary student brother both flaked out
on us." There she went again—blathering on about things.

"Go back a second. Astronaut brother?"

"Yes. That would be Will. He's commanding the next shuttle to
the ISS." Although the truth, Caty hoped that didn't come across as
bragging or boastful.

"That's the *Pursuit* mission, right? Coming up this later year?"

Caleb knew the name of Will's shuttle? That made her smile.
"Yes, it launches in late October. We're beyond thrilled for him.
Will's worked toward this goal his entire life."

"I can imagine. I had no idea you were related to Commander
Lewis. How many brothers and sisters do you have?"

"Five. In terms of age, I'm sandwiched between Will and
Carson, the youngest."

"In addition to the TeamWork brother, there's the astronaut and
the seminary student. Who are the other two?"

"Emily and Rachel, twins who've lived out on the West Coast
for years. Listen, I appreciate the call, but I should get back—"

"My apologies. I don't want to keep you. I mainly called to thank
you."

"Thank me?" That came out more an embarrassing squeak. "I'm
sure you're welcome but for what?" Shifting from one foot to the
other, Caty resisted the urge to chew on a fingernail.

Caleb didn't answer for so long she thought she'd lost the connection.

"For breathing fresh air back into my life." He chuckled again. "Maybe I should have thought that one through."

"No, no," she said quickly. "It was…very nice." She was thankful Caleb couldn't see her at the moment. So, his phone call wasn't motivated by business. Was this part of his new attitude in getting to know his employees?

"Enjoy the rest of your weekend."

"Thank you, Caleb. I'll hope to see you in the office one day this week." Maybe she shouldn't have said it, but it was true. Caleb might be her boss, but she genuinely liked him. When he wasn't in his full business mode, he was surprisingly humble and willing to make fun of himself. She liked talking with him. And yes, she'd also enjoyed flirting with him.

After disconnecting the call, Caty stared at her cell phone as if the device could somehow answer the burning questions in her mind.

Chapter 12

Parking his Porsche in the garage, Caleb cut the engine and climbed out of the car. As he entered the kitchen, he had one thing on his mind—cold water. He'd already drained his water bottle on the way home from the club after three rousing games of racquetball against a tough adversary. Grabbing a glass, he filled it with water from the fridge and downed it in three seconds flat. Then repeated the process a second time.

What had possessed him to call Caty at home? That'd been a harebrained move. His heart had pumped like a hormonal adolescent when she'd answered, and it wasn't from the energy he'd expended on the racquetball court.

Facing the window, Caleb rested his arms on the edge of the sink. Outside, the sun shone brightly. He loved this view of the backyard but made a mental note to hire a landscaping service. The pool was large enough for Lauren to swim laps and well-hidden from view. He cranked open the window so he could hear the soothing sound of the small, cascading waterfall. Rotating his right shoulder, he knew he should relax his muscles in the Jacuzzi at some point later in the day.

The home was older, built forty years ago, but as such, it held unique character and charm that a newer home lacked. That's one of the primary reasons he'd wanted this particular home. There'd only been one other family who'd occupied the home, an oil executive and his wife. They'd raised their family here, and after his death ten years ago, his widow had maintained and updated the residence. Several months ago, she'd moved to where one of the daughters lived in Arizona.

He'd snapped up the house after only one visit, armed with a glowing inspection. The mature trees provided natural shade and privacy. The owner's flower garden had been her pride and joy, her solace after her husband's death, according to his Realtor. The evidence of the widow's loving care, a lasting and beautiful memorial, bloomed in brilliant color outside the window. Oliver lived in the small guest cottage on the property and, in addition to being Lauren's driver, he was an expert gardener.

The need to pray seized Caleb. He hadn't prayed a legitimate prayer, something beyond the rote and routine, in so long he couldn't remember. Certainly not much since Helena's death. He'd listened to prayers here and there, but not so much in recent years. The words of the prayers of others had flowed over him, tickled his ears and warmed his heart, but they'd never made their way into his conscious mind or penetrated his heart. As a result, he'd been left empty and isolated. He had no one to blame but himself.

Lowering his head, Caleb started to pray. What was that sound? Still holding the glass, Caleb turned away from the sink. He almost spit out his last gulp of water, nearly dropped the glass, when he spied Lauren.

Leaning against the doorjamb, his daughter stared at him through big blue eyes—vacant and accusing—that reminded him of her mother. Otherwise, she resembled him with her height, shape of the nose and lips, and her dark hair.

He swiped the back of his hand over his mouth and set the glass on the counter. "I didn't know you were in the kitchen."

"Technically, I'm not *in* the kitchen." Lauren smirked, as much from being called *sweetheart* as anything else, he imagined.

"I don't know when you ever got to be smarter than me," he said. Not a great start to the conversation, but it was something. He'd tried his best to make it sound like a compliment instead of a sarcastic snarl. Whether or not the move to Houston was a good thing for her and their strained relationship was currently up for debate. All he knew was they'd both been dying a slow death in Dallas.

"What were you doing just now?"

"Well, Lauren, I thought it was time to start praying again."

In response, his daughter crossed her arms and stared at him. "Is it okay if I go out?"

Caleb's jaw clenched. "You know the rules."

Rolling her eyes, she let out a sigh of extreme disgust. "Why can't I go out with my friends?" She lifted her chin in defiance, an action that reminded him all over again of Helena and made it more difficult to escape the little things that niggled at him. The saddest fact? Even if she were still alive, Helena might not have been the best influence on their daughter. Maybe that wasn't fair. Everyone could change. Her death had certainly changed *him*.

"I'm happy to know you're making friends here in Houston." After refilling his glass again, Caleb carefully considered his next words. He couldn't push Lauren so far that he'd lose her permanently. He was precariously close to the precipice—or at least the point of no return—as it was. And she wasn't even a teenager yet. He was in big trouble.

Somewhere along the way his sweet little Lauren had morphed into this sullen preteen—dressed in somber colors and drab clothes—who rarely smiled and treated him with disdain. At least she hadn't started wearing makeup yet or she'd probably ring her eyes with black and look like a raccoon. Wear horrible black lipstick. Pierce body parts better left alone that should never have holes in them. If God didn't put it there, why make one?

Think positive. He couldn't tell her of the dangers of this new city until he had time to ensure her protection. No way would he allow her to go anywhere with someone he didn't know, hadn't met, or hadn't thoroughly investigated. He suppressed his sigh. Their situation was anything but normal. When did life get so complicated?

"Dad, don't you think I know what you're doing?"

Caleb's heart thudded in his chest. This should be enlightening. He was thankful she hadn't stormed away from him as per the norm lately. Had Lauren figured out what was happening? Did she know what *could* have happened several times in Dallas in the past three years? What almost happened at least once? The most frightening probability was that it happened more times than he realized. Detectives everywhere, not only in Dallas, had tons of cases and were short on manpower.

Finished with his water, he lowered the empty glass into the sink while he gathered his thoughts. "Why don't you tell me?" His stomach felt sour and his head ached from nothing to do with coming down from the natural high of his racquetball victory. The physical release had been welcome. Exercising his body was one of the best ways of dealing with his stress or he might have spontaneously combusted a long time ago.

"That's just like you! Half the time you don't even give me a straight answer." Lauren's voice was laced with derision, making

Caleb cringe. What had he done to deserve that from his daughter when all he'd tried to do was love her? Protect her?

"Lauren, baby, you've got to trust me."

"I'm not a baby, and you want to keep me a prisoner in this house! You might as well put bars over the windows and put deadbolt locks all over *me*."

Caleb shook his head. "No, that's not what I'm doing. And like it or not, you are—and always will be—my baby girl." Stiffening, he inhaled a deep breath. "Believe it or not, it's all about *protecting* you."

Blue eyes challenged him. "Tell me what's really going on. Or else I'm walking out of this house, and I might not come back." What was she going to do, scale the gates or climb the high brick walls around the perimeter of the property?

He'd had enough. "You're *twelve*, Lauren. You can't walk out of this house, and you won't." He tried to steady his breathing. If she pushed him hard enough, he might lose whatever control he still possessed.

"I have friends who are older. They said I can hang out with them. Or I can go back to Grandma Reid in Dallas."

"Hang out?" He started to step closer to her but stopped. Forced a few deep breaths. No way would he consider sending Lauren away. Anything but that. Although his mother was an infinitely better choice than anyone else, doing so would be the kiss of death to any relationship he hoped to have with her now or in the future. "Who are these friends?"

Lauren shrugged and dropped her gaze.

"Answer me." He'd spoken louder than he'd intended. "Please."

"Just some kids."

"Male or female? How old?"

"Both. A little older."

"How did you meet them?" They hadn't been in Houston long. He knew everywhere she went and what she did.

"Haven't you heard of the Internet?"

Caleb seethed. Lauren was an innocent. There were too many people out there with sexual perversions, pedophiles, and others with weird proclivities surfing the web on the prowl for vulnerable girls exactly like her. He shuddered at the thought. Although he hadn't had a drink in years, he felt like jumping in the car and driving to the closest liquor store. It was only a five-minute drive.

No. *Maybe it's time to tell her the truth.* He couldn't lose her. Not now. Not ever.

Caleb motioned to the chairs around the kitchen table. "Have a seat, please. We need to talk about some things." He'd picked up a Christian self-help book that encouraged dads of teenage girls to nurture them like a delicate flower. To use gentle words instead of acting gruff and unyielding, to be kind instead of overbearing. Maybe it was a bunch of hooey, but he had nothing to lose. *Following* the advice was the hardest proposition, and their situation was anything but normal.

"Why? So you can make more *rules*?" Lauren didn't budge but he could tell he'd gotten to her by the way her eyes widened. She appeared to be waging a mental debate. Finally, she lowered her hands to her sides and walked to the table. Pulling out the chair opposite him, she stared at him as she lowered into the seat. He did the same. He didn't like the idea of a face-off, but she was here. They were talking. In its own way, this was good. This was progress.

"Lauren, you seem to be under the impression that I don't want you to have friends or have fun. That's not true. I want all those things for you."

"Could have fooled me. I guess that's why you have those gates that could impale me and the walls with those pitchfork things on top?"

Leaning both elbows on the table, Caleb raked both hands through his hair. "I love you, Lauren. If nothing else, I hope you remember that."

"Then tell me the truth. Why do I feel like a prisoner?"

"You're not a prisoner. You go out with Lettie."

"Give me a break." Lauren lifted her eyes to the ceiling and crossed her arms. "Lettie's great, but she's like…ancient. She rolls her hair every night in those pink and black rollers and puts greasy green cream on her face. It's kinda scary." Thank the Lord he'd had Lettie's help with Lauren since Helena's death. Hired to help Helena, she'd been with him since before his daughter's birth. He didn't know how he'd have survived without her. She'd been a strong lifeline to the outside world in the months following Helena's death. His mother and Cordelia had been the other two women who'd helped to pull him through…and Lauren in her sweeter innocent years.

He'd been fiddling with his fingers, but at her words, Caleb nodded. Part of being a responsible parent was stepping back far enough to try and see this situation from Lauren's perspective. For what it was worth, she was his daughter in terms of character. She could always change, but for now she was a straight shooter—honest and forthright. He appreciated those qualities since Helena had always been more high-strung and nervous in temperament. If Lauren were the same way, he wasn't sure if he could handle her without resorting to some form of chemical dependency.

Get a grip. Tell her. She's old enough to understand. He hoped he wasn't making a huge mistake, but Caleb didn't know what else to do. No one ever said being a single parent was easy. No kidding. Being a father was the hardest thing he'd ever done. Yet the sight of his daughter's smile filled him with the more pride and made him happier than he'd ever been. If they could only get through this rough patch together, they might have a fighting chance.

Maybe it was time to loosen up on the reins a little and give more responsibility to others at Belac so he could concentrate on his relationship with Lauren.

"When I first held you in the hospital delivery room, I vowed to you then that I'd always protect you. As your father, that's an awesome responsibility that God entrusted to me. I've always upheld that vow, and I take it more seriously than anything else in my life. Lauren, you're more important to me than the business, this house, the Porsche. *Anything.*" He made sure she was listening and fixed her with his gaze. "*You* are the most important person in my life. Never forget that, sweetheart."

"What about Mom? You couldn't protect her from cancer." His daughter's words stemmed more from hurt than anger. He knew that, yet they still stung.

Caleb forced down the hard knot of bitterness lodged in his throat. "No, I couldn't. When I married your mother, I swore before the minister, God, and witnesses that I'd protect her *until death do us part.* I kept that vow until the day she died."

His eyes grew moist. Caleb swiped at them with the heels of his hands. "With everything in me, Lauren, I didn't want to let her down, but all the best doctors in the country couldn't stop the progression of her disease. That was beyond anyone's control. Except God's. He takes us in His time, and even though *we* weren't ready, your mother was ready to let go. She didn't want to live in pain anymore."

Lauren lowered her gaze and stared at the table.

He was depleted, out of answers. *Tell her.*

Caleb sucked in a quick breath. "You asked, so I'm going to tell you what's going on."

That caught her attention. Lauren glanced at him, clearly wary of what he'd say.

"Okay." Her eyes glimmered with unshed tears.

"I've received kidnapping threats. Six in the past couple of years to be specific."

Her gasp made him reach for her, wanting that connection, craving it for his sanity. His *heart*. Wrapping his hands around hers, Caleb held on for all he was worth without hurting her.

"You mean to kidnap *me*?" Her face crumpled, making his heart hurt. "Dad, why would someone want to do that?"

He breathed a silent prayer of thanks that she'd called him Dad. "Hard to say, but money is usually involved. I've made quite a bit of money in my lifetime, and there are people out there willing to break laws in order to get their hands on some of it."

"For what? To buy drugs?"

"I can't answer that. Perhaps. Or maybe to try and buy a better life. A lot of people mistakenly believe that having money will make them feel better about themselves. Or that they'll be happier. It doesn't work that way in real life. In some cases, having money makes life more complicated."

"Sometimes kids who are kidnapped aren't found…alive." Lauren's voice quivered and her trembling lower lip pierced his conscience. Was he wrong in trusting his instincts and telling her? Maybe she wasn't old enough to process the truth. In some ways, she was mature for her age, but in others, she was still a little girl. *His* little girl. That would never change. In spite of her big talk and behind the bad attitude, she was a twelve-year-old girl. She knew nothing of the evils of which men were capable.

What have I done? Guilt raced through Caleb, rendering him momentarily numb. Wouldn't telling Lauren cause her to be more observant and diligent? That was his only justification.

"Sometimes they're…murdered and bad people do horrible things…" Placing her hands over her eyes, Lauren burst into tears.

Heart wrenching, hard cries that he hated more than anything he'd ever heard in his life.

"Baby, I never meant to make you cry." Moving around the table, feeling like the worst father in the world, Caleb dropped into the chair next to her. He wrapped his daughter in his arms and leaned his head on hers. "I'm doing the best I can, and I'm sorry…" Not knowing what else he could say, he closed his eyes and hoped he could absorb the pain for her. If only he could.

Lauren leaned further into his chest, her shoulders shaking with hard sobs. He tightened his hold, never wanting to let her go. Never wanting her to know the harsh realities of life and how they could beat a person down, rob a person of joy and hope.

God can make everything right. He'd repeated that truth over and over in the past but come up empty-handed too often. Not that he'd expected an immediate answer, but he'd finally stopped asking God for help. Was God listening? He wanted to believe the Almighty heard his pleas.

God, if you're listening now, I could use a little assistance here.

Sniffling, Lauren glanced up at him with eyes innocent and trusting, a reminder that little girl was still in there somewhere beneath the mask of indifference and hurt. "Did we leave Dallas because someone was trying to kidnap me?"

"Yes, but that was only part of it," he whispered, smoothing one hand over her dark hair. "We both needed a fresh start, and Houston is ultimately a better location for the Belac headquarters."

All true. Reminders of his late wife were everywhere in the Dallas mansion. A change of scenery could only be healthier for both of them. Born and raised in a Dallas suburb, he'd loved it there, but it no longer held the same appeal it once had. His mother and Helena's mother had been upset about the move, but they both led busy lives and knew he'd make sure to keep the family connection in place. He had part ownership in a private jet. He could fly them to Houston for the weekend. When things settled down with Lauren, he could send her to Dallas for visits. He had to be optimistic and know that would eventually happen…a time when he wouldn't need to constantly worry about her safety.

Change was a positive step for his soul but, more importantly, better for his daughter's well-being. Especially since Helena's death, Lauren had become his sole focus in life. His reason for continuing to build his corporation as a legacy for Lauren and *her* future family. As long as he kept his eyes on that prize, they'd both be okay.

"But those people could have followed us, right? We're in the same state, not across the world. They could find us anywhere. Isn't that how it works?"

Caleb kissed the top of her head. "Such wisdom you have. Yes, they can follow us, but I'm hoping they'll move on. Not that I'd wish this on anyone else."

A deep frown slid over her features. "I wish you weren't rich. Then this wouldn't be happening."

"Being rich is a matter of opinion. There are different ways to be rich."

"Like what?"

"You can have all the money in the world but not have love. Trust me, it's much better to be rich in character than to live in a house full of things. Friends, family, and love are what's most important." Lauren couldn't know how long it'd taken him to reach that conclusion. Ten years ago, he wouldn't have been able to say such a thing. He'd gone through his own years of searching and making hasty, ill-advised decisions he'd later regretted. All part of the process of growing up and maturing.

Lauren's expression brimmed with skepticism. "Then you should go out and do stuff with people more. Make connections. You're still kind of young."

"I have a life, believe it or not."

"Not really. You never go out with people or have fun. Other than going to the health club and stuff. By the way, you stink." Wrinkling her nose, Lauren pulled away.

"My primary job is to watch over you, Lauren. Until I know the threats are gone, I need to focus on keeping you safe."

"Did you get ransom notes or something?"

He found it interesting how her preteen mind processed information, skipping from one train of thought and topic to another in a matter of seconds. Her voice sounded much stronger now, an encouraging sign. Her inner spark was igniting, reminding Caleb of himself. Ultimately, his daughter was a fighter. He liked that, but with all her youthful naiveté, she might unwittingly do something to put herself in danger.

"Ransom notes are sent when someone is actually kidnapped," he said. When Lauren's eyes widened as if in fear, he shook his head. That'd been the wrong thing to say, but it was too late to retract the words. "I've received a few messages. On my phone."

"How'd they get your phone number? You never give it to anybody." That wasn't true. He'd called Caty, so she had his number. Even now, he wasn't sure why it'd happened, only that he wanted Caty to have his number if she ever wanted it. He didn't look at it, subconscious or not, as a mistake.

"I don't know," he said. "Hackers must have tapped into my phone." He'd done everything he could to ensure they didn't crack the multiple passwords and safety precautions on his computers.

Three written messages had also been delivered in plain white business-size envelopes by a messenger service and left at the Belac front desk in Dallas. They'd been intercepted by Cordelia. He'd thoroughly checked out the messenger company and the kids who'd delivered the envelopes. At their request, he'd turned the notes over to the police, but...nothing. Frustration had settled in his gut long ago by the lack of solid leads or answers.

For whatever reason, he decided not to tell Lauren about the envelopes. Realistically, what purpose would it serve?

"Can I hear the messages?"

"No, you may *not* hear them." Caleb's words came out more harsh than he'd intended. "The police have them." Of course, he'd kept copies of the recordings, but no way would Lauren ever hear them. They were full of sick, twisted, perverted words about what they'd do to his daughter. He doubted any sane father in the world would have been able to listen to those messages and not take them seriously. If he'd known the identity of the person or persons, he'd go after them himself. Heaven forbid anyone would ever touch a hair on her precious head.

He'd never been a violent man, but after receiving the vile messages, Caleb could better understand the motivation behind those who chose vigilante justice to eliminate a threat to their loved ones. Didn't make it right, but it made some kind of sense for those who didn't have any basis in faith or belief in a just God.

You claim to have faith, but you're not living like you do. That truth saddened him.

Caleb had no one but himself to blame. He needed to get back on track with his prayer life. He needed to reconnect with the Savior he'd claimed all those years ago, sitting at the kitchen table with his mother. Asking Jesus into his heart had been the easy part.

"Chill," Lauren said. "I was just asking."

He tweaked her nose. "Do you like Greenbriar-Browne?" A high-priced private school that charged him a fortune but worth it all. Their security made the grounds a virtual fortress.

"It's okay." Lauren lifted her shoulders. "It seems safe enough, anyway. But now I know why you have Ollie drive me to school and then pick me up again."

"I don't know what else to do until I know for sure the threats are gone."

"But what if there are new threats?" Lauren's blue eyes grew wide again. "I mean, there are always crazies out there, right?"

"Unfortunately, that's true. I promise I'm doing everything I can to make sure you're safe. That's my utmost priority." What a sad world they lived in where a kid knew such things.

"One more question."

"What's that?" He almost dreaded what she'd ask next.

"When does it end?"

"I don't know, baby." Next to telling Lauren her mother had passed away, those were the most difficult words he'd ever said.

He hated feeling helpless. A total, utter helplessness was all he could feel. Until Lauren leaned into him again, needing him and his reassurance. And that gave him immeasurable comfort, more than his daughter could ever know.

Jesus, be with us both. Keep my daughter safe. Please.

Chapter 13

By the time Caty came back inside, the men had already brought in her dining room table and chairs. She heard a few grunts and muffled directions from Sam as the men, including her dad, carried the bottom part of her entertainment center into the living room.

Biting her tongue not to chastise her father, she asked them to set the heavy piece of furniture along the side wall across from the sofa. Even though her dad was in great shape for his age, she didn't want him to feel like he needed to keep up with the younger guys and overdo it.

That job accomplished, Sam removed his baseball cap and wiped his forearm over his brow. His dark waves were plastered flat on his head. He nodded in Josh's direction with a wry grin. "By the way, we're now addressing Josh as Your Excellency."

"I wish you people would stop that," Josh protested. "Not that I don't appreciate your support. I say let's go unload some more furniture."

"Not so fast," she called to Josh. "You've earned a break. What's this all about?" Caty figured this must be what Eliot had alluded to in the restaurant. Closing the front door, she then ran to the thermostat and cranked up the air conditioning.

Kevin grabbed water bottles from a cooler and tossed one to each of the guys. Then he handed Caty a bottle before taking another for himself. "Governor Collins mentioned Josh as a potential candidate for his short list of same-party candidates he'd like to see run for lieutenant governor in the next election." Twisting the cap off his water bottle, he took a drink and then toasted Josh. "Here's to my brother-in-law, ladies and gentlemen."

"Nothing's been said to me directly," Josh told her. "I'm shocked he suggested it. Although I appreciate the recognition, there are no guarantees, especially since the lieutenant governor is elected independently from the governor. It's not like a running mate kind of situation."

After taking a drink of his water, Sam nodded to his close friend. "Don't sell yourself short, Josh. You're qualified, and you'll be more experienced by the time the election rolls around in three years."

"From what I understand, the lieutenant governor is equally important as the governor, if not more so," Caty said. "Seems like a lot has happened while I've been serving my time in Lubbock. Josh, do you know Governor Collins personally?"

"I've met him a few times. I've served on two key committees and worked with a senator on a statewide initiative."

"And *that's* how it's done," Caty said. "Excellent! You've obviously impressed him."

"If I'm even on the ballot, I'd be the underdog with little possibility of being elected. There are people much more qualified than me."

"They also need fresh blood in Austin, and you'd be spectacular." Josh's wife, Winnie, stepped inside the living room with a box in her arms. "Move aside, guys. Drinking glasses coming through." The pretty blonde hip-bumped her husband. "You too, Your Excellency."

Catching his wife around the waist, Josh gave her a quick kiss.

Caty smiled. "Thank you for coming, Winnie. Mom's literally inside the kitchen cabinets putting down pretty shelf paper, bless her heart. I'll be in shortly." She turned back to Josh. "Premature or not, you'll get my vote when the time comes."

"Thanks, Caty, but that's enough of this talk." Josh motioned to the other men. "Time to bring in more furniture."

Sam Sr. came inside the front door, panting a bit, his face flushed.

"Dad, you're overdoing it," Caty scolded. "Come and sit down. Rest for a few minutes, and I'll get a low-sodium water bottle for you."

"I'm fine. Give me a second to catch my breath. The coffee table's sitting outside the door."

"I've got it. Dad, listen to Caty." Sam walked out the front door behind Kevin and Josh.

"That thing weighs a ton!" Caty slid her hands to her hips. "I can't have it on my conscience if you hurt yourself. Mom!" She felt like a teenager for calling her mother, not to mention tattling on her father, but Sarah was the only person who could talk sense into her father and make him listen.

"I'm not helpless, Catherine. I can get my own water. And no need to yell. I'm not deaf."

Caty watched as he strolled into the kitchen, tall, straight, and proud as ever. Once a military man, always a military man. He wore a hearing aid in one ear, the result of Ménière's Disease, a disorder of the inner ear diagnosed years ago when he'd served overseas with the Air Force. The condition had grounded him as a pilot. Coming home to tiny little Rockbridge, Texas, also led Dad into her mother's arms.

Sam and Josh lowered the coffee table to the floor and Kevin came back in with the second matching side chair. As the other two men headed out again, Sam turned to her.

"Dad's fine. Just a little sensitive about the increased hearing loss."

"How about the migraines? The vertigo?"

Sam grabbed his water bottle and took another quick drink. "Under control. You know he says that's why God led him to marry Mom." True enough. The effects of Ménière's could prove debilitating to some, but their mother had helped Dad to effectively manage the disease through the years.

Tugging on her ponytail, Sam gave her a concerned big brother expression. "I caught your smile when you came back inside after the phone call. Do you have a boyfriend?"

Caty pulled away before he could tug on her hair again. "Not telling. A girl has to have some secrets." Besides, how could she answer that question? She'd tell Sam when she had anything *to* tell. "Be sure and send me a bill for your services. I'm sure this expert TeamWork moving service doesn't come cheap."

Sam chuckled. "Special today only for Catherine Lewis. Help us out with a local TeamWork project sometime, and we'll call it even."

"I'm sure that can be arranged." An idea took root in her mind. Why not try to get something set up with Belac? An event that Caleb might attend and bring his daughter?

Sam chuckled. "We'll unload the dining room furniture next and then the bedroom."

"You're the best. I still can't believe you're doing this for me. Please don't *you* overdo it. I can't have it on my conscience if any of you strain anything."

"No worries." Sam wrapped her in one of his warm hugs. "Glad we can help. We old guys can always use the exercise."

"You're not old. No offense, but you *are* sweaty." Laughing, Caty fanned her shirt before going to check on her mother. Sarah was still working on the large lower cabinets while Winnie measured liner paper for the silverware drawer.

Winnie glanced her way. "Lexa wanted to come, but she's on deadline for her next book and sends her apologies."

"I know," Caty said. "She called and Sam also told me." Who could have known that both Sam and Lexa would be publishing books? It didn't hurt that another of their TeamWork members was a Christian publisher, but their talents never ceased to amaze Caty. The books sold, and they wouldn't continue to fly off the bookstore shelves if they weren't well done.

Caty set about unpacking a box containing small appliances. "Which thinly veiled, real-life TeamWork love story is H.L. Joseph, also known as Lexa Lewis, working on now?"

Winnie ducked her head but not before Caty caught her smile. "Oh, something about a man who finds his redemption in the child he didn't know he had."

"Ah, the old secret baby theme."

Beneath the counter, Caty heard a grunt from her mother. *Oh, oh.* She really should think before she spouted the first thing that came into her mind. "Winnie, I'm sorry if that sounded insensitive." Lexa's latest book was obviously patterned after Winnie's love story with Josh.

"No worries. Josh and I get to read it first and give our approval, just like Marc and Natalie did for their story. Have you read any of them yet, Caty? I think you'd really like them. She adds a lot of humor along with solid spiritual truths."

"No." Caty lifted her shoulders. "I need to remedy that, and I hope Lexa's not offended that I haven't. I suppose I'm still writing my own story."

"Now, *that's* a good line!" Sarah called from inside the cabinet.

Caty shook her head and leaned down to where her mother still worked beneath the cabinet. "Mom, how did you even fit all of you under there? That's got to be uncomfortable." Her mother was close to her own height. "You're going to be stiff and need Dad's help to climb out of there."

"Bite your tongue, Catherine Grace. Why do you think your dad and I walk every morning and play tennis or golf twice a week? I'm limber as ever."

Winnie winked. "Enjoy the best job in the house while you can. Directing traffic."

"Caty, come check out the dining room." This time it was the senior Sam who'd called her. "See if we have everything where you want it."

"Yes, sir. Coming!" The dining room was set up in short order, and then the men paraded inside with more boxes for the kitchen and other rooms. They started stacking them against the walls, and the sight almost overwhelmed her. Maybe she should have gotten rid of some things before leaving Lubbock. When had she accumulated so much stuff? It'd take her weeks, if not longer, to unpack all these boxes.

After helping more in the kitchen, Caty carried in more boxes from the truck that contained her personal mementos and collectibles.

"I'll come by this week and help you unpack," Sarah said when they stopped a short time later for a quick break. They munched on fresh fruit Winnie provided for them.

"I'd love that, Mom! Especially since I'm starting at Belac on Monday, I won't have a lot of time. It'd take me months to unpack everything. I'll figure out a way to repay you."

"Honey, no repayment is necessary. That's what mothers do for their children."

"Still, I'll send you and Dad to eat somewhere special to say thank you."

Her mother smiled. "We still love dinner at The Grotto."

"I'll keep that in mind." Caty made a mental note to pick up a gift card on her next trip to the grocery store. She continued working in the living room while the men arranged her bedroom furniture on the second level. She glanced up not long after to see Kevin coming down the stairs.

"Everything's coming together nicely," he told her. "I need to grab a tool from my truck to finish putting together the bed frame."

"Kevin? How are Rebekah and the twins? I can't believe I haven't met them yet."

A beaming, proud papa smile creased his face as Kevin paused in the doorway. "They're great. Elizabeth and Jacob turned a year old last week. They keep us busy, but we're settling into this parenthood thing. It's true what everyone says about how your life is never the same. In our case, it's even better. Rebekah's a natural mother, and it's been fun to see how the kids change every week."

"I'm sure," Caty said. "I don't want to keep you, but do you have a recent picture?"

"Of course." Stepping closer, Kevin reached into his back pocket and tugged out his wallet. "This was taken a few weeks ago before their first birthday."

Taking the photo, Caty moved one hand over her heart. "Oh, they're beautiful." Elizabeth, named for Kevin's late mother, was blonde like Rebekah while Jacob had curly, dark hair. Their features were a wonderful combination of the couple. "Are they walking yet? Talking?"

"They hold hands and walk together…or fall down together. They babble and say a few words and seem to have their own private language. Mom Grant said Josh and Rebekah used to do the same thing."

Caty returned the photo. "Is Rebekah still working with Sam and Josh full-time in the TeamWork office?" A former elementary school teacher, Rebekah now managed the educational division for the domestic missions.

"Part-time. Sam's a generous boss, and she's worked from home two days a week since the twins were born."

Caty's eyes misted. "I'm so happy for you, Kevin. Really, I am." *Silly girl.* Why did she have to tack on those last three words? Did Kevin have any clue how she'd crushed on him when she was younger? In her eyes, he'd been the ideal man—tall, handsome, quiet but strong in his faith. Musically talented, Kevin was a former youth leader turned part-time worship director. Successful, too, since he owned and operated the four Texas locations of his family's Louisiana-based lumber stores. Marta told her that he'd patented a gazebo design, called Rebekah's Heart, and it'd been a financial success for Kevin. From what Marta told her, consistent with his character, Kevin had donated a large portion of that money back into TeamWork.

"It'll happen for you, Caty." Ah, sweet, perceptive Kevin, another reason to adore this man. Maybe she should be embarrassed that he could read her emotions so easily, but not with him.

"God's got it all under control, right?" She hated how her voice quivered.

"You know it. Keep your eyes on Him, Caty. Sorry, but I need to keep moving. If the guys holler for me, tell them I'll be right back, okay?"

"Sure." Someone rested a hand on her shoulder as Kevin headed outside. Expecting her mother, Caty turned to face her father.

"Kevin's right, you know. God's *got* this." He lifted her chin. "*Trust*, sweet girl."

Caty blinked back her tears. "I know. Sometimes it's easier said than done, you know? I can't cry now. Kevin's coming back in here any second."

"Go back into the kitchen with Mom and Winnie for a few minutes." His voice, calm and gentle, always soothed her troubled heart. "I'll handle everything since I know the layout of the bedroom. If we have any questions, I'll ask."

"I guess you *were* listening when I discussed it with Mom earlier this week."

A small smile creased her father's handsome face. "I hear what's important."

Caty leaned into him, her solid rock, a man of unflagging honor. "I love you, Dad."

"Forever and always." He kissed her forehead. That's how they'd ended so many evenings together. Nights when he'd listen to her prayers and tuck her into bed. When she'd cry over a problem at school or a fight with her friend. When she'd think she was unlovable and that no boy would ever love her.

Yes, well, she was still working on that last one. *In God's time, not Caty's time.* She shivered and crossed her arms. Sometimes that concept was difficult to hold close to her heart since she'd always struggled with patience or the lack thereof, to be more accurate.

Watching her father head up the stairs, Caty sniffled and wiped beneath her eyes with her fingertips. How did she get so blessed to be part of such a loving, giving family?

Caty's thoughts strayed to Caleb. What was it about him that fascinated her? Something about the underdog had always attracted her. Maybe it wasn't so much the underdog as the walking wounded. How odd that she'd even consider Caleb an underdog in any sense of the word, but he was. It was in the depths of those soulful brown eyes as if he carried the weight of the world alone on his broad shoulders. In the tightening of his mouth when she asked him a personal question.

Was he still buried in grief over his wife's death? She'd known others who'd lost a spouse under tragic circumstances. Some reached out for comfort in their mourning, but others kept to themselves, preferring to retreat and work out their grief in their own way. If Caleb's last five years in the corporation were any indication, he'd taken the later route.

Lord, help Caleb to hold you close. To seek answers from you instead of trying to do things his own way. She sensed that trust might also be an issue for him, but for completely different reasons than her own.

Beneath Caleb's self-assured exterior, she'd detected a hint of the pain he carried deep in his soul. She'd also glimpsed his underlying warmth, his compassion. If he allowed himself to give his love to another woman one day, Caleb would be the type of man who'd do so with passion and the kind of uncommon devotion that would capture and hold a woman's heart forever.

Caty snapped out of her trance. "Someone's being awfully poetic today."

Enough daydreaming. Time to get back to work.

After promising her mother she'd go over to the house within the hour for dinner, Caty leaned against the front door and blew out a sigh. With the furniture in place, her townhome was beginning to take shape. Having some of her family and friends here today gave her a good start in *feeling* like she was home again. As cozy as her condo in Lubbock was, it had never been Houston.

"Back home where I belong." Caty started up the stairs to change her clothes. After carrying in boxes and doing some housework, her T-shirt and jeans had picked up some grime. A quick shower was in order. Hopefully she could find a box with clean clothes easily enough.

The doorbell rang as she reached the upstairs landing. Who could that be? Maybe one of the guys forgot a tool when they'd put together the bed frame. She'd better answer it. Back down the steps she went, smoothing one hand over her mussed hair.

A quick peek through the peephole revealed a man, half-hidden by something green and leafy, dressed in a polo shirt with a logo embroidered on it. He appeared legit considering a service van with a matching logo idled behind him in the parking lot.

"Delivery for Catherine Lewis," the man said in a bored tone of voice after she opened the door. An enormous potted plant stood on her front doorstep. Goodness. The thing was as big as a small tree. Big enough that—if it were the holidays—she might hang Christmas ornaments on its branches. Oddly enough, the tree reminded her of…a huge corn stalk. Why would anyone send her a corn stalk? She liked corn as much as the next person, but really? Her ignorance of plant life was showing.

"Do you know who sent this?" She scrawled her signature on the delivery ticket he thrust under her nose. Her mom and dad? Sam and Lexa? No, that seemed highly doubtful. Of all people, her family knew she killed most plants. Maybe Marta and Eliot?

The man sighed. "There's a card there somewhere. Check among the stalks."

"No worries. I'll find it. Do you mind bringing it inside?" Now that the guys were gone, she wasn't sure she could lift the plant by herself. Neither could she afford to be laid up with a sore back on her first day of work. At least she hadn't suffered from a sore back after her mishap downtown earlier in the week.

The man hefted the plant like it was lightweight. "Lead the way."

"The corner of the living room should be good." That seemed the best place since it would be shaded yet still catch rays of sunlight from the patio. "Let me get your tip. I'll be right back."

"Taken care of. I'm good." With one hand in the air, he was already halfway to the front door.

"Have a nice day!" After locking the door, Caty spied two white envelopes taped to the outside of the clay pot. The first contained her parking card for the building garage and her new Belac ID badge. Caleb was a thorough man and seemed to forget nothing.

When Caty opened the second one, it contained care instructions for the plant. She'd definitely need to study those.

"Okay, then. Let's see what I need to do to keep you alive and thriving, my friend." Caty tossed a glance at the large plant. "Well, I'll settle for alive, anyway." Growing up, her brothers had teased Caty for her tendency to constantly narrate her actions. She'd also been the Lewis kid who always read the cards first before tearing into her birthday gifts.

Caty darted a glance at the plant. "I really hope you're not hard to kill because I'm incredibly adept at it."

Time to read. "'This striking houseplant, actually a robust tree, is nicknamed the Corn Plant for its long, sword-like leaves that resemble the foliage of actual corn." Well, what do you know? "It's a member of the Dracaena group, known for its tenacious, rugged, and low-maintenance personality. The Mass Cane will thrive in an office or busy household, needing little attention and only moderate light to bring guaranteed lasting smiles.'"

Sounded like an easy care plant. "Tenacious, rugged, and low maintenance, eh?" An idea of the giver popped into her mind. Tenacious, yes. Rugged? Most definitely. Low Maintenance? That last one was a little suspect.

Spying another small envelope tucked into the side of the clay pot, Caty retrieved it. Seized it was more like it. "And now, ladies and gentlemen, for the envelope please…" Tugging out the card, she turned it over.

WELCOME HOME TO HOUSTON, CATHERINE. LOOKING FORWARD TO WORKING WITH YOU. *~Caleb Reid*

Hmm. The small scrawl looked a lot like Caleb's original signature. Had he handwritten this note and chosen the Corn Plant especially for her? Although he'd said nothing specifically about the delivery, maybe that had been the reason for his call earlier in the day.

"It's very nice to be back home, Mr. Reid." Tucking the card in her pocket with a smile, Caty climbed the stairs two at a time.

Chapter 14

Caty strolled into the Belac offices an hour earlier than expected on Monday morning. Not that she punched a timeclock, but it was always good to show up earlier rather than later.

Unable to sleep, she'd showered, gulped down cereal, and dressed. The Lubbock office had been much more casual, but now that she was in the main office, she figured she'd wear her professional suits most of the time. She'd managed to drive downtown, park in her designated space in the building garage, and make it up to the 35th floor without mishap. A minor miracle, perhaps, but life was good and hopefully back to her new normal.

"Good morning, Suma."

The receptionist glanced up from the switchboard and gave her a practiced polite yet cool smile. "Good morning, Miss Lewis." Did the woman possess emotions? Caty almost wanted to give that bare, toned arm a light pinch just to get a rise out of her.

Don't be irreverent, Caty.

"I hope you had a nice weekend."

Suma's dark eyes opened wider. "It was lovely, thank you."

Were office pleasantries discouraged here? In the Dallas office, the Belac employees were like one big happy family. Then again, if the boss was in the office, he'd always been behind closed doors. Speculating about Mr. Reid had been fun and a frequent topic of conversation before she'd actually met him. Now, things were different. Although she'd tried to avoid the gossip, she'd found the speculation rather intriguing.

"I finally got moved—" Caty swallowed her last few words as Suma lifted her finger and answered an incoming call. Why would she think Suma would engage in small talk?

"Good morning. Thank you for calling Belac. How may I help you?"

Today Suma's nails were painted a deeper red, closer to a maroon color. Everything about her appearance was perfection. How did women like this exist? Talk about a china doll. She actually looked rather fragile.

Be nice. No pinching.

Suma's phone manner was certainly professional and friendly. "Yes, Miss Randall. I'll put you through to Mr. Reid's private line."

Caty tried to ignore the questions the phone call raised in her overactive imagination. Miss Randall? Caleb's private line?

"You're welcome. Have a beautiful day." Suma glanced up at her again.

"Could you tell me if my office is on the right or left side? Any information to clue me in will be helpful." She felt silly admitting as much and recognized she was rambling again, not an attractive quality.

"I've already buzzed for Miss Bonner. She asked me to alert her when you arrived. I'm sure she'll be out momentarily." Suma's hand went in the air as though dismissing her.

"Great. Thank you." Caty walked into the client waiting area. The sun streaming through the windows was bright and warm.

Good morning, Caty. How are you today?" Cordelia marched toward her and grasped her hand warmly. Her smile reached her blue eyes.

"Ready for occupancy. I mean, I'm looking forward to inhabiting my new office." She might as well give it up. She wasn't making much sense today. Sequestering herself like a good little accountant, crunching numbers, and staying quiet might be advisable.

"We're glad you're here." Cordelia motioned for Caty to follow. "I'll take you to your office. I'm happy to report everything arrived intact on the moving van from Lubbock. I took the liberty of directing the placement of the furniture. If there's anything not to your liking, please let me know, and we'll have it rearranged for you right away."

"I'm sure it's all perfectly fine," Caty assured her. "Thanks for taking care of everything. As long as I have a desk, a chair, and a functioning computer, I'll be all set. My needs are simple." She waved to Suma as she passed by the reception desk and received a lukewarm smile in return. Apparently she didn't use that hand to wave to lunatic accountants.

You're losing it and it's only Monday. Lack of sleep was never a good thing, either. Whether it was her new townhome, new job, or her encounters with the enigmatic Mr. Reid, she'd tossed and turned most of the night.

Caty started down the right hallway behind Cordelia.

"Your office is the fourth one." When Cordelia stood aside, Caty noted the elegant gold nameplate on the door as she entered the office filled with her familiar furnishings—striped brocade loveseat in deep jewel tones, two matching chairs, a small cherry table with a lamp brought back from her parents' trip to the Orient, and miscellaneous decorative items from Sam and Lexa's mission trips.

"Thank you again, Cordelia." Opening the lower desk drawer, Caty dropped her purse inside.

Cordelia handed her a small key. "This is to lock your desk."

Caty frowned. "Is there a reason I should lock it?"

"Theft shouldn't be a concern, but due to the nature of your work, Mr. Reid wanted me to advise you to keep your desk and office locked when you're not here."

That was something she hadn't considered, but Caleb was right. In Lubbock, her office and computer had been accessible to anyone when she darted out for lunch. Of course, it'd never been a concern until the discrepancies began to appear. Perhaps she should have been more mindful.

"Then I'll certainly do that." Taking the key, Caty locked the desk for the moment and deposited the key in the pocket of her skirt.

"Your diplomas and personal photos are stacked against the far wall," Cordelia said. "We'll send someone by later today to hang them for you."

"Sounds great. You've thought of everything."

Cordelia's smile emerged. "Would you like some coffee or tea?"

"You know, I'd really like that."

"Why don't you get settled for a bit and meet me in the breakroom in fifteen minutes? We can have some coffee, I'll tell you more about the office, and perhaps introduce you to a few people."

"That sounds lovely. See you then." She didn't know where the breakroom was, but how hard could it be? She'd follow her nose. After Cordelia departed, Caty walked back to her desk and sat in her familiar chair. Same job, new surroundings, new people. That's all it was.

An image of Steve Robison popped into her head. She hoped she wouldn't encounter him today since she wasn't sure how she'd react. The man suspected her of wrongdoing. Other than going about her job and proving otherwise, Caty didn't know what else to do. Armed with Caleb's reassurances that her job was safe, she'd continue about her normal business.

Hearing a knock, Caty glanced up to see a blond young man standing in the doorway. He looked about twenty. By comparison to some of the stone-faced employees she'd passed in the hall, his friendly smile was a welcome sight.

"Hi, Miss Lewis. I'm Miles Durand, the mail guy." Medium height, slim build, he was dressed in dark khakis and a bright orange cotton shirt with BELAC, INC. embroidered across the top left.

Caty rose from her chair and crossed the room to shake his hand. "Hi, Miles. It's nice to meet you. Please call me Caty."

"Sure. Nice to meet you, too. I'll come by with your mail about eleven every morning. If your door's closed, that's my cue not to bother you. Then you can call me when you're ready, and I'll deliver it. My extension's 301."

"I'll do that." She assumed she'd find a phone list in one of the desk drawers.

"Do you have an assistant?"

Caty shook her head. "I've never asked for one." In truth, she preferred working alone.

"No wonder you're an accountant." Miles grinned. "You save the company money. I'm actually here with a special delivery."

"Oh?" Matter of fact, Miles *did* have one hand hidden behind his back.

He leaned closer and whispered, "It's from *him*. You know, The Head Honcho. The Big Kahuna."

"Mr. Reid, you mean."

"Right. I just like calling him those other things."

"Should I be scared?" This kid was fun. "Not of the Big Kahuna, but of what he's sent to me? Is this some kind of *Welcome to Belac* tradition?" Maybe it was a gift card to a nearby coffee shop. It couldn't be another potted plant unless it was much smaller than the corn stalk sitting in her home. What if he'd sent her a pretty yellow rose for her desk? That'd be a lovely gesture.

"I guess. Weirdest one I've ever seen, and sorry to say, it's pretty cheap."

Okay, not a rose. She needed to push the romantic thoughts out of her mind.

"Then Mr. Reid probably means whatever it is as a joke since I work with numbers. Like you said, accountants have reputations for pinching pennies and not wanting the company to spend money on frivolous things."

"Gotcha. I've never met the guy, so I couldn't tell you."

That might change, Miles. Caty raised a brow, waiting. When he didn't take the hint, she angled her head. "You have something for me?"

"Oh, right. Sorry. Just don't get your hopes up. Let's make it fun. Close your eyes and hold out one hand."

She followed his direction and then closed her fingers around something made from plastic—firm yet flexible with a handle.

"You can open your eyes now."

In her hand, Caty held an oversized red, white, and blue fly swatter. Not only that, but it was a Boston Red Sox fly swatter. She saw an envelope taped to the back, but she'd open it privately.

Laughing, Caty waved it in the air as though she'd been given a prize. "This isn't just any fly swatter, Miles. This is more valuable than you might think."

"If you say so." Miles shrugged and gave her a look like she was a little mentally off-kilter. "At least it might come in handy in case we get flies up here on the floor. I'll see you around the office, Miss Lewis—I mean Caty. Welcome to Belac."

"I'll see you soon. Thanks again." A fly swatter. Who could have known? The gift showed ingenuity. Yeah, the guy might be her boss, but she considered his gestures charming. Definitely unique.

As soon as Miles moved his mail cart farther down the hall, Caty opened the card.

GO GET 'EM, SCRAPPY! *~Caleb*

Chapter 15

Wednesday Afternoon, the Same Week

Caleb pounded a light rhythm on the steering wheel with his fists as he waited. Unfortunately, it wasn't because he was listening to a great song and drumming with the beat.

"Greenbriar-Browne Academy."

He leaned closer to the open window and directed his words into the intercom box. "Caleb Reid to see Mrs. Winthorpe. I have a two o'clock appointment."

"Yes, Mr. Reid. She's expecting you," a crusty, older-sounding female voice responded.

"Thank you." Seconds later, the massive iron gates opened. Gunning the accelerator faster than warranted, Caleb roared down the long driveway. Reminded him of The Biltmore Estate in Asheville, North Carolina. He'd visited with his mother once and joked about the three-mile long driveway. This driveway seemed every bit as long.

The landscaping of the grounds was equally spectacular with perfect rows of sculpted bushes and towering shade trees. If he didn't have lecturing his delinquent daughter on the brain, he might take a few seconds to appreciate and enjoy the view. When he spied a few students walking about the grounds, he slowed the car. Besides that, Lauren would be mortified if he was ticketed for speeding on the grounds of her school.

The private academy was housed in a former residence built by an eccentric billionaire who fancied himself a king. The place did resemble a small castle, again how he remembered Biltmore, and that made Caleb chuckle as he pulled into a VISITOR parking space. After slamming the car door with undue force, he stalked toward the front walkway. Although he didn't see them, he wouldn't be at all surprised to find a moat and drawbridge leading into the castle.

Pausing a moment, Caleb repositioned his red silk tie and buttoned his navy suit coat. He didn't wear a suit often, but he'd been courting Olivia Randall the last few months—strictly in the business sense—in the hopes of obtaining mineral rights for oil and gas exploration on her land. From all preliminary reports, the property in West Texas she'd inherited from her daddy promised to be quite profitable.

This meeting had better be worth missing his afternoon meeting with Miss Randall and her attorneys. He'd sent Steve in his place. Lauren was certainly worth it, but he hoped the school hadn't summoned him for a trivial reason. Likewise, he hoped his daughter hadn't committed some unforgivable offense. Squaring his shoulders, he headed inside the school.

Within a few minutes, Caleb was ushered into the Office of the Headmistress. Seemed the academy preferred the British terminology instead of simply calling her the principal. Considering the setting and its whole Pride and Prejudice vibe, he could understand the allure of this place for impressionable teenage girls. Although fairly modern in décor, the office seemed dim and cheerless. He folded his sunglasses and tucked them in the inside pocket of his suit coat.

"Mr. Reid, thank you for coming at such short notice."

Caleb rose to his feet as Lenore Winthorpe—a name befitting an Austenian character—entered the room. In her prim and proper black suit with a high-collared blouse, mid-fifties or thereabouts, not a stitch of makeup, and her hair severely pulled back in a bun, the woman was a walking stereotype if ever he'd seen one.

Mrs. Winthorpe took her seat behind a desk every bit as large and imposing as his own. Something about this woman gave him the creeps but, if pressed, he wouldn't be able to give a reason why. He wouldn't want to meet up with her in a dark alley, and he could only imagine what the students must say about her. For little girls more timid than Lauren, this woman must be downright frightening. *Forbidding.* That was a good word for her.

Caleb reclaimed his chair. "Will Lauren be joining us?"

"In a few minutes. She's completing a test in her English Literature class."

Threading his fingers together, he rested them on his lap. "Well, then, by all means, let's not interrupt her."

"It shouldn't be much longer. May I offer you something to drink?"

"No, thank you. This isn't a social call." Although honest, he could stand to tone down the flippancy. "I'd like to know about the incident you referred to on the phone." He didn't know much other than it involved contraband. Of course, here at Greenbriar-Browne, contraband might include chewing gum or a jawbreaker.

"Of course. I know your time is valuable, Mr. Reid. I'll give you the basic facts so you can digest them before Lauren arrives."

Digest? Caleb found himself slouching and forced himself back up in the uncomfortable chair. With the tuition this place charged, they should be able to afford decent chairs. No doubt it was an antique that impressed some of the parents passing through these hallowed doors.

"Lauren was found smoking in the restroom at the end of the lunch break today, Mr. Reid. The alarm picked up on it, and I assure you the cigarette was immediately extinguished."

Part of him wanted to shout *Is that all?* while another part of him cringed to know his daughter had ingested nicotine into her lungs. Hopefully, it was a one-time thing. Not that it excused Lauren's behavior. Kids experimented. Although it seemed a lifetime ago, he'd done the same thing. He'd also instigated some dumb pranks and done time in school detention. A classic overachiever, he'd been bored. It'd taken him years before he'd finally recognized his behavior was a manifestation of misdirected anger toward his absentee father.

The woman's gray eyes bore into him while she waited for his reaction.

"I'm afraid I was caught in the same offense when I was Lauren's age." Wrong thing to say. He could practically see the antennae rising from the back of the woman's head. The *Bad Dad* radar.

"I see," she said slowly. "Do you smoke *now*, Mr. Reid?"

"No, I do not. I hope it doesn't shock you that some of my friends smoke." Not many, but a few. He wasn't even sure why he'd said it since he didn't keep regular company with much of anyone these days. This woman brought out the worst in him.

"As long as they're adults, they're free to do as they wish." Disapproval oozed from the woman.

"Exactly. Look, Mrs. Windsocket…"

"That's *Winthorpe*." If it were possible, he'd be able to see the hackles rising on the woman's back.

"My apologies. I assure you that I will deal with this issue. Lauren will not smoke again."

"With all due respect, sir, how can you promise that? I trust you see the possible long-term ramifications of this incident. If you have friends who smoke, your daughter could be continually exposed to secondhand smoke. That's almost as dangerous for a child as if *she* were the one smoking."

Caleb had been tapping his foot on the carpet. Now it was going full throttle. If he had anywhere else to enroll Lauren, he'd yank her out of the academy. No wonder Lauren thought he'd imprisoned her.

"Dad?" He turned to see Lauren standing in the doorway. Her navy and green plaid school uniform hung on her thin frame, and she appeared on the verge of tears. So vulnerable and small. His heart wept at the sight of her.

God, I could use your help. Again.

He jumped to his feet. "Lauren, baby. There you are. We need to talk."

His daughter's expression transitioned into more of a smirk. "Don't call me baby around other mortals," she hissed under her breath. "Even Winthorpe."

"Sorry," he muttered, placing one hand her shoulder. "Thank you for the call, Mrs. Winthorpe. I'll be taking Lauren with me now. If you can make sure she's properly signed out for the day, I'll take it from here."

"We're not done quite yet, Mr. Reid. We have some business to attend to first."

His jaws clenched. "Of course. Is there paperwork to fill out?"

"Yes. Lauren is suspended for the rest of the week and you'll need to sign the necessary parental acknowledgment forms."

"Suspended? For a first offense? Isn't that a little harsh?" He barely kept his tone controlled.

"She's still in the enrollment probationary period. As such, her offense is weighted more heavily." Winthorpe rose to her feet and walked around her desk. It wasn't a stretch of his imagination that she didn't like him any more than he liked her.

"How many offenses is a student allowed during the probationary period? And how long does it last? Not that she'll have any," Caleb added. "Just for my own personal information."

"None, and it's for three months. In other words, if she does anything else warranting suspension, Lauren will be expelled. Permanently. Your deposit will not be refunded, Mr. Reid."

"Got it," he said.

Those intense pale eyes leveled on his daughter, and Winthorpe's tone was grave and foreboding when she spoke again. "Lauren, when you return to Greenbriar-Browne on Monday, you will be administered a drug test. If you pass the test, then your homework will be given to you. You'll have three days to make up your missed assignments."

"Yes, Mrs. Winthorpe." Lauren was smart enough to act appropriately repentant.

Caleb sucked in a breath. "I'd prefer you give my daughter the benefit of the doubt. We're not talking about a repeat drug offender here."

"I didn't mean to imply that was the case, Mr. Reid." He begged to differ. Her use of the word *if* as opposed to saying *when* she passed the drug test was proof enough.

Keeping his hand on Lauren's shoulder, Caleb gave her a reassuring squeeze. His daughter had been caught smoking, and her punishment seemed to fit the crime although the drug test infuriated him. Losing his temper in this woman's presence wouldn't help matters. "Is there a way to get her assignments online? She needs something to do while she's suspended, after all."

When he felt Lauren's shoulder slump, Caleb moved his arm around her waist. The glare from Winthorpe made him quickly withdraw, but he stood close enough for Lauren to feel the warmth of his presence. In a weird way, it gave *him* comfort having her so close.

"Online is not how we do things here at—"

"Yes, at Greenbriar-Browne Academy. I'm well aware." Caleb looked the headmistress in the eye. He bit his tongue not to advise her to join the rest of the modern age in regard to technology. "If you'll kindly provide those forms, I'll sign them, and then I'll be leaving with my daughter."

The woman nodded. "Very well, sir. Follow me."

~~♥~~

"Dad, you were such a bad—"

"Enough," Caleb growled, drowning out the last part of the word. "Don't add cursing to your growing list of crimes."

"That's not really a curse word."

"It is, and I don't want to hear you say it again. Understood?"

"Understood." Silence reigned as Caleb waited for Lauren to fasten her seat belt.

"I was trying to pay you a compliment," Lauren pouted. "You were pretty awesome back there standing up for me and everything. Winthorpe's a trip, isn't she?"

Caleb twisted his lips not to laugh. "I called her Windsocket. I feel safe in saying she's not a big fan of mine after this afternoon's chat."

"That's stellar." Lauren laughed. What a beautiful sound. Her long dark hair danced in the wind through the open window as he roared back down the driveway.

"What book was the test in your English class about?"

"Emma," she said. "Jane Austen."

He chuckled. "Of course." After exiting the gates, Caleb guided the car to the side of road and shifted into PARK. He pulled out his sunglasses and repositioned them on his face. "Lauren, I owe you an apology."

"For what?"

"For making you go to that God-forsaken place. Believe me, if I had anywhere else to send you, I would." He lifted his hands in a helpless gesture. "I'm fresh out of ideas. The school came highly recommended. I can investigate other options, but it'll take some time."

"It's not so bad when Winthorpe's not around."

"When is she *not* around?"

"That's the problem. She's always lurking. The kids are okay, though. And the teachers." Lauren twirled long strands of her hair around her index finger, over and over. Helena used to do the same thing.

"No wonder you feel like you're in a prison." Steering the car farther down the street, he turned into the first available parking lot, a medical facility of some sort.

He cut the engine, released his seat belt, and turned to face her. "Start by telling me why you were smoking in the first place."

"I wasn't the only one."

He arched his brows. "That doesn't answer my question, but how many others?"

She shrugged. "Two."

"Were they also suspended?"

"Not that I know of. They've been students here longer than me and told me they smoke all the time."

"On school property?" When she nodded, he slumped back against the seat. "Still doesn't get you off the hook, young lady. And you don't know that they're telling the truth. People—not just kids—brag all the time to try and impress people. A lot of the time, it's stretching the truth to suit their own purposes."

"Young lady? What are you, my mother now?"

"Look, Lauren. I'm trying to be both a mom and a dad to you, and that's not working out so well lately. You are, in fact, young, and I pray you stay a lady as long as possible. Meaning until you're married." Caleb shook his head. That hadn't come out right.

"Let me tell you something," he said. "When I was about your age, this cool new kid moved to town and starting coming to my school. His name was Wayne."

Lauren snorted. "Wayne's not a cool name."

"The right person can put the cool in *any* name. Wayne wore ripped jeans, chains, and black leather and claimed he'd done all sorts of stuff. All the guys wanted to hang out with him. So did the girls."

"He must have been hot."

Caleb grunted. Hearing her talking about a guy being hot made him uncomfortable in more ways than he could count. Ignoring it was best for now. "Anyway, my friend, Matt, and I started hanging around Wayne. One day he passed around a pack of cigarettes at the park. Everyone else was puffing away, so I tried it."

"Did you like it?" Lauren watched him with wide eyes.

"Not really, but I didn't hate it either. I didn't get the big deal about smoking, didn't understand the thrill. I think the idea of getting away with something illegal made us want to try it. At least we weren't at school, but we easily could have been. Anyway, when I got home that day, your Grandma Reid jumped on my case about being late and how I was supposed to be doing my homework. Then she caught a whiff of my breath, and…"

"Did she lay into you? Give you the big parental lecture about how smoking shaves time off your life?"

"Something like that. But she also did something I'll never forget."

"What?"

Caleb refastened his seat belt and then turned the key in the ignition. The Porsche roared to life. He loved that sound. "You'll find out soon enough." Reaching into the inner pocket of his suit coat, he pulled out his cell phone.

"Sir?"

Caleb started at the sound of someone standing beside his open window. Relief tempered with annoyance raced through him to find an overdone but attractive blonde woman standing beside the car. He must be jumpier than he thought. "Yes?"

"Excuse me, but do you have an appointment with Dr. Lewensteiner this afternoon?" Before he could answer, she continued in her honeyed southern accent. "He's had an emergency and had to go to the hospital, so all of his appointments are canceled for the rest of the day."

With a smile, the woman rested her left hand on the open window. No one could tell him *that* wasn't a strategic move. Then she tapped her manicured fingernails a few times. Yes, he wasn't blind. She was neither engaged nor married. Clearly looking for a man. He figured she wouldn't need to go far to find a willing participant for whatever she had in mind.

"I happened to be walking by and thought I'd mention it. Save you some time, perhaps."

"Thank you for the heads-up, but I don't have an appointment with Dr. Lewen…whatever. I only needed a place to sit and talk with my daughter for a few minutes. That's the only reason I'm here."

Caleb strategically adjusted his sunglasses with his left hand so she'd see his wedding ring. The ring he should finally remove and store away. For now, he was thankful it was still in place.

"I see." Disappointed laced her words as she tapped those fingers again. "I won't keep you. Bye now. I hope you have a lovely day." With a small wave and a parting smile, the woman sashayed away toward a nearby Mercedes.

"See now, *she* thought you were hot."

Caleb grunted. "She did not." Yeah, she did, but what was he supposed to do? He spied a business card balanced on the window ledge. Snatching it before Lauren could see it—if she hadn't already—he tossed it in a compartment on the door. He might be out of touch with dating, but he didn't appreciate a woman with strategically overinflated body parts making a play for him in front of his daughter.

"I'm not stupid, Caleb. And, for an older guy, you do look kinda sharp in your suit today. Do you have a hot date or something?"

"Lauren, can we please cut the *hot* talk? And what's with calling me Caleb?"

"Then how about I call you Abernathy?" She giggled.

"I'm the only one on the planet honored enough for you to call Dad. Use it, please."

"Okay." She kicked off her shoes, stripped off her socks, and propped her bare feet on the dashboard. Each toenail was painted a different metallic color. When had she started doing that? At least they *had* color and weren't black or gray.

"I'll call you Dad if you agree not to give me the *Lauren, you're only twelve* speech again."

"There's no negotiation with the Dad thing." Her statement gave him pause. "Do I say that a lot?"

Rolling her eyes, Lauren ramped up the twirling routine with her hair. "Try all the time." She waited as he looked up the information he needed on his cell phone. A visit to Dr. Paul was in order to put the fear of smoking in her.

"Dad, did you ever try anything else? Other than cigarettes, I mean?"

He sighed. What was protocol with these discussions? Still, Lauren had asked, and she deserved his honest answer. Maybe she'd recall this conversation in the future when she might be tempted to try something foolish.

"Stuff you can smoke. Alcohol." Too much alcohol in his undergrad days, but there were limits on what he'd share now. "Nothing hardcore or anything you can snort, and I was much older than you are. I'm not stupid, either, but I should have known better. I haven't touched any of it since before you were born. Smart people don't get sucked into thinking doing drugs is cool. And smart girls don't put their feet on the dashboard of their father's Porsche." He motioned to her feet. "Down. Now."

"But you're smart, and you still got sucked into it."

How to answer that one? "I also didn't have my priorities straight at the time, Lauren. You're a whole lot smarter than I was."

As he started to pull the car out of the lot, Caleb spied the sign for the medical office, surprised he hadn't noticed it before. He wanted to groan out loud but managed to restrain himself.

"What's a Donor Insemination Clinic?" Wonderful. Of course, Lauren had spotted the same sign. His observant daughter didn't miss much. She'd probably seen the woman's business card, too, but thankfully she hadn't mentioned it. He'd shred the card as soon as he got back to the office.

"Nothing you need to know about."

"Other than it might be a sperm bank, I really don't." She was teasing him now. How did Lauren even *know* that term? Did that overpriced school teach her these things? Short of cutting her off from the rest of the world, he didn't know what he could do.

Lord, help me.

The world was nuts. All he needed to prove it was the fact that he'd just been propositioned, more or less, in the parking lot of a sperm bank with his daughter sitting in the car beside him.

He needed to get his girl in church. Get himself to church. They'd go pray together. Listen to some good sermons. Think about the things of God instead of the warped ways of the world.

And think about looking for another school.

Lord, help us both.

For the second time that afternoon, Caleb couldn't speed away fast enough.

Chapter 16

Waiting in line for her sandwich at Anneta's Bakery & Deli on Thursday, Caty's eyes widened as she spotted a woman reading a magazine by the front counter. Was that Sam on the cover? Those two looked so much alike they were sometimes confused for the other. Although she thought it was Will, she couldn't fathom such an anomaly.

Caty stepped closer. "Excuse me. May I look at your magazine for a second?"

"Okay." With a curious expression, the woman handed it over.

She couldn't believe it. It *was* Will—full head of wavy, dark hair, piercing light blue eyes—gracing the cover of the national, tabloid-style magazine. Her brother rarely smiled as wide as in this photo, and would you look at that? His eyes positively sparkled. Will looked as handsome as she'd ever seen him.

She checked the headline and then read it again. *Have you met William Jordan Lewis?* Beneath it, the subtitle *America's Sexiest Astronaut Ever.* Oh, my. When she'd first looked at it, she hadn't noticed the "e" in *Sexiest* and thought it said *Sexist.* Big difference. She wouldn't want him to have *that* label.

Had Will consented to a photo shoot and interview? Highly doubtful. Caty wondered if he was even aware of the article and his cover boy status. If he *had* agreed, someone must have said or done something very amusing to coerce such a big smile from her brother. Not that he didn't have a sense of humor, but Will rarely allowed it to show through his customary stoicism. She felt certain he never would have approved a piece like this if he'd known about the whole *sexy* angle. Will would *hate* this. Not only would he hate it, he'd be spitting furious.

For all his aloofness, Will wasn't arrogant as much as anti-media. When he was a kid, he'd lived and breathed to learn all he could about the space program. He hung out at NASA, pestering the staff and any technician he could find with his endless list of questions.

His bedroom walls were covered with space posters and autographed astronaut photos, his ceiling plastered with glow-in-the-dark stars and planets. No one in the family, or anyone who'd known Will as a teenager, had been surprised when he'd become an Air Force pilot and then been accepted into the astronaut training program at NASA.

"Order up for Caty! Come and get it." With his booming voice and entertaining delivery, the deli counter guy sounded like he was auditioning for a sports announcer job.

Caty handed the magazine back to the woman. "Thank you." She'd try not to tease Will too much, but this was too easy. Wait until the rest of the family heard about it. She'd pick up a copy of the magazine on the way home.

Five minutes later, Caty found an empty bench in a small park sandwiched between the tall office buildings. Bowing her head, she said a quick prayer for her food. She ended the prayer with, *God bless Caleb and his daughter.*

After carefully prying off the lid from her tomato basil soup, she inhaled the rich aroma and then took a tentative taste. Sitting back on the bench, she reviewed her first four days at Belac. So far, so good. *Except you haven't seen Caleb.* Not one sighting, not even the downwind. Early in the week, Caty thought he might stop by long enough to make sure she'd received the fly swatter and the corn plant. What a weird thought. Perhaps she should have sent him an email or a thank you note, but in the back of her mind, she kept thinking she'd thank him in person.

She took another slow sip of her soup. Why should she *expect* to see Caleb? In spite of his resolution to become more human to his employees, and in spite of his unexpected *breath of fresh air* sentiment, it's not like a man could change his persona overnight even if he wanted.

"Hi, Caty."

Startled, she glanced up and tried to cover her shock. "Hi there. Care to join me?"

Without answering, Suma sat on the bench beside her. Caty watched as she pulled out a small bag of sliced apples and raw vegetables. Is that all she planned to eat? No wonder she was so slender. By contrast, Caty had just dipped her baguette into her soup and been happily gnawing away.

"Suma, do you ever eat a cheeseburger?"

A small smile twitched the corners of the other woman's lips. "Rarely." She darted a side glance at her. "You're thin, too."

"Genetics. I thank my parents daily for the blessing of height." Tummy-tucking undergarments were a fabulous invention, but no need to mention that now. "You're certainly a top-notch receptionist. I'm sure you see the world come and go sitting behind your desk."

"Sometimes it seems that way." After pushing her long hair over one shoulder, Suma took a dainty bite of a carrot stick.

"Even from my office four doors down, I've already heard a number of different languages spoken," Caty said. "Do you know if Mr. Reid is also multilingual?"

"No. Cordelia interprets for him when needed. I also speak four languages." At least Suma had volunteered that information.

"That's wonderful! I'm sure that makes you even more valuable to the company."

The other woman shrugged. "I suppose."

They ate in silence for a few minutes. After finishing her soup, Caty replaced the lid. The inevitable birds and pigeons gathered around the bench when she tossed crumbs from her baguette onto the ground.

"Be careful doing that or you might get...bird stuff on your shoes."

Caty grinned. "Then I guess it's a good thing I'm done with my soup."

Was that a giggle? Suma could giggle?

"I can't believe I practically fell at your feet the first day I came into the Belac office," Caty said. Nothing worked to bridge differences like a good old dose of humility. Might as well make fun of herself.

"I thought it was funny." Suma wiped her lips with a napkin although she'd only consumed tiny bites of carrot and a few apple slices. "You make life interesting. It's usually so quiet." A slice of cucumber slid between those red lips.

"Glad I can provide some humor." Reaching into the deli bag, Caty pulled out her wrapped sandwich. "Can I interest you in half a ham and Swiss sandwich on rye?"

Suma's eyes grew wide, and she appeared almost fearful. Scrunching her features into a frown, she bit her lower lip.

Caty unwrapped the sandwich and placed it on the bench between them. "Feel free to take half. Or all of it. Whatever you'd like."

"Are you making fun of me?"

"Oh, no. That wasn't my intention at all." Caty put one hand on Suma's thin arm and then withdrew. "I can't eat it all and thought you'd like to share." If she protested more, it'd only make matters worse.

"My nutritionist and therapist told me I need to eat more." Suma started to reach for the half sandwich before pulling back, her shoulders slumping. "I'm trying."

One of her roommates at Wheaton had suffered from bulimia so she knew a little about eating disorders. *If* that's what was happening with Suma. Offering her food wouldn't help. The underlying emotional issues needed to be treated.

"I'm glad you're getting help with whatever you're dealing with, and I hope you'll think of me as your friend. During the day, feel free to drop by the office." Reaching into her purse, Caty retrieved a card and offered it to Suma. "Miles brought my new business cards this morning. My cell phone number is listed on here. If you need to talk, or someone to listen, I hope you'll call me. Anytime, day or night."

Taking the card, Suma pocketed it. Her long hair fell over her face, reminding Caty of a veil masking her features, hiding whatever pain she kept hidden inside.

"I'd like to pray for you."

The other woman still wouldn't look at her. "No offense, but that makes me uncomfortable. I'm not a very religious person."

"You're not offending me, but you should know it won't stop me from praying for you on my own time."

"Suit yourself." Quickly gathering her things, Suma rose from the bench. A cloud passed over her pretty face. She started to walk away but then turned back. "How can you be so happy all the time?"

Caty smiled. "Trust me, I have my moments."

Lord, help me give Suma the words she needs to hear.

"My whole life, my parents taught me that I'm living on borrowed time," Caty said. "I'm only here by the grace of God, and I need to use that time wisely. I've learned that every person is special and has unique abilities and talents. *You* are important, Suma. To God and to me."

Suma's dark eyes widened. "How can you even say that? You don't know me."

"I know enough." Caty kept her voice low, quiet. "I know you speak four languages. You're always immaculately put together. You're quiet, well-spoken, and—"

"Do you think it's your job to tell me about God?"

Caty shook her head. "I don't look at it as a job so much as a privilege. Caring about your soul is more important than the work I do for Reidco and Belac. If I allowed my work or anything else to take control of my life, I'd be a bigger mess than I am now. I make a fool of myself a lot, but you know what?"

"What?"

"It's okay because God loves me in spite of myself. At the end of my life, I want to stand before God and tell Him I did the best I could in loving others. The biggest part of what that means right now, Suma, is that I love you enough to share how Christ offers you a peace you can't even begin to imagine."

"Why do you think I need peace?"

"You have a beautiful smile, and I'd love to see it more. True joy comes from deep inside a person's soul." Caty kept her voice calm and non-confrontational. "You asked why I'm happy all the time. Mostly it comes from the hope that after my time on Earth is done, I'll spend the rest of eternity in heaven. That's what keeps me going."

"You really believe in all that stuff, don't you?"

"Yes, I do. Life can be tough, but I've seen how God works in people's lives to transform them. No matter what, He's always there. Christ died for me, for my *sins*. When I was a kid, I told Jesus I was a sinner and needed His help, and then I invited Him to live in my heart."

Caty inhaled a quick breath. She'd gone this far, so she might as well keep going. "That's all you have to do. And something else I learned? If someone doesn't want to listen to me when I talk about God, they're not rejecting *me*, they're rejecting the message."

"I thought you weren't supposed to talk about religious stuff with people in the office." Defensiveness crept into Suma's tone.

"We're not in the office right now and on our own time. I won't mention anything about God again if it makes you too uncomfortable." She couldn't control the reactions of others, but neither did she want to beat her co-workers over the head. She'd said enough.

Lord, help Suma find you. Help her to see you in me.

The other woman's expression remained passive, her mouth unyielding.

"I'll see you back at the office." With that, Suma turned and fled.

Chapter 17

Caleb sat in his home office, checking his work email. Vaguely aware his housekeeper had entered the room, he greeted her without looking up as he typed a two-word response to the new head of the Dallas office. "Hey, Lettie."

"We missed you at dinner tonight."

"I know. Hold on a second. I'm almost done here." He sent the email and opened another message from a manager of a Reidco gas station in San Antonio. After typing a couple of sentences, he pushed SEND and then sat back in his chair. Scrubbing a hand over his face, Caleb closed his eyes. Man, he was tired in his *bones*. It'd been a long week, and it wasn't over yet.

"Perhaps I should come back later."

"No, stay." Opening his eyes, Caleb focused on Lettie. "Fair warning. I refuse to apologize because I wasn't at the dinner table. I'm there most nights unless I have a dinner meeting. Lauren's the one who hasn't made an appearance lately. You know that. Even if she was there tonight. Was she?"

"Yes." Lettie took a seat in the chair facing him. "I didn't say a word. All I said was that we missed you. I believe that's your own guilt and defensiveness talking."

"What do you expect me to do?" He raised his hands in the air. "I'm buried with work but spent a good portion of the afternoon hauling my kid out of her private academy. Then I took her to a doctor friend so he could show her what lungs look like when people smoke. Tried to put the fear of God in her for taking five puffs of a cancer stick."

"You could have taken her to the Museum of Natural Science instead. At least it wouldn't have cost you a consult fee."

Caleb shook his head with a slight smile. "Paul's a friend from Dallas. He was a golf buddy of Helena's dad. He didn't charge me, and it took twenty minutes, not the price of museum admission plus snacks and gift shop trinkets."

JoAnn Durgin

That statement only made Lettie's frown deepen.

"Give me a break," he muttered. "Given the circumstances, I'm doing the best I can."

Her brows lifted. "I know you are. Tell me what's got you more worried."

The force of his sigh puffed out his cheeks. Pressing back in his chair, Caleb crossed his arms behind his head. This woman could always read him, a mixed blessing. "Name a topic, and I've probably got a list. I'm assuming you mean on the personal front." A quick glance confirmed that's what she meant.

Caleb tilted his head, studying her. "What's different about you tonight?"

She smiled and touched her hair. "I had my hair cut and colored today. Working for you gave me too much gray."

He cracked a wry grin. "It looks very nice." Lauren's comment about how scary Lettie looked with rollers and face cream popped into his mind. That was on Saturday morning during their talk in the kitchen. Could Lettie have overheard that comment?

Caleb picked up the spongy Rangers baseball from his desk, one of those stress-reliever things. They'd tossed them to the crowd at one of the games a couple of years ago, and the gimmicky freebie turned out to be one of his best desk accessories. He had another one in the downtown office. He worked his fingers on the baseball, kneading and squeezing it in his right hand.

Like Cordelia, Lettie knew him better than anyone. Knew the vulnerabilities and insecurities he kept hidden from the rest of the world. Sometimes he suspected these two women knew him better than he knew himself. Besides Cordelia, Lettie was the only other person who knew about the kidnapping threats. He hadn't even told his mother. She'd only worry too much and that wouldn't be good for her weakened heart.

"Lettie, are you aware Lauren feels like she's a prisoner here? In the house, in Houston?"

"Yes, I've gathered as much." She shifted on the chair. "A child her age sometimes feels that way no matter what the circumstances."

Caleb dropped the baseball and propped both elbows on the desk. "It was foolish of me to think a change in scenery would make a difference." He leveled his gaze on her. "Did she feel the same way in the Dallas house?"

"I think she started to feel that way in the last couple of years after you stopped allowing her to go to normal activities like birthday parties, sleepovers, school events—"

"Point taken," he snapped, his tone unnecessarily harsh. "I'm sorry, Lettie." The woman possessed the patience of a saint and didn't deserve his anger.

"The move to Houston made sense in a number of ways," she said. "The Dallas house had too many reminders of Helena."

Lettie spoke quietly but with respect. Lettie had gotten along well enough with Helena, but the two women had never been as close as he'd hoped. His wife had never shared the bond he did with Lettie. Helena had never embraced relationships with those in their employ, and she'd treated them like servants, a fact that had never set well with him.

"As important as Helena was to you and Lauren, it's difficult to move on with your lives when you're surrounded by constant memories," Lettie said.

Unexpected emotion clogged Caleb's throat. "I hope I haven't pushed Lauren so far away that she'll hate me."

"I seriously doubt she hates you, Caleb. Tell me what you're thinking?"

That's one of the aspects he loved most about Lettie's character. She allowed him to talk it out. "Lauren threatened to leave the other day. Can you believe that?" He snorted. "As if she'd even know where to go."

"And *that's* what scares you?"

"That's one of the things, but I don't think she'd leave voluntarily." He pinched his nose between two fingers. "I'm scared of one of those nut jobs out there who-knows-where making good on their kidnapping threats." He leaned forward and met Lettie's gaze. "That's a nightmare I hadn't even considered, and it's got me wondering if this entire move to Houston was a mistake. Who's to say that in Lauren's shoes, I might feel the same way? I uprooted her and yanked her away from her friends in Dallas, not to mention her grandmothers. I understand she might be angry with me, but I hope in time she'll understand it was best course of action for both of us. It wasn't just the house, it was…everything. I can't lose my daughter. I'll do everything in my power to prevent that from happening."

"You won't lose her."

Silence passed between them for a long moment. "I told Lauren about the kidnapping threats," he said finally. "When she talked about leaving, I felt as though I had no other choice."

Lettie gasped although she attempted to deflect it by coughing.

"If Lauren knows there are people out there who want to kidnap her, then it might make her stop and think before she's tempted to run off without making sure she's adequately protected."

Lettie gave him the motherly look she'd perfected the past thirteen years. "I think you should work on the reasons why she'd want to run away in the first place."

"Am I such an ogre, Lettie? Such an overbearing parent?"

"Of course not. You know that."

"You should have seen Lauren today as we drove away from the academy. She was happy and carefree. Almost as though she were a different kid and more like she used to be. A girl Lauren's age shouldn't be burdened with the problems of adults."

"I agree, but no amount of protection in the world will make up for your lack of trust, Caleb."

He snapped his gaze to hers. "Trust in what?"

"You are the most capable man I know, but when it comes to your daughter, you wear blinders."

Caleb could only stare at her, slack-jawed. "What are you saying?"

"I'm saying that in trying to protect her, you're pushing her farther away. Lauren's not the only one who feels like she's in a prison."

"You?" he barked. "Do you feel that way, too?"

"No, of course not." Lettie shook her head. The sadness radiating from his dear friend pierced his soul as deeply as Lauren's tears.

"It's time to let go of your fear. You can build higher walls, install more security, and hire guards. I'm not saying not to protect her. That's your responsibility as her father. I'm suggesting you do what you can to keep her safe, but place your trust—and surrender Lauren—to a higher power and then trust she'll be okay."

"I believe in God. I gave my heart to Jesus a long time ago. Please don't start with me." Raking one hand through his hair, Caleb frowned. "I'm trying to figure it all out. Part of that is coming back to the Lord and giving Him total control. I realize that. It's the only way

I can get through this thing unscathed. You know me well enough to know that's something I find difficult to do."

Right or wrong, at times he questioned God's motives. He'd never blamed God for taking Helena. More likely, it was more a matter of questioning his own ability to parent Lauren, keep up with the corporation, and somehow manage to be a halfway decent man. He'd learned the lesson long ago that trying to be all things to all people was an impossible challenge.

Not that he hadn't tried.

"You know, I founded Belac on a solid biblical foundation. I'm beginning to feel as though I've tossed those principles aside."

"I don't believe that's true," she said. "I think it's more that you've neglected them. You're also too strong of a man to allow personal tragedy to define you."

He jutted his chin and narrowed his eyes. "Is that what you think I've done?"

"Yes," she said. Her voice, calm as always, held firm conviction. "I've witnessed how strong you can be, but I've also seen you retreat into a shell because you feel that somehow you failed Helena. God gave her life, and in His time, He took her home. You were by her side the entire time, and she died with dignity and grace."

"I don't want Lauren to be defined by her mother's death." Caleb lowered his gaze. "You and I both know life wasn't always easy with Helena. Then again, I'm not the easiest man to be around. I want my daughter to remember the good about her mother. To understand Helena, to know she did the best she could for her, and to know that it was more than enough."

"Lauren knows those things, and the cancer wing at the hospital in Dallas is something you'll always have as a living memorial to her memory. As far as Lauren, you've invested yourself in that child. Many men in your position would have sent her off to boarding school or hired someone full-time to take care of her every need."

The phrase *men in your position* had always amused him, and he'd heard it enough. "I've always thought that's why I was paying *you*."

She harrumphed. "You're a father to that child, and you always have been, even when you thought you weren't." Lettie's confidence flowed over him, giving him comfort.

After a lengthy pause, she spoke again. "Trying circumstances can bring someone closer to God. At other times, it brings about the opposite response. For some, it simply requires the passage of time. I think you're ready to move forward with your life, professionally *and* personally."

She was right. Lettie usually was. Caleb blew out his sigh, prompted by frustration but also a sadness he couldn't seem to shake. He was tired of that, too.

It was time to reclaim his life. Remember what was most important and get on with living instead of dwelling on past regrets. An image of Caty popped into his head, but Caleb pushed it aside. Lauren needed to be uppermost in his mind now.

Maybe Caty is the way to move on for both you and Lauren. Perhaps, but he'd think about that later. Where had that thought come from? It was too early to know. He'd only just met Caty although he'd been observing her from a distance for a few years, strictly in a professional sense. Now that he'd met her, shared conversation with her, grown to like being around her, he found himself thinking about her more than he should. That confounded him yet, at the same time, knowing Caty gave him hope he could find his way out of that confining, narrow tunnel where he currently lived.

"Giving your heart to the Lord and living for Him can be two different things." Lettie's words brought him out of his musing. She knew exactly what tone to use when he was at his moody best.

Caleb grunted. "I've always thought those things go hand-in-hand."

"Ideally, they do. There are people who claim Jesus owns their heart, but they don't look to Him for the most important decisions. I'm not saying that's what *you've* done, Caleb. But the Lord demands your obedience and a full-time commitment. Walking with Him isn't a part-time option. I think you've lost sight of the fact that no one man can do everything on his own. That's not your job."

Caleb's gaze fell on the framed verse on the wall. When he'd moved into the new house, he'd given instructions for it to hang on the wall opposite his desk where he couldn't miss it. The same verse he'd established for Belac, Inc. all those years ago.

FOR BY YOUR STANDARD OF MEASURE IT WILL BE MEASURED TO YOU IN RETURN. ~LUKE 6:38

"One of the hazards of being a business owner, I fear. I'll tell you one thing." He reached for her hand. "You are a blessing in my life, and in Lauren's life. We couldn't have done these last few years

125

on our own without you, Lettie, and it's to my regret that I don't tell you enough."

"Loving you and Lauren is the easy part." When he glimpsed the tears in Lettie's eyes, his heart jumped.

Caleb released her hand. "So, any advice on how to go about relinquishing control of the reins?"

A smile curved her lips. "You could start by showing up at the dinner table."

"I can do that."

Chapter 18

Caty startled when a hard knock sounded on her front door. Who could that be? No one had called to say they were coming over. She peered through the peephole on the front door and spied Carson. Someone else was with him, but she couldn't tell who it was—only that it was another guy, a little taller, dressed similarly to Carson in jeans and a Dallas Cowboys cap pulled low on his forehead.

She swung the door wide. "To what do I owe the honor of this visit? You could have called—" She gasped. "Will!" She lifted the baseball cap. "What are you doing?"

"Apparently failing in my attempt to go incognito." Will brushed past her. "Sorry to drop in unannounced." Grabbing Carson by the arm, he tugged him inside and then shoved the door closed with his free hand.

"Hello to you, too." She couldn't help her laughter. "I'm sorry, Will, but you look ridiculous. For *you*, I mean. I don't think I've seen you in jeans"—Caty darted a glance at his feet—"tennis shoes, and a baseball cap since you were like…ten."

These days, Will's customary wardrobe consisted of a NASA jumpsuit or khaki slacks and a white or light blue work shirt with his name embroidered on the right pocket. Will had never cared two licks about what he wore, so Mom used to spot check him before he left the house. She checked them all, but more likely than not, Will had been the one sent back to change.

"This is what a science geek looks like in civilian clothes. Carson shopped for me." As if an afterthought, Will gave her an awkward hug. Just as quickly, he released her.

"Love you, too," she murmured.

"We had photogs chasing us." Carson walked over to her front window and pulled the drapes closed. "I think we finally lost them."

"Photogs?" Caty's brows lifted.

Will laughed, a welcome sound, and he nodded to Carson. "Now he's talking the press lingo."

"Photographers?" Crossing her arms, Caty grinned. "Well, now, that's pretty exciting, Mr. Affirmative. Time to face the facts. You're a rock star in the scientific world. Budding scientists everywhere admire and emulate you. Not to mention you're America's Sexiest Astronaut. *Ever.*" Caty crossed her eyes at her older brother.

She loved teasing all her brothers, but Will was the easiest target. Women were attracted to the strong, silent, handsome type. Will was introspective, cerebral, and he couldn't talk to a woman to save his life. For some reason, that made him more irresistible to the opposite sex. Half the single women in the large pipeline of Lewis family friends would drop everything for the opportunity to date bachelor Will. Not that they hadn't tried. The fact that he *didn't* date only increased his appeal.

Will scowled. "I'm guessing you saw or heard about that so-called piece of yellow journalism?"

"Yellow journalism? Wow, I haven't heard that term in forever. I saw a lady reading the magazine in a deli downtown at lunch today and bought a copy on my way home. You can rest easy that it was a flattering article, and you looked absolutely *amazing,*" Caty drawled like a fawning female fan. "I wondered how they got you to smile like that."

"They caught me at an aeronautical convention." Will pumped his fist in the air. "Geeks, Freaks, and Nerds United." He lowered his arm. "I had no idea they'd use that particular angle for their misguided article."

Caty smiled. "I hope these people chasing you tonight are at least cute and female."

"Sadly, they are not," Carson answered for him. "They were burly with lots of facial hair." Whipping off his hat, he smoothed one hand over his hair.

Of all her siblings, Carson looked the most like Mom with his blond hair and brown eyes. He jokingly referred to himself as the male runt of the family since he was the shortest at just shy of six feet tall. Caty always told Carson that God compensated by giving him those charming, deep dimples.

Girls loved her outgoing youngest brother, and he'd never had a problem finding a date. She'd never understand how he'd managed to get through four years of seminary without getting married somewhere along the way. Any number of the Baylor nurses he'd dated would probably have loved to walk down the matrimonial aisle beside him, but Carson was having too much fun being single.

Walking over to the front window, Caty lifted the corner of the curtains and peeked outside. Then she turned back to Will and parked her hands on her hips. "Seriously? I don't see any *photogs* lurking about, but you might want to rethink driving a Mercedes with a Johnson Space Center frame and PURSUIT plastered across the Texas license plate. Dead giveaway, Commander Lewis."

"I've earned the right to drive that vehicle, Caty."

"Of course, you have. That's not my point. Tell me, Will. You *can* install a light bulb, right?" Perhaps that was unkind, but sometimes she wondered if Will's common sense brain cells had gone missing.

Will snorted. "Should I get a girly car to throw them off my scent? Drive around in a yellow beetle bug like Winnie Grant used to have?"

"That was borderline sexist, but it's nice to hear you have a sense of humor. I'm suggesting you rent another car until after the mission. Something nondescript like an old brown Buick. Maybe one with a few dings that backfires to throw people off your trail." With a bright smile, Caty snapped her fingers. "I know! Have Sam resurrect the bomb."

"No thanks. I'll take my chances," Will said. "It has nothing to do with pride."

Carson plopped onto her sofa. "Of course not. We all know Will promised himself that fancy car as his reward for being named commander of the Pursuit mission."

Caty smirked. "Like I said, I'm not disputing that."

"You know my route is from Point A to Point B these days—condo to Johnson Space Center, and then in reverse. This whole thing will blow over soon enough when someone more interesting comes along." Will consulted his absurdly expensive watch that performed untold functions. "That should happen any time now. T-minus 30 and counting."

"Listen to this, Caty," Carson said. "Some woman started to strip off her top at dinner the other night. Reputable restaurant, too." He sounded shocked but more than a little impressed.

Will raised his hands. "I'm not saying a word. Anytime you want to forget that incident is okay by me."

Carson held up one hand to hold off Will's protests. "Sorry, brother, but this is too good. She told Will he could explore her heavenly body anytime. It was pretty obvious she'd had a few cocktails."

Caty shook her head. "Some people have no sense of decency. I hope that kind of thing doesn't happen often." She motioned to Carson. "Feet off the coffee table."

"A few times, but I've learned to ignore it. Another reason I don't go out that often. Leave it to the seminary student"—Will shot a glare at Carson—"to focus on that episode."

"Promise this is the last time I'll tell the story," Carson said. "Sam and Lexa were there, but I'm glad Mom and Dad sat this one out."

Caty grinned. "Are you kidding? Mom would love it. She'd chase the woman away from the table and give her a lecture. What did Sam do? Toss her a few Bible verses or a New Testament?"

Will chuckled. "Sam looked the other way while Lexa threw her sweater around the woman and escorted her from the table."

"Yet another reason why I love that woman," Caty said with an emphatic nod. "She always watches over our Lewis men. Listen, since you're here, come into the kitchen and let's hang out. It's been a long time."

Caty led the way, and they followed. "Want to watch a movie or play a game of Parcheesi?"

"You still have *that* game?" Will's tone was incredulous. "I don't think I've played Parcheesi since middle school."

"You mean since the last time you wore jeans and tennis shoes? I've also got Battleship—we can give the ships names of space shuttles if you want—Monopoly, Scrabble, Clue, Life, plus some newer games. Name one, and I've probably got it. Are you hungry?"

"When am I not?" Carson gave her a sheepish grin. "Truth, Cates? We were feeling guilty for not helping you move in last weekend."

"Likely story," she scoffed. He was the only one that called her Cates on occasion. She rather liked it.

"It's true. So to appease our shared guilty conscience, we came by to mooch." Will ruffled her hair with one hand like he used to do eons ago. In a weird way, she liked that, too.

"Then that whole photog thing was a big ruse? You two are hopeless, but sit down, anyway." Caty motioned to the table and set about getting snacks.

"No, that was real," Carson assured her. "They had these huge cameras and everything. One guy almost fell out the car window trying to get a shot of Will's profile."

"Then tinted windows on the Mercedes might be advisable, too," Caty said. "No matter what brought you two to my doorstep tonight, I'm glad you're here."

"Same here." Will grunted. "Where are those games? Have you unpacked them?"

An hour later, Carson won their rousing game of Parcheesi, and Caty accepted Will's challenge to play a game of chess. Quickly enough, she was reminded why she rarely played this particular game with Will. He and Sam were the family champs.

Their younger brother guzzled his can of Diet Coke and munched on chips while reading her most recent copy of *Kindred Spirit*, the magazine produced by Dallas Theological Seminary. She couldn't believe the baby of the family would graduate with his Master of Theology degree from DTS at the end of the year, another important milestone in their family. Combined with Will's mission, and her move back to Houston, it was shaping up to be quite the eventful year.

Will took precise bites of an apple and worked on his third water bottle while analyzing the chess board. This brother took everything in life seriously, even games.

Caty resisted rolling her eyes after Will refused more snacks. "I hardly think a handful of chips and a Coke will negate your survival training, Commander Lewis."

"You'd be surprised how easy it is to slip off the diet. I can't take any chances. Especially now." Will's voice was resolute and *I take no prisoners* firm. She almost slapped his hand when he took another measured bite, but who was she to question an astronaut-in-training?

Getting up from the table to get a second Diet Coke for Carson, Caty gave Will a light pat on the back instead. "I admire your fierce determination." Nothing would jeopardize his shuttle mission, including his diet. He'd worked too long and hard to blow it now.

Carson shot him a look. "Yeah, blowing up that spacesuit from eating junk food wouldn't be good, especially for Commander Lewis."

"If only the people of America knew the next shuttle commander spends his evenings playing Parcheesi and chess with his brother and sister," Caty mused. "Not that it's a bad thing."

Carson closed the magazine. "Don't let that get around or it'll spoil Will's whole sexy image."

Will ignored that comment and concentrated on his next chess move. Tiny lines showed around his eyes. At thirty-eight, he was the youngest shuttle commander in NASA history, and he'd been training extra hard in recent months.

She might joke and tease him, but Caty was so proud of him she felt like she could burst. Whenever she thought of her brother blasting into space on *Pursuit* in a few short months, she teared up and usually allowed the tears to fall—except when in Will's presence. As the time of his mission neared, she prayed she'd be able to keep her emotions in check. Mission Control better have plenty of tissues on hand. Wow, she got dizzy just thinking about it.

The entire family—including Rachel and Emily—had attended three preparatory sessions at NASA over a period of five days last November, almost a year before Will's scheduled launch. They'd been advised of the potential risks for the shuttle crew—emotionally, mentally, and physically—both pre-launch and after their return to Earth.

Watching Will now, Caty bit her lip as she thought of the enormity of his mission. To some, the work and experiments they'd perform on the International Space Station would be routine, but the knowledge they'd gain while earning a place in the history books was nothing short of awe-inspiring. Who could possibly call that *routine?* Routine was driving into the city for her job every morning, Monday to Friday. Routine was going to Mom and Dad's for dinner once a week. Calling Sam or Lexa to check in with them every few days.

"Will, promise me you're getting enough rest."

A few seconds of silence passed. After making his next move on the chessboard, Will finally spoke. "I try, but my body doesn't always cooperate at this stage of the training." He started to push aside dark strands of his hair.

Catching his hand, Caty gently brushed them away from his forehead. "I hope you know how proud I am of you. How proud we *all* are."

Will's gaze settled on her. "Thanks, Caty."

"I'm sure you'll get that hair cut before the mission."

"Affirmative. NASA requirement. I'm letting it grow until they cut it."

She checked the back of Will's head and smiled. "You have the beginning of a curl on the nape of your neck. Girls like that."

"They do?" That made Carson sit up straighter. Popping another potato chip in his mouth, he eyed Will. "So, tell me something. Is it true your body ages faster while you're up there at the International Space Station?"

"That would be a negative, Carson. We actually age slower when we're at the ISS because of gravitational time dilation."

"Layman's terms, please." Carson pushed the bowl of chips aside and then planted his elbows on the table.

"Space time isn't flat, it's curved," Will said. "It can also be warped by matter and energy."

"Not helping." Caty feigned a yawn.

"Let me see if I can explain it so you earthlings will understand."

"Right. With our feeble brains and all." Carson ducked when Will tossed a chip at him. Grabbing it from the table, he chomped it down.

"Time moves slower as gravity increases," Will said. "Technically, your head ages faster than your feet. For instance, time passes faster for people living on a mountain than those living at sea level. Then there's relative velocity time dilation which means that time moves slower as you move faster."

When Carson made snoring sounds, Caty placed a finger over his lips to shush him. Then she crossed her arms on the top of the table. "Tell us more, Astronaut Will."

In his element, Will grinned. "In the ISS, we'll be floating 260 miles above where the Earth's gravitational pull is weaker than at the surface. Time should speed up for us relative to people on the ground, but this is the key: we'll be whizzing around the Earth at nearly five miles per second. Which means time slows down for astronauts relative to people on the Earth's surface."

Will smiled, looking from Caty to Carson and back. "Got all that?"

"Einstein had it right all along," Caty observed. "Time *is* relative."

"Time is *weird*, and you scientists like to throw around the word 'relative,'" Carson added. "If my pea brain understands it correctly—because velocity time dilation has a bigger effect than gravitational time dilation—when you return to Earth after all that whizzing around in space, you'll be a marginal fraction of a second younger than if you'd stayed right here in Houston all along?"

"Excellent, little brother. Not bad for a pea brain." Will high-fived Carson and then finished his apple.

"Is whizzing a scientific term? I always thought it meant something else." When Will and Caty both looked at him, Carson laughed. Jumping up from his chair, he grabbed the trash can from beneath the sink and held it up. "Okay, space man. See if you can put that apple core in here." He winked at Caty. "Let's see how good he is at aiming. That has to be a very important skill for a space shuttle commander."

Will ignored Carson and motioned to her. "It's your move. I'm waiting."

"At least promise me you're dating every now and then and getting out among the human race," Caty said. "We're not such a bad sort, you know."

"I'm here with you and Carson now. And *you're* here and not out on some hot date."

Sitting back in her chair, Caty frowned. "What's that supposed to mean?"

"I figured you'd have a cowboy dangling on a string by now."

"What? Like a puppet?" She made her next play and immediately recognized her fatal mistake. Unless he was off his game, Will wouldn't miss it, either. "I can't think about a relationship right now."

"And checkmate." With a triumphant smile, Will sat back in his chair.

"No fair," Caty protested. "Did you bring up that whole dangling cowboy image to distract me? No wonder you wanted to play this game. I should have remembered how you used to mop the floor with the rest of us."

"Except for Sam." Was that resignation in Will's tone? Ah yes, there was always more of a rivalry between those two, although more on Will's part than Sam's. With all her brother had accomplished in his life—and still had yet to accomplish—why would he feel inferior to Sam? Not that it was a competition.

Carson nodded. "Even I know better than to get in the middle of that one."

"Sam has his talents, you have yours"—Caty angled her head at Will—"and so does the young one here. Now, let's get back to the subject of *your* romantic pursuits."

Will blew out a sigh. "I can't think about dating right now."

"Because you have more important things to do."

"Yes, I do, as a matter of fact." Will's blue-eyed gaze pinned her down. "A woman, especially a woman who's not my wife, would only complicate things."

"So, you're saying that—for an astronaut—it's easier having a wife than a girlfriend?" Carson popped a chip in his mouth and then downed another long drink of his Diet Coke.

"Yes, but having neither is best. For me at this juncture of my life." Will shot another pointed look her way.

Caty placed her hand over Will's. "Trust me, I know how important the *Pursuit* mission is to you, and I admire and respect you more than you can possibly know. All I'm suggesting is that when you come back down to Earth—and I *do* mean that quite literally—I hope you'll try to find a nice girl and settle down. I need some more nieces and nephews."

"I'm not buying into that reasoning. You have plenty of those with Emily and Rachel's kids, not to mention Sam and Lexa's growing brood," Will countered. "Unlike the mindset of some people in this kitchen, procreating is not high on my list of things to do."

"Will, you are so smug but brilliantly so. Sometimes I don't understand how you could have come from the same womb as the rest of us. How do you plan on passing on all your intelligence genes to the next generation? Wait." Caty held up one hand. "I respectfully retract the question. I don't think I want to hear the answer."

When Will chuckled, it relaxed the lines around his eyes. "I'm interested in space exploration for the next generation, Catherine.

That might be my contribution to the world instead of actually *making* children."

"Well, okay then. Tell a woman *that* line and you're golden." Caty nodded to Carson. "When he returns from his mission, we should give him some lessons. *How to Talk to a Woman 101.*"

"Hey, I'm all for the cause of young love," Will said. "When the time is right."

"I have to agree with him there." Carson sat up straighter. "Cates, did anyone tell you about Will bringing that Army soldier home from Afghanistan last year?"

Caty searched her mind. "Now that you mention it, Lexa said something about it. Emma and Ryan? They live somewhere near Cleveland?"

"*Ellie* and Ryan." A small smile etched the corners of Will's mouth. Customary to his nature, he'd never brag on the fact that he'd personally flown Ryan back to the States. Hearing about moments like that made Caty proud of him all over again. He was a quiet hero, stalwart and strong. The *best* kind of hero.

"That *was* very romantic," Caty agreed. "You flew him home so he'd make it in time for his Christmas wedding, right?"

"He sure did," Carson said. "Going back to the *having a wife is easier than a girlfriend* discussion, what Will says makes good sense for a pastor, too. You can't bring your relationship issues to the pulpit just like you can't be stewing about a woman when you're sitting in the commander's chair. Right, Will?"

"You got it." Will shot her a wink. Who knew the man could wink? Encouraging. Maybe there was hope for the space scientist yet.

"Which means you'd better get busy, too, little bro," Caty said. "For now, we'll be content in our singledom."

"Is singledom a word?" Carson appeared genuinely puzzled. "Hey, at least I'm dating."

"Yes, it's a word," Will said. "I think Caty's the only one who cares. She needs to focus on her own love life and think about giving us more nieces and nephews to spoil."

Although Will and Carson both chuckled, Caty didn't feel much like laughing. She only had herself to blame. Why *had* she started this discussion? "So, who's up for a rousing game of KerPlunk?"

Will's jaw dropped. "You still have that game, too?"

"I do," she said. "It's in the same box where you found Parcheesi. Do the honors and go get it for us, will you?"

Will pushed back from the table, shaking his head. "You're fun, Caty. Weird, but fun."

"I know. That's why you love me."

"Sounds about right." Will headed back to the living room.

Carson rubbed his hands together. "This should be fun. Think they'd ever do a cover story on the Sexiest Seminary Student?"

She swatted his arm. "Don't even suggest it. Why? Is that someone you know?"

Those dimples made an appearance. "You know it, sista." When she burst out laughing, he shrugged. "Can't get away with that one, can I?"

"Not a chance."

"Will, stop orbiting and get back in here!" Carson called.

All Caty could do was laugh. These two were good for her *soul*.

Chapter 19

"Dad, do you own the whole building?" Lauren walked beside Caleb on Friday morning as they headed toward the private elevator in the parking garage. Twirling in a circle, she opened her arms. Still facing him, she took short, backward steps.

"I don't own any of it. I only lease space for Belac on the 35th floor."

"The whole floor?" She still sounded impressed. "That's like...huge!"

Caleb smiled at her enthusiasm as Lauren turned around and bounced the rest of the way to the elevator. *Bounced.* Not slouched, dragged, or plodded. Her attitude today was much improved, and he'd lost count how many times she'd called him Dad.

He'd taken the time to say a prayer—granted, while he was soaping up in the shower—and acknowledged his gratefulness for Lauren's recent shift in attitude. Her outlook had also encouraged him, and he hoped it'd continue.

The night before, they'd sat together at the dinner table and talked. They'd shared a decent conversation even if it was only about movies and TV shows. Sometimes the inconsequential discussions were every bit as good for the soul as deep, meaningful talks. He'd turned off his phone and insisted Lauren did, too. No work papers were scattered on the table, nothing to distract either one of them. He'd focused on what she'd said and Lauren answered his questions without resorting to any *you're so old* or *you're so out of touch* comments. He suggested watching a movie together one night and she hadn't flat out refused. Again...progress. Baby steps.

As they waited for the elevator, Lauren looked up at him. "So, if you don't own the building, do you *rent* it? Is that what lease means?"

"You've got it." Caleb angled his head and gave her a stern look. "I think you like being suspended. Is that why you smoked in the bathroom? To get out of going to school for a few days?"

Although he'd never admit it, he couldn't blame her if she had. In her shoes, he might have done the same thing. Maybe he was being unfair, but he wouldn't wish Windsocket on anyone. *Winthorpe.* Usually he was a stickler for using someone's proper name. Calling her by the wrong name had started as a joke, so why couldn't he get it right?

"No. I didn't like smoking that much, anyway. And that model thingee with the black lungs that Dr. Paul showed me was disgusting."

"Good." If smoking one cigarette was the least of her—make that *his*—problems, she'd be blessed. Still couldn't hurt to ramp up the prayer time. "Lauren, I hope you realize I'm not saying people who smoke are bad. It's like anything else. What they do is their own business, but every person is accountable for their own actions before God."

"I know. Grandma Reid used to smoke."

How could he have forgotten? Momentary lapse. She'd smoked after he'd gone away to college and hadn't kicked the habit until Lauren was about four. After Lauren spent time with his mom, Helena had been furious when she'd come home reeking of tobacco—in her hair, her clothing, even in her skin.

Addiction could be a horrible thing. He'd finally paid for his mother to go to a fancy clinic somewhere in southern California to kick her by then two-or-three-pack-a-day habit. If he were honest, he'd done it to be the hero to his wife as much for his own mother's health. By that time in his marriage, he'd have done almost anything to help salvage his lackluster marriage.

With its faint ding, the elevator finally arrived. The private service elevator was a courtesy provided to exclusive building tenants, but it was unbearably slow. Taking out his pass key, Caleb waited as Lauren entered the elevator. He followed and then quickly slid the card through the slot.

Lauren grabbed his arm as the doors closed. "This is fun. Like *bring your daughter to work* day."

"You know the rules, Lauren. Cordelia will watch over you when I'm not there." At least he only had one appointment this morning. "After I'm done with my meeting, we'll do something together." He hadn't figured out what that was, but Cordelia could help him come up with something. As long as she wasn't confined in the house, Lauren might be less inclined to sulk.

"You and your rules." Lauren pouted for all of three seconds before brightening. "Maybe I should have smoked before, huh?"

"Bringing you here isn't a reward. Taking you to lunch and then somewhere later isn't a reward, either. Keep that in mind, please. However, in spite of the circumstances, I like having you here with me today." He smiled at her. "Very much."

"Me, too." Slipping her hand in his, Lauren leaned her head against his shoulder. His heart skipped a few beats. When was the last time she'd spontaneously expressed her affection like this?

"Dad, do you think the kidnappers know I'm here?"

What? Caleb slammed his hand on the STOP ELEVATOR button. "Lauren, please promise me you won't say anything to anyone about the threats." She looked up at him with those eyes that had captured his heart from the moment she was born.

Deep breathing a few seconds, Caleb fought to rein in his emotions. "The most important thing to know is that this isn't a game. You need to stay close until I can figure out what to do. Don't worry. I'll think of something." Those statements were more for his own benefit than Lauren's.

"I know it's not a game. I just don't want to be old, like twenty-five or something, and not have a life."

Caleb swallowed hard. "I have the feeling that won't happen. I want you to have a life."

"Like I said before, you need one, too." After Lauren punched the elevator button, it resumed its ascent.

If only he could push aside his worries as readily as his daughter. On the other hand, he'd thanked God that morning for the optimism of youth and the fact that he hadn't scarred her for life by telling her about the kidnapping threats. Hopefully, that's all they'd ever amount to—threats on paper—but he couldn't take any chances.

"Wow. That was really fast!" she said when they reached the Belac floor and the elevator doors opened into his private offices.

As usual, Cordelia waited for him by the elevator. "Good morning, Mr. Reid." She smiled at Lauren. "Good morning to you, *Miss* Reid." In private, Cordelia addressed him by his first name but always with "Mr." whenever others were around. Even Lauren. Probably had a lot to do with her military background.

Lauren giggled and released his hand. "Hi, Delia." She saluted her. "Put me to work."

His daughter was the only one Cordelia permitted to call her by that nickname. "Lauren, be good," he cautioned. "Don't be a nuisance."

"I'll take good care of her. Danica's off today. Lauren, you can sit at her desk." Cordelia gave him a reassuring nod.

"Oh, you've got food!" Lauren's blue eyes grew wide and she lunged toward the serving cart near his second assistant Danica's desk. "Can I have a cinnamon roll?" Dangling one hand above the cart, she flashed a mischievous grin.

"You ate breakfast at home. You know what? It's Friday. Have at it. Why not?" At least she'd asked his permission. In his mind, Caleb imagined Lettie giving him the *pushover* expression. Admittedly, he was a pushover when it came to Lauren. Making rules was much easier than enforcing them. He was fumbling his way through this single dad gig one challenge at a time.

Caleb turned to Cordelia. "Do you have some filing or an easy task Lauren can do?"

"What do you mean by *easy*? I'm not dumb." Lauren assumed a battle stance, feet apart, hands on her hips. Hips that would probably start filling out and looking more like a woman's any day now. He wasn't ready. As it was, he'd barely made it through the training bra stage. After Lauren begged for one, he'd implored Lettie to take her shopping. The thought of anything else Lauren might ask him for in terms of womanly stuff made *him* blush. Female adolescence might very well be the end of him.

"Trust me, I know you're not dumb," Caleb said. "I didn't mean it that way."

"I'm sure I can come up with the perfect job for Lauren." Cordelia checked the clock on the wall. "Your meeting starts at ten. The green folder is on your desk."

"Excellent. Thank you." With a nod, Caleb strolled into his office. Shrugging out of his leather jacket and removing his Stetson, he hung them both on the coat tree. Unfastening the top button of his shirt, he slid into the leather chair.

In addition to the usual files, there was something extra on the desk this morning. Looked like a bakery box. Pulling it toward him, he caught a faint whiff of something delicious. Man, it smelled irresistible.

Using his thumbnail, he slit the tape and opened the box. Peach pie? Looked homemade since there was no bakery name. Caleb couldn't remember the last time someone had baked him an honest-to-goodness homemade anything. Although peach wasn't his favorite—apple held top honors—any fruit pie ranked high on the list.

He pushed the intercom. "Cordelia, where did this peach pie come from?"

"Caty Lewis brought it for you. She said she made it first thing this morning. I thought you might like a slice with your morning coffee. You'll find a knife, napkins, forks, and a short stack of paper plates in the top right drawer of your desk. My assistant, Miss Reid, will be bringing your coffee to you shortly."

"Thanks for taking good care of me. Please send Miss Lewis a thank you email."

"Yes, sir. I'll take care of it."

"Scratch that. I'll send the email to Caty myself."

"Whatever you'd like."

His brow furrowed. "Wait a second. I'll tell Caty in person. Something as special as a homemade pie warrants a personal visit." He hesitated. "Don't you think?"

"Whatever you'd like, sir." Was that amusement in Cordelia's voice? Small wonder since he was waffling like an insecure teenager with a crush on the prettiest girl in school.

He missed seeing Caty, oddly enough, and it was only her first week in the Houston office. He didn't *want* to miss her, but he did. Several times, he'd stopped himself from sending her a quick email, calling her, or dropping by Caty's office. He'd already sent her two gifts albeit nothing extravagant or too personal. If he started hanging around her office, she might question his motives. She wouldn't be the only one.

He'd heard from Cordelia how Caty was already endearing herself to the other employees with random acts of kindness. Or a well-placed word or expression of caring. Seemed she had a tradition in Dallas and Lubbock for leaving birthday cupcakes and cards on desks. She'd made it her mission to motivate employees and generate goodwill and a feeling of family. He supposed that made sense from a woman with five siblings.

Some people might consider her Pollyanna Do-Gooder attitude irritating. With Caty, it wasn't an act. He'd met a lot of people in his lifetime, and she was one of the most genuine. Intelligent, witty, and feisty all rolled into one beautiful woman, an alluring combination.

Okay, enough of this. Caleb buzzed Cordelia one more time. "Would you like a piece of the pie? I'm willing to share."

"That's not necessary, sir."

"Are you sure? It looks and smells delicious. It's just Lauren and me at the house this weekend. We can't eat an entire pie by ourselves."

Was that a sigh from his assistant? "Sir, Caty left a second one in the breakroom. Please stop trying to give away your pie and enjoy it."

He grinned. "Yes, sir. I mean, ma'am." Through the intercom, he heard Lauren giggle. He'd make a fool of himself every day if it made his daughter laugh.

Opening the desk drawer, Caleb withdrew a paper plate and cut himself a medium-size piece of the still-warm pie. He savored the first bite—warm, fresh, and mouth-wateringly delectable. His second bite tasted even better. She must have used fresh peaches, not the canned kind. Seriously one of the best pies he'd ever tasted.

A quiet knock sounded on his door. "Come in!" he said around another mouthful.

Lauren walked inside his office with a steaming mug of coffee. "Ow ow ow. This is burning my fingers."

Caleb rushed to her side. "Here. Let me get that. You're a great assistant." He rescued the mug.

"You're welcome, Mr. Reid. Will there be anything else?" Oh, she was cute.

"Yes, as a matter of fact. You can sit with me and eat a piece of this fantastic pie. Come join me at the conference table." He carried the box over to the table along with his pie, a second paper plate, and a fork.

Lauren eyed him warily. "Are you feeling okay? You never eat something this sweet for breakfast." The massive leather chair swallowed her small frame as she dropped onto it.

"Yes, but this is a special occasion." After cutting a small piece of the pie and sliding it onto a paper plate, Caleb handed her the fork. He'd try to forget she'd already consumed a cinnamon roll, and she'd be on a sugar high all afternoon. Fun times.

"What's the special occasion?" Lauren took a bite and gave him a thumbs-up.

He sat down beside her and nudged her shoulder. "Bring your daughter to work day."

~~♥~~

Caty fully intended to ignore her ringing cell phone on her desk until she noted it was Marta. With a smile, she clicked it on. "This is Caty. Not looking for a man today."

"Very funny. Any sign of the boss yet?"

"Nope." Caty rose to her feet and crossed the room. "Hang on while I close my office door."

"Good thinking," Marta said. "I guess it wouldn't be good to be caught gossiping about the boss."

"No, it would not." After closing the door, Caty kicked off her shoes and then curled into the corner of the loveseat. "I'll take five minutes, but then I need to get back to work. You've done a great job on the late night newscasts. Did you find out what's up with Brandy?"

"She's pregnant. The question is whether or not she'll be back. She's having a rough time of it, and I heard a rumor she might sit out this entire pregnancy, if not longer."

"That's unfortunate, I guess," Caty said. "Of course, I'm sorry she's sick but happy she's pregnant." She rolled her eyes. "That made no sense, did it?"

"You sound like you did at the restaurant the other night. Are you flummoxed again?"

"I guess you could say that. It's true there are different ways to look at any situation. So, did the station offer you the interim job?"

"Yes, you're talking to the full-time *weeknight* meteorologist. One of the producers confided it might work out for the best since I'm trained as a meteorologist and, well, Brandy's not. She was hired first, so she has seniority, though. I'm not sure how I feel about all that, but for now, I'll do the best job I can. The station management will have to figure out the rest."

"That's all you can do," Caty agreed. "Keep me posted."

"I will. Now, how's that handsome cowboy treating you?"

"He's not. I haven't seen Caleb since our dinner."

"Well, that's a pity. He's retreated into that secluded cave again?"

"Funny you should say that. His office *is* kind of like the Bat Cave. It takes up space in the middle of the floor with entrances on both sides. I didn't get a lot of sleep, so I got up at four a.m. and made peach pies, one for Caleb, and I left another one in the breakroom."

"Quite the ambitious woman. Kissing up to the boss?"

"No kissing involved, I assure you." Why had she said anything about the pie?

"You miss him."

Caty squirmed a bit. "How can I miss a man I barely know?"

"Because Caleb wasn't the only one infatuated at dinner the other night. Deny it all you want, girlfriend, but subconsciously? Admit it, Caty. You made that pie hoping Caleb would swagger into your office in all his cowboy manliness and thank you in person. I'm telling you, there's something between the two of you just waiting to be explored."

"I… I…" Caty wasn't sure how to answer. "Mom gave me a bag of fresh peaches. I had to do something with them so they wouldn't go to waste. Marta, the man is a widower and has a twelve-year-old daughter. I've barely had relationships let alone with a man who's been married and has a child of *any* age."

"Do we need to go over this again? Where's that Lewis optimistic spirit? It's been five years, and the man's had time to grieve. Not to sound insensitive, but a handsome man like Caleb needs to be married."

Caty couldn't stop her grin. "Yes, Caleb is handsome, but how do you figure that?" Maybe she shouldn't ask.

"If you think about it real hard, I'm sure it'll come to you."

"Don't start with the whole *a man has needs* discussion." Caty slapped her forehead and rolled her eyes. "I can't even believe I'm having this conversation." Thank goodness she'd closed her door. Still, she'd be humiliated if anyone passing by her office overheard her comment.

"Okay, then, how about the fact a girl that age desperately needs a mother? You remember being twelve, don't you? The age when you're on the cusp of *becoming a woman*," Marta said with an overly dramatic flair, making Caty smile. "Gawky as anything, braces, liking boys one minute and hating them the next, getting all tongue-tied, starting to think about going to school dances."

"I remember it all too well, my friend. Listen, I couldn't be more thrilled that you called, but I need to get back to work so they don't think I'm a lazy, man-deprived accountant."

"May it never be!" Marta laughed. "*Chop chop* then. I'll talk with you later, Caty. Have fun."

"You, too. Thanks for the call."

Jumping up from the loveseat, Caty opened the door and moved back to her chair. She clicked on the computer file she'd been working on before Marta's phone call. A faint sound made her glance up from her desk. What was that? Sounded like something brushing over the carpet. Or maybe her lack of sleep was finally catching up with her? Concentrating on her report, Caty went back to work. Thank goodness no discrepancies crept up as she downloaded the latest ledgers.

Another few minutes later, she heard another noise.

Please, Lord, don't let it be a rodent. Anything but that.

She could handle a little mouse, but on the 35th floor of a downtown high-rise? Maybe it came from down the hall. Overall, the office was quiet, but occasionally sounds from next door or the main lobby floated down the hallway. Then she heard it again. No, it definitely came from somewhere in her office.

As quietly as possible, Caty lifted out of the chair, thankful she hadn't yet put her shoes back on. First, she peeked along the wall behind her desk before tiptoeing across the carpet. She scanned the baseboards around the perimeter of the room. Nothing unusual. Maybe she *was* hearing things. Heading back to her desk, she heard another sound. Hard to say what it was, but maybe a sniffle?

She eyed the loveseat. That was the only remaining option. Wouldn't she have noticed if anyone else was in her office? It wasn't that large, after all. Surely she wasn't that oblivious.

Dropping to her knees, her pulse racing, Caty peeked beneath the piece of furniture. Because it sat so low to the ground, she couldn't see much. She'd need to go around to the back. "Please don't be a mouse, please don't be a mouse." Repeating it seemed to ease her unrest.

Feeling silly, Caty crawled around the loveseat on all fours.

"Please don't be a mouse...*ohhh!*"

Chapter 20

A young girl stared at Caty through luminous blue eyes. Knees drawn to her chest, her wavy, dark brown hair reached almost to her waist. Dressed in black jeans and an oversized gray sweatshirt, she was a pretty girl. Striking, really, although her long hair threatened to overwhelm her delicate features. She looked to be in her early teens if not younger.

"You're not going to tell on me, are you?"

"That depends," Caty said, trying to catch her breath. "Have you recently escaped from jail?"

"No." The girl's eyes rounded.

"You didn't take anything that didn't belong to you, did you?"

"I don't steal if that's what you're asking."

"Is there something you need on my office floor? Did you lose something?"

The beginnings of a small smile surfaced. She shook her head.

"Then no, I don't suppose I'll tell on you."

Her features visibly relaxed. "You're not mad?"

"No, I'm not mad. At the moment, I'm immensely thankful you're not a rodent."

The girl giggled, and Caty knew. *Lauren.* This had to be Caleb's daughter—the dark hair, the nose, the face shape, everything but the eye color belonged to him.

She offered her hand. "I'm Caty. You must be Lauren."

"How'd you know?" Lauren gave her hand a brief shake.

"You look like your father." *Oh, no.* Dread settled in Caty's stomach. Had Lauren overheard her conversation with Marta?

"You're the lady who made the peach pie." It wasn't a question.

"That's right." She'd said something about a man having needs. If Lauren had overheard that statement, would she know its meaning? At twelve, Caty had been pretty naïve, but kids these days seemed to grow up a lot faster in many respects.

Oh, no. She'd also mentioned Caleb being a widower with a child. She had the feeling that might not have sounded good. How was she supposed to know Lauren would hear it? At least Lauren didn't seem to dislike her, no matter what she might have said...or not said.

"Your pie is really good. Dad shared some with me. Did you make it?"

"I did. Peach pie is a favorite in our family. My grandmother passed down her recipe, and it's kind of a given we'll all learn how to make it." Not that Lauren needed to know all that.

"So, you've met my dad?"

Caty nodded. "Yes, I met with him in his office last week."

"But you had dinner with him, too, right? Was it a date?"

"No, it wasn't a date. Turns out your dad and I have mutual friends. He didn't know I'd be at the dinner, and I didn't know he'd be there." Based on her question, Lauren must have overheard her conversation. What a great start to the day. Tired of being on her knees, Caty settled on the floor facing Lauren and stretched out her legs. Sitting cross-legged didn't work well wearing a pencil skirt.

"But do you *like* him? You know, not because he's your boss or anything?"

Oh, goodness. How to answer that question? Caty remembered being Lauren's age, but she'd never been Lauren's age without a mother. "Yes, I like him. Your dad is extremely smart, kind, and he's very good to his employees."

"But do you *like* him, like him? Do you want to kiss him and stuff?" She frowned. "Lots of women like Dad, but he doesn't seem interested."

What was with all the talk of kissing? First Marta, now Lauren. She'd ignore the *and stuff* part. Caty looked her in the eye. "Lauren, were you here in my office when I was on the phone with my friend?"

Lauren's lowered gaze answered her question. "Sorry."

"That was a private conversation." Caty tried not to come down too hard on the girl. This wasn't her child and was, in fact, her *boss's* child. "I hope you don't make it a habit to listen to what others say without their knowledge."

"I came to meet you, but you were busy and didn't see me. Then you got the phone call and said you were closing your door. That's when I hid behind the sofa—on the end—so you wouldn't see me. I swear I didn't mean to eavesdrop, Caty. I hope you believe me." A tear slipped down Lauren's cheek, and she swiped it away. She hadn't expected tears, but Lauren appeared sincerely apologetic.

"Tell you a secret. I did the same thing a couple of times when I was a kid. Doesn't make it right, but I know it can happen."

"You did?"

"Sure did. I remember hiding behind our living room sofa once while my parents made plans for a surprise party for me. I'll tell you one thing. It totally ruined the surprise." Not that it was quite the same thing, but it was the first example that came to Caty's mind.

A cell phone rang, but its ringtone was unfamiliar. "That's my dad," Lauren said. "He's probably freaking out. I'd better answer it." Lauren tugged a cell phone from beneath the cuff on her sweatshirt. "Hey, Dad." As soon as Caleb began to speak, Lauren held the phone away from her ear. From where she sat, Caty could hear the agitation in Caleb's voice.

"Calm down, okay?" Lauren said when he stopped. "I'm in the office. You can call off the wolves now. I'm safe."

Call off the wolves? Caty lifted a brow. Why would Caleb be so upset? And why would Lauren feel the need to tell him she was safe? Being protective was one thing, but he sounded more than irritated. Not angry, exactly. *Frightened* almost, but that made no sense. Not coming from Caleb Reid. What could be running through the man's mind?

Not that it's any of your business.

"I'm in Caty's office." Lauren lifted her gaze to Caty's. "We're talking about kissing."

Caty wanted to laugh and groan at the same time. So, Lauren liked to repeat things. She feared that might not bode well for either of them.

"Okay. Bye." Lauren disconnected the call and shrugged. "He worries about me too much."

"That's a father's responsibility and what parents do."

"Do you have any kids?"

"No."

"Do you *want* kids someday?"

"I come from a family of six children. If I get married, I'd love to have at least one or two. Perhaps you should head back to your dad's office, Lauren. He sounded worried."

"I'm suspended from school." Lauren didn't appear especially remorseful or apologetic. Neither was she in a hurry to leave, apparently. With her arms still wrapped around her legs, the girl rocked back and forth.

"For how many days?"

"Until Monday. Dad didn't know what to do with me since Lettie's in Dallas visiting her sister for the weekend. That's why I'm here in the office today."

"Lettie?"

"My housekeeper. Well, she's a lot more than that. She's been with us since before I was born. My mom died, so Dad depends on Lettie. She's kind of like my third grandmother. She cooks and does laundry, those kinds of things."

"I'm very sorry about your mom, Lauren."

"Thanks." Lauren shrugged. "It's been five years."

"I'm sure you must miss her."

"Sometimes." The girl nodded. "I smoked at school yesterday, and my dad had to come and get me." Her face crumpled. "At least he came."

Caty resisted the urge to hug her. Had she smoked to get Caleb's attention?

Lauren glanced up at her again. "Caty, what's a Pollyanna?"

"Where, um, did you hear that name?" Caty shifted her position.

"Dad called you that."

He did, huh? Caty drew in a quick breath. "Well, from what I know, a Pollyanna is someone who tries to see the best in people. There's an old Disney movie by that name." She'd probably been called worse things behind her back, so she'd look at the nickname as a positive one.

"He acted kind of stupid when he got the pie you brought for him. That's what guys do, right? They act all weird and say dumb things when they like a girl. He said he couldn't remember the last time someone other than Lettie made something homemade for him."

"I'm glad he liked the pie, but I can't imagine your father acting weird or saying—"

"Lauren, there you are!" Caleb flew around the corner of her office. Crouching in front of his daughter, he took firm hold of her arms. "Sweetheart, you have to let me know when you leave the office. I didn't have any idea where you were, and neither did Cordelia."

Was he panting? Even if he'd sprinted the short distance from his office to hers, a guy in top physical shape like Caleb shouldn't be winded. He seemed to be overreacting, but what did Caty know of his life? A sudden thought struck her. Could Lauren be ill with some kind of disease? She prayed that wasn't the case, but it might explain his extreme reaction.

Lauren raised her cell phone in the air. "That's why you gave me this, remember?"

"Yes, but you didn't *use* it to tell me you'd left my office." His voice was firm. Dressed in jeans, boots, and a light blue oxford shirt, Caleb looked masculine and appealing, as always.

Her office suddenly felt very warm. No, more like *she* was a little overheated. Caty resisted tugging on the collar of her blouse.

"On your feet," Caleb ordered his daughter. "I'm still in my meeting, and you're coming back to the office with me."

As Lauren scrambled to her feet, Caleb glanced at Caty as though seeing her for the first time. "I'm sorry for the interruption, Miss Lewis. I hope my daughter didn't interrupt your work for too long."

"Not at all. She livened up my morning." Caty smiled at Lauren. "It was very nice to meet you, Lauren. If you're in the office again, feel free to come and see me anytime you'd like."

"Thanks. I think my dad would really like it if you kissed him sometime. He's been kind of lonely and grumpy lately."

"That's enough, Lauren." An adorable flush invaded Caleb's cheeks.

Caty avoided his gaze. Getting up from the floor in her skirt would be a challenge, and she didn't look forward to doing it with an audience. "Don't let me keep you." Still seated on the floor, she made a sweeping motion with one hand. "You should get back to your meeting now."

"You can stop shooing me." Caleb's lips twitched. "They can wait another minute or two." He was beside her in seconds. Positioning one hand beneath her elbow, he assisted Caty to her feet. The man was nothing if not a gentleman.

"Thank you kindly. The designers of pencil skirts weren't thinking of sitting on the floor, that's for sure." Trying not to laugh at the silliness of it all, Caty smoothed a hand over her skirt, now irreparably wrinkled. No matter since no one would ever accuse her of being a fashionista. Accountants were usually rumpled as a general rule.

She pulled back slightly when Caleb leaned close enough to catch a whiff of his intoxicating cologne. What was the name of that scent—*Illegal? Irresistible?* Combined with his appreciative glance—not *in*appropriate but certainly not businesslike—Caty nearly swayed.

I'm in such trouble here. She opened her mouth to speak but then closed it again.

"Can we discuss this later, Caty?"

"If you'd like, but I'm not sure we have anything to discuss." She should have known better than to look directly into those warm brown eyes. The man made her positively dizzy.

The corners of his mouth lifted in a charming grin. "I think we do."

"I have Lauren with me, sir." Cordelia stood in the doorway. "We'll be in my office."

Caty flinched. How long had they been watching this little exchange?

"I'll be there in a couple of minutes," Caleb called over his shoulder, never moving his gaze from Caty's.

Taking a quick breath, she lowered her voice. "Caleb, I didn't invite Lauren into my office." Matter of fact, his daughter had been eavesdropping on her private conversation, but she'd keep that tidbit to herself. It would seem the father-daughter duo had deeper issues. She could have done without Lauren's kissing remark, but other than that, no real harm had been done.

Crossing his arms, Caleb tilted his head with an arched brow. "You seem to have a disconcerting habit of telling me what you believe *I'm* thinking."

"Oh." Caty lowered her gaze. "Sorry."

"I wasn't thinking you invited Lauren into your office, but I *am* wondering how she got here in the first place."

She lifted her chin. "Lauren's smart and inquisitive. From what I can tell, she's a perfectly normal twelve-year-old girl. I'm sure your daughter was bored and only wanted to do a little exploring. She mentioned the pie I'd made and said she wanted to meet me. You can't blame her for any of that, can you?"

"No, I suppose not. In other words, lighten up?" Caleb lowered his arms to his sides.

"Well…yes, in so many words."

"Are you saying I'm boring?"

"I'm not saying that at all. My dad is one of the most fascinating people I know, but he was a banker. I was bored to tears whenever I visited his office yet look at me now. I work with numbers all day. Imagine that."

"Sounds like you had an interesting discussion with my daughter."

"You could say that. Caleb, did you call me a Pollyanna?"

He chuckled. "Only in the best possible sense. I happen to believe the world needs more Pollyannas. Thank you for the pie, Caty. Hands down, it was the best peach pie I've ever tasted. I should get back to my clients now, but are you free to join Lauren and me for lunch?"

"Well, I—"

"I'll swing by here at noon to get you."

She fought the urge to grin. "I didn't say yes."

"You didn't say no."

Her smile emerged. "You're very sure of yourself, aren't you?"

He stepped closer, bringing all that intoxication with him. "Please say you'll come."

"When you put it that way…yes. I'll come to lunch. With you and Lauren." That cleft in his chin fascinated her. His smile mesmerized her. That masculine cologne did untold things to her senses.

"I'll see you then." He headed for the door.

"Caleb?"

He turned back to face her. "Yes?"

"Wouldn't it be a better idea if we meet downstairs in the building lobby?"

The muscles in his jaws flexed. "Right. Perhaps that's best."

"And maybe one o'clock when the noon-hour lunch crowd might have thinned out? I mean, you should probably ease back into the world gradually after being so reclusive." Caty hoped he wouldn't take offense. Had she really just said *ease back into the world?*

"I'm glad you're thinking for both of us." Hesitating, Caleb ran one hand over his brow. "I'm sorry for snapping at you in the parking lot of the restaurant last week, Caty. That was…rude and obnoxious. I trust you'll accept my apology."

"Of course. No need to worry," she said. "I wasn't exactly a Pollyanna that night. We both said things we didn't mean, but you don't need to take me to lunch to apologize."

His eyes softened. "That's not what I was thinking, and that's not why I asked."

"Then I'll see you at one o'clock."

Caleb nodded. "Looking forward to it."

As he departed, Caty couldn't help but think how much she *didn't* understand about this man.

You are one fascinating man, Abernathy.

Now that she'd met his daughter, she had even more questions.

Caleb stopped by his assistant's desk as he strolled back into the offices. "Cordelia, can you find a place nearby for lunch within a three or four block walk from the building?"

"Certainly. What time and for how many people?"

"Make it one o'clock. My meeting will be done by then. There'll be three of us—Lauren, Miss Lewis, and myself. "

"I guess you found a way to thank her." Spoken half under her breath, Cordelia had to know he'd heard.

He quirked a brow. "Your point?"

The smile Cordelia gave him was as wide as any he'd seen in recent memory. "I'm absolutely delighted, sir. I'll be happy to make the lunch reservations."

"I can stay here with Delia if you want to go with Caty, just the two of you," Lauren suggested. "A man has needs, right?"

Caleb did a double take so fast his neck popped. "What did you just say?" At her desk, Cordelia pretended to be inordinately occupied with something although she couldn't seem to stop smiling.

Lauren giggled. "Something I heard recently."

"You listen too well," he grumbled as he massaged the back of his neck. What was he going to do with her? He could only imagine what she might have told Caty. Hopefully, an intervention wouldn't be necessary to deprogram whatever ideas his prepubescent daughter might have planted in Caty's mind.

Not to mention she'd planted the idea of kissing Caty in *his* brain. *You've already thought about kissing her.* No, he couldn't blame that one on Lauren.

Lauren obviously liked Caty. That was encouraging. Caty had been gracious to her, but if his suspicions were correct, there was more to that story. Why had they been discussing kissing? He had no doubt Lauren initiated that conversation. On the other hand, having Lauren along for lunch would be a safeguard against him saying, or doing, anything which might not be in anyone's best interest. Something flirty or romantic like the dinner last week with Caty. That'd been fun and as close to a date as he'd had in a long time. *Better* than any date he'd had in recent years.

Apparently, he'd gone delusional. Why was he even thinking about these things? Because of their previous flirting and Caty's proven pie-making skills? Because Caty was a beautiful woman and his daughter seemed drawn to her the same as he was? He needed to get a better handle on his emotions before they spiraled completely out of control.

Caleb turned to Lauren and restrained himself from pointing. "I'm giving you the final say on where we go for lunch, but no hot dog vendors, taco stands, burger shacks, pancake houses, or pizza joints. Cordelia can help you."

"Aye aye, captain." Lauren saluted him and then plopped on the chair at Danica's desk. He could only hope she'd stay put during the remainder of his meeting.

"Mr. Reid?"

He focused on Cordelia. "What?" Realizing he'd snapped, he forced calm into his tone. "Did I forget something else?"

She pointed to his office. "Your meeting? They're waiting on you."

"Right." This was getting serious. Five minutes in Caty's presence, and he'd already lost his senses. The woman was dangerous.

Opening the door to his office, Caleb strode toward the conference table where his clients patiently waited. Ah, Cordelia had shared some of the peach pie with them. Smart woman. He should give her another raise.

"My apologies for the delay. Now, where were we?"

Chapter 21

As she walked through the Belac lobby, Caty was surprised to see another woman behind the desk—the blonde she'd seen near the elevators the day of her first meeting with Caleb.

"We haven't been officially introduced." She stretched her hand across the desk. "I'm Caty Lewis."

"Nice to meet you, Caty. Quinn Howland. I'm Suma's backup during lunch." That explained why she hadn't met this woman since Caty was usually squirreled away in her office during the noon hour.

"Would you like me to take your calls while you're out?"

"That's not necessary, thank you. I let them go straight to voice mail. Which division are you in?"

"I'm Martin Hillyard's new personal assistant."

Caty's radar shot to high alert. "I wasn't aware Martin had transferred from the Lubbock office."

"It's a recent development. His assistant decided not to make the move, so I've been assigned to work with him." Leaning closer, Quinn lowered her voice. "May I ask you a question?"

Caty nodded. "Of course."

"Martin seems very private and prefers to handle everything himself. Do you know if he operated that way in Lubbock?"

"I don't really know. Sorry. You could contact Lesley, his former assistant in Lubbock, and ask her. I'm sure she'd be happy to talk with you."

"That's okay." Quinn smiled. "I just thought it couldn't hurt to ask."

"Please give Martin my regards. Nice to meet you."

"You, too." An incoming call took the other woman's attention.

Lost in thought, Caty departed the office and waited for the elevator in the outer lobby. So, Martin had transferred to Houston. Interesting. A Reidco executive vice president, he'd been one of the men she'd considered a possible suspect in falsifying entries on the Reidco ledgers. As Caleb had suggested, she'd been keeping a close eye on the numbers all week. Nothing else had seemed out of place since their initial meeting. For that, she was extremely grateful. She hoped nothing else would happen although her intuition told her it was inevitable that something *would*.

When Caty exited the elevator on the ground floor lobby, Caleb waited with Lauren. With his leather jacket casually tossed over one shoulder, smiling, he presented a more relaxed image from the tense man who'd run into her office not that long ago.

Something was going on with him in terms of his daughter. Not that it was her business, but she cared about these two. They'd suffered a major loss in the past few years, and she couldn't begin to imagine how difficult losing Helena had been.

"I'm glad you could join us." Caleb fell into place beside her. "I thought we'd try out one of the local restaurants. Familiarize ourselves with the area." He motioned for her and Lauren to go ahead of him into the revolving door.

"Did your meeting go well?" Caty said as he joined them on the sidewalk.

"It did. We're investigating potential new properties for mineral and oil rights, and the reports were encouraging. I hope you're settling into the office now. Have you met the others in the offices around yours?"

"Yes, have *you*?" Caty tossed him a smile. "Sorry, I couldn't resist." As they waited at the crosswalk, Caleb rested his hand on Lauren's shoulder. She'd noted his vigilance in keeping his daughter within his close range of vision.

"Caleb, do you realize what this means?" Caty said as they crossed the street to the next block together.

"No, I guess not. Why don't you tell me?"

"You're actually walking down the street with one of your employees. Going to lunch. Sharing small talk and casual conversation. That's a significant breakthrough."

He chuckled. "You're not only an accountant, now you're also my psychologist. I don't think I need psychoanalyzing, thanks very much."

"Maybe not, but I *do* think you might need a friend."

"Is that so?" He shot her a curious glance as he opened the glass door of a restaurant.

Japanese?

"Isn't this great, Caty?" Lauren said. "Do you like Japanese? Dad let me pick where to go and he said this would be fine."

Caty swallowed. "Peachy."

Caleb watched her carefully. "It *is* okay, isn't it? If you'd rather go somewhere else, say the word." His lips, so close to her ear, sent shivers *everywhere*. Good shivers, but even with his daughter-in-tow, this man could be dangerous.

"I'll be fine. Let's do this." Caty followed Lauren into the restaurant. She could be a daredevil when it came to sports, but when it came to food? How could they know she was more a meat-and-potatoes kind of girl? Even on family and church mission trips, she'd always stuck with the tried-and-true or gone without. Sam and Carson used to always tease her about her "refined" food tastes while they'd scarfed down anything put in front of them. Ugh, but they'd lived to tell the tales.

A young hostess, wearing a bright pink silk kimono, greeted them with a sweet smile. "*Nan mei sama desu ka?*"

Lauren tugged on Caleb's sleeve. "Let me, okay?"

"By all means. Have at it. You're much better at Japanese than I am."

"*San nin desu.*" Then Lauren said something else Caty could only assume was about a reservation since she gave the woman their last name.

They followed the hostess down a long, narrow hallway. Stopping halfway, she slid open a screen partition that led into a small, private dining room.

"The floor is made from tatami mats," Caleb told Caty in a low voice. "Which means they're straw and hard to clean, so we're expected to remove our shoes. Put your hand on my arm to keep steady."

Doing as he asked, grateful for his assistance, Caty quickly slipped off her pumps and placed them beside Lauren's flats. *Please, Lord, don't let this be a disaster.* The potential for that very thing was all around her, and that's what scared her.

Caleb tugged off his cowboy boots with practiced ease and set them on the floor. Placing one hand on the small of Caty's back, he escorted her into the room. She appreciated the gentlemanly things he seemed to do so naturally.

The hostess pointed to the seating area and the low-to-the-ground table. "*Kochira e douzo.*"

"*Arigatou gozaimasu,*" Lauren said as Caleb removed his jacket and Stetson. Taking them from him, the hostess hung them on a rack in the corner.

"Ladies are supposed to sit with their legs on the side," Lauren whispered. "We should sit together, side-by-side. Caty, you sit between me and Dad."

Legs on the side? That sounded odd enough. How could that possibly be comfortable for an hour? Now Caty really wished she'd worn pants today. And why on earth would she want her feet next to Caleb? Sure, she'd showered that morning, but had she known she'd be in a Japanese restaurant, she'd have made time for a pedicure.

Oh, the predicament.

Caleb nudged her arm. "You can kneel if it's more comfortable."

"I can do that. I just haven't done it for an entire meal." Still, it would save her from the side-sitting dilemma.

Marta was right. She *was* a nut. One thing was a given—life with Caleb Reid was anything but boring.

"Only men are allowed to sit cross-legged. It's totally not fair." Dropping onto the cushion to Caty's left, Lauren sat back on her haunches. "Sitting like this is called *seiza.*"

Following Lauren's lead, Caty lowered onto the cushion next, and then Caleb took his place to her right. Cross-legged, of course, the privilege reserved only for men.

The hostess handed each of them a menu. "*Menyuu ni narimasu.*" Then she departed, sliding the partition closed behind her.

"I think I actually understood the first word of that," Caty whispered. For the second time today, she found herself sitting on the floor in her pencil skirt. The fact that her handsome boss sat only inches away, so close she felt the warmth from his body, certainly wasn't helping her equilibrium. Something about it seemed almost intimate compared to dining in a restaurant. On a chair. At a table.

"I've never been to a Japanese restaurant before," she confessed. "I have no clue what to do. I'll be honest—the thought of using chopsticks kind of terrifies me."

"It's not that hard. We'll teach you." Lauren seemed so animated compared to earlier. No wonder Caleb wanted to indulge his daughter by bringing her here.

"There are a few rules for using chopsticks," Caleb said. "The major *faux pas* is sticking them upright in your rice. It's similar to a ceremony performed at funerals. Lauren knows some of the other rules."

Lauren nodded. "Don't put your chopsticks in the air when you're thinking about what you want. That's considered greedy. Don't eat directly from the shared dishes. Take food from the top of the dish only. Oh, and don't lick the ends of chopsticks. That's considered rude." She giggled. "Remember, Caty. Chopsticks are not a toy."

"I'll try to restrain myself." Caty grinned at Lauren. "Thanks for the helpful tips."

Caleb slapped his hand on his forehead in dramatic fashion, no doubt for Lauren's benefit. "How could I forget this one? Never share food with your chopsticks. That's probably the biggest taboo. It's a reminder of another custom at Japanese funerals where cremated bones are transferred to the urn."

"Lovely." Caty shook her head. "Let me guess. You got the funeral tidbits from Cordelia?"

"No, I learned it on a business trip to Japan about seven years ago. Why?"

"I got a lesson in the most expensive coffee beans in the world—weasel-digested, as a matter of fact—when I first visited your office. Cordelia has all sorts of fun facts to know and tell."

Caleb burst out laughing. What a great laugh. "Cordelia was an Army brat, and then she and her husband both served overseas in the armed services."

Lauren frowned. "She told me about eating eyeballs once. In some African country or something. Gross stuff. But she's cool otherwise."

"Yes, well. If you see me breaking any rules during lunch, I trust you'll let me know. Transferring food from the plate or bowl into my mouth is my biggest concern at the moment," Caty admitted. "Or else I might be hitting that peach pie myself when we get back."

Caleb turned to her. "Are you okay if Lauren and I make the menu decisions for all of us?"

"Please do. As long as there's no liver on my plate, I'll be fine. I'm not a big fan of sushi, either. Or eyeballs." Caty winked at Lauren. While they discussed what to order, Caty sat with her hands demurely on her lap, hoping it wasn't against the rules and that she wasn't being offensive.

A different young woman entered the room and offered Caty a small, palm-sized, hot towel. "*O-shibori?*"

"You're supposed to use this on your hands," Lauren said. "Not on your face. It's not polite."

After thanking the woman, Caty took the towel and wiped her hands. "I'm guessing I shouldn't ball this up and toss it in a basket somewhere?"

Caleb grinned. "You can either fold it or roll it up and leave it on the table. You mentioned sushi. Most people have a misconception about it. Have you ever actually tried it?"

"No." Caty frowned. "You weren't supposed to ask that question."

"Take a wild guess what sushi is." Lauren lifted her brows up and down.

"I'm guessing raw fish isn't the right answer?"

Lauren shook her head. "Nope. Sushi is rice with vinegar in it. *Sashimi* is sliced raw fish."

"Sushi is usually served with toppings like cooked or raw seafood, and that's where the misconception comes from," Caleb added. "It didn't originate in Japan, by the way."

"I'm learning all sorts of things today. Obviously you two have done this before. Multiple times," she murmured under her breath.

"I have a kimono. Dad took me to Japan a couple of years ago," Lauren told her.

"That must have been a fabulous opportunity for you to experience another culture. Do you like traveling?"

Lauren nodded. "It's fun. I've been to Germany, England, and France."

"Lauren's gone along on a few of my trips in the past. I'm hoping to take a few more extended trips for fun in the future."

"I think I'd like to be an interpreter someday," Lauren said. "Sit in on big important meetings with world leaders, and get the early scoop on what's happening. Doesn't that sound exciting?"

"I think it'd be great." Caty smiled at the girl's enthusiasm. "From what I've seen, you're well on your way."

"She learns easily and retains it well." Caleb leaned forward to address Lauren. "Keeping things confidential is also a valuable quality in someone who wants a position like that."

"Yes, Father. No more talk about kissing. I get it."

Caleb chuckled. "That's right. Best to leave the talking, and the kissing, to others."

"Don't worry. I hate boys. I'll never kiss them."

"That's the spirit." Caleb nudged Caty with his elbow.

Hot green tea was delivered to their table. As they waited for their food, Caty wondered if Caleb normally prayed before meals. "Do you mind if we say a prayer?"

"I'll do it." Caleb reached for her hand and Lauren did the same.

"Dad, you haven't—"

"Lauren, bow your head. Time to pray now. Dear Lord," he began before she could say more. "Thank you for this special meal. We're glad Caty could join us today. We ask that you'd bless this food to our bodies and our conversation that it might glorify you. In Jesus's name we pray. Amen."

"Amen." Caty squeezed Lauren's hand and then gently withdrew her other hand from Caleb's. He probably didn't realize that he'd run his thumb over the side of her hand several times during the prayer, making it difficult to concentrate. Not that she was complaining. In fact, she'd liked it *too* much.

The door opened again, and a trio of servers brought in their food and proceeded to set what Caleb explained was a traditional Japanese table—a bowl of rice to her left, a bowl of miso soup on the right. Behind those, each main course—an *okazu* according to Lauren—was served on individual plates. Pickled vegetables were on another plate on the side as well as a dipping dish with soy sauce.

"The presentation of the food is just as important as the taste," Caleb said. "Traditionally, there are three main dishes served—one raw dish, one grilled, and one simmered, steamed, or deep fried."

Caty leaned forward to take a closer look. "And what do we have here, Mr. Reid?" At first glance, they looked safe enough.

He introduced her to the various dishes on the table. "We have *tempura* consisting of battered and deep-fried seafood and vegetables. *Yakitori*, grilled chicken, and finally, *nikujaga*, which are potatoes and beef stewed in sweet soy."

"Yummy. Really," she insisted after Caleb gave her a look of skepticism. Now, for the dreaded chopsticks. They were only wooden sticks, after all.

After Lauren showed her how to hold them, Caty's cheeks flushed as she fumbled with her chopsticks. She might as well accept that would be a common occurrence around her boss. Experiencing new things and a different culture was a *good* thing. Beads of perspiration broke out on her forehead. If she kept this up, her hands would be so clammy the pesky wooden sticks would slip out of her hands and clatter on the floor. And that would inevitably be a horrible offense or remind them of funerals.

Calm the sarcasm, woman.

"Here. Let me help you." Caleb leaned around her and wrapped his right hand over hers. "Hold the chopstick in your right hand with your pointer, middle finger, and thumb. Try moving it up and down like so." He demonstrated. "Now, you try it."

He expected her to think with his hand over hers? He released her, and Caty tried her best to hold it like he'd shown her.

"That's great except you need to try and keep your thumb still," he said. "Only the pointer, middle finger, and chopstick should be moving. Now, for the second chopstick, hold it like this between your thumb and your palm. This chopstick shouldn't move at all while you're using it."

"Okay." Maintaining her focus was the most difficult task. "Watch this." Caty managed to pick up some rice and a piece of grilled chicken. By the grace of God, the food made it from the chopstick into her mouth. Well, she did lean forward quite a bit, but somehow she managed to feed herself so she wouldn't starve.

"I have to say, the Japanese make you work for every bite," she said, sitting back on the cushion. "I might need the rest of the day off after this meal. If I'm not sitting here all afternoon trying to eat it, that is. I have to say, this meal is a little exhausting. But fun," she added quickly.

Caleb chuckled and started to feed her from his chopsticks.

"No, no." She laughed. "That is forbidden."

"Oh, right. You're doing fine. Keep at it, and it'll get easier. Promise."

Lauren was a pro at using her chopsticks, and Caty watched her in awe for a few moments. "You are my hero."

"Thanks." Lauren grinned around a bite of tempura.

As they continued to eat, Caleb asked her if she was settling into her new townhome.

"Oh, I can't believe I haven't thanked you yet for the potted plant and the BoSox fly swatter! They're fabulous. I've decided to decorate the Corn Plant for Christmas this year, and Scrappy will be armed and ready for fly season."

Caleb chuckled. "I'm glad you find them both practical."

Lauren laughed. "Dad, you are so strange. Have you ever heard of flowers? Who's Scrappy? And what's a BoSox?"

"Scrappy is a very important fly swatter," Caty told her. "BoSox is a nickname for the Boston Red Sox professional baseball team."

Lauren still looked befuddled. "So, wait. You're supposed to swat baseball players with Scrappy?"

Caleb and Caty both laughed.

"That would be interesting to watch," Caleb commented as he effortlessly moved chicken to his mouth with his chopsticks. Show off.

"I get it," Lauren said, smiling. "It's one of those adult things, right?"

"Kind of." Caleb shrugged and shot Caty a helpless grin.

"I ended up going to Mom and Dad's on Saturday after the big moving extravaganza," Caty said as they continued eating.

"They sound wonderful," he said with what sounded like an edge of sadness in his voice.

"Do you have any brothers or sisters?"

"I'm an only child."

"I can loan you some." Caty hoped to make him smile.

"What's it like to be part of a big family?" Lauren piped in.

"Most of the time it's great. I used to feel like I had no privacy, but if I needed a friend, I always had one nearby—whether under the same roof when we were little or by phone or email later on."

"Even your brothers?"

Caty smiled. "Yes, especially my brothers. I'm very close to my oldest brother, Sam. He's a great listener, and no matter where we are in the world, we've always kept in close communication. Except for when he was on an overseas mission for a year, but that's another story. He's married to a great woman named Lexa, and they have three kids. Sam gives great advice, and he's come to my rescue a few times."

"Rescued you from what?" Lauren took another bite of her food and chewed slowly, watching her with wide eyes.

"Well, he once picked me up from a disastrous date. He took me home and danced with me in our living room because I'd never even made it to the dance. Sam couldn't dance very well, but he knew my heart was a little bruised. He wanted to reassure me that my date wasn't rejecting *me*."

As soon as the words escaped, Caty wished she could take them back. Perhaps that wasn't the best example for a girl Lauren's age.

"Why did you think he was rejecting you?"

"Lauren, that might be too personal." Caleb took a drink of his tea and darted a chastising glance at his daughter.

"It's okay. That's a valid question deserving of an answer." Caty stabbed a bite of tempura to stall for time while she considered the best way to answer. "He wanted things from me that I couldn't give him."

Lauren's jaw dropped. "He didn't hit you or anything, did he?"

"Nothing like that, Lauren. He just didn't like it when I told him no."

"Oh, he wanted you to have sex with him." Caty tried not to look shocked but didn't succeed.

On the other side of her, Caty heard Caleb's deep sigh. With him so close, she felt the lift of those broad shoulders. Although he kept his voice low, she sensed his frustration. "Lauren, how do you even *know* these things?"

"I have eyes and ears. People talk, and things are in the media all the time."

"That doesn't mean you have to listen." He sounded a bit testy. "Or read. Or pay attention. Take notes or whatever."

Lauren smirked. "I'm growing up. I've faced it, Dad, and you should, too. Wouldn't you rather I be prepared for things like that?"

Caty heard his low groan at that question. She turned to Caleb before her feelings of guilt could overtake her for bringing up the subject in the first place. "So, what do you think the chances are for the Astros to make it to the World Series this year?"

The glance he shot her was filled with sweet gratitude and tugged on Caty's heart. "Probably no better than any other year."

Caty grinned. "Ah, but we made it to the World Series in 2005, and ushered in the first-ever World Series game in Texas. We don't need to talk about what happened, but it goes to show you that there's always hope."

"That was also the longest game in World Series history, but I like your optimism." Caleb toasted her with his water glass. "To baseball and...new friendships." As he sipped his water, his eyes locked with hers.

Caty was thankful for Caleb's focus on things other than the corporation during their meal. He needed a break the same as everyone else did, and when he relaxed, he was an engaging conversationalist. Not that she was surprised, but he'd always seemed so serious.

As a father, Caleb was clearly devoted to Lauren. Raising a child in a two-parent household was hard enough, but a man trying to do it alone with a precocious preteen daughter? That had to be one of the most difficult tasks of all.

Lord, if there's any way I can help him, please clue me in.

Chapter 22

"Thank you for lunch," Caty said as they all exited the restaurant together. "It was very good, but the company and the funny stories you two shared were the best part."

Her compliment brought back his ready smile. She'd missed it during the last part of their meal. Even though Caleb carried his share of the conversation, he'd seemed somewhat subdued.

"I'm glad we could go. Still want a piece of peach pie or do you need to hit the sub place in the next block?"

"I think I'll make it to dinner. Caleb, it's my turn to apologize. I obviously wasn't thinking when I brought up that story."

"No worries. If your story hadn't triggered a remark like that, something else probably would have." He rubbed a hand over his brow. "I warned you that Lauren's twelve going on forty-five. I joke about it, but I'm afraid it's painfully accurate."

"Kids that age say provocative things to get our attention." Caty said. "She might be testing the waters with you to see how far she can push you. Not that I'm an expert, by any means."

"I think there's a lot of truth in what you're saying." Caleb's brow creased. "I'd like to keep her young and innocent for as long as possible. In today's world—with phones and advanced technology—that seems like an impossible task. Even though I've installed parental controls, she still knows things that shock me."

"Unfortunately, all she has to do is turn on a television, a radio, or look at a magazine these days," Caty said. "If she's grounded, she'll make the right choices."

He glanced her way. "I'm sorry that guy was such a jerk to you all those years ago. Sam sounds like a great big brother, and I'm glad he could be there."

"I was afraid to tell my mom and dad, but I did learn from that experience. It's all part of growing up, I suppose."

Lauren darted here and there during the three-block walk and peeked in store windows. "Caty! Come over here and look at these cute shoes."

Caleb encouraged her to go with Lauren. "I'll sit this one out."

"As you can tell, she's getting very interested in fashion," he said when Caty rejoined him. "Lauren understandably doesn't want her father trailing along on a shopping trip although I come in handy to pay the bills." He blew out a sigh. "I'm afraid I've overindulged her since her mother died."

Caty shook her head. "I don't think that's true. If you'd *over*indulged her, Lauren would be crying or begging for the shoes she's looking at in that store window right now. Then you'd go inside the store and plop down your credit card so she could buy them. Do you know someone who might be able to take Lauren shopping?"

Surely Caleb wouldn't think she was fishing for information about his personal life. Well, maybe she *did* wonder a bit, but that wasn't her primary motivation for asking.

"Not really. The average age of the four closest women in my life is sixty—Lettie at the house, Cordelia in the office, and my mother and Helena's mother in Dallas. Not that they don't have a sense of style, especially the ladies in Dallas, but..."

"I'd be happy to take Lauren shopping sometime," Caty offered. "I used to take women and their daughters shopping as part of my ministry in Lubbock." The shopping for the Montford Mission had been at a mix of discount clothing stores, consignment shops, and local charity thrift stores, but the theory was the same.

Caleb stopped walking. "That means a lot that you'd be willing to do that, Caty. Not to be pushy, but would you have some time in the next week or two?"

She nodded. "I'll make time."

Caleb appeared relieved that Lauren was still preoccupied with her window shopping. "I had to pick her up at her school yesterday because she was caught smoking in the bathroom. Now she's suspended until Monday."

"She told me."

"She did?" When he resumed walking, Caty fell into step beside him.

"I'm glad she feels comfortable confiding in you. That's not something she usually does with someone she doesn't know well."

His smile emerged. "I shouldn't be surprised since I feel the same way about you. I hope that's not awkward for you because we work together."

"Not at all, and I wouldn't offer to take her shopping if it did. I'm sure it's not easy being a single parent, Caleb, and I like to believe we're becoming friends."

"We are." He lifted his arm but then lowered it, leaving Caty to wonder what he'd planned on doing with that arm. She liked how he'd phrased it as *working together* instead of making the distinction that he was her employer.

"I'd like to pull Lauren out of her private academy, but I'm not sure where else I can send her."

"May I ask why?" Suspension seemed a logical and fair punishment for smoking on the school grounds.

"It's one of the best private schools in Houston and came highly recommended, but something's missing." They walked in silence, but it wasn't uncomfortable. "I guess the best way to describe it is that the atmosphere is oppressive. I didn't meet any students, and Lauren says it's not all that bad although the headmistress is rather...interesting. They're subjecting Lauren to a drug test on Monday, and if she violates any other rules during her initial enrollment period, she's out."

"I'm sorry, Caleb." She could tell he wanted to say more.

"Homeschooling is an option, but it's not the best one for us. Lauren needs the social interaction with the other kids."

Caty hoped he wouldn't be irritated by her next comment. "Not to sound like...well, like a snit, but rules are made for a purpose."

"I understand. Eliot and I discussed that the other night at dinner, as a matter of fact. My question was whether rules serve to confine us or whether they actually challenge us to be our best."

"I think the answer is both. Rules are made by men to keep order and peace just as God gave us His commandments," Caty said quietly. "I don't want to sound like I'm a know-it-all Christian, either. I'm not perfect in any sense of the word, and I definitely don't have all the answers. Not by a long shot."

Stopping, Caleb turned to face her. "Your faith is part of who you are, Caty. A big part." With a warm smile, he leaned close. "I get that, and I admire you for it." He chuckled. "If it helps, I know you're not perfect."

"Well, that's a relief. Now I can relax. Were you a troublemaker in school?" Tossing him a grin, Caty increased her steps and forced him to catch up to her. With his long strides, it only took a few steps. Lauren kept pace with them, still peering in shop windows, but Caty suspected the little matchmaker had made herself scarce for their benefit.

"I guess you could say that." Caleb pushed his Stetson farther back on his head and then shoved his hands into the pockets of his jeans. "I initiated and participated in more than my fair share of stupid pranks."

Caty mock gasped and moved one hand to her cheek. "Were you a *bad* boy, Abernathy?"

"The answer depends on your definition of bad. I never did anything that created lasting physical or emotional damage. It was more about getting together with my friends and making mischief. Nothing to do with loving and leaving the girls if that's what you're thinking."

One hand moved to her hip. "Now you're telling me what *I'm* thinking?"

The corners of his mouth quirked. "I guess I am. Sorry."

"No problem. I'm only teasing you," she said. "Did you go to a private school like Lauren?"

"Not at all. My mom, Jennifer, couldn't have afforded it. Not that I cared. I didn't know anything about private school, didn't know anyone who went to one. My dad—his name was Charles—left us when I was ten. I think partly because I saw how hard my mom had to work to provide for us, I had these grand dreams of working in the oil industry one day."

"Because you wanted to take care of her one day like she'd taken care of you?"

Caleb nodded. "Exactly. I also wanted to show her that not all guys would run off and abandon her. She didn't deserve that. No one does. He didn't go off with some other woman, and he didn't have substance abuse issues, nothing like that. He just decided he didn't want to be married anymore."

"That's tough. I'm sorry," Caty said.

"As weird as this might sound, I think Mom would have preferred it if he *had* left her for someone else. That way, she'd have an answer. Something definitive instead of the unknown. He got his

CDL license and spent the rest of his days driving frozen foods cross-country in a semi with a big dog on the seat beside him. We heard that from a guy back home who ran into him in a truck stop diner a couple of years after he took off."

Caleb's voice had grown quiet and a frown creased his brow. "He never bothered to contact us again. We heard from a family friend that he died of cancer three years ago. I don't even know where he's buried except that it's somewhere in West Texas." He heaved a heavy sigh. "For all I know, he was cremated and his ashes scattered along the highway."

Caty's heart hurt for Caleb and Lauren. Not knowing what else to do, she reached for his hand, lacing their fingers together. She sensed he needed that connection. "I don't know what to say. I'm sure that carries its own kind of pain."

He removed his Stetson and held it in one hand. "As selfish as this sounds, I hope he somehow knew that I was able to eventually make a good life for mom. Not to stick it to him, as some would say, but to prove that I didn't allow his influence to negatively affect my life. To prove that I was able to make something of myself without any help from him. And to prove that, at least in some respects, I was a better man."

Caleb glanced into the distance and his Adam's apple slid up and down in his throat. "What a pitiful waste of a life, you know? He walked away from and threw away the relationships he could have had with a wife who loved him and a son who wanted nothing more than to adore him." Scuffing his boot on the sidewalk, Caleb's voice caught and his gaze temporarily strayed from Lauren. Up until that point, his gaze had never veered away from his daughter.

He cleared his throat and focused on Lauren once more. "He never met Helena, and he had a granddaughter he either never knew about or never cared to know."

Squeezing his hand, Caty waited until he looked at her again. How true it was that no one knew what sadness lurked in someone's soul. Caleb had been through so much. "Not to sound flippant or to make light of it, but I'll be happy to loan you my dad sometime. I happen to think he's a pretty awesome guy."

Caleb studied her for a long moment without speaking. "Does he fly model airplanes?"

Caty smiled. "He used to fly jets in the Air Force, so I'm feel pretty confident you could talk him into flying a model airplane. Want me to ask him?"

A slow-moving smile creased Caleb's handsome face. "I might ask him myself. When I give him a tour of my baseball collection." He glanced down at their joined hands with obvious surprise as if he didn't remember when that had happened.

Suddenly self-conscious, Caty slowly withdrew her hand. Please continue your story."

"One of my high school teachers saw potential in me, and he recommended that I apply to Princeton," he told her. "In my mind, I didn't have a prayer. To be honest, I did it on a dare from a friend. Turns out Princeton looked at my grades and figured I might be a worthwhile risk. When I looked at their catalog, I liked what I saw and thought it would give me a solid business background."

Caleb lifted his shoulders with a boyish grin. "You'd think I would have gone to UT, but something about the Ivy League appealed to me. My mom was so proud, and I knew it meant something to her that I go there, too."

"I think you like doing things others don't expect," she said.

He smiled, and the faint lines around his eyes showed. "And *I* think you know me pretty well. Anyway, Princeton offered me a decent scholarship, but my mom still had to scrimp and save to pay the incidentals. I worked in construction all through high school, in the summers during college, and then into graduate school to help out with the expenses. By God's grace, I was able to get it all done in five years and with only a small amount of debt, a minor miracle in itself."

Caleb's steps slowed again. Caty didn't want their time together to end and wondered if he felt the same way. This felt like more like a first date—the *getting to know you better* part shared in the beginning of a relationship—than an office lunch with her boss. Instead of making it more *im*personal, Lauren's presence had somehow made their time together even *more* special.

The office building loomed ahead in the next block. Running ahead of them, Lauren checked out a purse boutique. It was the last shop before they'd cross the street and then head into the building.

"My parents sent me to public school," Caty said. "I used to think if they knew half of what I heard or saw there, especially in high school, they would have yanked me out so fast my head would spin."

"Did you ever tell them?"

"Yes, but not until I was at Wheaton College." She smiled. "I wasn't really surprised to learn they'd sent me to public schools on purpose. Even in the small hometown where they grew up, Mom told me those same things went on. Private schools aren't immune or isolated from any of it, either."

"I doubt any school is immune," Caleb said. "I'm sure your parents trained you well, and they trusted you'd make good decisions. My mom did the same thing. I made a lot of mistakes, but I tried to hold true to the values she'd taught me. Didn't always work out so well, but I eventually came around."

"From what I can tell, you turned out pretty well." Her compliment prompted another smile from Caleb. She was quickly growing accustomed to his smile. "I remember my dad telling me that time and place doesn't matter. Sin has existed since Adam and Eve. It's part of life and always will be. I remember he said, 'Most people are going to do whatever they want, whenever they want, and with whomever they want. But you have the Lord in your heart, Caty. Follow His lead and He'll never steer you wrong.'"

"Wise advice. Your life has been blessed, but you don't take it for granted, Caty. I admire that."

Caleb called for Lauren, and together they crossed the street and entered the building. With a number of other occupants in the elevator, it was a quiet ride up to the 35th floor.

As soon as they walked into the Belac reception area, Suma's surprise was almost comical as her gaze bounced between the three of them.

Caty stepped up to the desk. "Mr. Reid, have you met Suma?" Did she have a last name?

"I haven't had the pleasure." Caleb moved forward and offered his hand. "Caleb Reid. This is my daughter, Lauren."

Lauren asked to see Suma's nails and then gushed over them, generating a rare smile from the quiet woman.

"Thank you again," Caty said quietly. "I had a wonderful time." Something about saying that made it seem like the end of a date. At least she wouldn't need to worry about the old *will he try to kiss me?* dilemma. With a parting smile, Caty headed for her office.

"Hold up a second," Caleb called after her. "It was very nice meeting you, Suma."

"Did you see that telephone board thing?" Lauren caught up to them. "With all those lights and beeps going off, it must be hard to keep everything straight."

"I know I couldn't work the switchboard," Caty said. "I'll stick to numbers. They're much less complicated."

"I need you." When both Caty and Lauren looked at him, Caleb flushed. "To stick to numbers. For Reidco." He cleared his throat. "Lauren, go on ahead and tell Cordelia we're back."

Her lips twisted. "Dad, if you want to be alone with Caty, all you have to do is say so."

"That *was* what I said, more or less." He grinned and ran one hand over his jaw. "Fine. I'd like a moment alone with Caty. Please."

"Okay." Lauren giggled and waved. "Bye, Caty. Remember…"

Caty pulled the souvenir chopsticks from her purse and held them up. "Chopsticks are not a toy, and they are my friend. Bye, Lauren. It was fun. Hope to see you again soon." She hoped that statement wasn't too presumptuous.

Caleb stood in the doorway and watched his daughter in the hallway. "I'm going to stand here until I see you go back into my offices."

"Dad, you can trust me."

"Keep walking, Lauren." A few seconds later, seemingly satisfied, Caleb's gaze found hers. "May I come inside your office?"

"Of course." Caty's heart pounded. Now *this* felt like the end of a date. Leading the way, she wondered if he'd close the door. He did, pushing it with one hand. Not all the way but enough so that anyone passing by in the hallway wouldn't be able to see him. Was this wise? At the moment, she couldn't care less.

Be still, my heart.

Appearing deep in thought, Caleb draped his jacket over the back of the loveseat. Then he removed his Stetson and carefully placed it on top of the jacket. "I seem to be breaking a lot of personal rules since you've come into my life."

Her pulse was out of control. "Is that a bad thing?"

"I'm not sure if you know, but there's no rule at Belac, Inc. prohibiting employees from socializing with one another. Spending time with one another."

"Considering that's what we've been doing for the past hour or more, I'd say we've already crossed that threshold."

Stepping closer, Caleb's nearness made it difficult to think, to breathe. "Specifically, *dating* one another. As long as it doesn't interfere with business in terms of negatively impacting on-the-job work performance."

"Understood." Caty swallowed hard. "And do those rules also apply to the boss?"

"*Especially* to the boss." He traced his fingers lightly along her jawline. "The problem is, I'm not quite sure what to do with this very real, very *strong*, attraction I feel for you."

"I'm sure you don't need me to tell you." Caty lifted her chin. "You strike me as a very capable man."

Caleb's eyes lit, the depth of color deepening. "Do you feel the same?"

"I think that's a safe assumption." When he seemed to want her to say more, she nodded. "Yes, I feel the same."

He brushed his thumb over her cheek. "I'm not sure I deserve you. You're so good, so…"

She shook her head. "I have plenty of faults, Caleb. I'm not without sin. I'm outspoken, stubborn as all get out, selfish… What? You're looking at me funny."

"Even when you rattle off a list of your faults, you're irresistible." He looked deeply into her eyes. "Is it too soon, Caty?"

"If you're asking me to run away with you for the weekend, yes, it's too soon. I wouldn't do that, anyway. Just so you'll know. But if you're asking me to go on a *date* with you, I'd say yes. I mean, no, it's not too soon." She breathed out a sigh. "Am I making any sense?"

"Adorably so." His lips curved in a heart-stopping way. "In that case, Miss Lewis, would you do me the honor of coming to dinner at the house one night next week?"

Yes, please.

Caty struggled to find her voice. "I'd like that very much," she finally managed. Every nerve ending in her body was on high alert, her breathing shallow.

"Tuesday night?" His voice turned husky.

"I think that can be arranged." This might be a bad idea, but she didn't care. The annoying voice of reason could take a hike. They were both adults. Caleb had traveled this road before although she never had. Everything else faded into the background, replaced by promise and the hope of something new and completely wonderful.

"I'll send my driver for you at six on Tuesday. His name is Oliver."

"I'm not sure I can be ready by six. My boss can be demanding, and I need to make sure my work is done first." Dinner at the house? That seemed to be jumping a big step. Not that it mattered.

Caleb's chuckle was low in his throat. "I don't think your boss will mind if you leave the office a little early. Oliver will give you a keyword when he arrives so that you'll know it's him." Those gorgeous brown eyes searched hers as if asking permission. Then his gaze dropped to her lips, lingering there, before he dropped a light, tantalizing kiss on the corner of her mouth.

"Should I be worried that you seem to know so much about me, including where I live?"

In response, he brushed his lips over hers again, teasing her. "One of the perks of being the boss."

"And, um"—hard to think with him so close—"what is this keyword of which you speak?"

"Scrappy," he whispered. His lips warmed her skin. She felt his smile on her cheek.

Caty blinked. "That's not very romantic, Mr. Reid."

In response, his arms slid around her waist and Caleb tugged her close. "I don't play games, Caty. I'm completely out-of-touch when it comes to dating. However"—he brushed his mouth over hers again—"I hope that's about to change." He lowered his head and chuckled. "I trust you know what I meant by that."

"I do. I'm a firm believer in change." She appreciated Caleb's openness. He wanted her to understand things about his past. Get to know him. *Trust* him.

"So am I." His lips nuzzled hers. If he didn't kiss her—*really* kiss her—soon, she might just lose her mind. "Part of that whole new attitude change I was talking about."

"Change can definitely be a good thing." Caty moved her hands up his chest to his broad shoulders, appreciating the journey. "Healthy and...productive."

"Stop me now if you need to, but I'm falling. Hard and fast." If Caleb hadn't spoken the words, the softness in his eyes, the caress of his voice, and the tenderness in his touch would have told her.

When Caty's eyes closed, his lips found hers, settling in. Claiming her. His kiss was surprisingly gentle yet firm. Not demanding, in control. Beyond perfect. She felt the tautness in his chest, the restrained strength of his muscles, as he held her in his arms.

As he released her, Caleb's smile seared straight through her. "I hope that was more romantic. More to your liking, Miss Lewis."

"Hmm, yes," she murmured. "Much better."

Chapter 23

"Caleb, I'm sorry to disturb you."

"Then don't. Go away and let me enjoy my moment." He softened his words with a smile to let Cordelia know he was teasing, but her features were solemn. Not even a hint of a smile.

"You need to see this."

His heart dropped. *Can't I have one afternoon free of worry?* He'd come back to the office full of optimism and now...this. Thoughts of Caty Lewis would have to wait. Caleb motioned for her to bring whatever it was to him.

Approaching his desk, his assistant offered him a plain white business envelope with his name typed in all capital letters on the front. Black, bold letters, centered. He'd seen similar envelopes to this one before. Cheap quality. No distinguishing marks except for the company name. The other envelopes had contained nothing good. Nothing he'd ever wanted to see again in his lifetime.

His head pounding, blood rushing to his ears, Caleb reluctantly reached for the envelope. It'd been four months since the last delivery. Why had he been foolish enough to think this nightmare might be over by moving to Houston?

"Stay," he said when Cordelia turned to leave. He probably shouldn't be touching the envelope in case he eventually surrendered it to the authorities as evidence. Evidence of *what*, he didn't want to consider.

He tapped it on the top of his desk. "Did you look at it? Read it?" He'd hoped she *had* read it and could tell him.

"No. You'll note it's still sealed."

"You've intercepted them in the past, so I thought perhaps…" He tossed it on the desk in disgust.

"I shouldn't have done that. It wasn't my place."

"I was out of the country for the last one. In my absence, you had every right, Cordelia. Perhaps I shouldn't open this one now." Caleb frowned and lowered his fist on top of the envelope. "It's nothing more than opening the door and inviting the devil to get a foothold on my deepest insecurities concerning Lauren."

Cordelia took the chair across from him. "I think you should open it. If nothing else, you can show it to the authorities. If you don't open it, won't you be curious what's in it?"

Sitting back in his chair, Caleb rested his head on the back of his chair. "You should know by now a Pandora's box doesn't tempt me. All it does is complicate a situation over which I have zero control."

"That's your biggest fear, isn't it? Losing control?"

She knew him, all right. "You could say that, yes. Beyond that, the authorities won't do anything with idle threats. The sad reality is that they won't take action until something actually occurs. By then, it might be too late." He tapped the desk with his fist. "Does Lauren know?"

"No. She's playing a game on her phone and doesn't suspect a thing."

"Thank you for that." Caleb hoped he could mask his emotions around Lauren as well as Cordelia. "You never knew when you signed on to work for a nineteen-year-old, snot-nosed kid that you'd be dealing with things like this, did you?"

"I've never regretted working for you, Caleb. If I did, I wouldn't be sitting here now. I've seen you grow in so many ways. As a man, as a husband to Helena"—Cordelia dropped her gaze—"and especially as a father to Lauren. If you'll pardon my saying, your wife's death forced you to take more notice of Lauren and spend quality time with her. You didn't have to, but you did, and I know how much you love your daughter. Losing someone doesn't mean our lives stop. It just means we go about our lives in a different way."

She'd lost her husband to cancer when her boys were teenagers, and together with Lettie, this dear woman had also ministered to him in his hour of deepest need after Helena's death. Counseled him on the days when he sat and absently stared at the wall in his office as though in a catatonic state. Pushed him to meetings and made him care about living again.

Hanging his head, Caleb clasped his hands together on top of the desk. "You showed me how to pick myself up and keep moving forward. I asked Caty what she was afraid of. Perhaps I should be asking myself that question. For one thing, it's time for me to stop running. Or at least to slow down. In order to do that, I need to figure out if there's anything more I can do about the threats." His gaze fell on the envelope while his thoughts waged a fierce inner battle.

"You're an important man in a position of power," Cordelia said. "The authorities should know you'd be a likely target of such schemes. Perhaps if you go to them, they could provide some kind of security for you and Lauren."

"Without knowing who it is we're dealing with? I doubt it. Besides, what would that do? I refuse to give into intimidation." He held all the admiration in the world for law enforcement but not in the way things had been handled when Lauren was almost snatched from under his nose in Dallas at her private academy.

They'd attended an evening school event. She'd gone back to her classroom to get something. The hallway had been quiet, dark. Caleb had discovered a man hunched in a corner outside the classroom—lurking, waiting, watching. Not wanting to alarm Lauren, he'd taken off after him on foot, but the man had escaped into the night.

Caleb had somehow managed to keep calm and Lauren had never even known. But *he'd* known. He'd called the police when he'd returned home that night. The detective made a report and filed it away with the hundreds, maybe thousands, of other reports. The school had been alerted. During the day, the Dallas academy's security had been top-notch—just like at Greenbriar-Browne—but after hours, they'd been much more lax.

He didn't like being told there were no guarantees. There were always guarantees of one kind or another. He couldn't risk his daughter's life for no guarantees. Someone was still waiting for him to make a false move. Which meant he needed to be one step ahead to keep Lauren safe.

"In its own way, maybe you're giving into the intimidation by not turning this matter over to the authorities." Tilting her head, Cordelia gave him *the look*. Like Lettie, she'd perfected it through the years. Two completely different women, but he loved them both.

"I have an alternative." Armed with a plan, Caleb sat straighter in his chair. "I met a man for dinner last week who's ex-military. Owns a private security company now. I'm thinking of calling him. If you ever get a call from Eliot Marchand, put him straight through no matter what I'm doing. Don't record his name anywhere—not on the computer, not in the files. Just remember it."

"Understood." Cordelia angled her head to the envelope. "It's time."

With a grunt of frustration, Caleb used his letter opener and slit the seal. His fingers shook as he pulled out the single white sheet of unlined paper and read the words that could not be traced. Words that chilled him to his bone marrow and shook him to the core of his being.

YOU CAN'T PROTECT HER FOREVER.
SHE WON'T BE YOUR LITTLE GIRL MUCH LONGER.
IN MORE WAYS THAN ONE.

Chapter 24

The paper in Caleb's fingers floated to the desktop while he stared straight ahead, glassy-eyed. *Dear Lord, not again.* The words on that paper replayed in his mind, over and over. If he allowed them, the words would haunt him. He had a few choice words for people who threatened something so heinous and vile.

No more! He could not allow the intimidation to continue without making an effort to stop it.

You pray, Caleb. Prayer was the answer, not violence. He knew that, but for the moment, he wanted to strike back. But how did he fight an unseen foe?

Clearly alarmed, Cordelia jumped out of her chair. Seizing the paper, she quickly scanned it. "This is enough. Caleb, you have to do something. Call your friend or whatever you need to do. Should I make the call or will you?"

He snapped out of his trance. "I'm going to call Eliot. He'll know what to do. Or at least give me some solid advice."

"I'll keep Lauren with me for now. Let me know if you need me to do anything else."

"I will. Thanks, Cordelia." She departed his office and closed the door.

Locating Eliot's card in his wallet, Caleb started to dial from the office phone then thought better of it. He reached for his cell phone instead, and his fingers continued to shake as he dialed. They shook so bad he almost dropped the phone. The call went straight to voice mail, making him frown, even though he shouldn't be surprised. It was Friday, after all. Eliot might have already started his weekend.

Collapsing back in his chair, Caleb stared at the ceiling. The only sound in the room came from the clock.

Tick tock.

"Oh, be quiet," he muttered. He still sat in the chair, stewing, when Eliot returned his call. Only a few minutes later, it seemed more like days.

"Hi, Caleb. Tell me how I can help you."

That statement gave him momentary pause. "How did you know?"

"It's my business to know. This is my work number, so I figured this wasn't a social call."

Caleb told him in brief terms about the previous threats and then read the newest one to him. "If you have time, can we meet somewhere to discuss it?"

"Sure," Eliot said. "How about in an hour? I'm in the office." He relayed the address and told him it wasn't far from downtown. "Will Lauren be with you?"

Lauren. He rubbed his hand over his jaw. She'd be safe if she stayed with him for the meeting, but he didn't want her to go. Where could he take her? Cordelia would be willing, if he needed her.

"I'm guessing it's better not to bring her along?"

"Correct."

Could he persuade Caty to take his daughter shopping *this* afternoon? She'd probably think he was a lunatic, or a schizophrenic, but he could try. Caty was a smart woman. Based on his earlier behavior when he'd rushed into her office, especially, she probably guessed something was going on.

"I'll figure out something," he told Eliot. "Better give me an hour and fifteen."

"You've got it, buddy. Call if you're running late, but I'll be here. I'm not going anywhere."

"Thanks, Eliot. See you soon."

After pocketing his cell phone, Caleb lifted out of the chair and headed for the door. The need to pray washed over him, stopping him. Walking across the room, he fell to his knees and rested his elbows on one of the chairs in front of the fireplace.

Closing his eyes, he bowed his head. "Father, you promise to watch over us and protect us from evil. You know how much I love Lauren, how fiercely I want to always protect her. I need your help."

His voice broke. "I know I don't deserve it, and I'm not asking for me. I'm asking for my daughter. I'm sorry I've been away so long. I don't feel worthy to ask anything from you. I hate this unrest in my heart, this war in my soul, but I don't know how to fight back against this unseen evil, and this person or persons who threaten to harm her. I don't know what to do, Lord. I'm a sinner saved by your grace, and I'm trying my best to trust in your promises. You know how hard it is for me when I can't control things, and it's absolutely *killing* me"—his voice caught again, and he scrubbed a hand over his face—"that there's absolutely nothing I can do. I don't *do* helpless."

Tears rolled down his cheeks. It'd been a five-year drought since he'd cried. Not since the day of Helena's funeral. Then the well had gone barren. Bone dry.

Surrender Helena. That thought stopped him cold. Had he truly surrendered Helena to the Lord? In his heart he thought he had, but maybe he'd only mouthed the words, and they hadn't penetrated his heart, his soul.

Although he'd never outright rejected Helena, he'd buried himself in work. He'd sacrificed as much of his time as he could for his wife, but it was never enough. When they'd married and then the business expanded rapidly, Caleb thought she understood the demands on his time and energy. She'd been active in several local charity groups in Dallas, but they didn't fill much of her time. Nothing else he suggested seemed to work, and she'd grown increasingly weepy, needy, and clingy.

One of his grandmothers had long-suffered from depression, and he began to recognize the same behavior in his wife. When he'd dared to suggest she seek professional counseling, Helena's response was to run off to Paris—whether by herself or with someone else he'd never known—and not returned until a week later.

He'd remained faithful to Helena. Even in his lowest moments, he'd never succumbed to temptation. Although he'd had a number of opportunities with other women, that wasn't the kind of man he was. In all areas of his life, he'd stayed faithful to a God he welcomed as a presence in his life. Even though he'd temporarily lost sight of Him, he'd always known marital infidelity wasn't the answer to his discontent. It would only be a temporary physical release that masked deeper problems and led to more complications.

When Lauren was four, the relationship between them deteriorated to its lowest level. Helena had been pampered her entire life, but she'd been the best mother she knew how to be, and Caleb couldn't fault her parenting skills and love for their only child. But when Helena came home unusually late the second time in a week— the masculine scent of a man's cologne lingering in the fabric of a dress Caleb had picked out for her—he vowed to resurrect his marriage. He'd left the office early, wined and dined his wife, paid her compliments, lavished her with attention and expensive gifts. Jetted off with her for long weekends and spent time with her like he hadn't in years.

At one point, he'd hoped another child might be the answer, but that had been *his* dream, not Helena's. His efforts to revive a dying marriage, no matter how impassioned, seemed to come too late. The sad fact was that he hadn't lived up to her expectations. Even more than being a mother, Helena wanted Caleb to be her entire world. No one person could be that for another or they'd surely fail. His young wife had a void inside her that only the *Lord* could fill.

Then she'd found the lump in her breast. Actually, *he'd* found the lump in a moment of intimacy. The discovery had only fueled Helena's angst and spurred on his overwhelming guilt. The relationship slowly declined from there.

Two years later, she was gone. And he'd failed her.

His deepest regret, the one he kept hidden in the darkest part of him, was that he should have loved Helena more. Loved her *better*. Not that anything he could have done would have saved her from the ugly ravages of the horrible, hideous beast that was cancer. The banks of the river between them had grown farther apart each year, and the bridge he'd tried to build was a few feet short of reaching the other side.

He'd loved his wife when he married her, and he'd loved Helena when she died.

That was what he needed to remember.

He'd closeted himself away from the world. By doing so, he'd only made things worse by focusing and dwelling on the grief. That hadn't been good for him or Lauren.

Mopping the moisture from both cheeks with the heels of his hands, Caleb continued his prayer. "I surrender Helena to you, too, Lord. She was sick and couldn't be healed. I understand that. Taking her home was your way of healing her. I'm asking you to show me the way. If Eliot can help me, please give him wisdom to help me face down these threats with courage and strength. Above all, Father, please keep my little girl safe."

His voice cracked again. More tears fell, and he let them go. Moving his hand over his mouth, Caleb stifled his quiet sobs. "If anything happens to me, please watch over Lauren. I want her to grow up and have a wonderful life, family, friends, and *love*. I pledge to you that I'll train her in the way she should go, and in your ways. I've neglected that responsibility, and I know how that grieves you. I surrender her to you because I know you love her even more than I do. But I'll do my best as long as you've entrusted her care to me."

Swallowing hard, he pushed on. "Show me *how* to trust in you, Lord. Show me how to give you *all* of me, and not just the parts I'm willing to give. I ask these things in the name of your Son, Jesus. Amen."

He needed to get moving, but Caleb inhaled several deep, cleansing breaths and released them slowly. His time of prayer helped to calm his nerves, and a quiet peace flooded his soul. Blessed grace and sweet comfort from the heavenly Father who could take all his human faults, fears, insecurities, and weaknesses upon Himself and give Caleb the confidence *he* needed to face whatever might come, armed with truth, and the sword and shield of righteousness.

Hauling himself to his feet, Caleb exited his office through the main corridor. He slipped out and began walking down the quiet hallway, grateful no one was around. He hoped he could make it around the lobby and over to Caty's office without being stopped.

"Hey there, Mr. Reid!"

Gritting his teeth, Caleb glanced over his shoulder but kept walking. "Nice to see you, Miles."

"Sir, do you have a quick minute? Caty—Miss Lewis—suggested that I bring a couple of my ideas to you."

"I'm sorry, but I don't have time right now. Make an appointment with Cordelia. We'll meet one day next week."

"No fooling? I mean, seriously?"

"Seriously." Caleb kept walking. "I'll see you then."

"Yes, sir. Thank you. You have yourself a great weekend, Mr. Reid."

"You, too, Miles." Waving one hand in the air, Caleb hastened his steps.

As usual, Caty's office door stood open, but he paused in the doorway when he realized she wasn't alone. The receptionist he'd met earlier. Suri? Suki? *Suma.*

"Hi, Suma. Caty, when you have a moment, I'd like a word with you, please."

As expected, Suma had risen to her feet when he'd made his appearance. "My break's almost over, and I need to get back to the switchboard. Nice to see you again, Mr. Reid." Suma nodded with a small smile and departed.

Stepping farther into the office, Caleb stopped a few feet from Caty's desk and lowered his voice. "Caty, I realize this might sound a little bit nuts, but are you free to take Lauren shopping this afternoon?" She probably thought he was pushy and obnoxious. He couldn't blame her.

Cheeks flushing, Caty fiddled with the ink pen in her hand. "As in right this minute?"

"Sorry. I should have asked if you have plans after work."

"I don't have plans."

"I—" He was bungling this. "Something's come up, and I need someone to watch Lauren while I go to an important meeting. It might take a couple of hours." He raked one hand through his hair and then crossed his arms. "I have a credit card in her name that I'll give you to buy her some new clothes, shoes, that kind of thing. Whatever she tells you she needs. One of the malls might be good." Malls were well-lit, lots of people around, security patrols. Yes, that would be best.

Caty stared at him with clear compassion in her expression. "I'll be more than happy to spend time with Lauren. Shopping for someone else is more fun than shopping for myself." He appreciated how she didn't question his motives.

"I'll call you when my meeting is over. We'll go from there."

"Sure," she said, hesitating a moment. "Caleb, you look like you're tied up in knots. Are you okay?" Her concern touched him. He needed to leave before he became unplugged and the rest of the story tumbled out of him. With Caty looking at him with those trusting eyes, he *wanted* to tell her everything.

What are you doing? Fear struck him all over again. How could he possibly put Caty in danger? In wanting to protect Lauren, was he being foolish? Putting both of them in danger?

"Okay, this is going to sound even crazier, but would one of your brothers be available to go with you? Meet you there?"

Her jaw went slack. "On a shopping trip to the mall?" Rising from her chair, she walked across her office and closed the door. "Sit down, and tell me what's going on."

"I don't have time now."

"Yes, you do. Take three minutes. I want to help you, but I can't do that if you won't tell me what's going on."

He didn't even hesitate and dropped onto the loveseat. She sat down beside him and pulled him into her arms, holding him close. She rested her cheek against his and whispered, "Abide, Caleb." Pulling back, she took his hands, covering them with hers. "'Abide in Me, and I in you. As the branch cannot bear fruit of itself unless it abides in the vine, so neither can you unless you abide in Me.'"

Caleb nodded. "From the Book of John."

"Yes," she said quietly. "It's one of my favorite verses of Scripture. In times of stress, I repeat that verse, as many times as needed. It never fails to help keep me calm. I've always found that giving Christ complete authority over my life brings an *unbelievable* freedom. The kind of freedom that nothing, or no one else, can."

What a godly woman, as lovely inside as she was beautiful on the outside. How was it that Caty seemed to understand his deepest struggle? "A few minutes ago, sitting in my office, I prayed that I can be strong enough to surrender to His authority. *Fully* surrender." He swallowed hard and met Caty's gaze. "That includes Helena. The past five years, I've lived in fear of my own making. It stops here. Now. I need to move forward with my life, Caty, and I hope that includes you. I *need* you in my life. You can't even know how important you've become to me."

Her eyes misted. "Strong men recognize they can't do life on their own, Caleb. Thank you for entrusting Lauren to me. I know what a huge step that is. I don't plan on going anywhere, and I'll watch over her for however long you need."

"Thank you."

You need to tell her everything. Then Caty could make the conscious decision to walk out of his life or stay with the knowledge of what he was facing.

"I've called Eliot to help me. Sorry to blurt it out like this, but I've received six kidnapping threats over the past few years, and I had another one waiting for me when we returned from lunch today." Caleb hoped she wouldn't ask what the note said. He might be strong, but if he had to repeat those words, he might break down.

"Oh, Caleb." Caty's concern was obvious as she rested her hand on his arm. "Have you also called the authorities?"

"No, and I'm not sure I will. I went that route in Dallas when someone came too close to Lauren at an after-hours school event. Without anything further to go on, they can't do anything, even if they want to help."

"You could still try."

"I need to go," he said, rising to his feet. "Forgive me. I shouldn't have kissed you without first telling you what's going on in my life. I shouldn't ask you to do anything now. I wouldn't be able to live with myself if anything happened to either you or Lauren. You should stay clear of me. I don't want to drag you into something potentially harmful."

Jumping off the loveseat, Caty moved ahead of him and barred the way to the door. "Maybe that's not your decision." Crossing her arms, she stared at him through defiant blue eyes.

"Please move. I need to leave."

"I can see you're also one of the most stubborn, infuriating men I've ever met in my life."

"I'm not going to argue. Step aside."

"I will not."

"I've never manhandled a woman. Don't make me start now."

Taking hold of his shirt by the collar, Caty pulled him close, her eyes searching his. "Caleb, you trusted me enough to share what's happening, so now you need to trust me to help you. Don't you think I could tell that something is weighing heavily on you where Lauren is concerned? I'll call Carson. He's here in Houston through the weekend."

"You realize by doing that, I'll be dragging someone else into this mess?" Shaking his head, Caleb groaned with frustration.

"For once, could you please stop relying on yourself and depend on God and your friends?" Caty released her hold on his shirt. Stepping back, she smoothed her hand over the collar of his shirt.

"I feel helpless," he admitted. "That's not something I handle well. I never have, and I doubt I ever will."

"Not many do, especially men, if you don't mind my saying. You can't give into the fear, Caleb. That's what they want. Be stronger than they are. Put your trust in the Lord, but also go see Eliot. Like you said about the accounting discrepancies, we'll figure this out. But this situation is so much more important because this time, it's *personal*. If anyone can help you, Eliot can. From what Sam says, he's like a well-trained bloodhound. Even better, he'll pray with you every step of the way."

Caleb swallowed hard. "I don't know what to say except...thank you for being willing to help with Lauren. That means more than you'll ever know."

Her smile was compassionate. "I *do* know."

Taking out his wallet, Caleb handed over a credit card. "If you can, convince Lauren to branch out in her color choices. No black. No gray. Some color might be nice for a change." Even though a maniac threatened his daughter, he had to maintain some sense of normalcy. He was accustomed to going through the motions.

Caty took the card. "I'll do my best. Promise me you won't drive too fast."

"Define fast." When she shot him a frown, he nodded. "Promise."

After planting a kiss on his cheek, Caty stepped aside. "Call me when you're finished with your meeting. We'll figure out where to meet."

"I will."

"Abide."

He nodded. "Abide. Thanks again, Caty." With that, he opened the door and departed.

As he'd expected, Lauren was ecstatic at the prospect of spending time with Caty. He'd grabbed his jacket after telling Cordelia the plan. Only a few minutes behind schedule, Caleb exited the parking garage. If the traffic cooperated, he should still be able to make it to Eliot's in decent time.

On and off during the past five years, he'd wondered if he'd find another woman to love. More like a woman who could love him. Did he have much to offer anymore? He'd noticed some gray hairs mixed in his beard lately, and that gave him more of an impetus to shave every day. Not that he minded getting old and gray.

He just didn't want to grow old and gray alone.

"Abide," he said in the quiet of the car.

Chapter 25

Caleb stared at Eliot. "You're telling me to get a dog?" That was definitely something he'd never considered.

"I'm *advising* you to get a guard dog. For your situation, it makes better sense than putting 24-hour security on Lauren. From what you've told me, you live in a fortress, and Lauren's driver is a black belt. The cars are nearly as secure as a presidential motorcade, and Greenbriar-Browne is tantamount to a castle with top-of-the-line security."

"The only thing missing is the moat and drawbridge." He'd leave Lauren enrolled in the school since he had no other valid options. Hopefully, she wouldn't do anything to violate the terms of her probationary period. Given the latest threatening note, short of confining her to the house, Greenbriar-Browne was the best place for her. Lauren was making friends there, and she seemed to like her classes. He needed to get over his personal misgivings about the headmistress since Mrs. Winthorpe seemed to have Lauren's welfare uppermost in her mind. He needed to suck up his pride and not question or second-guess his decision in that regard.

Caleb shifted in his chair. "This isn't about money. I can pay whatever you're asking in order to protect Lauren. You read what was in this most recent note." He'd also made Eliot aware of the contents of the previous notes since he could recite them word-for-word from memory.

Calm down, man. At the moment, he sure didn't sound like a man who trusted in the Lord's protection.

Eliot checked his calendar. "I know it's not about money, Caleb. I'm flying out of the country on an assignment early next week, and my available men are already contracted for other assignments. Even if I *had* a man available, I'd give you the same advice about getting a guard dog. For another thing, it wouldn't be advisable to put male security detail on a girl Lauren's age. It's not an ideal situation."

"That makes sense. Do you have any female agents?"

"Not for an assignment like this. I don't give my female agents the dangerous assignments."

Caleb lifted a brow. "You consider my case dangerous?"

"Insofar as there are existing threats, yes. As far as assigning women to a case, it has nothing to do with capability. I've served alongside plenty of females in the military." Eliot's gaze met his. "Attending a funeral for a woman killed in the line of duty was one of the toughest things I've ever done, especially since she had kids."

Caleb shook his head. "I can't even imagine."

"If you'd still prefer to hire a security firm, I can give you some recommendations. You're welcome to call them if you'd like."

He didn't hesitate. "That's not necessary. I trust you. You're the man I need to help me." Call it the nudging of the Holy Spirit or discernment, but in the lives of Caty and Eliot, it was as though Caleb could practically *see* the hand of the Lord upon them and working in their lives. A few short years ago, even as a Christian, he would have mocked the idea. But faith was real, and these people *lived* their faith.

"I've dealt with a number of kidnapping cases in the past." Eliot's brow creased. "You can't allow threats to paralyze you with fear. For now, we're dealing with words on paper. I understand how emotionally upsetting they are, but we can't know the intent behind them. Unfortunately, there are kids and teenagers out there who get their kicks through intimidation. I'm not saying that's what's happening in this case, but it's still a possibility. We can't rule anything out."

"*Kids?*" Caleb couldn't hide his outrage. "You're telling me some underage minor could be responsible for instilling this kind of unimaginable fear in people? For making a father doubt his ability to protect his own daughter? What kind of kid *does* something like that?"

Disgusted, Caleb slumped back in his chair.

"Unfortunately, it happens all the time. A kid who hasn't had a good homelife. A kid with one or more parent absent from the home. A kid who craves the power he can exert over someone's life anonymously."

Eliot met his gaze. "A kid who hates authority and embraces the idea that he can singlehandedly bring a rich man to his knees in fear."

"That's sick." Running his fingers through his hair, Caleb leaned forward in his chair and rested his elbows on his thighs.

"Threats from a benign source like a bored kid are preferable to the alternative, my friend. There are savage monsters out there without a conscience that thrive on making innocent people suffer. I'm sure I don't need to elaborate."

"I get the picture," Caleb muttered. What a twisted world. "Give me your gut instinct here. Where do *you* think the kidnapping threats are coming from?"

"It's impossible to say at the moment. I have a few more questions." Eliot pulled out a piece of paper and jotted something down. "Any known enemies in business or otherwise?"

"None that I'm aware of, no."

"Any hostile takeover attempts or anything along those lines?"

"No."

"Anything unusual happen in the company since the threats began?"

"Unusual? Like what?"

Eliot sat back in his chair. "An employee acting out of character. Petty theft. Sudden, unexplained outbursts of anger, provoked or not. Squabbles between employees. Tensions running high. Faulty work performance from a normally reliable source. Anything along those lines?"

Caleb shook his head but then a thought came to mind. "Would suspected accounting discrepancies count?" Surely that had no bearing on the matter at hand, but this was why he needed Eliot—in case it did.

The other man nodded. "That could definitely qualify. Tell me more."

"We've had a handful of accounting discrepancies which were allocated to theft and damage in the Reidco gas stations. The most substantial amount was an oil payment supposedly paid to a supplier we no longer use."

Eliot's expression indicated he might have hit pay dirt with that revelation. "How much?"

"Eight thousand, more or less."

"Who brought these discrepancies to your attention?"

"Steve Robison, my Vice President for Belac, noticed them a couple of months ago. Are you suggesting the two might be connected? If that's the case, I can't believe one of my trusted employees could be capable of writing those notes and making threats."

Eliot rubbed his hand over his brow and paused a moment to gather his thoughts. "I'm not suggesting that, but again, you have to consider everything. I'm sure you've been in business long enough to know that, as much as we think we might know a person, that's not always the case."

"You're right, unfortunate and sobering as it is." He'd personally hired Steve. Plenty of other current employees—including Catherine Lewis—had been interviewed and hired by others. Any one of them could potentially be responsible for trying to steal from him.

"Is anyone else other than you and Steve aware of these accounting discrepancies?"

Caleb was reluctant to mention Caty. He assuaged his conscience somewhat with the fact that Eliot knew her, and full disclosure was necessary. "Caty Lewis. Off the record, when I first met her, she'd requested a meeting with me in private to point them out and make me aware of the discrepancies. She's my chief accountant for the Reidco division."

"Caty's worked in the Lubbock office the past two years, correct?"

"Correct. Before that, she worked in the Dallas office for three years."

"But you'd never met her until recently? Here in Houston?"

"That's right." He should explain further. "After my wife died, I more or less retreated from life, Eliot. I worked behind closed doors, kept to myself, pretty much pushed a lot of people out of my life. Caty came to Belac around the time of my self-imposed seclusion."

"Before that time, were you more accessible to your employees?"

"I was a constant presence." Caleb's chuckle held no mirth. "More than some liked, I'm sure." In the years leading up to Helena's death, he'd talked with employees in the hallways or breakrooms. Attended weddings, baptisms, funerals. Known most of the employees in the various offices by their first names. Known the names of their children and even some grandchildren.

Guilt snaked its way through Caleb's conscience. He missed those connections. During the past five years, his relationships with his employees had become a casualty of his personal and professional withdrawal. Cordelia, Steve, and a few others stuck by him during those dark days while others opted to leave. In spite of it all, the corporation had continued to thrive. God had seemingly chosen to bless his efforts even while he'd been at his personal worst.

Eliot continued to record notes. "So—as far as you're concerned—Steve Robison and Caty Lewis are the only two employees of Belac, including all its divisions, with any knowledge of these accounting discrepancies?"

"Correct, although I prefer to call them intentional errors that someone's tried to cover, hoping they wouldn't be discovered and exposed."

Eliot snapped his gaze to Caleb's. "Embezzlement?"

"Correct." The word *embezzlement* made him sick.

"Have you ever personally suspected Caty of having anything to do with the discrepancies?"

Eliot's question startled him back to reality. "No, but Steve considered it a possibility." A rather *strong* possibility. Caleb shook his head. "Anyone who's met Caty Lewis can tell after five minutes the woman doesn't have a dishonest bone in her body."

"Agreed, but you're not exactly unbiased," Eliot said. "Neither am I, for that matter."

The sudden need to defend Caty rose within Caleb. "She has an excellent work record with Belac. I didn't get where I am by misjudging character and making decisions based on feelings or emotions." Caleb didn't care how high and mighty that sounded. It was truth.

"If Caty weren't so attractive, would you be so quick to defend her?"

"Give me a break, Eliot." Anger stirred in his gut. Rising from the chair, Caleb began to pace in front of Eliot's desk. "That hardly seems a fair question, and this discussion has nothing to do with Caty's attractiveness. Whose side are you on?"

"Don't make this personal," Eliot said.

"Excuse me, but I think that's what *you* just did." Caleb stared at him, unflinching.

"I need to examine all possible angles." At least Eliot kept his cool, more than Caleb could say for his own defensive attitude.

"I'm not trying to agitate you," Eliot continued. "Trust me, I know the Lewis family. Caty's one of my wife's best friends. This is a formality I go through with all my clients."

Eliot was right. He was only doing what he'd been trained to do. Caleb stopped pacing and approached Eliot's desk. Planting both hands on the edge, he looked the other man straight in the eye. "I can state unequivocally that Catherine Grace Lewis has nothing whatsoever to do with the accounting discrepancies. I admire her for coming to me directly with what she'd discovered. She didn't have to do that, and she put her job on the line by doing so. She was well aware of that and yet she came to me, anyway."

"Good enough. Did you discuss a course of action with Caty if the discrepancies continue?"

"We agreed to keep a close eye on them. She's going to alert me at the first sign of anything out of order. It's been quiet lately."

"Have you considered that Steve Robison could be responsible for the discrepancies?"

Caleb dropped into the chair. "Steve's been with me almost from the start of Belac. I can assure you he has nothing to do with it, but neither could I discount his initial suspicions without further consideration and investigation."

Eliot's brows arched. "In terms of Caty Lewis, you mean."

Caleb blew out a sigh. "Yes. I've told him Caty has nothing to do with them."

"And does he concur with your opinion now?"

That one was tough to answer. "I don't know. We haven't talked about it lately. The bottom line is that Steve follows my direction. I told him to focus on the other divisions, and I'll personally take control of overseeing Reidco."

Eliot stared him down. "He still suspects Caty knows something."

"I believe he does, yes. But I don't believe that's the case."

Eliot nodded. "We're clear on that point. Are there any other employees with access to the Reidco financial records?"

"I'm sure there are a few. Unfortunately, those files can pass through a number of hands. We've never had a security breach before, so it's never been questioned. I could have my assistant, Cordelia Bonner, put a list together for you."

"Yes, have her do that," Eliot said. "Have her call me on her cell phone or a non-corporate phone when it's ready, and I'll send someone to pick it up from your office. Don't email them in case someone's wired into your computer, and don't fax it either."

Eliot made a few more notes. "We're almost done. Since Caty came to you about this matter, did she share her thoughts regarding any employees *she* believes might be behind the discrepancies?"

"I know she has her suspicions, but she refused to share them with me. I agree with her that unsubstantiated accusations might do the corporation more harm than good."

"That might be true," Eliot said. "On the other hand, I hope that decision doesn't come back to bite you. Keep your eyes and ears open. That's my best suggestion. Other than getting the guard dog for Lauren's extra protection."

"I'm willing to try anything. Even a dog," Caleb muttered. Was he nuts? Who'd take care of a dog? They required a lot of work—feeding, visits to the veterinarian, walking, picking up their messes. On the other hand, if Lauren had a companion at the house—canine or not—that might be a viable solution. Kids loved animals. The idea grew more appealing by the minute.

"Have you ever had a dog before?"

"I had dogs growing up, and I love them. I just haven't had one in a long time since Helena was allergic. Lauren went through a stage when she was about eight where she begged for a puppy almost every day. For a few weeks, I considered it, but at the time, I considered her too young for the responsibility that goes with having a pet. All things considered, and armed with your specific recommendation, now might be the right time." No doubt in his mind, Lauren would wholeheartedly embrace the idea of getting a dog.

"Okay then. I'm in touch with some top local breeders." Eliot pulled a file from a drawer and put it on the desk, studying it for a few seconds. "There are some older dogs available that are already trained. That might be more suitable for you." He handed the list across the desk.

Caleb glanced at the paper. "What exactly do you mean by older?"

"Three to six years. Still excellent guard dogs, but I'd say the younger the better, ideally around three or four. If you want, give a few of the breeders a call, ask them your questions, and see what you think. Let me know what you decide."

"Is there a particular breed you'd recommend?"

"The Bullmastiff is physically strong and has protective instincts. They're fearless and extremely loyal. If someone tries to get near

Lauren, a Bullmastiff will knock them over and pin them down in a heartbeat. Otherwise, they're docile and make a great family pet. There's also Doberman Pinschers, Rottweilers, German Shepherds. All smart, protective, highly trainable. Shepherds are used by the police and would be a good choice. The Giant Schnauzer is powerful and dominant but requires strict training."

"Sounds like I have some homework to do."

"I'd caution you about the Rhodesian Ridgeback," Eliot said. "They're lion hunters. They don't bark often, but when they do, they'll wake the neighbors. They're not naturally obedient and seem to think they're a lapdog."

Caleb chuckled. "How big do they get?"

"Anywhere from sixty-five to ninety pounds, depending on gender."

"Thanks for the tips. Is there anything else you need from me?"

Eliot scanned his notes quickly. "We've gone over everything. Sounds like you're prepared and alert. I want you to call me immediately if you receive any more notes or phone messages. Look, Caleb, I know you want answers. You can rest assured you're doing everything you can."

"What do I owe you for your time?" Caleb reached for his wallet.

"Save your money for now. We're friends."

"Well, be sure and send me an invoice for the consult fee."

"You can take us to dinner instead."

Caleb smiled. "Even better." He rose to his feet. "How long will you be gone on your trip abroad?"

"A week, maybe less, depending on how it goes."

"When you return, then we'll all definitely go to dinner together."

Eliot grinned. "We'd like that. Does 'all' include Caty?"

"Sounds about right. Caty's with Lauren right now, as a matter of fact. Lauren likes her, and my daughter doesn't freely welcome most people into her life. I'm afraid I'm to blame for creating an atmosphere of distrust with my…fences and high walls." Eliot would understand he meant it figuratively as well as in the literal sense.

"I want Lauren to be diligent and aware of the dangers in the world," Caleb said. "At the same time, I'm afraid I'm doing her a great disservice by sheltering her to the point where she feels like she's a prisoner."

Eliot's expression was compassionate. "You're a protective father, Caleb. She might not always act like it, but I'm sure Lauren knows how much you love her. Have you told Caty about the threats? From what you've said, it's pretty clear the two of you have gotten to know one another better."

"You could say that. I finally told Caty about the threats before coming here. I couldn't lie to her, Eliot. She's a smart woman and could tell something was wrong. To be honest, it's nice to share the burden even though I hate like anything to drag her into this mess." Caleb blew out a long sigh. "And she asked her brother Carson to go along and watch over both of them."

From Eliot's creased brow, Caleb could tell he was weighing his response. "I think the important thing is that you trust her," he said finally. "I know Caty well enough to say with full certainty she wouldn't do anything she didn't feel was right. As you said, you have good instincts. I can tell you from personal experience that you don't get any better than the Lewis family. They're one of the best families I've ever had the privilege of knowing."

"I haven't met any of her family members, but from what I've heard about them, I agree. Do you share any of your cases with Marta?"

"No. Even if it's one of her best friends. The fewer people who know, the better."

Caleb nodded. "Agreed. Caty's aware, too. It's in her nature to share things with people. Listen, thanks for your time. I'd be honored if you'd pray for me, especially for patience. That's not my long suit."

"You've got it, buddy. Patience is tough for a lot of people, and this type of situation can pull at a person from all directions." Eliot opened his office door. "You and Lauren are welcome to join us for church on Sunday."

"Thanks. I can't commit right now, but could you email me the church info?"

"Hang on. I've got a card here on my desk." Within seconds, Caleb had the church's card in his pocket.

When Caleb offered his hand, Eliot did something unexpected. He curled his fist and held it, waiting. Following suit, Caleb fisted his hand and Eliot bumped it with his, saying, "Everything according to His purpose."

"Everything according to His purpose," Caleb repeated.

"Call if you need me or if anything else comes up."

"Will do." Climbing back into his car, Caleb's heart was lighter. The knots in his stomach had eased somewhat. In terms of the threats, the Lord knew he hated playing the wait-and-see game. Then again, what was the sense in being tied up in knots about something that may or may not materialize?

Trust, Caleb. Just…breathe. He knew the Lord was in control. He did. *Abide.*

"I'm trying, Lord. Bear with me." Caleb chuckled under his breath. "Looks like I'll be adding a dog to the family. Lauren's gonna love this."

Chapter 26

"What do you think of this one?" Lauren paraded past Caty, dressed in a brightly patterned, multicolored tunic and black leggings, imitating a high fashion model on a catwalk. Third outfit in the last fifteen minutes. Caty had lost count of all the different combinations, but it'd been a fun process. Thankfully, Lauren hadn't protested her less-than-subtle suggestion to add colorful pieces into the mix.

Lauren twirled and then parked one hand on her hip. She puffed out her lips in a mock pout. "Tell me dahling, is it me?"

"It's fabulous. Very nice." If it weren't an upscale department store, Caty would stick her fingers in her mouth and whistle. Growing up with a sports-minded family, she could whistle with the best of them. Instead, she opted to clap.

They'd shared a lively conversation on the way to the mall. Other than trying to prop her bare feet on the dashboard, Lauren had been polite. Whatever was going on in their lives seemed to weigh heavily on Caleb. His daughter, however, seemed either unaware or unconcerned. More likely, she didn't know about the threats. Maybe she should have asked Caleb, but for now, Caty would remain silent and hope Lauren didn't mention them even if she *did* know. As much as anything, Lauren needed normalcy in her life. Talking about the threats wouldn't benefit either one of them.

Lauren's smile evaporated. "Caty, I need your help deciding which clothes to get." With Caleb's credit card, this girl could probably buy one of everything in the department. She seemed surprisingly considerate about spending her father's money.

"Start by telling me where you'll wear your new clothes."

A frown clouded Lauren's pretty face. "I don't get to go anywhere, so I'm not sure. I wear a uniform to Greenbriar-Browne."

Don't get to go anywhere? That statement tugged on Caty's heart.

"I think this outfit is my favorite of the ones you've tried on, but I really liked the green top with the capris," Caty said. "And the yellow top with the matching skirt. Plus, you can mix and match some of the tops and bottoms. If you want, we can ask the clerk to remove the tags, and you can wear this outfit tonight. How about that? It might be a nice surprise for your dad."

Granted, the leggings were black, but Caleb would have to live with it. He'd learn soon enough that basic black was good for a woman of any age.

"That sounds okay. Hey, can we buy something for you, too?" Lauren's eyes lit. "Do you ever wear jeans? You don't wear suits all the time, do you?"

"I'm all set, thanks. I wear suits for work, but when I'm at home, I'm usually in jeans, shorts and T-shirts, or workout clothes."

"Dad works out all the time. Like a fiend, Lettie says." A grin spread over her features. "He thinks you're gorgeous."

Don't ask. No matter how curious, Caty had already learned her lesson with Lauren. On the other hand, Lauren's comment to her dad earlier in the day had brought an unexpectedly wonderful response. A response she still couldn't quite believe had happened. Caty touched her fingers to her lips for a brief moment before lowering them. Goodness, the man could kiss.

"Don't you want to know *how* I know that?"

"Come with me, please." With a gentle hand on Lauren's arm, Caty positioned her in front of the three-way mirror. "I want to show you something. Do you mind if I try something with your hair?" The preteen's long hair was lovely but too long and heavy.

Lauren shrugged. "What are you doing?"

"You'll see." Working quickly, Caty draped the girl's long strands of dark hair over her hands. Twisting her wrists, she gave it the illusion of a shoulder-length cut, almost like a bob. "Imagine a few layers along the side of your face and maybe some light wispy bangs." Caty smiled at Lauren's reflection in the mirror. "What do you think?"

"I think I like it." Lauren moved her head from right to left and then turned to the side. "I haven't had my hair cut in a long time. I guess I don't think about it. New clothes, new look, right?"

Caleb's words about adopting a new attitude rang in Caty's ears. First the father, now the daughter.

"Change is good every now and then," Caty said. "Do you ever wear your hair in a ponytail or pull it back?"

"Sometimes. Usually, I wear it down. I don't know how to fix it or what to do with it."

"If you don't want to cut much off the length, you could have it trimmed to even out the ends," Caty said. When she released Lauren's hair, it fell almost to her waist. "I'm sure a stylist could find a style that works with your natural wave so it'll be easy for you to do at home."

Lauren gave her a thumbs-up. "Can we do that now? If we don't, I might chicken out."

"You? Never. Let's pay for the clothes, and then I think it's a good idea to call your dad and get his opinion on the haircut." She didn't wish to step over Caleb's parental boundaries.

"Let me get my cell phone," Lauren said.

"I have your dad's phone number."

"You do?" Lauren seemed surprised but not upset.

Caty retrieved her phone from her purse. "He called me once, so I have it."

"I thought he had some kind of block on it. Dad must think you're really special."

Seemed Miss Lauren had romance between her and Caleb on the brain. Would she feel the same about *any* woman? If Lauren knew about the kiss, she'd probably have them married by next weekend.

Caty quickly scanned the list of contacts in her cell phone and dialed the number.

He picked up on the first ring. "Caleb Reid."

"Hi, Caleb. It's Caty. I'm sorry to interrupt if you're still in your meeting."

"Not a problem. I'm leaving downtown now. Is everything okay with Lauren?" At least he sounded calmer and not at all agitated.

"We're having a great time, but Lauren has an important question to ask you."

When Lauren gestured for the phone, Caty handed it over.

"Hey, Dad. I picked out some cute new things. Can I get my hair cut? Please? Okay. Hold on." She nodded and then returned the phone to Caty. "He wants to talk to you about it."

"Nothing too short is all I ask," Caleb told her. "When Lauren tries something new, she has a tendency to go for extremes. I still want her to look my daughter if you know what I mean."

Caty couldn't resist teasing him. "I'm guessing that means no bright streaks of color in her hair? Purple or pink? They have temporary color that washes out quickly."

He laughed. "I'd prefer not. I hope you didn't just give her the idea."

"I don't think you need to worry." Lauren stood by the register and talked with the salesclerk while Caty gave him the name of the mall and basic directions.

"I should be there in about forty to fifty minutes, depending on traffic. I suppose it's like Dallas on a Friday afternoon. You never really know. Was Carson able to make it?"

"Yes," she said, lowering her voice. "Call when you get to the mall since I'm not sure where we'll be at the time."

"I'll see you soon, Caty. Thanks again." The affection in Caleb's voice made her smile.

Lord, if this isn't right, please help me not to fall headfirst into something with this man.

Caty had the feeling it might be too late to stop that fall.

After Caty approached the counter, Lauren tugged on her arm. "I really need some new underwear, too."

"All right, but your dad's on his way to meet us now. If you make it quick, we might still have time to get your hair cut."

"Can we go to that fancy underwear store where they sell thongs and stuff?"

Caty turned to the waiting salesclerk. "Can you please help us find some age appropriate underwear?"

The woman smiled. "I'm sure we can find some things for her, Mrs. Reid."

Mrs. Reid? Caty did a double take and widened her eyes at Lauren.

Lauren pouted. "I really want to go to the other store." At least she hadn't called her Mom.

Caty pulled out her phone again.

"Who are you calling?"

"Your dad." Caty started to dial the number. No wonder the salesclerk thought she was Lauren's mother.

"Okay, okay. I'm just teasing you. I don't wear those things, anyway."

"Good." With a satisfied smile, Caty pocketed her phone. "Keep moving."

Testing the limits, Caty. She's just testing the limits.

"Pssst! Cates!"

Startled, Caty turned in the chair. Lauren was in the back fitting room of the lingerie department.

Carson peeked out from behind a mannequin. Creeping closer, he hunched down beside her chair. "How am I doing?" This whole spy thing was like a game for him, but her brother was physically strong. Carson wouldn't hesitate to defend them if needed.

"You're like the Pink Panther's protégé. You've only knocked over one display so far."

"Hey, that thing just jumped right out at me," he protested. "No harm done. Do you think Lauren suspects anything?"

"No, but you'd better stay clear." Her eyes misted. "Thanks for being here even though you have no idea why."

"That's what brothers are for, right? I'm glad you called me." Carson grinned. "Makes me feel useful. Sam's writing books and leading TeamWork, and Will's the space hero, but I'm not sure what my niche is yet." He waggled his brows. "Or should I say my superpower?"

"No doubt in my mind you'll have a great ministry one day, little brother. I happen to know you have unique qualities that Sam and Will can't touch."

"Yeah?" Carson's dimples appeared. "Like what? I could use some positive reinforcement. It'd be nice to have a permanent job when I graduate, anyway."

"You relate incredibly well to people. I know how important the jail ministry is to you in Dallas. I know you've given men hope and led souls to Christ. That's a special gift."

"Thanks." He crossed his eyes and gave her a comical grin. "I can't believe I'm in the ladies underwear department. Will's gonna love this story."

"Remember you can't say anything about this." *Boys will be boys.*

"And spoil my fun? Will's such an easy target."

"I know, but—"

"Caty!" Lauren called from the fitting room. "Can you come here for a minute?" At least she wasn't demanding, didn't sound like a diva.

"I'm being summoned. You'd better scoot before Lauren comes out and sees you."

"How long do you want me to follow you?"

"Until Caleb meets us. He's on his way now." Caty checked her watch. "If we have time, we're going to the hair salon first."

He chuckled low in his throat. "Sounds like fun. So, who is this guy? He must be pretty special for you to be so secretive."

She sighed. "I wish I could tell you, Carson. I really do. He's Lauren's dad is all I can say."

"I figured that, but I didn't mean to pry. Sorry." He raised his hand. "Lewis Honor?"

Caty smacked her palm against his like they'd done when they were kids. "Lewis Honor." She hadn't done that in forever and yet it came back to her like they'd done it yesterday. After digging out her wallet, she pulled two crisp, fifty dollar bills and handed them to Carson. "When we're done, take this and go buy yourself something nice."

"Now I'm a kept man." He waved the money in the air. "Nice and crisp. What'd you do, print these bills this morning?"

"It's called visiting the ATM, silly."

"Alrighty, then. Thanks, Cates. The poor seminary student will accept your charity. I'm not too proud." Folding the bills, he pushed them down in the pocket of his jeans.

"You've done me a huge favor. Love you." Caty kissed her fingers and placed them on his cheek. "I've got to go. Later."

"Take care. I'm on the case."

With a wave over her shoulder, Caty headed toward the fitting room.

Chapter 27

Sunday Morning

Caleb pulled back the curtains covering Lauren's window and then raised the blinds. Bright sunlight flooded the yellow and blue bedroom. "Good morning, sunshine!"

Rolling over, Lauren tossed him a dazed-with-sleep look. "It's Sunday morning. Go away."

"Lauren, I told you I wanted you up by eight. It's now 8:15. Rise and shine time." Caleb fumbled with fastening his right cuff link as he approached her bed.

She eyed him. "Do you have a meeting? You're all dressed up."

"I told you last night. We're going to church."

"We are?" Yawning, she slapped one hand on her forehead. "Why?"

Because I'm a negligent father when it comes to your spiritual upbringing. Because you and I both need to reconnect with Jesus. So many reasons.

Standing beside her bed, Caleb opened and then closed his mouth. He didn't want to pull the old *because I'm your father and I say so* card, but he would if that's what it took to get her to church.

"Here's an idea," Lauren said. *"You* go and then come home and tell me about it."

He shook his head. "No deal. You told me not all that long ago that you feel like a prisoner in this house. This is the inmate's chance to escape."

Her forehead creased. "As long as I can get out of the house every now and then like on Friday night with Caty, it's not so bad. Hey, is Caty coming to church with us?"

"No. I assume she goes to the church where her family attends." Why couldn't he get the cuff link fastened?

"Did you know one of Caty's brothers is the next space shuttle commander?"

"For real? Have you met him?"

"No." He grinned. "Maybe we can invite him to dinner sometime."

"Yeah, right." She rolled her eyes. "Like *that's* ever going to happen."

"Hey, you never know. I invited Caty here for dinner on Tuesday night."

As he knew it would, that statement caught his daughter's attention. "Seriously? Cool." Then she surprised him by giggling. "You should serve her liver with chopsticks. She'd love that."

Caleb chuckled. "Not if we want her to come back again." He gave up on the cuff link.

"Here. Let me do it for you." Lauren got on her knees and gestured for his sleeve. "You always have a hard time with the right one."

"I guess I'm not as talented with my left hand."

She fixed it for him with impressive speed then patted his wrist. "There you go. All set."

Eyeing it, Caleb gave her a nod of approval. "Thank you." Helena had always helped him with the cuff links and then Lettie. Now it seemed his daughter had assumed the task. Lauren's willingness to help him touched him in that place deep inside reserved only for his child.

"I like Caty, Dad. She's fun. Easy on the eyes, too, don't you think?"

He'd ignore that comment. Sounded like something a guy would say to another guy, and he didn't appreciate it. "Glad you think so. I like her, too. She did me a big favor the other night."

"By babysitting me, you mean?"

He shot her a frown. "Did Caty *treat* you like a babysitter?"

"No, not that I've ever had a babysitter other than Lettie."

"You're not a baby, Lauren. I trusted Caty to keep you safe, and she did. If she hadn't been willing, I would have sent you somewhere with Cordelia."

Lauren giggled. "Delia's nice and everything, but..." She shook her head. "Not the same thing." She glanced up at him, her smile disappearing. "Does Caty know about the kidnapping threats?"

"Yes. I told her on Friday afternoon. It was either that or risk her thinking I was certifiably crazy, based on my behavior." He was thankful Carson had been able to watch over them while managing to stay out of sight. He'd caught a glimpse of Caty's youngest brother, and they'd shared a glance and a wave at the mall.

Lauren seemed surprised. "Caty didn't say anything. Neither did you. I guess that's for the best, huh?"

Caleb nodded. "I think so. For now. Caty's a strong Christian, and she refuses to give into fear. She believes it's better to move forward instead of looking over our shoulders, wondering who or what might be out there. That's the kind of positive attitude we need to adopt."

"Yeah. She's really smart." Lauren laughed a little. "Not that you're not."

It'd been a testament to Caty's strength of character that she'd managed to spend time with Lauren and not let on that she was aware of the threats. They'd found a quiet corner table in one of the mall restaurants and shared a nice meal for the second time that day.

Lauren stared at him. "Are *you* afraid, Dad?"

With a sigh, Caleb moved his hands to his hips, stalling for time as he pondered how to answer her pointed question. Again, she deserved his honest answer. "In some ways, yes, but it's more the uncertainty of not knowing who's behind the threats. I hate the fact that we're *both* being forced to live like prisoners. You're not alone in feeling that way."

Grabbing the chair by her desk, Caleb straddled it and crossed his arms on the back. "As far as Caty is concerned, relationships need to be honest from the start or they're doomed to fail."

"Are you dating Caty now?"

"I haven't known her long enough to be dating her. While it's true she's worked for me for five years, I only met her recently for the first time."

Lauren gave him a knowing smile. "Now who's not being straight, Dad? The way I see it, you've known Caty long enough to fall in love with her."

Shaking his head, Caleb avoided her probing gaze. Not bad for a twelve-year-old. He must be more transparent than he thought for her to see past his emotional walls and straight into his thoughts.

"Caty is a very special woman. The reason I invited her to dinner here at the house is so that we can get to know each other better. From my perspective, this isn't just a casual dinner date."

"I can tell because you hardly ever go on a date, and you've never invited a woman to the house. What am I supposed to do while Caty's here? I mean, you probably want me to get lost, right? So you can play kissy face with her." Grabbing two stuffed animals from the shelf above her bed, Lauren smushed their furry faces together and made smacking noises.

"Very funny. You're welcome to stay and eat dinner with us."

She tossed the animals on the bed. "And then get lost?"

He chuckled. "I'll leave that up to you. I don't know that we'll be doing any kissing." That response wasn't completely honest, either. He enjoyed kissing Caty. Very much. Judging by her impassioned response, she seemed to like kissing him. They were *good* together and not only in the physical sense.

"I'm okay if you date her, Dad. You know when you were talking with Caty on the phone on Friday afternoon? When we were at the store? The saleslady thought Caty was my mom."

"She did?" His pulse jumped. With Caty's coloring, dark hair, and blue eyes, he could see where someone might assume they were mother and daughter.

"Caty's a little young to be your mother. If she *were* your mother." This conversation was silly.

"How old is she?"

He cleared his throat. "Not as old as me."

"Are you saying you might marry Caty someday?"

"You should be a reporter, Lauren. You ask the hard-hitting questions. I only came in here to get you up for church, not an inquisition." Rubbing his hand over his jaw, Caleb glanced toward the window. A bird landed on one of the tree branches outside her window. He began to sing, and that made him smile.

"Talking love and marriage is premature. I *will* tell you that Caty Lewis is the first woman since your mother where I believe our feelings for each other could develop into something long term."

"Like marriage." She grinned. "Just admit it already."

"You'd be okay with that?"

"I can tell she makes you happy, so…yeah. I like it when you smile instead of being all tense and stuff. You get a goofy look on your face around Caty. You can be kind of fun when you let yourself relax."

"Thanks for that. Coming from you, that's high praise." Caleb fixed her with his gaze. "Not a word to anyone about this discussion, *especially* Caty."

"Okay, but I can tell she really likes you, too. I think you confuse her, but she thinks you're handsome."

"She does, huh?"

Lauren nodded. "She called you that on the phone with her friend."

"I see. The call you 'inadvertently' heard, I suppose? I hope you apologized for eavesdropping."

Lauren hung her head. "I told Caty I was sorry. It was kind of an accident."

How could he chastise her when he'd allowed someone else to pretend to be him? Were the situations all that different? He should never have allowed Steve to talk him into that ridiculous charade, but that still didn't excuse Lauren's behavior. She'd been in the wrong.

"You made it worse by repeating something Caty said in a private conversation with a trusted friend. That's wrong, Lauren. Don't ever do that again."

"I won't." Lauren sniffled. *Please, Lord, not the tears.* Helena's tears could alternately be a manipulative tactic or the result of genuinely wounded feelings. Without fail, hearing her cry always twisted his gut. The problem? Reality and dramatics got all jumbled together when his wife cried, making it difficult for him to differentiate between the two.

He'd always been a "fixer" who tried to make everything better. Sometimes a problem couldn't be fixed without divine intervention. Caleb only wished he'd learned that lesson long ago. Caty didn't strike him as the type of woman to cry easily. Neither did she seem the type of woman to *scare* easily.

Caleb lowered his voice. "When Caty comes to dinner on Tuesday night, I don't want her to hear anything that'll send her running out of our lives. Understood?"

"My lips are sealed. Promise." Lauren made a zipping motion across her lips. He hoped he could bank on that promise.

Crossing the room to the bed, Caleb removed the bed pillow and then tossed it at her. "If you go with me to church this morning, I'll take you to lunch."

"I thought bribery was against church rules."

He'd ignore that barb. "Whatever you want although a place with plates and silverware might be nice." Then he'd drive them out to the country to meet with a dog breeder. For now, he'd hold off on that announcement or she wouldn't listen to a word in the church service.

Lying on her stomach, Lauren propped herself on the mattress with both elbows. "Here's an idea. How about I go with you to lunch wherever *you* want and then you let me repaint my room?"

He surveyed the room. "What's wrong with this room? It's bright and happy. Optimistic."

"There's nothing wrong with it except it looks like a six-year-old lives here."

"Since you're twelve, it's like *two* six-year-olds live here." Caleb laughed when she groaned and crossed her eyes.

"You are sooo corny. And stop with the twelve-year-old stuff already. We've had this discussion." Lauren plopped back down on the bed and then flipped over on her back. "You might as well add daisies or"—she danced her fingers in the air—"little smiley faces and cartoon characters."

Time to compromise. "Fine, then. Let's talk. Tell me what colors you like." Walking over to the closet, Caleb opened the door and started working on his customary Half Windsor knot in front of the full-length mirror. "Black's not allowed. It's not a color."

"Yes, it is."

"Not in my house, it's not. Anything but that."

Giggling, Lauren kicked off the sheets with one foot. Caleb did a quick double take. "I see you've decided to paint your toes all one color." Red was preferable than the metallic mishmash.

"Thanks for noticing. A lady painted them for me while another one cut my hair at the mall."

His daughter had some new clothes, a cute haircut, and painted toenails without major damage to his credit card. He'd expected a much higher bill and would have paid a lot more. Caty's influence, no doubt. Lauren had talked about Caty whenever he'd seen her in the house yesterday. He hadn't seen his daughter smile so much in months.

Lauren eyed him. "How do you feel about gray?"

"Short answer? I don't. It's another non-color, and a dull one at that."

"Gray is better than boring beige. It's a good backdrop. At least I think that's the right word."

"Let me get this straight. You want to paint the walls gray just so you can cover them up with something else?" Caleb could envision her hanging posters of long-haired, tattooed guys, but he'd deal with that later. One hurdle at a time. The concept of *pick your battles* he'd heard from other parents began to take on personal meaning.

"You are hopeless!" Lauren propped her back against the headboard. Wrapping her arms around her knees, she yawned again. "How about all that stuff you told me about how this is my house, too?"

"It *is* your house, sweetheart. But until you pay the mortgage, I have the final say on what colors the rooms are painted."

"You don't even *have* a mortgage, Dad."

Caleb groaned. "How do you know anything about that?" When he was her age, all he cared about was sports and model airplanes. His mother had used that line on him, and it had always worked. Lauren was too observant.

"Can I paint my bedroom myself?"

Caleb stilled his fingers on his necktie. "Why would you want to do that?" Wow, he sounded high-handed. When had he become so spoiled? He'd worked construction for years to help pay his expenses from high school through grad school. Together with a couple of his buddies, he'd renovated the first house he'd bought before he married Helena—painted, wallpapered, installed lights and ceiling fans—everything but the most sophisticated wiring. After his dad left, he'd basically taught himself, with minimum guidance from an older neighbor, how to do home repairs. He'd always found a certain catharsis in working with his hands.

"You're spoiled."

Caleb frowned. How ironic coming from his privileged daughter.

"You know something?" He turned to her, dropping his hands to his sides. "You're absolutely right, not that I need my daughter pointing out my deficiencies. Another reason I need to be in church. Time for a change in attitude." His subtle meaning being that *Lauren* could also use a change in attitude.

She gave him an impish smile. "So, how about that gray?"

Returning to the tie, Caleb swallowed his sigh. "Next to white, gray is the most boring color ever. For that matter, I'm pretty sure white's not a color, either."

"Sure it is. Anything that isn't clear is a color." Lauren tossed a pillow at him. "Would you finish that tie and leave me alone so I can get dressed? It's taking you forever. We'll be late."

"One of these days you'll be begging me to show you how to tie a man's necktie," Caleb teased. "Goes along with fastening cuff links. Valuable skills for when you get married one day."

She groaned and pushed her face into her pillow. "I hate boys. I'm never getting married."

Good answer from a girl her age. Guaranteed, in another year— two tops—she'd change her tune. Based on recent comments, Lauren was more focused on getting *him* fixed up with a woman, but he wasn't about to bring up the subject.

After finishing the knot, he straightened his tie. What was he saying? Lauren was growing up way too fast as it was. Caty was right in that kids Lauren's age liked to say things to get their parents' attention and then some. His daughter had certainly accomplished that. Likewise, the smoking had probably been a ploy of some kind, or else a desperate attempt to spend more time with her.

He turned to her. "Compromise time. I'll help you paint your bedroom a new color if you mix another color with the gray. To give it a hint of color."

"You and your colors. How about purple?"

"You'd end up with lavender if you mix purple with gray."

"I could live with that," Lauren said. "I think. Ask me tomorrow."

Caleb nodded. He'd accept that response as a victory. Hiking his sleeve, he checked his watch. Knowing he might have trouble getting Lauren out of bed, he'd allowed an extra thirty minutes. As it turned out, that rationale had been providential.

"We'll talk about it more later this week and maybe visit a paint store. For now, I'll meet you in the kitchen in ten minutes. By the way, I'm making chocolate chip pancakes."

Lauren's brows shot up. "Why didn't you say so in the first place?" As he left the bedroom, Caleb heard her scrambling behind him. There wasn't much Lauren wouldn't do for his pancakes.

Granted, it was one of the few foods he'd managed to master, but it was becoming tradition whenever Lettie was off for the weekend.

Caleb bounded down the front staircase, smiling the entire way. Today was off to a very good start.

Chapter 28

After greeting church members and taking a bulletin, Caty spotted Marta sitting on the left side of the sanctuary near the front. She walked down the center aisle and stopped by the end of the pew. "Good morning."

Marta looked up with a bright smile. "Hey there! I'm so happy you could join us. Have a seat." She scooted farther down the pew and moved her purse to the floor.

"Is Eliot here?" Caty sat beside her and gave Marta a quick hug. In her chic blue dress and high-heeled sandals, her friend looked every bit the professional television meteorologist.

"He's ushering this morning and will join us once the service starts. How is the Lewis clan dealing with your defection?"

"Defection?" Caty laughed under her breath. "They understand I need to find my own place to worship. Contrary to popular opinion, we're not all joined at the hip." Caty glanced around the sanctuary. "Have you seen Rebekah? I talked with Kevin the other day and told him I need to meet their adorable tykes."

"Oh, those kids are precious. Beck might be working in the nursery, but I'm sure you'll see her." She leaned close. "Eliot had a fun surprise waiting for me this morning, and I could use your help."

"Well, if that's not a multilayered statement. Is it PG-rated?"

Marta winked. "This one is. He's put together clues for me, sort of like a scavenger hunt. Supposedly there's a surprise after I solve them."

Caty grinned. "I'll bite. Sounds like fun. How many total clues are there?"

"Three, I think. Maybe four. I'm not sure. I only have the first one so far."

"Do you have any idea what the surprise is?"

"Of course not. What would be the fun in that? It could be a plastic ring or a chew toy for Barney for all I care."

"What's the occasion?" Marta's birthday was last month and their anniversary was in October.

"No special reason. Eliot doesn't do what's *expected*. That's one of the things I love most about him. Take notes, my friend. I'm telling you, this is the kind of thing that keeps a marriage fresh."

"A creative mind is a definite plus in a relationship," Caty said. "I'm guessing you need my help with the first clue?" Caleb seemed to be the same type of man from what she could tell.

"You read me so well. Are you game?"

"Why not? I'll look forward to living vicariously through your romantic love games or whatever, but it might be better to wait until after church to discuss it."

"Why? The Lord is the greatest promoter of romance there is, especially in a marriage."

"You've got me there." Spying Kevin on the platform at the front of the church, Caty waved.

After digging through her purse, Marta retrieved a small white piece of paper and handed it to her. CLUE #1: IT GOES AROUND THE NECK AND GIVES ONE IDENTITY.

Caty puzzled over it for a few seconds. "What do you think this means?"

"My first thought was that it has something to do with my swimming medals."

"That would make sense." Marta had been a swimming champion all through school.

"Then I checked every last one of them. Nothing."

"It seems like it'd have to be a necklace, or maybe a collar of some kind," Caty said. "Let me think about it, and I'll get back to you."

Marta leaned close. "Don't look now but the handsome cowboy just walked in the door."

"Handsome cowboy?" Couldn't be Caleb. Why had her pulse shot to the rafters?

"*Your* handsome cowboy, Caty. Caleb Reid is in the house and talking with Eliot."

"Why am I sensing a set-up?" Caty couldn't even pretend to be mad this time.

"I know nothing. This is the first time I've seen him here in church, same as you. Imagine that. Praise the Lord and scoot on down the pew." Marta glanced over her shoulder.

"You could stand to be a little more subtle," Caty whispered.

"There's a time and place to be subtle. This isn't it." Marta turned and waved. "Caleb, hi! Come and join us."

Caty twisted her lips. "That'll teach me to tell you what *not* to do."

"There's a pretty young girl with him. Do you think that's his daughter?"

Caty refused to turn around. "If she has dark hair and looks a lot like him, it's Lauren."

"That's a pretty name." Marta shot her a look of surprise. "Have you met her? Why didn't I know this?"

"Calm down. I haven't talked with you since Friday morning," Caty said. "You could say some things have transpired." That was a vast understatement. Even if she could, where would she begin?

"It was that peach pie you made for him, wasn't it?" Marta laughed. "I'm telling you, you Lewis women and that peach pie. Your baking skills just reel a man in." She gestured as though she were tossing out a fishing line and then reeling in a big fish. "By the grace of God, Eliot fell in love with me even though the *only* thing I could make at the time was blueberry muffins."

"At least you know he didn't marry you for your culinary talents." Caty laughed. "No wonder we get along so well. You're as nuts—and as challenged in the kitchen—as I am."

"You know it, girlfriend. Here comes Eliot with Caleb and Lauren. Put on your best smile."

Eliot stopped at the end of the pew and introduced Lauren to Marta. "I have more ushering to do, and then I'll come back to join you." He said something to Caleb under his breath and then gave him a man-slap on the back before heading down the aisle.

"Glad you two could join us," Marta said.

"Morning, Caleb. Hi, Lauren." Caty gave them both a bright smile.

Caleb nodded to Marta and then his gaze found hers. "Best surprise of the week to see you here, Caty." He carried a navy sport coat over his arm and wore a blue and white striped dress shirt, opened at the neck and tucked into khaki slacks. She knew he was more comfortable in his jeans, leather jacket, and boots, but the man cleaned up incredibly well.

"The week just started, Dad." Brushing past her father, Lauren sat down beside her. "Does my hair look okay, Caty? I tried to fix it like the lady at the salon."

"It looks even better than it did on Friday." Caty ran her fingers lightly over Lauren's bangs. "You did a great job."

Lauren beamed from Caty's praise and turned to Caleb. "Dad, doesn't Caty look especially gorgeous this morning?"

"That she does." With an amused grin, Caleb settled on the other side of Lauren and draped his jacket over the empty pew in front of him.

Lauren leaned across her and stared at Marta for a few seconds. "Now I know why you look so familiar! You do the weather on TV, don't you? You're so funny, and you make weather fun."

Marta's cheeks pinked. "That would be me. Thanks, Lauren."

"What do you have there?" Lauren leaned over Caty's shoulder to see the clue she still held in her hand.

Marta quickly explained the game to Lauren.

"Can I help you solve the clues?"

"Of course." Marta lowered her voice when the keyboardist began playing the opening prelude.

Eliot walked toward them from the opposite end of the pew and sat beside Marta. Caty counted under her breath. *One, two, and three.* As expected, his arm slid around his wife, and he tugged her close. Eliot might not be traditional, but when it came to Marta, he was predictable in all the best ways.

Sensing Caleb's gaze on her, Caty tried to focus on the church bulletin. The list of services and ministries blurred. Caleb definitely wasn't traditional. Since she'd met him, nothing he'd done could be classified as predictable. Although she liked her job to be boring and traditional, she liked how she never knew what her boss would say, or do, next.

As the beginning strains of the first hymn began, Caty rose beside the others. Sitting together with Caleb and Lauren—all of them lined up on the pew together—felt *right.*

Chapter 29

Caleb stumbled through the opening praise choruses.

Gripping the back of the pew in front of her, Lauren swung back and forth until Caleb placed one hand over hers to still her movements since they weren't in response to the praise and worship going on at the front of the church. She was so much like he'd been at the same age that he recognized the obvious signs. His mother thought he should have Lauren tested for ADD, but that wasn't it, and her doctor had agreed. Lauren was highly intelligent, and she became easily bored. His daughter didn't need medication. She needed to be challenged and mentally stimulated.

The guy leading worship had a good singing voice, and his guitar playing was equally impressive. Before the service, Eliot told him his name was Kevin Moore, and he was another one of Caty's brother's TeamWork volunteers. Seemed a lot of talented, diverse people were in that missions group.

Like he'd told Caty, he'd heard of TeamWork Missions, but Caleb didn't know details or how many ministries they were involved in around the country until recently. After their dinner with Eliot and Marta, he'd done some research, enough to discover the scope of TeamWork was worldwide and far-reaching. The missions organization was solid and financially sound, and he'd look into it for future investment purposes.

As the Domestic Missions Director of TeamWork, Sam Lewis was featured prominently on their website as was Joshua Grant, TeamWork's general counsel. He'd smiled at the photo of Marta and Eliot in New Mexico on the mission where they'd married. Then he'd read poignant testimonies from a sports advertising agency owner in Boston, the owner of the *Leather* stores in Texas and Louisiana, and a Christian publisher and an investment banker, both from New York. Considering their wives were also quoted, it would seem TeamWork boasted a number of husband/wife teams.

The keyboardist began playing "It Is Well With My Soul," a hymn Caleb knew well. His mother loved it, and it was one of his favorites. Considering the unrest in *his* soul in his current situation, the irony of this particular hymn did not escape him. The lyrics were printed in the bulletin, and Caleb shared with Lauren as he began to sing.

He *needed* to sing this hymn. *You always know, don't you, Lord?*

At the end of the hymn, the musicians effortlessly transitioned into "When I Survey The Wondrous Cross." Kevin's voice resonated with passion as he led the music. This was a talented man who loved the Lord with everything in him. An inspiration.

As he sang, Caleb moved his gaze to the large wooden cross mounted on the wall at the front of the sanctuary. An imperfect cross, it was crudely made. A crown of thorns hung where the wood crisscrossed. "…On which the Prince of glory died," he sang. His eyes unexpectedly grew moist but he pushed on in singing, "My richest gain I count but loss, and pour contempt on all my pride."

Powerful words. Convicting words. The remaining verses talked about pride and how man should boast or glory in the Lord and His sacrifice, not trust in wealth or boast about his own works. As he neared the end of the hymn, Caleb poured more conviction into his singing. "Love so amazing, so divine, demands my soul, my life, my all."

Lauren looked up at him with surprise. She'd rarely heard him sing with such enthusiasm. She didn't cringe or shrink away from him. The fact that they were together in church was enough of a breakthrough for the day, although he'd started out the morning on his knees at home. His biggest fault as a parent had been sliding into apathy and not taking Lauren to church more after her mother died. That was the time when they both *should* have been in church.

But you're here now. Yes, that was a very good thing.

"Great singing, everyone!" Kevin strummed a few quiet chords on his guitar. "Now, let's bow our heads and continue our worship this morning by thanking the Lord for this glorious day He has made."

After a few announcements, the pastor strolled across the platform. Charles Baldwin was a middle-aged man, soft-spoken, with a pleasant demeanor. He nodded to the assembled congregation with a welcoming smile. "Morning, folks."

Gripping both sides of the podium, he looked out over the congregation. "I'd like to tell you a little more about the first hymn we sang this morning, 'It Is Well With My Soul.' The lyrics for that hymn were written by a man named Horatio G. Spafford in 1873. Spafford was the son of a gazetteer author, Horatio Gates Spafford and his wife, Elizabeth Clark Hewitt Spafford. What is a gazetteer, you might ask? I had to look it up myself. A gazetteer is a geographical dictionary or directory that's used in conjunction with a map or an atlas. It contains information about the geographical makeup, social statistics, and physical features of a country, region, or continent.

"Young Horatio married Anna Larsen of Norway on September 5, 1861, in Chicago. They were a very well-known couple in 1860s Chicago. He was a prominent lawyer and a senior partner in a large, thriving law firm. They were also prominent supporters and close friends with an American evangelist some of you might have heard of named Dwight L. Moody. The same D.L. Moody who founded several entities including Moody Bible Institute and Moody Publishers.

"Mr. Spafford had invested in real estate north of an expanding Chicago in the spring of 1871. You might recall that the Great Fire of Chicago reduced the city to ashes in October of that same year. Along with it, the fire destroyed most of Spafford's sizable investment and ruined him financially."

The pastor moved away from the podium and pushed his hands into the pockets of his slacks. "Never a man to be beaten down, Horatio managed to rebound financially. Two years later, in 1873, he decided to take his family on a holiday in Europe. Partly based on the fact that D.L. Moody would be preaching in England that fall, he booked passage for his wife and four daughters on a steamship called the *Ville du Havre*. Delayed because of business, Mr. Spafford sent his family ahead—Annie, age eleven, Maggie, age nine, Elizabeth, age five, and Tanetta, his youngest at the tender age of two.

"On November 22, while crossing the Atlantic, the *Ville du Havre* was struck by an iron sailing vessel. In that horrible event, 226 people lost their lives, including all four of Spafford's children. Anna survived, and upon her arrival in England, she sent her husband a telegram that has since become very well-known. That telegram simply said, 'Saved alone.'

"Several weeks later, as Spafford's ship passed near that same spot where his daughters had perished, the Holy Spirit inspired those words: 'When peace like a river, attendeth my way. When sorrows like sea billows roll. Whatever my lot, thou has taught me to say, it is well, it is well, with my soul.'"

As the pastor recited the lyrics, Kevin sang them softly in the background, a nice effect.

"Ladies and gentlemen, those lyrics speak to the hope all believers share. No matter what pain and grief you may suffer here on earth, and no matter how difficult your challenges may be, with God's help, you *can* overcome them."

Scooting closer on the pew, Lauren rested her head on Caleb's arm. "That's really sad," she whispered. Prompted to reassure her, Caleb put his arm around her and tugged her close. In a spontaneous move, he pressed his lips to her forehead. She didn't pull away or give him a look of disgust, and that it itself was encouraging, In truth, he needed the reassurance as much as she did. He couldn't imagine ever losing Lauren in such a horrific tragedy. He'd known a few children who'd died under tragic circumstances, but to think of any man losing *four* children?

The idea was unfathomable, and the story behind the well-known hymn was incredibly *powerful*. For a man who'd lost almost everything, Horatio Spafford found *joy* in the midst of his suffering.

"Anna went on to give birth to three more children, a son, Horatio Goertner Spafford, who died at the age of four from scarlet fever. They also had two daughters, Bertha born in 1878 and Grace, born in 1881."

The pastor glanced at his notes and took a quick drink from a glass of water he retrieved from a small stand behind him. "Unfortunately, the church the Spaffords attended regarded their tragedy as divine punishment. In response, the couple formed their own Messianic sect, called 'the Overcomers' by the American press. In August 1881, the Spaffords set out for Jerusalem as a party of thirteen adults and three children, and they set up what they called The American Colony."

Pastor Baldwin looked over his congregation. "Listen up, folks, for there's a lesson in what I'm about to tell you."

Caleb sat up straighter on the pew. "Those Colony members, later joined by Swedish Christians, engaged in philanthropic work amongst the people of Jerusalem regardless of their religious affiliation and without proselytizing as their motive. Through their efforts, they gained the trust of local Muslim, Jewish, and Christian communities. Finally, Horatio Spafford died on October 16, 1888, of malaria. He is buried in Mount Zion Cemetery in Jerusalem.

"The work of the American Colony continued on. During and immediately after World War I, they played a critical role in supporting these communities through the great suffering and deprivations of the eastern front. They ran soup kitchens, hospitals, orphanages, and many other charitable ventures."

Caleb's mind wandered a bit as the pastor continued. Grabbing the Bible from the pew rack in front of them, Lauren flipped through to the passages of Scripture the pastor referenced. Good to see she remembered where to find them. He'd need to find their Bibles at the new house or else buy them both new ones.

From the corner of his eye, he sensed Caty watching him. He gave her a slight nod and returned her smile. *Thank you, Lord, for leading me here today.*

"In closing, this is what I'd like to impress upon you," Pastor Baldwin said. "God knows your burdens, your fears, and your deepest insecurities and vulnerabilities. The key, ladies and gentlemen, is *surrender*. Full and complete surrender to our worldly desires, whatever they may be, and giving complete lordship over all to the heavenly Father.

"This is my challenge to you today: review your life this week. As you do that, ask yourself this question: do I keep such a tight control over my finances, my family, my emotions, and everything else that I'm unwilling to give the Lord His full and proper place? It's my prayer that if you find yourself lacking in any one of those areas, friends—and few of us *don't* fall victim to one or more of those things since it's part of what being human is about—then acknowledge it's time to reevaluate your priorities and goals.

"Search your heart. Read the Scriptures. Pray. A lot of it is mindset, and focusing on the good, the pure, and the righteous. Giving Him the glory and control over your life. And then, may all be well in *your* soul."

Caleb rose to his feet as Kevin took the platform to sing a last praise song. He'd been in services where the sermon topic applied in some way to his life. This morning, it was as though Charles Baldwin was speaking directly to him, an audience of one. Caleb didn't need to search his soul to know he was lacking in so many ways. But he was making a concerted effort to reconnect, pray, and include the Lord in his plans, both personal and professional.

"Dad." Lauren nudged him. "It's over." He'd completely missed the closing prayer.

After he stepped out into the aisle, Lauren darted around him. "Stay in the front vestibule," he called, but he doubted she'd heard him. Eliot stood near the front door. Catching his eye, he nodded and mouthed, *Got it covered.*

Caty rose to her feet and moved toward him. In her business suits with those pencil skirts and heels, she was a beautiful woman. This morning, in her feminine, retro-looking brown and white polka dot dress and high-heeled sandals, she stole his breath. The dress, modest yet fitted, revealed her pretty feminine curves to their best advantage. Normally, brown was another non-color he didn't like. Seeing Caty in this dress changed his opinion. In fact, brown might be his new favorite color.

"Fancy meeting you here." She graced him with a surprisingly shy yet also confident smile. Interesting. She was an intriguing woman, alternately demure and confident. It took all of his restraint not to pull her into his arms and kiss her. He didn't want to move too fast, but once he made up his mind—whether in business or his personal life—he wasn't a patient man.

"Great service this morning," he said. "Pastor Baldwin touched on some things in his message that I've wrestled with on a personal level. As recently as this past Friday, as you know."

"Same here. This is the first time I've ever visited this church. I have the feeling I'll be returning. You?"

"Definitely. Eliot invited me. I'm assuming Marta invited you?"

"Yes." She laughed. "We probably shouldn't speculate on whether the right hand of the Marchand Cupid Brigade was aware of what the left hand was doing."

"Whatever the reason, I'm always happy to see you, Caty."

She dipped her head. "Likewise. I used to always go to my home church whenever I was back home in Houston. Now that I'm back, hopefully permanently"—Caty darted a glance at him—"I'd like to try and find a different church."

"Makes sense. You want to establish your identity separate from your family, and not follow tradition simply for the sake of…tradition." Caleb scratched the side of his head and gave her a wry grin. "Okay, that sentence made sense in my mind. You have a way of confusing me but in the best possible way. Caty, if Lauren and I didn't already have plans, I'd love to take you to lunch. I wasn't aware you'd be here—"

"That's okay," she said quickly. "I have a standing invitation to go over to Sam and Lexa's on Sundays, so that's where I'm headed today, anyway. That is, as soon as I stop by the deli and pick up the salad I supposedly made last night."

Caleb stepped closer and lowered his voice. "Eliot advised me to get a guard dog. We're driving out to the country to meet with a breeder this afternoon, but Lauren doesn't know it yet."

"Has Lauren ever had a dog before?"

"No, but she used to beg for one. It'll be a crash course. We're going to see a three-year-old Bullmastiff named Max. I wasn't sure I could deal with—or ask Lettie to handle—training a puppy. So, I guess you could say Max is like a ready-made family member."

"I'll look forward to meeting Max on Tuesday night."

He nodded. "This will be an experience for all of us. By the way, on another subject, when Pastor Baldwin talked about The American Colony, did that remind you of something?"

Her blue eyes lit. "TeamWork?"

"Exactly. I might call Sam and chat with him sometime about investment opportunities or a way to get involved." He hadn't planned on saying anything but the words slipped out of their own accord. "I'm always looking for solid organizations to support, and what better one than a missions-minded one?"

Caty appeared pleased. "Sam would love to chat with you. Not to be presumptuous, but I was thinking we could put together a group from Belac to help out with a local TeamWork mission. Sam coordinates a lot of downtown events." When he didn't respond immediately, she continued. "It's just a thought. Please don't think I'm going to come up with all sorts of *getting to know you activities*."

"That's a wonderful idea." He loved her enthusiasm for her family, TeamWork, and Belac. He liked how she rambled on when she was nervous, trying to explain herself. Most of her suggestions were solid. No doubt she and Miles the mail guy had bounced ideas off one another, and that only endeared her to him more. She didn't closet herself away like some of his executives. Caty was the type of person who invested herself in others. How many people had he ever met who put the needs of others above their own? So few he could probably count them on one hand.

"You're looking at me funny again. Is something wrong? Should I be worried?" With a quick frown, Caty glanced down and touched her dress. "Do I have a rip or a stain or something?"

"Nothing like that," he assured her. "Forgive me. It's just that you look—"

"Like a breath of fresh air?" Her smile grew.

"That, too." Caleb's brown eyes settled on her. "You're breathtaking."

Chapter 30

Caleb's compliment hit its intended target when he caught Caty's quiet intake of breath. He hoped she understood he didn't freely bestow compliments on women the way some men did, and he enjoyed the sweet bloom of pink in her cheeks and the deepening blue in her eyes.

"Thank you. Believe it or not, this dress belonged to my mother, Sarah. She wore it around the time my parents got engaged back in the early sixties. I'm sure she could still wear it, but she insisted I take it. We have a framed photo of her standing in front of Dad's vintage airplane wearing this dress. It's one of those retouched photos that looks like an oil painting."

Walking side by side, moving slowly, they made their way down the aisle. Marta was keeping Lauren occupied, and they seemed to be sharing a lively discussion in the outer vestibule.

"I love how your family values tradition, and you all seem so close," he told her. "Does your dad still have the airplane?"

"No." Caty breathed out a quiet sigh. "After a while, he donated it to a local museum. He goes to visit it sometimes since they still have it on display. Dad has Ménière's Disease, a disorder of the inner ear, and it grounded him as an Air Force pilot not long before the Vietnam War broke out. Growing up, we heard all the stories about his missions flying overseas. Anyway, the plane was a two-seater, and he gave all of us rides in the plane when we were old enough to go up with him."

He smiled. "Great tradition."

"It really was," she agreed. "He waited to retire from flying until Carson could ride with him. It was sort of a rite of passage in the family, one of those things that was bittersweet. We all stood and watched as they flew around the countryside together, knowing it was Dad's swan song. I know my mother was secretly—or maybe not so secretly—relieved, but giving up that part of his life was quite difficult for Dad."

Caleb heard the lingering sadness in her voice. "I'm sure your parents must be proud of Will for carrying on the family love for aviation."

"They are. My Grandpa Lewis loved to tinker with airplane engines and obviously my dad picked up on that love for aeronautics. My parents have known each other since Dad's family moved to Rockbridge when he was a teenager. His sister, Rachel, had been killed in a car accident, and the family needed a fresh start."

She appeared slightly embarrassed. "I hope that didn't sound insensitive."

"Not at all," he assured her. "If anything, I can identify with the need for a fresh start." He assumed her older sister, Rachel, had been named for her father's late sister. Namesakes seemed important in the Lewis family.

"I don't want to keep you, Caleb. I don't know why I started that trip down memory lane."

He tipped her chin. "I'd like to believe that, subconsciously or not, you understand that I want to hear everything there is to know about you."

Caty glanced up at him with that same shy smile that completely captivated him.

"I've got time if you do." He lowered his voice. "If you're willing, tell me more about your parents." He leaned against the back pew, his jacket draped over one shoulder.

"Even though they're my parents, I consider their love story one of the most romantic I've ever heard. My mom's six years younger than my father, and most of the citizens in their small town had picked him to marry her older sister, Tess. Even before they started dating, Mom and Dad would meet at Thornton's Creek and dream about the future. After he came back home from serving in the Air Force, Dad worked in my grandfather's bank. Mom wanted to go to nursing school.

"They'd spend hours at the creek together, swimming and sunbathing on the rocks or on the banks of the creek. What I love is that it was actually my *mother* who had the avid interest in NASA, and it was still in its infancy. Dad said Mom speculated on what it'd be like to one day have a child in the space program."

A faraway look came into Caty's eyes. "They fell in love, and my dad helped my mom win a softball scholarship to the University of

Texas. They married in Rockbridge on Christmas Eve one year, and then he moved with her to Austin so she could pursue her dream."

"You're right," Caleb said. "Their story is romantic, not to mention admirable on the part of your dad. He demonstrated sacrificial love."

"My father has always been my hero. My brothers are wonderful, and so are my sisters, but there's something so special—or should be—between a girl and her daddy."

"I hope Lauren will admire me the way you do your father." Caleb's jaw tightened. "I doubt she does now, but maybe in the future."

Caty clasped his hand. "I'm sure she does. We had our tense moments, but I never doubted for one second that Dad loved me. You're a great father, Caleb. Never doubt *that*. When I was shopping with Lauren, all she could talk about was you. You should have heard all the times she mentioned something you'd said or done. She's proud of you even though she might not always act like it."

He swallowed hard, touched by her words. "Thank you."

"Going into space is every bit my brother's dream as it was Mom's dream all those years ago." Caty glanced up at him, wonder in her eyes. "Something about that seems so *right*, you know?"

"I know."

"Will is named after Mom's father, William Jordan, although he went by Bill. Mom was also the one who first told Dad about TeamWork, too. They did some early missions when they were newlyweds and lived in Austin, and then they took us kids on a number of missions."

"So TeamWork also holds a rich history in your family, and Sam caught that vision," Caleb observed. "What's *your* vision, Caty?"

"Sorry, to interrupt, but I need to give Caty a hug." A tall, attractive blonde approached with an adorable blonde baby girl nestled in her arms.

Caty broke into a wide smile. "Rebekah, it's so great to see you!" She threw her arms around the other woman, and they exchanged a warm hug. "It's been too long. I've missed you."

"I know. I was in the nursery this morning, but Marta told me you were here."

"Kevin was such a big help moving me into the townhome. I told him I couldn't believe I hadn't met your twins yet, and they're already a year old." Caty smoothed the baby's soft, straight blonde hair. "This must be your sweet Elizabeth."

"Yes. Kevin will be over in just a minute with Jacob." Stepping back, Rebekah gave Caty an approving onceover. "You look absolutely terrific, my friend. I think I recognize that dress you're wearing. Moving back to Houston definitely agrees with you. I'm glad your company finally wised up and brought you back home where you belong."

Caleb twisted his lips not to laugh.

"Sorry. Where are my manners?" Caty turned to him. "Rebekah Moore, I'd like you to meet my friend, Caleb Reid." Her eyes widened as though she realized maybe she shouldn't have given his full name.

Hoping to reassure her, Caleb nodded. "It's very nice to meet you, Rebekah. I'm a...co-worker of Caty's." He didn't offer his hand since Rebekah held Elizabeth and the largest diaper bag he'd ever seen was slung over one shoulder. He sensed Caty's amusement as he waved at Rebekah's daughter. The child gave him a shy smile before burying her head against her mother.

"Great to meet you, Caleb. My husband is the worship leader here. We both think the world of Caty. She must be a great co-worker, and I'm sure she's an asset to the company."

"Oh, she is. I don't know what I'd do—what *we'd* do—without her."

"What do you do at the company, Caleb?"

At Rebekah's question, Caty turned to him with an arched brow, waiting. She was enjoying this.

"One of my responsibilities is coming up with ideas for promotional items. My latest idea is having some of those spongy stress-reliever things made in the shape of a baseball. They'll have the corporate name on them, and they can be handed out at the entrance or tossed to the crowd at Astros games."

Caty smiled like that was the best idea she'd heard in a long time. "I love that!" He'd come up with it off the top of his head, but even he could admit it wasn't half-bad.

"Well, the fly swatter idea was such a hit, I figured why not?" Caleb turned to Rebekah. "Your husband is a talented musician. I enjoyed the service."

"Thank you. I hope you can both join us again soon. Caleb, I met your daughter. Lauren's such a cute girl. I'm guessing she's about twelve?"

"Thirteen in November. I'm bracing myself now."

Kevin walked up to them with Jacob in his arms, and Rebekah made the introductions.

Reaching around his sleeping son, Kevin shook his hand. "It's great to have you with us this morning, Caleb." Moving beside his wife, he lifted the heavy-looking diaper bag from her shoulder.

That simple action brought to mind the days when Lauren was a baby. He'd loved kissing her soft, baby powder-scented skin after her bath, giving her a bottle, and then rocking her to sleep. Recalled the times when he'd hold her and dream about the future. He'd made lots of promises to his infant daughter. He'd kept the most important ones.

"Do you two have lunch plans?" Rebekah's question broke into his musing. "Marta and Eliot are coming over to the house. Nothing fancy, but Kevin's going to throw some burgers and hot dogs on the grill. We'd love it if you could join us."

"I told Lexa I'd come over today," Caty told them. "Let's get together soon, though."

When was the last time anyone had invited him to a cookout? "I'm afraid I have a prior commitment," Caleb told them with sincere regret. "Perhaps another time."

"Our door's always open," Kevin said. "Stop by anytime."

Rebekah gave Caty another quick hug and then gave him a warm smile. "Caleb, it's great to meet you. I hope we'll see you again."

"Likewise. I'm sure you will." If he had anything to say about it, they'd see him with Caty. Judging by the look in her eyes, she'd be agreeable. A week ago, he couldn't fathom wanting to be part of a couple again, but here he was embracing the idea.

God, you know best. I'm following your lead here.

"We'll look forward to it," Kevin said. When the little boy shifted in his arms, Kevin kissed his dark, curly head. Caleb felt a tug inside at the display of open affection between father and son. He was being more sentimental than usual, but their body language spoke volumes—the way Jacob moved his arms around his daddy's neck, the way Elizabeth burrowed into Rebekah.

Lauren used to do those things with him, too. What could he expect? Part of growing up was becoming independent from your parents.

Lord, I'd like to have another child one day. Wow. That thought stunned him, something else Caleb hadn't thought of in years. He'd begun to think it was too late for him to start again. His gaze strayed to Caty again as they rejoined Lauren and said their good-byes. Caleb made a point of thanking Pastor Baldwin for his convicting message.

He walked beside Caty to her car a few minutes later while Lauren ran ahead in the parking lot. "I hope that wasn't a colossal mistake handing her my car keys."

"I don't think she'll try anything."

"I didn't think she'd smoke, either, but that didn't work out so well."

"Caleb, I might be overstepping my bounds, but like I mentioned the other day, I'm pretty sure Lauren was testing you. She wanted to see if you'd come to the school and get her, and you did." She touched his arm. "That was important to her."

"If nothing else, the experience taught me that I need to spend more time with her. I can't have her resorting to drastic measures to get my attention." Caleb slanted a glance her way, thankful for the cover of his sunglasses, allowing him to openly admire Caty without being rude. He liked looking at her—long legs that looked even longer in heels, gorgeous feminine curves, dark hair falling in soft layers framing her face and flirting about her shoulders.

Lauren's squeal caught his attention. Alarm shot through him as he turned his head, following the sound.

"She's fine." The calm in Caty's voice soothed him. "She's discovered Eliot's mode of transportation." She nodded across the parking lot to where Lauren climbed into a white Hummer. "That should keep her occupied for a few more minutes."

He chuckled. "My SUV can't compare to that tank."

"The SUV?" Caty glanced around the parking lot. "How many cars do you have, Mr. Reid?"

"A few. They're one of the few things I collect." He angled his head a couple of rows over. "The white Toyota FJ Cruiser over there is mine."

"Well, that doesn't exactly help."

"The one that sort of looks like a jeep. Short of strapping him to the hood, a dog might not fit in the Porsche. Guaranteed, I'd be the ASPCA's man of the year—*not*—if I did that."

Caty laughed. "No doubt. The Lewis family has a weird obsession with Volvos. Dad had one of the first ones back in the early 60s. We all drive them except for Will. He's a Mercedes man."

As they reached her car, Caty opened her door and tossed her purse on the passenger seat. After closing the door, she leaned back against the car, hands behind her back. "You asked me about my vision. That's difficult to answer since you're my boss."

Caleb planted one hand on the roof of her car, pinning her. Leaning close, he whispered against her cheek, "I think we've effectively broken down the walls of an employer-employee relationship between us, don't you?"

She could have no idea how difficult it was to be this close and resist her. However, kissing Caty in the parking lot of the church wouldn't be appropriate.

"If you're asking me where I hope to be in ten years, I *could* say that I want to be the CFO of Belac, Inc."

A grin lifted his lips. "Now there's an intriguing theory."

"But I won't say that because it's not what I want."

Caleb withdrew his hand from the top of her car. "Let me guess. You want to be the CEO."

She lifted her chin. "Nothing could be further from the truth. The man who holds that job now does a great job, and he's not going anywhere for a very long time."

"Oh? I thought he might buy a yacht and disappear on a journey around the world. From what I know, he seems like the oddball, reclusive type."

"No." Caty shook her head slowly. "I doubt that will ever happen."

"Why not?"

"Odd or not," she said, "there are people who depend on him. People who care for him, and people who wouldn't want him to leave."

Taking her hand, Caleb pressed a gentle kiss to her palm. "Can you see yourself hanging around this weirdo long enough to get to know him better and find out if he's as odd as everyone says?"

Caty's smile emerged. "That's one way of putting it, and I'm sure that can be arranged." The wind tossed her dark hair across her cheeks, and he tucked the long strands behind one ear.

He helped Caty inside the car before closing her door. "Don't forget Oliver will pick you up on Tuesday evening. Lauren will be joining us for dinner, and then she's graciously volunteered to make herself scarce."

"I'm looking forward to it." Caty started the car. "If I don't see you in the office until then, I'll see you on Tuesday night. Let me know if I can bring anything."

"Just yourself."

"What's the dress code?"

"Wear anything you'd like. Casual's fine. Have a great rest of the day, Catherine."

"Bye, Caleb." She waved, and he watched until she turned out of the parking lot and out of view.

Lauren bounced over to him as he returned to the SUV. "*That* was fun. You wanted to kiss Caty. I could tell. So could Marta and Eliot and the worship leader dude and his wife."

"You know what, Lauren? I care a lot about Caty, and life's too short to worry about what other people think. I might do or say some things that others won't like, but that's their problem."

"Yeah? That's kinda cool, but they seem all for a relationship between the two of you. I like this new fearless attitude thing, Dad. It seems to be working for you."

Caleb chuckled. "You think so? I have to admit, so far it's working pretty well."

Lauren wiggled in her seat as she removed her lightweight sweater. She had on a yellow top and matching skirt, the first feminine outfit he'd seen on her in as long as he could remember.

"New dress?" Repositioning his sunglasses, Caleb headed out of the church lot and toward the highway that would take them out of Houston. Today was definitely a day for new beginnings. Fittingly, the sun was shining, and its warmth was encouraging for his *soul*.

"Uh huh." Lauren sounded pleased. "I got it on the shopping trip with Caty."

Score another one for Team Caty. "It's very pretty. For a color you don't really like, it looks nice on you. Good choice."

"There's a difference between *wearing* yellow and painting my walls this color, you know." Lauren twisted in her seat to face him and leaned against the passenger door. "Are you going to tell me where we're going?"

"First to lunch, and then I have a surprise for you. Sit up in your seat and don't lean on the door, please."

"I like surprises." Caleb didn't need to look at her to see Lauren's smile.

Spying a number of restaurants advertised for the exit a quarter mile away, Caleb accelerated from the fast lane to the far right lane in seven seconds flat. Lauren whooped it up from the passenger seat. The SUV didn't have the same pick-up as the Porsche, but she loved it when he gave any of his cars a burst of speed. He did, too, but he hoped a cop wasn't nearby.

His daughter had no clue she'd have a new friend by the end of the day. No question in his mind they'd be going home with a Bullmastiff later this afternoon.

As great as the day had been so far, he wasn't about to allow the reminder of *why* he needed a guard dog to spoil his new positive outlook.

Bring it on, Lord. I'm ready.

Chapter 31

"Mommy! Aunt Caty's here!" Sam and Lexa's oldest child, Joseph, swung the front door open as Caty approached the house.

"You're quite the door greeter, partner. Thank you." Stepping inside, Caty closed the door behind her. Her gaze dropped to her five-year-old nephew's feet. "New boots?"

"Yep. Just like Dad's." He pulled up his shoulders and gave her a smile destined to break hearts when he was older. Already a clone of his father, Joe was uncommonly tall for his age, with the same dark, wavy hair, intelligent blue eyes, and ready smile. "They'll call me Commander Cowboy one day."

"I'm sure they will." Caty started to ruffle his hair then decided against it. Joe might not appreciate the gesture so much anymore.

After grabbing his toy spaceship, Joe zoomed around the living room, making swooping noises and saying things in his "Mission Control" voice.

"What do you have there, Joe?"

He stopped in front of her and held up his toy. "It's *Pursuit*, Uncle Will's space shuttle." He continued zipping about the room.

Caty's eyes widened as Lexa pushed through the swinging door from the kitchen. Slender as ever in a pale pink cotton dress, Lexa's hair was loose around her shoulders instead of in its usual long braid. Fresh-faced as always, she looked more like a college-aged girl than a woman in her mid-thirties with three small children.

"Hey, Lexa. Does Will already have a commander action figure?" That'd actually be pretty cool. Her family and friends would be sure and snatch up that merchandise.

Her petite sister-in-law laughed. "Not yet, but give him time. It's a generic shuttle, and I used black stick-on letters to put PURSUIT on the side."

"Uncle Will promised to take me to Mission Control again next week," Joe announced. "I might get to meet some of his shuttle crew. There's seven of them."

The pride in the little guy's voice made Caty smile. Kids loved her astronaut brother. Part of it was the whole astronaut thing, but Will was unbelievably patient and related surprisingly well to kids. He didn't talk in overly scientific terms around them, and they loved hearing him talk about planets and the research they planned to do at the ISS. A popular, in-demand speaker, Will made it a point to travel to the local schools.

Caty offered her salad to Lexa. "Here's my offering for today's meal. I'm sorry it's not homemade, and I hope it'll go with whatever you're making."

"We're just glad you could come, Caty. Sam and I know you've got a lot going on. Come into the kitchen with me while I finish getting everything ready. I'm keeping it simple and just made chili and cornbread. So, tell me how you're settling in at your new home and in the office."

"I'm getting there. More than anything else, I'm just thrilled to be home in Houston again." Following Lexa into the kitchen, Caty was thankful the other woman couldn't see her smile. What would Lexa say if she told her that she'd kissed her boss on Friday afternoon? Sat with him and his daughter in church this morning?

"Joe reminds me so much of Will," Caty observed. "Eat, sleep, and breathe the space program. That was his motto. It's gratifying to think Joe might continue the Lewis love affair with aviation. By the way, where's that husband of yours?"

"Sam's on a phone call in the study. The girls are with him. I'm sure they'll be out soon." Lexa retrieved a bowl for the salad and put it on the large island in the middle of the kitchen. "I invited Jensen Callahan to join us for lunch today, too." She darted a glance at the clock on the wall. "She's been coming to the church lately, and I thought it'd be good for you two to meet."

"The Jensen-of-all-trades for Doyle-Clarke Catering?" Opening the salad, Caty dumped it into a bowl and then pulled out serving utensils from the drawer. "I look forward to it."

"One and the same. I'd better check on my chili." Lexa scooted over to the stove, picked up a long-handled spoon, and began to stir. "Jensen does a fantastic job with booking our events, and she's coordinating all the advertising now. We were more than happy to turn it over to her. Time flies, and she's been with us since before the Albuquerque mission. Winnie and I are so busy with the kids, and

I'm busy writing my book series, that we don't have time to do as much other than overseeing the business."

"Understandable." Caty pulled out a small silver pitcher for the salad dressing. "Do you miss it?"

Lexa sighed. "You know, I do. I know Winnie does, too. We still work a few events here and there, especially for friends. Our staff has grown—both full-time and part-time—and we have an off-site catering kitchen now, four managers, and five delivery vans."

"Awesome blossom," Caty said. "Sounds like it's grown more in the past year or so. How's the New York catering branch coming along?"

"Still building a solid client base. Cassie's doing a great job managing it for us. It's been a huge blessing that Mitch, Amy, and Landon have tons of contacts, so it's growing steadily through lots of referrals."

"Amy and Landon had their baby around the same time as Kevin and Rebekah had their twins, right?" Caty stole a carrot stick from the salad.

"Right. Ava was born two weeks after Elizabeth and Jacob. The latest photos are on the side of the refrigerator. As you might imagine, Ava's gorgeous with tons of dark hair, and she's spunky and smart. She got the best attributes from both Amy and Landon. Sam and I were in New York a few months ago for book tours, and we got together with that side of the TeamWork family. Oh, Mitch and Cassie called a few days ago, and they're expecting their first baby, a boy due sometime in late September. As you can imagine, they're ecstatic and currently trying to agree on his name."

Gnawing away on a second carrot stick, Caty pushed aside thoughts of Caleb, and wondering what he and Lauren were doing this afternoon. "I adore both Amy and Cassie. I'm going to have to meet their illustrious husbands one of these days."

The photograph of Marc and Natalie Thompson and their kids laughing and romping in the snow made her smile. Even though she'd never met Marc, Caty was acquainted with Natalie. Her love story with Marc had touched her deeply. Marc's devotion to his wife after a horrible fall when they were still newlyweds was a strong testament of God's faithfulness. She loved how Sam and his TeamWork crew traveled to Montana to rally around the couple.

Close to Thanksgiving, no less. The close friendships they all shared were rare and precious.

"Marc and Natalie's girls are beautiful," Caty said. "I think you need some more boys in the TeamWork gene pool. I'm glad to hear that Mitch and Cassie are doing their part. I have the feeling Marta and Eliot will have an announcement one of these days, too. Those two have already agreed on names."

"Oh?" Lexa grabbed an oven mitt from the drawer and peeked on the progress of her cornbread. Caty's mouth watered. Lexa's cornbread was one of her favorite things in life. Her recipe had won a few cooking contests.

"Jalapeño?" After plucking a cherry tomato from the salad, Caty popped it into her mouth.

Lexa laughed. "Surely that's not one of the names Marta and Eliot picked out?"

"No, silly woman," Caty teased. "Your cornbread. Henri and Sophie are the names. Subject to change, of course. Hey, I heard about the possibility of Josh running for lieutenant governor in the future. Wouldn't that be something?"

"Yes, and everyone but Josh seems to think it might actually happen."

"Continuing on with the TeamWork roundup, where in the world is Gayle these days?"

"Funny you should ask. Gayle was offered the opportunity to live and work overseas for a year. She left right after the first of the year. It's a very exciting opportunity for her since she's been commissioned to paint a number of family portraits across the European continent. Last time we heard from her, she was in Austria. She lives with a family until their portrait is done, and then she moves on to the next. Kind of a referral thing, but it's a great way to get to know the culture and to get to travel around Europe."

Caty sighed. "Tough job, but someone has to do it, right? She must be very talented."

"She is. Gayle made a portrait of Sam for his early birthday gift and gave it to us before she left. We couldn't wait and unveiled it, and it's hanging in the study. Be sure and stop in to see it while you're here today."

"I'll definitely do that," Caty promised. "What about Sheila and Dean? Angelina and Felipe?" The foursome lived in San Antonio and came to Houston for occasional weekend visits.

Lexa broke into a wide smile. "Sam married Sheila and Dean last month in San Antonio. Angelina gets prettier every day, and Felipe's completely enamored with her. He's doing well and keeping himself out of trouble. Angelina's focusing on her art, and she's encouraging Felipe to work on his stories."

"I'm sure you are, too. Seems there are some wonderful writers in the TeamWork family. It's a talented group of people." Another thought popped into Caty's mind. "Wait a second. Wasn't Felipe living with Dean? I can't help but wonder how that's working out."

"Felipe's living with the pastor and his wife from their church now. They're a lovely older couple. Their children are grown, and they adore Felipe. All things considered, it worked out best for everyone. Sheila doesn't allow Angelina to date one-on-one yet. Felipe knows the rules, and he's going with her to the youth group at the church. They do supervised activities together and are really cute together." Lexa smiled as she stirred the chili again. "I think the time in New Mexico on that mission was the start of another beautiful TeamWork romance., but they have plenty of time."

"Who's in this photo?" A darling, dark-haired young man and woman, dressed in wedding attire, stood on the steps in front of a white church. Fat snowflakes fell around them, and their love for one another was clearly displayed in their clasped hands and the joy in their faces.

Lexa peeked around her shoulder. "That's Ellie and Ryan, the young couple I told you about before. Remember, I told you how Will and Eliot flew to Germany to escort Ryan home after his helicopter was shot down in the war zone in the Middle East?"

"Ah, yes. Are they part of TeamWork now, too?"

A smile curved Lexa's lips. "They have a ministry they started together before they were married. It's called Perchance to Dream, and they provide toys, clothing, and Bibles for kids in the Cleveland area. The ministry's been growing by leaps and bounds each year, and Sam's been talking with Ellie and Ryan about TeamWork coming onboard as a silent partner."

"Hello? Lexa?" They heard a knock on the side door leading into the kitchen. A tall, pretty blonde with long, straight hair appeared at the side door.

"Come in, Jensen. You don't need to knock."

The other woman nodded to Caty and set a grocery bag on the counter. "I picked up saltines and oyster crackers, as well as a few varieties of shredded cheese for chili toppings."

"Jensen, I'd like you to meet Caty, Sam's youngest sister," Lexa said. "Caty, this is Jensen."

"I've heard some wonderful things about your work at Doyle-Clarke Catering," Caty said. "You sound like a native Texan, too."

Jenson's eyes were an unusual shade of pale yellow gold. Honey-colored is probably what it was called. "I'm originally from Justis, a tiny town in the western part of the state."

"Justis," Caty repeated. "Why does that sound so familiar?"

Jensen retrieved small serving bowls from an upper cabinet. She must have spent time in Lexa's kitchen, too. "Our town's claim to fame is a soccer phenom named Dante Moretti. It's all very recent. He just got drafted straight from West Texas A&M to the Italian Soccer League. It's a pretty big deal."

Caty snapped her fingers. "That's it! I saw an interview with Dante on *Good Morning America!* Do you know him? I was very impressed. He seemed quiet but surprisingly humble."

"It's such a tiny town that everyone in Justis knows everybody else." A slight frown creased Jensen's brow as she opened the bags of cheese and began to fill the bowls. "Dante's story is rather tragic, and I'm sure that's part of the draw for the media outlets. His parents and little sister were killed in a plane crash a year or two ago. He was playing in a tournament and their private plane crashed. The whole town rallied around Dante, and we're all rooting for him to make it big in Italy."

"How awful for him, but I wish him the best." Caty swiped another cherry tomato.

"Will Dante be living near Rome or Florence?" Lexa moved back to the stove to check on her chili again.

"He'll be living in Rome. His family's roots are Italian, and I'm sure the ladies will love him. He's a gorgeous man."

"Hi, ladies." Sam walked into the kitchen with blonde-haired Hannah and dark-haired Leah skipping on either side of him. Caty smiled since she often called the four-year-old twins his little shadows.

"If you heard what Jensen just said, we weren't talking about you," Lexa teased.

Sam laughed. "I didn't hear a thing."

"If success doesn't spoil Dante, I'm sure he'll be fine. All things considered, he had a good childhood, and he's a man of faith."

"You must be talking about Dante Moretti," Sam said. "I heard about his story earlier this week. I'll be watching for him in the Italian Soccer League. Sounds like he has a bright future."

"Aunt Caty!" Running to her, the twins wrapped their arms around Caty's waist. She hugged each one of them in turn and then peppered their faces with the silly, noisy kisses they loved. One of the things she'd missed most in living away from Houston was the birth of Joe and then the twins eighteen months later. Although she'd visited them as often as possible, Caty wanted to make up for lost time. They were only this young for such a short time, after all.

After she released them, the girls smiled shyly at Jensen.

"Girls, you remember Miss Jensen from church?" Lexa said.

"You're pretty." Leah beamed at Jensen.

Hannah slipped her hand in Caty's. "You're bee-u-tee-ful, too, Aunt Caty."

Caty squeezed her niece's hand. "Thanks, Hannah Banana."

A short time later, they all sat around the table. The meal of salad, chili, and cornbread was delicious and satisfying. Caty liked how Lexa was a low-stress hostess. Keeping it simple allowed her to sit and enjoy the time around the table with her guests. Joe entertained them with stories of his make-believe space adventures, and the girls chattered away about their latest activities. Lexa answered Jensen's questions concerning ministry opportunities at their church. Caty told them what she could about her new office and a few amusing anecdotes about her co-workers. Joe thought Miles sounded like a cool guy. He was, actually.

After asking the blessing, Sam had seemed content for everyone else to carry most of the conversation. She knew her oldest brother loved Sunday afternoons with his family when he didn't have to deal with the day-to-day responsibilities of the TeamWork office. More than once, Caty caught his loving gaze on his wife. That might explain why Lexa had worn her hair down today. And why Marta had worn red lipstick again today, now that she thought about it. Yes, she could take lessons from her married friends.

Caty declined dessert, and Leah climbed onto her lap with her bowl of vanilla ice cream and fresh strawberries. "I have a new baby doll."

"You do?" Caty pressed a kiss to her niece's dark head. "What's her name?"

"I named her Caty, just like you, and she has black hair like us. Hannah has Lexa, and she has yellow hair. Like Mommy." She darted across the table. "And Miss Jensen, too."

"That's nice, sweetie," Caty said. "Did you get the dolls for your birthday?" The girls had been born on Valentine's Day which always made the date easy to remember.

"Dolls are for sissies." Plopping his elbows on the table, Joe made loud slurping noises as he tried to suck a piece of strawberry through his straw.

"Elbows off the table, Joe." Lexa motioned to him, and he reluctantly obeyed.

"You're sposed to set the sample," Leah reprimanded her brother.

"*Ex*ample," Hannah quietly corrected.

Taking her spoon, Caty swiped a strawberry from Leah's ice cream. Giggling, the little girl picked another piece of fruit from Hannah's bowl and hand-fed it to Caty.

"I used to have a doll," Sam said, sitting back in his chair. "Aunt Caty can tell you."

"Yes, he did have a doll. An Army guy, wasn't it?"

"Air Force," Sam said.

"Of course, it was." Caty tried not to laugh at Joe's expression as he sat up straighter and shoved a huge bite of ice cream into his mouth.

"I think they called it an action figure, but he was awesome," Caty said. "I tried to play with him a few times, but your dad wouldn't let me."

"There's dolls for boys?" Joe shook his head. "Dad, how old were you?"

"Six or seven." Sam smiled at his son. "Your Uncle Will had one, too."

Joe clamped his hands on his cheeks. "No way."

"Dolls aren't so bad, Joe." Sam gave Lexa a wink as he finished his bowl of ice cream with fresh peach slices. Did the man ever eat a meal without peaches?

"If Uncle Will has a *Pursuit* action figure, you're going to get it, aren't you, Joe?"

Caty's question appeared to stump her nephew. "Not sure," he said, lifting his bowl to his mouth. "Maybe I'll just play with my shuttle."

Caty stole another bite of Leah's ice cream so she wouldn't laugh out loud. Life was never dull in this house.

"Joe, did you leave your manners at church today?" Shaking her head, Lexa handed her son a napkin. "Wipe your mouth, please. You don't see your father eating like a horse at the trough."

"I saw Daddy drink out of the milk carton," Joe protested. "At breakfast yesterday."

Lexa's brows lifted and she looked at Sam. "Oh?"

Sam chuckled. "I only drink from the carton when I know I'll finish it. Next time, use the straw for its intended purpose, Joe, especially at the dinner table."

"Yes, Daddy."

"It might be time to put away the straws," Lexa said. Joe's eyes widened at that statement.

After helping Lexa and Jensen clean the dishes, Caty slipped into Sam's study to see the portrait Gayle had painted. It was quite large and occupied a good portion of the side wall. In the painting, Sam was seated on a backless counter stool with his signature black Stetson perched on his right knee. His head was angled to give a glimpse of his face even as he studied his well-worn Bible balanced on his other knee.

"What do you think?" Sam came into the study and stood behind her.

"Gayle captured you well. Isn't this pose similar to the one in your author photo?"

Sam nodded. "I believe that's what she used to paint the portrait. It was a complete surprise. She presented it to us right before she left for Europe. I'm not sure how I feel staring at a picture of myself while I'm working here in the study, but Lexa loves it."

"Stop being so humble and enjoy it," Caty teased. "It's a precious labor of love and, from what I hear, this painting might be valuable one day. Lexa tells me Gayle's work is in demand. You really are the Papa Bear of a terrific group of people, Sam. You've made such an impact on them."

"No more than they've made on me. They're a great group. I'm just their temporary shepherd."

"Yes, but the shepherd guides them. In your case, you help them tap into their unique talents. You mentor them and lead by example. In case I haven't told you lately, I'm proud of you."

After Caty dropped into a chair in front of his desk, Sam sat down beside her. "One of the most gratifying aspects is seeing how they get involved in ongoing TeamWork ministries wherever the Lord's planted them. Fulfilling the mission He's given each one of them."

"They're making a difference," Caty agreed. "Speaking of which, our brothers unexpectedly dropped by the townhome the other night. Carson was pretty impressed by the woman at dinner who approached Will, and I couldn't resist teasing him about that magazine article naming Will"—she held up two fingers to make air quotes—"America's sexiest astronaut. Have you seen it?"

Sam chuckled. "Amy called to tell us about it. She saw the magazine on the newsstand in New York. When she first saw it, she thought it was me on the cover."

"Same here! That's why I had to take a closer look. For one thing, I don't know when I've seen Will smile like that. The article was decent, but it stressed that Will's a confirmed bachelor. I'm sure that angle will make women more determined than ever to meet him and get his attention."

"Will's so focused on the mission right now that he views it as a minor irritation. Something like that won't distract him." Sam shifted in the chair. "Time to talk about you, Caty Bug. How are things going in your new downtown office?"

"They're going well. It's the same job, just a different location, and some new staff from the ones I've worked with before."

Sam nodded. "I'm sure that makes it easier in some respects."

"It does. Mom and Dad have been unpacking more boxes at the townhome for me. I don't know what I'd do without them. I'm getting a gift card to send them to The Grotto for a nice dinner as a small way to say thanks."

"They love helping you out, and I know Mom's ecstatic to have one of her girls back in Houston." Sam smiled. "They also love The Grotto. I'm sure they'll really appreciate it."

"As far as I'm concerned, I'm home to stay."

"I hope so," Sam said. "It's not the same without you here."

Caty started when a loud clap of thunder sounded outside the window, and she moved one hand over her heart. "Oh, that scared me. I wasn't expecting rain today."

Her brother leaned close, elbows on his thighs. "Now, why don't you tell me what's *really* going on?"

Chapter 32

"Come on, Max. Be a good boy."

Caleb watched with faint amusement as Lauren tried to coax the dog from the cushy comfort of the SUV. He wasn't sure why, but he'd parked in the circular driveway by the front door instead of pulling the car into the garage.

"I think he's enjoying his lazy Sunday afternoon nap." Walking closer to the vehicle, Caleb leaned over and peered inside. "You're supposed to be a guard dog, Max. Don't forget that. Come out and...guard us or something."

The dog only gave him a sleepy-eyed look, his tongue hanging out. At least he'd had the foresight to bring along a red plaid blanket and laid it out on the backseat before Max had taken up residence. He'd forgotten how dogs could drool, and Max's output seemed in direct proportion to his large size.

"He'll need to get used to our voices when we give him commands," Lauren said. "And you need to speak in a firm, commanding voice, Dad. Not in a *Hi Max, how are you doing?* way. That's too casual."

"Then I'm putting you in charge of telling me what to do." Caleb frowned. "Within reason."

Having a dog was going to be an interesting experience. Maximillian Lancelot Reid—Max's full title once they got him registered with the American Kennel Club—was three years and four months old in human terms, stood 26 inches tall at the withers, whatever that was, and weighed 112 pounds. The breeder told them that Bullmastiffs were slow growers, so there was a possibility that Max could continue to grow a bit more until he'd be considered fully grown. His color was described as "brindle," the color preferred by gamekeepers who used the dogs in the 19th century to guard estates and capture poachers because of its effective camouflage, especially under the cover of darkness.

"Hey, Max, want to go around back and see the pool? You can swim in it."

"He will *not* swim in our pool," Caleb groused. "Or do anything else in my pool. The pool is for humans only. This isn't a resort and spa, and he's not on vacation. What happened to being firm? We need to let him know who's boss."

"Don't listen to him, Max. He's just being grumpy. Be nice and maybe Dad will build you a doggie pool."

"We've had him less than two hours, Lauren, and you're already spoiling him." He could stand to lighten up a bit, but Caleb didn't want her indulging Max to the point where he got soft. He wasn't a lap dog, and he had a job to do the same as a hired security guard.

As if on cue, thunder rumbled across the sky. Ten minutes ago, it'd been a gorgeous afternoon. They hadn't had any rain in recent days, so they were due. He just hadn't expected it. Great timing.

While Lauren tugged on the leash and alternated between soft endearments and frustrated sighs to try and coax Max to leave the cushy comfort of the backseat, Caleb retrieved the bulging packet of materials and registration paperwork.

They'd managed to drive the fifty miles south of Houston back to the house without any major incidents. Max tried to stand up on the seat early on, but once he seemed to understand he couldn't stretch to his full height, he'd plopped back down. In another instance, he'd made a weird nose.

"Bullmastiffs rarely bark," the breeder had told him. That might be the case, but Max had definitely let out a sigh or something similar. Lauren thought he'd been snoring, but focused on his driving, Caleb hadn't been able to investigate. As long as the dog didn't get carsick…that would be the worst case scenario.

"He won't come out, Dad." With a deep sigh of frustration, Lauren's shoulders sagged and she handed him the leash. "I give up for now. Can you try it? You're good at getting people to do stuff for you, so maybe you can get Max to cooperate."

"I don't know that I'll have any more success than you. Here, hold this folder." Caleb took the brown leather leash wondering how this was going to work. He tugged on it a few times, but nothing worked. Max sat on the back seat, tongue wagging, staring at him. Looked a bit too smug for his liking.

"Okay, so this is how it's going to be, is it?" Another clap of thunder, this one much louder and closer, made him jump. "Enough. You're coming with me." Caleb pulled on the leash. Max must have known he meant business and finally lifted off the seat and emerged from the SUV.

"Yay, Dad. You did it!" Lauren ran ahead of him, punched in the security code, and swung open the front door. "Come on inside, Maxie boy. Let's check out your new home."

"No Maxie boy stuff, either!" he called. "It's Maximillian or Max. We want him to be a fierce guard dog, not a wimp." He hated sounding like a taskmaster, but he needed to set the ground rules from the start.

Once inside the house, Caleb disconnected the leash and curled it in his hand. Glancing around the front hall, his gaze landed on a fancy wall sconce. He'd never liked those things. Now it would serve a worthwhile purpose. He quickly looped Max's leash around it. "There we go."

Lauren clapped. "You go get the stuff out of the car, and I'll take care of getting Max settled."

"Looks like it's going to pour any minute, so I'll pull into the garage. When I bring in the dog food and Max's dish, you should go ahead and feed him now."

"You're putting me in charge of him? Then can he sleep on my bed?"

"Meet me in the kitchen in five minutes, and we'll discuss it. Don't get your hopes up." As he darted back outside and pulled the SUV into the garage, Caleb considered Lauren's questions. Those were only the beginning of what he knew would be many. Maybe they should have discussed some of these things on the way back home, but he'd been preoccupied with thoughts of Caty while Lauren talked to Max. He'd loved listening to her happy chatter. If nothing else, getting the dog was healthy for his daughter's well-being. Max might give her a sense of calm that a regular neighborhood police patrol and top-of-the-line home security system couldn't.

Who was he kidding? Lauren was mad about the situation, but he was the one who needed the security more than she did. There was something to be said for the optimism of youth.

"Dad, can I call Caty?" Lauren said as soon as he closed the garage door and entered the kitchen. Max was sitting on the floor, staring at him, no doubt because the intelligent dog anticipated what he was about to do with the dog food and feeding dishes in his hands.

"Yes, but not until after we take care of Max. Is there something in particular you need to ask her?" Caleb lowered the bag of dog food onto the floor along with the dishes. "You give him some food while I get his water. Remember what the breeder said about food—no more, no less, than what he's supposed to have. And no table scraps. We need Max to be in top form, not get lazy and fat."

"Wow, you're a strict dog daddy." After he stared her down, Lauren giggled. "Okay, but I still love him, and he's a member of our family now." Grabbing the food dish, she started to unzip the bag of food while Caleb carried the water dish to the sink.

Her words *I still love him* resonated with him. His daughter's affections were already involved. Amazing, really, but not in a negative way. Then again, before he'd met Caty, he wouldn't have believed it possible to love someone in such a short period of time.

I love Catherine Lewis.

Standing at the kitchen sink, staring out the window, he smiled. Huh. Why should he surprised by this revelation? In his heart, he'd known it from the start. He'd been through enough in recent years to recognize the difference between fantasy and reality, to distinguish between physical desire and romantic love.

To anyone else, it would sound crazy, but his life had become intertwined with Caty's from the first moment he saw her on the street. He'd stopped the car because God brought her into his range of vision. She was a beautiful woman, but there was more to it than that. A conscious decision to offer his help, if she'd accept it, made him step out of his car that afternoon. Like everything else in his life, the Lord had paved the way, and then offered *him* the choice to follow His ways or reject them.

Lowering his head, Caleb said a quick prayer ending with, *I choose you, Lord. With your help, I want Caty beside me in the journey.* "I ask these things in the name of your Son, Jesus. Amen," he whispered. Then he chuckled. Standing in front of the kitchen window was a place where he could connect with the Father, it seemed. He'd make it a daily habit, beginning every morning during breakfast.

"You're not going crazy on me over there, are you?"

Caleb turned around with a wide smile. "I was praying again. You should try standing in front of this window. I've discovered it's a great place to discover things about yourself. More importantly, it's a great place to pray."

Tilting her head, Lauren eyed him not like he was crazy but...not such a bad father, either. That swelled his heart. Another prayer answered. He darted a glance at Max. He was already halfway through his bowl of food and seemed quite content.

Crossing the room to the kitchen table, Caleb sat beside her. "I choose not to be afraid of these threats. Say the words out loud, Lauren. Say the words with conviction and *mean* them. Know that God will take care of us."

"You mean they might go away?" His daughter's blue eyes searched his.

"They might. But if they don't, it's a conscious decision we're making not to allow anyone or anything to call the shots and rule our lives. That's living in fear, Lauren. God doesn't want us to live in fear, like Caty said. That's defeating and giving into the lies and deceit of the devil."

"The devil? I've never heard you talk about the devil before."

He nodded. "I believe he's out there, and very real—also referred to as Satan, the enemy, and the evil one—and he wants nothing more than to defeat us."

"I remember hearing about the devil in Sunday school. He's the one who tempted Jesus, right?"

"That's right. But Jesus could not be defeated."

"I'm not afraid, Dad, but I choose not to be afraid of the threats. How's that?"

"Lauren, you know God loves you more than anyone else, right? Even more than me, and that's with a ferocity you can't even begin to imagine."

"Ferocity?"

"A whole lot of love."

"Caty talked to me about Jesus the other day," she said. "Even though I asked Jesus to live in my heart a long time ago, when I was really little and we used to go to church, I wasn't...well, I wasn't sure."

"And now?" Why hadn't he talked about these things with his daughter before? Important things, more so than anything else they could have discussed.

"Caty prayed with me even though she told me I didn't need to ask Jesus to live in my heart again if I'd already done it. She said once is all it takes, but I wasn't sure if it *took* or whatever."

"Oh, baby." Tugging her close again, Caleb smoothed one hand over her hair and gently kissed her temple. "Caty's right. All it takes is that one time. There's a verse in Ephesians that says believers are sealed with the Holy Spirit of promise."

He cupped her face between his hands. "I hope I get it right, but there's a verse I remember. It's John 10:27, and it goes like this, 'I give eternal life to them, and they will never perish; and no one will snatch them out of My hand.' The thing is, Lauren, once you put your trust in Christ, you're sealed with Him in an eternity in heaven. He's got you in His hand, and he'll never let you go. Just as I'll never let you go. Never doubt that security."

Lauren nodded, and he could tell she understood what a comfort her decision was for *his* heart. "Mom's in heaven, right?"

"She wasn't outspoken about her faith, but yes, I believe in my heart that she's in heaven. Your mother accepted the Lord when she was in her mid-teens at a summer camp."

"But she never really talked about God even though we went to church."

"A lot of people don't talk about God, either with their kids, or when they're anywhere but in church. For that matter, a lot of people who talk about God in their home raise kids who eventually leave the church and reject God. Parents do the best they can, but there's something called free will, and then there's also the sin nature inside men. But for those people who walk away from His teachings, they might eventually come back to Him one day."

"They'll be in heaven, too. Right?"

"If they made a true profession of faith, confessed their sins, and invited Him to live in their heart, yes. I don't have all the answers, Lauren. No one does. Only God."

"Caty talks about God a lot. She's like the best Christian I know, but it's not like she pushes it down your throat or anything." Lauren's lips curved. "Tell me the truth. Do you love Caty?"

"Are we back at this again? I love *you*."

She smirked. "Answer the question."

Caleb's smile grew wider. "I love everything I know about her, and I care for her a great deal. Put it this way: I could very easily love Caty Lewis." In his heart, he was already there, but he wanted to tell Caty first, not risk having Lauren tell her first, a very real possibility.

"I said I choose not to be afraid for you." Lauren pressed one finger on his shirt. "Say it."

"You drive a hard bargain." Caleb chuckled and shook his head. "Fine. I love Caty Lewis."

"Then you should tell her. Tuesday night when she's here for dinner." Lauren would make a decent lawyer one day if the interpreter thing didn't work out.

"She might think I'm out-of-my-mind crazy."

"Maybe. But I think she's worth the risk." Never taking her gaze away from his, his daughter studied him. "I think she loves you, Dad. She might even already love me just a little bit. I'm going to call her now." Lauren pulled out her phone. "You know that game Eliot put together with clues and stuff for Marta?"

Caleb nodded. He'd seen Lauren reading something on a white piece of paper in church. Preoccupied with thoughts of Caty, he hadn't thought much about it.

"I think I might have an idea how she can solve the first clue—if Marta and Eliot have a dog."

He chuckled. "Go ahead and call Caty then. I'm curious to see how it all works out."

Chapter 33

Caty spilled the story to Sam, every last detail—Caleb was her boss, his connection with Eliot, the initial meeting when Steve Robison stood in for him, the lunch at the Japanese restaurant, Lauren's suspension from the academy and the reason behind it, the trip to the mall, church this morning…

She shared everything with Sam *except* the kidnapping threats. While she hated keeping things from him—and she'd sworn Carson to secrecy about watching out for them at the mall—Caty knew Caleb wouldn't want her to tell anyone, even her closest family members. She understood his reasoning, although more prayer warriors on the case would be even better.

When had her life suddenly become so complicated? No brainer answer on that question—since she'd met Caleb. Now she could better understand his reclusiveness the past few years. The death of his wife must have been devastating, but kidnapping threats might make any man go underground. So many people thought the wealthy led privileged lives with no worries, but Caleb's financial success had only complicated his situation.

Leaning her head against the back of the wingchair, Caty exhaled a long sigh. "Sam, you can't even know how *great* it feels to tell someone else these things! You also have to understand I just violated my Belac contract." When he said nothing, she motioned with one hand. "Well? I'm sure you have a comment. I'm waiting."

"I'm absorbing," Sam said. "That's a lot to happen in the relatively short time you've been back in Houston."

If only you knew.

"Since I've met Caleb. I'm telling you, the man lives larger than life." That was an understatement. Another clap of thunder sounded outside, but this time it made her laugh. "See, even God agrees with me!"

The door of Sam's study flew open and Joe ran toward her. "Phone for you, Aunt Caty. Mom said to bring it to you." After thrusting her cell phone into her hand, the little tornado of energy tore back out of the room.

By the time Caty glanced at the screen, the call had already gone to voice mail. "I don't know who it is. It can wait until later." The phone buzzed again while she still held it in her hand.

"Go ahead and answer it," Sam said. "If it's the same person, they obviously want to speak with you."

Two minutes later, Caty ended the call. "That was Caleb's daughter, Lauren. She sat next to me in church this morning when Marta told us about a game that Eliot's set up for her."

"Game?" Sam sat back in the chair and threaded his fingers together.

"Right, with clues that lead up to a gift or something. You know as well as I do that life with those two is always interesting. Marta shared the first clue with us, and Lauren just told me her idea to solve it."

"Sounds like you've already developed a good rapport with Caleb's daughter," Sam observed. "Bonding with Lauren is a surefire way to encourage the relationship if that's what you want. What's she like other than the smoking incident?"

"She's adorable, but precocious. She's a pretty girl who looks a lot like Caleb except she has her mother's blue eyes. I never know what she's going to say next, and she seems to like saying things for shock value."

"Probably seeking her dad's attention," Sam said. "They've both had a lot going on in their lives the past few years. I'm sure she's trying to find her way, especially with the move to Houston after she's lived in Dallas her entire life. Kids that age have a lot going on without losing a mother and being uprooted."

"That's more or less what I thought, too, and what I shared with Caleb."

Sam nodded. "A lot of people can't see what's in front of them because they're too close to the situation. It impairs their judgment and rationale. Even someone as smart as Caleb. I'm not saying it was a wrong move. Obviously, he's extremely intelligent to have achieved such a high level of success in the oil industry."

"Sounds like our brother Will." Caty shared a smile with Sam.

"Caty, if you don't mind my armchair observation, I think you've fallen in love with Caleb."

Her older brother's statement momentarily stunned her. "I can tell you there are definitely things I admire about him. He's a strong man in many ways yet vulnerable in others. He's relatable and flawed. He's an excellent father, alternately strict and lenient, and he's trying to find a balance. Caleb's funny when he lets down his guard, and he can laugh at himself. He's also surprisingly down-to-earth for someone who's achieved so much at a young age…"

Caty stopped and met Sam's gaze. "Okay, Sam. Yes, as crazy as it seems because I haven't known him long at all, not to mention he's my boss—which is like one of the biggest taboos in the corporate world—I am *falling in love* with Caleb Reid." She raised her hands. "There, I admitted it. Happy?"

"Yes." Sam's deep smile lines emerged. "I hope you can introduce Caleb and Lauren to the family at some point."

"Let's see what happens first. If anything even happens."

"Sounds to me like it already has," Sam said, his smile still in place. "Technically, I was Lexa's boss when we first met. There are people who can't believe lasting love can happen quickly, but a few of my TeamWork couples can testify to that—Landon and Amy, Mitch and Cassie, and your friends Marta and Eliot most recently, although those two had known each other a few years but never spent much quality time together until the mission in Albuquerque."

"Any theories on why that is? The falling in love quickly part?"

He considered her question for a moment. "I think when two people are in God's will and open to the possibilities—meaning they're able to set aside their own pride and selfish ambition—it can happen. Of course, physical attraction is part of that initial draw toward someone else. When neither party wants to play the relationship games prevalent in today's culture, and both acknowledge a common desire to serve the Lord. But that's the beginning, the easy part. From that point on, both need to make a commitment to nurture that love.

"They have to give the relationship time to grow and flourish, to blossom into a full-fledged, abiding love. I'm talking about beginning with day one and continuing from that point forward. It's a continual, evolving process, where marriage comes into play somewhere in the journey. After three kids and almost ten years since we first met, I'm more in love with Lexa than before. You add kids, church, work, and everything else into the mix, and there are times when you're too exhausted to do much of anything but pass each other coming and going. Lexa and I work hard to keep the spark going, but it's worth it all. I'm sure Mom and Dad could give you the long-term perspective."

Caty nodded. "They're my inspiration, just like you and Lexa. I guess I've always thought Mom and Dad's story was so romantic and special because it developed over time, the idea of being friends first that slowly developed into something more. And, I suppose I thought that's the way it would happen with me."

"That's true, but there's something else to remember about their relationship," Sam said. "Because Dad was a few years older than Mom, he looked at her like a younger sister for years. But after he'd been overseas flying with the Air Force, and then returned home to Rockbridge, he saw her through the eyes of a more mature man. A man who was looking to find a wife and settle down."

"And, by that time, Mom had grown up to become a woman he found irresistible."

"Exactly." Sam's eyes softened, and he reached for her hand. "Dad had the *moment*. That moment when he knew Mom was the woman God intended for him."

"Although most of the town thought he should marry Aunt Tess."

"Right," Sam agreed. "But God knew that Uncle Charlie was the right man for her. And He led Dad to move to Austin with Mom so she could pursue her dream of becoming a nurse."

"Love is not self-seeking or self-serving." Caty smiled. "With all that said, Sam, are you saying you believe Caleb is the right man for me?"

Sam strengthened his grip on her hand. "I'm saying I believe he *could* be, but only the Lord knows. Let's pray about it."

"That's the best idea yet."

Chapter 34

"Mr. Reid?"

"This is he." The voice was female, non-threatening. The phone call had come through on his private home landline. He darted a glance at the clock. Almost eight o'clock. Where was Lettie? She should be home by now.

"This is Rhonda Billings, Lettie's sister in Dallas."

"Yes, of course." He closed his eyes with a sense of foreboding. "Is everything okay?"

"I'm sorry to tell you, but my sister's had an accident. Nothing serious, but it will delay her coming back to Houston."

Caleb opened his eyes. "What kind of accident? Is she all right?" Lettie was one of the safest drivers he'd ever known. Over and over, she'd reminded *him* to watch the posted speed limits, especially after he'd bought the Porsche. She'd thought he was going through an early midlife crisis. Then he'd taken her for a ride, and she'd changed her tune.

"A few scrapes and bruised ribs, but she's fine otherwise," Rhonda told him. "Nothing broken and no internal bleeding, thank goodness. The doctor said she was lucky for a woman her age."

"That's a relief. I'm thankful she wasn't hurt worse. Do you have any details? Know how it happened?"

"She was driving back to the house from the grocery store earlier today, and her car ran off the road and veered into a ditch." A long pause ensued on the line. "There's something else, Mr. Reid. Lettie didn't want me to say anything, but I feel you have the right to know."

His head throbbed. "Tell me."

"The police believe she was purposely run off the road by another driver."

Curling his right hand into a fist, Caleb lowered it to his desk. He could read between the lines to know what Rhonda *wasn't* telling him—she believed the accident was no fluke. Neither did he. It was purposeful with the intent to scare her, and to send *him* a message.

Lord, she's an older woman. Who would *do* such a thing?

"For the sake of my sister's health and well-being, I hope you can understand that I'd like to keep her here until things smooth over," Rhonda said. "Of course, Lettie's fighting me on that decision, but I'd feel a lot better if I can keep an eye on her."

"I understand, and thanks for letting me know. Give Lettie our love and tell her to take as long as she needs. If you don't mind, I'd like to come to Dallas with Lauren and pay her a visit later this week."

"Lettie would love that, I'm sure."

"I'll have Cordelia call you with the details sometime tomorrow. Thanks again."

As soon as he hung up the phone, Caleb left a message on Cordelia's voice mail at the office. "Cordelia, order a dozen yellow roses and have them sent to Lettie at her sister's house in Dallas. You should have the address. If not, let me know, and I'll get it for you. Have them delivered as early as possible tomorrow morning. Next, I'll need a rundown of my schedule for the coming week. I also need to schedule the plane to fly to Dallas with Lauren sometime later this week, whatever seems to work. Thanks. See you soon."

He'd called Eliot to tell him about the incident with Lettie, but no doubt being in the early morning abroad, he'd left a voice mail message.

Not long after, Caleb slipped into the Jacuzzi and adjusted the settings. Stretching out his arms, he leaned back and closed his eyes as the pulsating jets massaged the cramps and knots in his stressed muscles. Once they'd gotten Max settled, and he felt fairly confident the dog wouldn't tear up the house, he'd been able to get a workout in the pool. Lauren had joined him, and they'd played a few water games.

The night was quiet except for the light rustling of the wind through the trees. He glanced up at the house, dark except for the hall light upstairs. Houston was beginning to feel like home in spite of everything else, a blessing in itself.

Thinking about Caty and their growing relationship was a comfort...to a point. Lying in his bed the night before, he'd thought a lot about her. Pure thoughts for the most part until they'd ventured into dangerous territory—wondering what she'd feel like in his arms, thinking of the softness of her lips and how they'd felt on his, remembering her touch… When he envisioned Caty's tousled hair on that pillow, the length of her stretched out beside him, he knew he needed to get a grip on his emotions and his thought life. He'd learned long ago to put a block on his cable television and not to have any magazines or reading material that could pollute his mind with impure images.

He was a man, and he was weak. Although he'd abstained from anything improper since her death, he'd indulged in premarital relations with Helena. The guilt had eaten away at him for years. They'd both willingly engaged in reckless behavior, and he'd wondered at times why she hadn't already been pregnant when they'd married. He'd discounted the insinuations from his friends that she'd tried to "trap" him into marrying her. Yes, he'd been blinded by his physical desires, but they'd had a good marriage for a few years before everything started to go south. Not that his guilt had prompted him to marry her. He'd loved her, but in his way of thinking, he'd atoned for his sin by putting a ring on Helena's finger and doing the right thing in the eyes of man and God.

Only in the past few years had he finally accepted God's forgiveness for his sexual weakness. By the grace of God, he'd resisted the ongoing sexual temptation. But he'd also given himself too much credit. When it came down to his most basic, primal instincts, it was all God who'd saved him from his own sinful actions. God and God alone.

Thank you, Jesus.

Crawling out of bed, Caleb had gone into the bathroom for a brisk cold shower. And then he'd prayed for a long time. The Lord would have to forgive his thoughts, and he'd confessed them. The Lord knew better than anyone how much Caleb missed being married. Missed the companionship, the physical intimacy, the private times of talking and sharing. The loneliness was always worse in the middle of a restless night, lying in the empty bed, staring at the empty pillow beside him.

Sitting in the Jacuzzi now, he needed to stop feeling sorry for himself or he'd repeat the same routine as the night before. He needed to stop thinking about Caty Lewis.

Business.

Right. He'd think about the corporation. Good. That should keep his mind occupied and his thought life straight.

The idea to remove tobacco sales from his Reidco convenience stores had been simmering on the back burner for months. A radical move, he was more convinced than ever this was the right thing to do, especially since Lauren's smoking incident. How did he know the cigarette she'd smoked hadn't come from one of his own stores? That pierced his conscience. How many other people got hooked on cigarettes after buying them from Reidco?

As a matter of personal conviction, they'd never sold alcohol or pornographic magazines. He'd been widely criticized by his competitors, but it hadn't hurt his business. A large majority of his faithful customers respected that stance and proved their loyalty with their patronage and dollars. Now maybe it was time for the next step. He'd made more money than he'd need in a lifetime, and not that he was out to save the world, but what did a potential loss of revenue matter compared to the health of his customers?

"Lord, can I do this?" He prayed and laid the decision at the foot of the cross. This was the right thing to do, he could feel it in his gut. He'd always trusted his instincts, and now that he was back on track and praying again, Caleb knew in his heart that the Lord would honor and bless the decision.

By the time he pulled himself out of the Jacuzzi, he'd resolved to call a meeting of the board for late in the week. Sitting on the side of the pool, he smoothed his wet hair away from his face and then leaned back on the heels of his hands. Sure, he'd face an onslaught of criticism, no doubt from some members of the board, shareholders, and perhaps a few Belac officers. They should know by now their objections wouldn't daunt or stop him once he'd made up his mind.

No, Caleb, you're not the ultimate boss. True enough. He was only the caretaker of what God had entrusted to him. To the best of his ability, he'd do his job. Even so, he couldn't deny there were definite perks to being the boss.

A smile creased his face as Caleb dried off with his towel, grabbed his bottle of mineral water, and headed back into the house.

If anyone wanted a fight, then he'd give it to them.

Chapter 35

"Caleb, Mr. Robison is here to see you."

He nodded. They didn't have an appointment, but Steve was one of the few people who didn't need one. "Sure. Send him in, please."

Cordelia had never liked Steve. She was respectful, and although she'd never said anything, her tone and expression belied her true feelings.

Steve strolled into the office, and Cordelia closed the door behind him.

"Good morning, Steve. Did you get my email?"

The other man dropped into a chair. "About the tobacco ban? Yes. That was a surprise, and I can't say that I agree."

"I knew you wouldn't. I'm sure I'll have a battle on my hands with the board, but it's one I'm willing to fight."

Steve's face was serious and expressionless as always. He could stand to smile every now and then. "Caleb, where's this decision coming from?"

"I've been thinking about it for a while, and it's time to implement the change."

"I'm sure you realize this is more than a simple, uncomplicated change," Steve said. "I'm not sure you have a full grasp of the significant amount of revenue generated by the tobacco sales. I'd venture to say they're upwards of thirty-five to forty percent in some of the West Texas Reidco convenience stores, maybe higher. They're second only to the oil revenue. I'll be happy to provide sales reports to back up that statement if you'd like. I'm sure you're aware that Reidco is our most valuable entity."

"Of course, I am." Caleb shook his head. "I reviewed the up-to-date sales reports early this morning. The percentage is actually closer to thirty-seven percent across the board." He'd been prepared for this discussion. "This decision isn't based on revenue."

Steve planted both hands on the arms of the chair, his knuckles white. "Then why don't you tell me what it *is* about?"

"It's about taking a stand against sales of a product that could potentially harm our customers."

Steve snorted. "That description could fit any number of things we sell in the stores. We're not forcing anyone to buy anything."

Caleb steepled his fingers and breathed out a deep sigh. "True, but the reports with figures of how many people become addicted to tobacco products each year, and how many *die* from lung or mouth cancers due to those products every year, overwhelmingly support my decision that it's the worst thing we can sell."

"Since when is that our problem, Caleb?"

"Not our problem that people are becoming addicted to tobacco products from something they buy at a Reidco station?"

Steve met his gaze. "That's stretching it. You can't be responsible for someone else."

"That's true, but if I can prevent one kid from getting addicted to cigarettes, or prevent one pregnant woman from inhaling nicotine, then I can sleep better at night."

"Isn't that being overdramatic?"

Caleb sat back in his chair. "Perhaps, but it's called going with my gut, doing the right thing, following God's leading, and keeping my conscience clean."

Steve removed his glasses and cleaned them with the corner of his suit coat before speaking again. "Know what I think? You're allowing a skirt to sway your business decisions. You've gone soft, and that's not the Caleb Reid I've known and admired all these years."

Tamping down his anger, Caleb forced calm into his tone. "This has nothing to do with Catherine Lewis if that's what your lewd insinuation is meant to imply. I'll ask you not to disrespect her, or me, by saying things like that. It's enough that she forgave me for that ridiculous impersonation trick we pulled on her the first day she came to the office."

Steve's forehead creased, and his lips thinned. "Try to see it from my perspective. You've been in hiding since your wife died, and now all of a sudden you're parading around with the Lewis woman like some stupid college kid in the throes of his first affair. And, as long as I've known you, you've rarely mentioned God, much less making him some kind of partner in Belac. It's good to see you smile again, but all I'm saying is…don't be blind and foolish."

"First of all, I'm not having an affair with Catherine Lewis. If I hear anything to that effect, I'll start eliminating people from the payroll. Is that understood?"

Steve held his gaze. "Yes, sir."

"The decision to remove the tobacco sales has nothing to do with her." Neither did he want to divulge anything regarding Lauren and the kidnapping threats. That was no one's business but his. The less people who knew, the better. "Furthermore, Miss Lewis has nothing whatsoever to do with the ledger discrepancies. I'd stake my reputation on it."

"Then be prepared to have that reputation sullied by your poor decisions and bad judgment."

Caleb sighed. *Lord, give me the words. Keep my patience in check.* "Her work record has been excellent for the five years she's worked for Belac and Reidco. As far as God being a partner in Belac, look at Him as a silent partner. He's going to be around a lot more often. Steve, talk to me. We've worked together a long time. Tell me why you suspect her of falsifying records."

"Because she has the ways and the means to do it. She has something to prove perhaps."

Caleb stared at the other man, unwilling to believe what he'd heard between the lines of that statement. Caty was one of the few female accountants working for Belac, and the only woman in the Reidco division. "That's all the proof you have? Because she's a woman or for some other reason?"

The muscles in Steve's jaws flexed. "Don't accuse me of sexism."

"I didn't imply that. *You* did." Caleb sat back in his chair. "This meeting is over. I'm having Cordelia schedule the quarterly board meeting for Thursday morning, and I plan to announce the withdrawal of tobacco sales. I'm pulling rank on this one, and I'll expect you in the meeting. Thanks for your time." Caleb turned his attention to the computer screen to indicate his dismissal.

Steve rose slowly from the chair. "You built this company by being smart, Caleb. Don't tear it down by acting stupid over a woman and allowing your emotions and physical desires to take over your business decisions."

Caleb looked at Steve and felt nothing but pity. "I don't want to let you go at this stage of the game, but I will if your behavior warrants it, and if I feel it's necessary. You've got one foot over the edge of the cliff as it is, Steve. I don't want to hear you say—so much as *hint* of anything improper—about Miss Lewis again. Are we understood?"

Without another word, Steve left the office.

~~♥~~

In the breakroom, Caty stirred cream into her coffee. She smiled, thinking of Marta's reaction to Lauren's clue-solving ability.

"That girl is brilliant!" Marta proclaimed after she'd checked Barney's collar. "Lauren was exactly right. Barney's collar has a locket, and the second clue was written on a piece of paper folded up inside it. Here's what it says: It's NOT TICKING, BUT IT'S PRECIOUS TO THE TEAMWORK CREW.

Caty wondered if the answer to that clue could be as deceptively simple as Sam's old, white Volvo station wagon, affectionately nicknamed by Lexa as "the bomb." The car he'd driven for years for missions, including the 1997 mission in San Antonio where he'd met Lexa.

Sensing someone else had entered the breakroom, Caty glanced up and met the hard gaze of Steve Robison. "Good morning, Mr. Robison." She'd managed a pleasant tone although she couldn't quite muster a smile.

"Miss Lewis." With his coffee mug in hand, he walked to the coffee maker. His appearance was a surprise since she assumed his assistant usually delivered coffee to him.

Stepping aside to make room for him at the counter, Caty debated whether to take her leave. What could she say? The man had worked for Caleb a long time, and he trusted him. Steve obviously didn't trust *her*.

"I hope everything is going well for you." She added a packet of sweetener to her coffee since her first sip had been stronger than the usual brew. Suma normally made the coffee, but someone else must have made it this morning.

"No, it's not, as a matter of fact." His voice was low, controlled, and could in no way be construed as friendly. His facial features were expressionless.

She looked up at him in surprise. "I'm sorry to hear that."

Brushing up beside her, he put one hand on her arm, applying firm pressure. "Caleb might be fooled by your charms, but I'm not."

Caty swallowed her gasp, but Steve Robison had already departed.

"Caleb, Miles Durand is here to see you."

"Right." Caleb sat back in his chair. What a day, and it was only ten a.m. He didn't want to see Miles at the moment. He wanted to see Caty so she could reassure him that the world hadn't indeed gone crazy. He was flying to Dallas with Lauren on Wednesday to see Lettie and staying overnight, then returning early on Thursday morning in time to drop off Lauren at Greenbriar-Browne. Shortly afterwards, he'd walk into his board meeting where he'd announce the decision to discontinue all tobacco sales in the Reidco convenience stores. He was still the one in control of his corporation, and he'd assert his authority for the decision. He would not accept a vote or a compromise. His decision was final.

"For what it's worth, in my opinion, you're doing the right thing regarding the tobacco sales," Cordelia said, breaking into Caleb's thoughts. She stepped closer to his desk. "Do you have any idea how much I admire you?"

Caleb glanced up at her with grateful eyes. "No, I guess not. Thanks for that. I already sent through the paperwork for your latest raise, by the way." His assistant rarely got overly sentimental. Was she about to start now? Still, he appreciated her words.

Cordelia laughed. "That's not why I said it, and you know it. Don't let it get around, but I'd probably work for free. You've been very generous through the years, and my family has benefitted greatly from your generosity."

"You deserve every bit of what I pay you and more. For the moral support if nothing else."

"Caleb, not that this has anything to do with it, but I'm one of the few people other than your personal accountant who knows you pour the majority of your personal profits from the tobacco sales into the cancer center for Helena."

"Let's keep it that way. Ironic, though, isn't it?" Sitting back in his chair, Caleb stretched his arms high above his head. "I'm taking sales from cancer-inducing cigarettes and other tobacco products and donating them to a research hospital named after my late wife to *prevent* cancer and to treat cancer victims. Doesn't matter what type of cancer, but the principle's the same. That's the reason I haven't pulled the products from sale before now." He lowered his arms and crossed them over his chest. "That's a whole lot of funding."

Cordelia's expression softened. "Your motives have always been honorable, and I know how many other fundraisers you've done for cancer awareness, but I'm curious. Why *now*, Caleb? What finally prompted you to make this decision?"

He looked at her for a lingering moment. The answer was simple. "I'm finally learning to give it all to God and know He'll take care of the details. That money was never mine in the first place, Cordelia. I'll still pour money into the cancer center, but it'll have to come from another source. My own pocket, if necessary. I'll figure out something."

She nodded. "You have other investors for the cancer center, of course, but it's a *good* decision, Caleb. God will bless you for it, I have no doubt. Everything will work out. I'm glad you spoke with Eliot on Friday, and I'm relieved you and Lauren have Max. And"—Cordelia's eyes sparkled as she started to take her leave—"I'm thankful you have Caty. She's a wonderful young woman."

"And I'm thankful I have you." That was an understatement. "Don't ever leave me." He pushed up in his chair again. "Okay, now. Enough of this mutual admiration society. Please tell Miles to come in."

"Of course. I'll send him right in." With a parting smile, Cordelia quietly left the room.

"Hey, Mr. Reid. Thanks for agreeing to meet with me, sir. I appreciate it." Caleb suppressed his smile as the young guy practically bounded into the office. The kid had enthusiasm, he'd give him that much.

"Don't mention it, Miles. Have a seat and tell me what's on your mind." He'd checked the personnel file. Miles was twenty-two, still lived at home, and he was taking business courses at night from one of the local universities. Made good grades and showed promise. Miles had worked for the Houston office for two years. Picking up the Rangers baseball, Caleb began to knead it with his fingers.

"I have some forward-thinking ideas for the corporation. I won't take much of your time, but I'd like to discuss them with you." Miles put a plain manila file folder on top of the desk and opened it. "I had to write them down to keep them straight and in some kind of order."

Caleb's mind wandered a bit as he listened to his young employee. In some ways, Miles reminded him of himself when he'd started the corporation—full of energy, eager to learn, lots of ideas, some valid and others ready for the garbage pile. This was a vastly different mentality than Steve Robison presented. Steve was old school. He needed fresh ideas like Miles presented. He needed positivity surrounding him, not negativity.

"In closing," Miles said, recapturing Caleb's full attention, "I'll leave this folder with you to look over. If you have any questions, feel free to let me know."

"I'll be sure and do that." Caleb opened the folder and perused it a moment. "I like your ingenuity and loyalty to Belac. I'm glad you came to see me today, Miles…" *Wait a second.*

"You bet." As Miles rose to leave, Caleb quickly reread one entry.

"Hold on just a second. Can you tell me more about this entry?" Flipping the folder around on the desk, he pointed to one of the items on the list. "Explain this one to me, please."

Miles leaned closer. "Oh, yes. I hope you don't mind, but there are certain people in the company who seem to be using the company interoffice system to send personal gifts. I know I'm not in charge of the mailroom—and I don't mean to overstep my bounds—but I can tell they're sort of valuable. If anything got lost, misplaced, or God forbid, stolen, who do you think the first person would be to get the finger of blame for theft?" Miles jabbed a finger at his chest. "Me, that's who. The low man on the seniority list, and the expendable one."

"Sit down, Miles." Caleb softened his tone when he saw the fear in the kid's eyes. "You're not in trouble, I assure you."

"Okay then, sir." He returned to his chair and fidgeted.

"Are multiple employees sending gifts to one another or would you say it's mostly the same people?"

"One person, but he's sent things to some of the women here in the office."

"Did this start before or after I transferred here to the Houston office?"

"Before." Miles lowered his gaze. "Although the envelopes came from the Dallas office."

"I'm going to ask you to give me names, Miles. This information could be significant to me personally as well as the corporation. But this needs to remain between the two of us, and no one else. Do I have your word?"

Miles nodded and raised his right hand as though in a courtroom. "Yes, sir. I understand, and I solemnly swear, so help me God. You have my word."

Chapter 36

As expected, Oliver arrived at Caty's townhome on Tuesday evening. She felt silly giving him the password *Scrappy*, but he'd smiled and offered his arm before escorting her to a waiting black Cadillac Escalade. How many vehicles *did* Caleb own?

"Do you go by Oliver or do some call you Ollie? What should I call you?" Caty settled back into the plush leather backseat.

"Whatever you wish, Miss Lewis. I go by either name."

"Hang on just a second, Ollie." Opening the door, Caty hopped out, closed the door, and then scooted into the front passenger seat. "This is much better." She blanched. "Unless you'd rather I *not* sit up here. I guess I should have asked first." She was being forward, but she hated sitting in the back and being driven by someone paid to do it.

"Not at all." A wide smile creased the older man's smile. He was a rather large man, mid-sixties or so, she estimated, with a kind face and a calm demeanor. "It's my honor to have your company."

"Call me Caty, please. How long have you worked for Mr. Reid?"

"Ten years. I was originally hired as Mrs. Reid's driver."

"I see." Caty didn't feel comfortable asking questions about Helena. "I understand you drive Lauren to the academy?" Lauren had mentioned Oliver, calling him Ollie, during their shopping expedition. She knew he'd never married and lived in a guest cottage on the property. One of his hobbies was horticulture, and now he tended to the garden planted by the home's previous owner.

"That's right." He hummed a tune under his breath and darted a glance her way. "Except when Miss Reid was suspended most recently."

Caty nodded. "Lauren's a very spirited girl, and I'm sure she keeps her father busy."

"She's got a good heart," Oliver said. "As does Mr. Reid. I've enjoyed working for him."

"How long will it take to reach the house? I have no idea where he lives."

Oliver smiled. "That must be the grown-up version of *are we there yet?*"

"You caught me," Caty admitted. "I'm nervous, Ollie. Going to the man's home for dinner is a big step. *Huge.*" She hadn't even told her parents although she'd told Sam and Marta.

"No reason to be nervous." Oliver continued to hum as he turned onto the highway.

"Not to interrupt, but what is that tune you're humming? It sounds familiar."

"It's called 'Younger Than Springtime' from *South Pacific.*"

"Aha! That explains it. My mom adores musicals. I think 'Some Enchanted Evening' was her favorite song from that movie. Do you know that one?"

"I do, as a matter of fact." He punched a succession of buttons on the dashboard. The strains of the familiar song began to play, and Oliver began to sing in a quiet, smooth tenor. "…And somehow you know…somewhere you'll see her again and again."

Caty smiled. "There's such a sweet longing, an innocence, in that song, don't you think?"

"Yes," he agreed. "The song speaks to a simpler time, when love is fresh and new."

Love is fresh and new indeed. The sentiment seemed fitting.

Glancing out the tinted side window as the music continued, Caty snapped mental snapshots of their surroundings. The traffic was moderate, and the surroundings grew increasingly more elite and upscale as they neared their destination.

Twenty minutes after they'd left her townhome, Oliver pulled through black wrought iron gates and parked in a circular driveway in front of a large, stately, three-story red brick home with a three-car garage.

After helping her from the Escalade and escorting her to the front door, Oliver turned to leave. "I'll be around later to transport you back home."

"You're very kind. Thank you." On a whim, she kissed his cheek.

"Enjoy your evening, Caty."

"Thanks, Ollie." Was that a twinkle in the man's blue eyes?

Lauren answered the door wearing a bright green kimono. That was a surprise. Bowing low, she said something in Japanese before speaking in English. "Good evening. We've been expecting you."

"Are we having Japanese tonight? I dressed for comfort and look more like I'm ready to go out and do some two-stepping." Caty glanced down at her white eyelet skirt, red cotton blouse, and favorite denim jacket. Knowing Caleb liked her red cowgirl boots, she'd worn them, as well.

"No, I just wanted to see the look on your face," Lauren said. "I told Dad we should make you eat liver with chopsticks."

"Very funny. You don't dislike me *that* much, do you?" Caty stepped inside the grand foyer and Lauren closed the front door behind her. She tried not to gape in awe at the luxurious home, one of the most elegant she'd ever been inside except for the home tours she'd taken. This was the kind of home that probably had a home theater and a popcorn machine. Maybe a pool in the backyard.

"Nope. I kind of love you."

Caty turned her head and did a double take. Did Lauren say *love?* Before she could respond, Lauren asked for her jacket.

"I'll keep it with me for now if that's all right."

"Certainly. Follow me, please, Miss Lewis. Your table is waiting." She giggled and motioned for Caty to follow as they walked past the living room and formal dining room.

Although elegant and tastefully furnished in muted earth tones, the house wasn't yet fully decorated. Caty would never say as much to Caleb, but the rooms could use a woman's touch to lend more warmth and personality, not to mention some much needed splashes of color.

"We decided to be informal tonight," Lauren explained. "We haven't used the dining room yet, but it's stuffy and formal, anyway. Dad figured we'd eat in the kitchen, like a family."

Caty swallowed her surprise. "I see." Not that the mentions of *love* and *family* intimidated her, but they were unexpected. "Where's Max tonight?"

Hearing a noise behind her, the next moment, Caty was flat on her back on the hardwood floor, somewhere between the dining room and what she assumed was the kitchen at the back of the house. Dizzy, she brought one hand to her forehead. "What just happened?"

"You met Max." Caleb leaned over her, concern in his eyes. "I'm afraid my bodyguard dog knocked the wind out of you. I'm sorry, Caty. If it helps, I think he likes you. I had Lauren take him to the backyard."

Caty struggled to sit up and propped herself on her elbow. She had to take this in stages. Being knocked out was a brand new sensation she'd never experienced before. "Are you…wearing a tuxedo or am I imagining this entire thing?"

"Rest for a minute." Caleb shrugged out of his jacket and then rolled it into a ball. "Here. Put this under your head." With gentle care, he lifted her head and slid the makeshift pillow beneath her.

"Thank you, kind sir. How do you figure Max likes me?"

"Well, for one thing, you're still intact and have all your original working body parts." His cheeks colored. "At least I think—"

"One hundred percent natural girl here, Cowboy Abe, but you'll have to take my word for it." Maybe Helena had undergone plastic surgery? A lot of wealthy women in Texas with money had enhancements.

Trying to focus, Caty squeezed her eyes closed. How had this conversation even started?

Opening her eyes again a few seconds later, she avoided looking at him. "How long do you figure I'll need to stay here supine on the floor?"

He chuckled. "You must be okay if you're using a word like supine. I thought it was prone or prostrate."

"No, no," she said. "Prone is lying face down. Supine is lying with your face in an upward position."

Caleb shook his head with an irresistible smile. "You've got me beat on that one."

"Not really. You see, supine is the word that broke my perfect record with vocabulary tests in fifth grade. I'm weird. Things like that stick in my mind."

With a start, Caty's eyes grew wide. She fumbled for the hem of her skirt. Of all nights to wear a shorter skirt! She'd smack her forehead if that wouldn't lift her skirt higher again. Had she left herself open to humiliation? The hem of her skirt seemed to be where it should be, and she blew out a sigh of relief.

"No worries. Your modesty is intact. I already knew you had great legs."

"Please, Caleb," she groaned. "I'm embarrassed enough as it is. This floor will open up and swallow me whole now, right?"

He raised his hands. "I'm only stating fact. I like your outfit. You know I really like your red boots, and the—"

"Stop right there!" Holding up one hand, Caty mock glared at him. "Don't you dare say I look *cute* or like I'm ready for a hoedown, hootenanny, barn dance, or a shindig."

"I wouldn't dare. Spectacular as your suits are, it's a nice change to see you in something else. For instance, your dress on Sunday singlehandedly changed my opinion of the color brown."

She laughed. "That's quite enough compliments, but thank you. I appreciate them."

When she tried to sit up, Caleb planted a firm hand on her shoulder. "I'll help you get up in just a minute. For now, humor me and take another minute to catch your breath."

Little could Caleb know it wasn't only Max jumping on her that knocked the breath out of her. The master of the house had every bit as much to do with it.

Lowering to the floor, Caleb stretched out beside her, resting on his side, propped on one elbow—crisp white dress shirt, black bow tie, cuff links. Her gaze traveled the length of him down to his feet. Barefoot?

"You seem to have forgotten your socks and shoes."

"Lauren thought it would be fun for me to dress like this and play the role of your server during dinner. And I wholeheartedly embraced the idea." Leaning across her, Caleb planted his hand on the other side of her. She couldn't escape if she wanted, but why would she *want* to?

"That still doesn't explain the bare feet."

Caleb's lips curled. "Are you complaining?"

"No, but your cowboy boots might be a nice touch." Why were they talking about footwear or lack thereof? Her pulse spun out of control. "You seem to like pinning me down. Should I worry about your intentions?"

"Quiet, please. You're obviously delirious."

"I think I might just be."

"Shhh." He brushed his lips over hers. Gentle. Completely in control yet enough to drive her out-of-her-mind crazy. "Welcome to our home. I'm glad you could come."

"Me, too. I'm glad to be here, but if this is the way you greet all your guests, I might have cause to worry."

"Only a beautiful, honored guest named Catherine Grace Lewis."

Oh, my. She enjoyed Caleb's playful side and adored flirting with him. With a smile, she patted one hand on his cheek. "Enough with the flattery. Now that the handsome prince has given me a kiss, it's time for me to get up now. Apparently, the floor in your home can be dangerous."

Chuckling, he helped her to her feet. "Better me kissing you than Max."

"Agreed," she said. "You don't drool nearly as much, either."

Taking her by the hand, Caleb led her into the kitchen and pulled out a chair. Caty glanced around the large room, admiring the stone floor and beamed ceilings, and its state-of-the art fixtures and countertops. The dinner table was covered in a white linen tablecloth, set with fine china and silver, and a single candle was lit beside a vase with fresh peach-colored roses.

"This is beautiful. I'm getting special treatment tonight." Caleb pulled out a chair, and she took a seat. "How's Lettie doing?"

"Improving," Caleb said. "She's being stubborn as usual and is insisting on coming back sooner than later. Lauren and I are flying to Dallas late tomorrow and staying the night."

A frown creased Caty's brow. "I hate to bring it up, but do you think there's a connection between what happened—"

"I do, but what good is worrying about it? Lettie's sister is right. I'm going to insist she stay in Dallas until we know what's happening."

Caty turned more serious. "Steve Robison spoke with me in the breakroom yesterday morning, Caleb. He had a few choice words. If I didn't know it before, I know now that the man doesn't trust me." When Caleb didn't answer immediately, she glanced up at him. "You knew?"

He tipped his head. "Steve shared his suspicions with me. Then I called Eliot. He's in Europe on an assignment, but he talked with me for a few minutes."

"Did he have any helpful suggestions?"

"He believes Steve might be involved or else he really doesn't like you, I'm sorry to say."

Caty's mouth went dry. "Do you mind getting me a glass of water?"

"Where are my manners? I'm sorry." Caleb quickly grabbed a glass, and then he filled it with ice and water from the most impressive refrigerator she'd ever seen.

"Thanks." Caty took a long drink. "I was going to say that, in all fairness, it could be that Steve is fiercely loyal and believes he's protecting you. I mean, if you look at the facts on paper, I *am* the most likely suspect. After all, that's the reason I came to you in the first place. I suppose Steve interpreted that meeting as my way of trying to deflect you…or to sway you with my feminine charm or something."

"I had a meeting with Miles yesterday," Caleb said. "He has some decent ideas, and I'm going to take a few of them into consideration. One of the things that came to light from his list was unexpected." Caleb planted both hands on the back of a chair and appeared to be weighing his words carefully. "Seems Steve has been sending gifts to various women in the company through interoffice mail."

"What?" Caty set down the glass. "How odd. I assumed he's married since, as I recall, he wears a wedding band."

"He's been married to a lovely woman named Barbara for over thirty years. They have four children and a handful of grandchildren."

"Hmm." Caty took another sip of her water. "Do you know what kinds of gifts?"

"Jewelry, according to Miles. I guess one was a pearl necklace. It came out of the pouch it was in, and was loose in the interoffice envelope. Since those envelopes have holes in them, Miles could see what it was. He was afraid he'd get in trouble by telling me, but I forced it out of him. I assured him he wasn't in trouble. I needed to know."

Caty frowned. "If he wanted to send gifts like that, why would he send them through interoffice mail? Is he sending them anonymously or is his name on them?"

"Anonymously. Miles picks up Steve's mail, so he knows the envelopes are coming from his office."

"That's just…"

"Sloppy and highly inappropriate," Caleb finished for her. "I'm beginning to believe my second-in-command needs to be put out to pasture, as insensitive as that might sound."

"Have you talked with him about it?"

"I haven't had a chance, no. Depending on my mood, I might address it with Steve after the board meeting on Thursday morning." The meeting where Caleb would announce his plans to discontinue the cigarette and tobacco sales. Caty was glad he'd shared that news with her before the public announcement.

"By sending the envelopes anonymously, I'm assuming he doesn't really know these women." Caty glanced up at Caleb as he tugged on elbow-length mitts and opened the oven door. Whatever was baking smelled delicious. "Did Miles give you the names of the women?"

"He told me there've been five women, although he can't be sure how many times Steve's sent something to each one. Suma's one of them. And Quinn."

"Attractive single women," Caty said.

After removing a large, oval ceramic bowl from the oven and sliding a tray of rolls inside, Caleb closed the door and carefully set the piping hot dish on the dishtowel-covered counter. "I'm not suggesting it has anything to do with the accounting discrepancies, but I suppose I shouldn't discount anything. I'm also not assuming the women have anything to do with them."

Lauren scurried into the kitchen. She'd changed into her new black leggings and colorful tunic. "No serious talk, you two. Time for your romantic dinner!" She clapped her hands. "First off, some music for ambiance to get you in the mood."

"Lauren! Keep it up, and I'm going to ask Cordelia to get me a list of boarding schools." Caleb shook his head with a deep frown.

"You'd miss me too much, Dad." Lauren scooted over to a control box of some kind in the corner of the kitchen. "Caty, do you like jazz?"

"I'm sure Louisiana has plenty of decent boarding schools," Caleb called to her. "That's not so far away." Caty glimpsed the beginnings of a grin teasing the corners of his mouth. She couldn't help but smile as soft jazz began to play.

Caleb ordered her to remain seated while he and Lauren finished their dinner preparations. They both seemed relaxed and happy, teasing one another with an easy rapport as they worked together.

After he prayed for their meal, Caleb served Caty a tossed salad on a separate plate with Italian dressing on the side. Father and daughter sat side-by-side on the opposite side of the table. As they ate, Lauren made sure Caty's water glass was filled and that she had everything she needed.

Caty found it cute how Lauren fussed over both her and Caleb. Then Lauren told her about the drug test at the academy. "I'm looking at it as an educational experience," she said. Based on his frown, Caleb didn't share that opinion, but he remained silent.

"I asked Sam if he has any upcoming TeamWork projects that Belac could plug into," Caty said as they finished their salads. "If you'd like, I could give you a list of upcoming events in the Houston area. There are a few in the next few months that sound promising."

Caleb nodded and wiped his mouth with his napkin. "Give me your personal recommendation, and we'll go with it. Unless you specifically need my input, I trust your judgment. Cordelia can help. If you want, put Miles in charge of the event. I think with the support of a few others, he could handle getting it set up."

"That's commendable," Caty said. "I know Miles will do his best. The vote of support from you will mean a lot to him."

"We all have to start somewhere, and I'd like to see him have more responsibility at the corporation. To some extent, he reminds me of myself." Pushing back from the table, Caleb gathered their empty salad plates and took them to the sink. "Now, for our next course. Fettucine with fresh cream sauce, mushrooms, and snow peas." He lowered the bowl into a warming dish on the table.

Lauren jumped up and gingerly transferred the hot rolls from the tray to a basket before bringing them to the table. Next, she pulled a butter dish from the refrigerator and put it beside the rolls along with a knife. "Am I forgetting anything, Dad?"

"I think you've got it all. Thanks." After making sure Lauren was seated, Caleb returned to his chair.

"You are my kind of people." Caty smiled. "Fettucine is one of my favorites."

Lauren grinned. "Dad knows."

Caty lifted her brows. "Been spying on me, Mr. Reid?"

"I asked Marta." He shot her a grin as he wrapped pasta around his spoon.

"I suppose you've been to Italy, and they taught you how to do that?" Mimicking his actions, Caty had little success.

He chuckled. "I'll show you." Caleb moved around the table to stand behind her. Wrapping his arms around her, he placed his hands over hers and proceeded to wrap pasta around the spoon. He had her practice a couple of times then whispered against her cheek, "Got it?"

"I think so, thank you." Surely he could feel how fast her heart was beating. He seemed to like showing her how to eat things. How oddly romantic.

"And that's my cue. You two lovebirds are on your own." Giggling, Lauren put her empty plate in the sink. "I'm going to grab a bowl of sorbet, and then I'm out of here. I'll be up in my room."

"Where's Max?" Caleb moved back to the other side of the table and took his chair.

"Outside. I'll bring him in, but can he sleep in my room tonight, Dad? Pretty please?"

"I don't know if that's such a good idea."

The girl rolled her eyes. "Dad thinks it'll make him soft, and Max won't be an effective guard dog if I pamper him."

Caleb's gaze implored hers. "I'm open to any suggestions."

"I think it'd be okay for Max to sleep in your room, Lauren. It'll make him feel like part of the family. What I wouldn't advise is having him sleep on your bed."

Caleb burst out laughing. "Definitely not on the bed. Off with you. I'll be up later to say good night."

"Is Caty staying the night?"

"Go *now*," Caleb growled. As Lauren scampered out of the kitchen, Caleb shook his head. "See what I have to deal with? I think she needs an intervention."

"Let me help you." Caty gathered their sorbet dishes and took them to the sink.

"Leave them. It won't take but a few seconds to put them in the dishwasher later," he said. He had things on his mind besides washing dishes.

"Let's do them by hand. My parents always said that washing dishes together can be very romantic." Slipping out of her jacket, Caty draped it around the back of a chair.

"Is that right? I'm willing to test that theory." Sounded promising, and he was willing to try it.

After locating a bottle of dishwashing liquid beneath the sink, Caty positioned the stopper and began to run water into the sink. As they worked, she admired the view of his backyard, and they talked a bit about their childhoods. She'd run track and played softball in school, and he'd played basketball and baseball. She told him what it was like being one of six kids, and he shared his perspective on being an only child.

"There were a lot of times where I wished for an older brother," he said. "I don't mind saying I envy the relationship you share with Sam. I can tell how special it is for you."

"You know," he said after she'd picked up the last pan and submerged it in the water, "with your hands in the dishwater like that, you're very vulnerable to me. I could take advantage of this situation if I'm so inclined."

Caty laughed. "I wouldn't advise it unless you want a water fight on your hands."

"Maybe I do. Let's see if you're ticklish." Sidling over to her, Caleb planted his hands on her waist and turned her to face him. And then he began to tickle her. The feel of her in his arms was irresistible.

Biting her lower lip, Caty tried not to laugh. The more she squirmed and laughed, the more he increased his efforts. He was relentless, and he adored the sound of her laughter. Loved her native Texas drawl as she begged him to stop. Seemed her drawl was more pronounced when she was riled, either in a good way or a not-so-good way.

"Okay, you asked for it." Grabbing the sprayer, Caty aimed it at him.

"Oh no, you don't!" He lunged for her too late as she pressed the lever long enough to douse him. At least the water was lukewarm.

"Now, see what you've done," he accused in a mock-threatening tone, advancing on her. "You shall pay."

"I'm so scared. Ohhh." With wide eyes, Caty pretended to shudder. And then aimed again and pulled the nozzle trigger.

"You!" Laughing, Caleb grabbed a dishtowel from the drawer and held it up in front of his face. "Truce, okay? Just stop the assault."

"You totally deserved that." As he lowered the dishtowel, Caty's eyes met his. Her smile faded, her laughter gone. She licked her lips, moistening them, and her eyes dropped to his mouth. Age-old clues that she wanted his kiss. He suspected she wasn't even aware. He'd been ready from the moment he'd first spied her coming through the door in her cute outfit and those terrific red cowgirl boots. In his imagination, he'd actually been ready *long* before she showed up on his front doorstep.

The air between them was charged with energy. Dipping his head, Caleb pressed his lips to hers, keeping the kiss light and playful. He pulled back slightly, and Caty's eyes searched his for a long moment before he lowered his mouth to hers a second time. Hungry for her, he caressed her lips with his, threading his fingers through her soft, silky hair.

"You are so beautiful," he murmured, moving one hand to cup her cheek. "My shirt's a little damp."

"I don't care." Sliding her hands around his neck, Caty returned his kiss. His groan escaped his throat, and he deepened the kiss, making sure to keep his hands anchored on her waist. Kissing Caty made him feel alive again in more than in the physical sense. He needed to be careful and keep himself in check. He was in love with this woman.

Skimming his thumb over her cheek, Caleb leaned his forehead on hers. He felt the rise and fall of her irregular breathing. His lips brushed her temple, and as he dipped his head, their gazes locked. He'd always thought talk about losing oneself in the eyes of another was silly romanticism, but now…he understood. He'd never expected to feel this way again about another woman, but Caty was a woman who commanded his attention. He could only pray she'd consider him worthy of her affections. Her love.

"Caty," he whispered. "I've fallen—"

"What are you *doing*?"

Chapter 37

Dazed, Caty's lashes fluttered as she pulled out of their embrace. Caleb withdrew his hands from her waist with obvious reluctance, and they both turned. Lauren stood in the doorway. She didn't appear so much upset as surprised. Judging from the expression on Caleb's face, he wished his daughter's timing had been better. So did she, but they should address her concerns.

"I thought you were giving us time alone." Caleb scratched his head, mussing his hair.

Caty smoothed a hand over her blouse and tried to slow her breathing. Lost cause. Nothing like being caught in a close embrace. She'd never been kissed like that before. Never kissed a man with such…passion. She felt dizzy and overheated. Maybe Lauren's timing was better than she'd thought.

"I came down to get a cold water bottle. For me and Max."

A cold water bottle to press against her own cheeks sounded like an excellent idea, but Caty said nothing.

Caleb walked to the refrigerator. After retrieving a bottle, he handed it to Lauren. "Do we need to talk or are you okay?"

Lauren darted a glance at Caty without answering.

Caleb squeezed her hand. "Caty, would you mind waiting for me in the garden?"

"Not at all. Take as long as you need."

"Dad, can I maybe talk to Caty instead?" Lauren shifted from one foot to the other. "I'll be gentle. Promise."

Caleb appeared surprised, but he nodded. "Sure, as long as it's okay with Caty."

"Of course." Releasing his hand, Caty crossed the room. She put one arm around Lauren's shoulders and gave Caleb a reassuring glance over her shoulder.

Caty followed Lauren up the staircase off the kitchen that led to the upper level. At the top of the stairs, Lauren turned to the right and headed into a yellow and white bedroom. From what Caty could tell, there were a few guestrooms, and the master bedroom was on the opposite end of the house.

Plopping onto the bed, Lauren opened her arms. "This is my room."

"It's lovely, Lauren. Cheerful."

She snorted. "That what Dad says. I wanted to paint it gray, but we compromised, and he talked me into mixing purple with it. So, it'll be lavender. We were supposed to talk about repainting my bedroom this week, but with Lettie's accident, we couldn't. We're flying to Dallas tomorrow to see her, so now we'll have to wait until next week." Stopping, Lauren took a deep breath.

"Your dad's a busy man. I'm sure he'll make time soon." Caty sat on the bed beside her.

"He told me he used to work construction where he painted houses and everything," Lauren said. "Did you know that?" The way Lauren's eyes lit, she seemed more impressed by the idea of her dad doing manual labor than being an oil man. Something about that struck Caty as very sweet.

"He mentioned it to me after our lunch last Friday." Caty shifted on the bed. "Lauren, I hope you weren't upset by what you saw tonight."

"What's it like?"

Caty hadn't expected that particular question, but Lauren was unpredictable. That much she knew. "What's *what* like, exactly?"

"Kissing."

Caty suppressed her smile. "When you care about the other person, like I care about your dad, it makes kissing them all that much more special."

"Do you see fireworks?"

She nodded. "Yes, I do, as a matter of fact."

Lauren drew her knees to her chest, resting her chin on them. "Justin Connors wants to kiss me. I can't tell Dad or he'll freak."

"Is that a boy in your school?"

"Greenbriar-Browne is only for girls. I met him through my friend, Britt."

"You said you don't get to go anywhere. How did you…where did you…?"

"I met him online, okay?"

Caty knew kids spent a lot of time online, but Lauren was right. Caleb wouldn't be happy to hear this news. "So, you've never met Justin in person?"

"Right. I mean, no, I haven't. Here's the thing. He wants to meet me. We have a dance at school in a few weeks, on May 12th. It's a boy-girl thing. Britt thinks I should ask Justin."

"Forgive me if I'm wrong, but I thought you hated boys. If I'm remembering correctly, you never wanted to kiss a boy, or words to that effect, when we were at the Japanese restaurant."

Lauren rolled her eyes and moved into a cross-legged position. "Do you have to remember everything?"

Caty laughed. "I remember saying I hated boys, too. And then Grant Sims moved to town."

"Yeah? How old were you?"

"A little older than you. Maybe fifteen."

"Tell me about Grant," Lauren said. "What was he like?"

"He was taller than me, which was saying a lot. I was one of those awkward girls because I was taller than most of the boys until I was in high school."

"Tragic," Lauren murmured.

"I thought so. My petite friends hated being short, but there were times I would have willingly traded places with them. I guess there are advantages and disadvantages either way. Grant moved with his family from Los Angeles to Houston. His dad had been in a few movies. He was very handsome, and Grant looked a lot like him. All the girls fell in love with him immediately. He had dark brown hair with one strand that never stayed in place, and all the girls wanted to be the one to push it away from his forehead. Gorgeous, deep brown eyes, and a little dimple but only on the right side. He walked me to my locker after English class one day and asked me to the Fall Festival Dance."

"Did you go?"

Caty nodded. "I did. It was my first boy-girl dance."

"Did he kiss you?"

"No," she said. "I found out he mainly asked me to go with him so he could get my help with English."

"That's just wrong." Lauren shook her head. "I'm sorry, but you know what?"

"What?"

"If he *had* kissed you, and if it weren't for his being dumb, you might have married Grant Sims. Then you wouldn't have met my dad."

They shared a smile. "What's Justin look like?"

"He's just a boy." When Lauren caught Caty's sidelong glance, she smiled again. "Okay. He's not real tall, kind of medium height. He has blond hair, and it kind of sticks up weird sometimes. I like his blue eyes, though. And he has a nice smile."

"You have a great smile, too," Caty told her.

Lauren blushed. "I got my retainer off last year."

"So, how do you know Justin wants to kiss you?"

"He told me."

"He did?"

Lauren laughed. "Yeah, but I think he's kind of scared."

"Maybe he wants to get to know you first. You're a pretty special person and worth getting to know."

"Thanks." Lauren shrugged. "How did you know you wanted to kiss my dad?"

"It's something you feel inside. It's rather hard to describe, but I'll try. Your dad is very kind and caring. He takes good care of you and is a terrific father. He's a gentleman. He opens doors for me, and he listens to what I say. He looks to the Lord for guidance in his business and personal life. He puts my needs before his, he puts *your* needs before his, and he looks awfully cute in his tuxedo tonight. Lauren, you know you need to ask your dad about the dance, right?"

"I know. With these stupid threats, he doesn't let me out of his sight."

"Does the school need parent chaperones for the dance?"

Lauren shrugged. "I guess." She propped an elbow on her leg and rested her chin on it, studying her. "Will you come, too? Then you can dance with my dad."

"Let's start by asking your dad's permission first."

"You can mention it to him if you want."

Caty rose from the bed. "Did you bring Max in yet?"

"I put him in Dad's room. He's a good dog, but I didn't want him jumping on you again. Once is enough for one night."

Caty smiled. "Thanks. Good night, Lauren. I'm sure I'll see you again soon."

Jumping off the bed, Lauren threw her arms around her neck and kissed her cheek. "I meant what I said. I know we haven't known each other long, but I know I love you."

Caty's eyes welled and she hugged her back. "I love you, too, sweet girl."

As Caty descended the staircase to the kitchen, she wondered where she'd find Caleb. The kitchen was quiet and dark. She moved into the living room, and her heart caught in her throat. Caleb was sprawled on the sofa, fast asleep. He'd changed out of the tuxedo and now wore jeans and a red polo. Still barefoot. His arms where crossed over his chest, emphasizing some very nice muscles in his upper arms.

Caty watched him for a long moment. Walking over to the picture window, she rubbed her hands over her arms. Then she strolled across the large room, focused on a bookcase full of family photos. A woman who must be Caleb's mother smiled at her in a black and white photo. Blonde and regal-looking, she had a lovely smile. Several photos of Lauren through the years. What a sweet little girl she'd been—there were photos of her a ballet costume, riding a horse, swimming, and in a gymnastics outfit.

Caty's breath caught when she spied a photo of a beautiful blonde woman.

This must be Helena.

She heard Caleb stir and turned. His eyelids fluttered open and a long, slow, lazy grin surfaced on his face. "Hi there." He sat up and patted the place next to him. "I kept it warm for you. "Is Lauren okay?"

"She's fine. There's a dance coming up at her school in May, and she wants to ask a boy."

"A date?" He shook his head slowly, his smile gone. "You can't be serious. What happened to my little girl who said she hated boys and was never getting married? That last part was only this past Sunday morning."

"Calm down, papa. She has a lot of questions, and she's naturally curious. As much as you might not want to face it, she's wondering about things like kissing. Don't worry," Caty added when she glimpsed his deepening frown. "You've raised a smart girl. She'll be fine."

"She hates it when I point out she's only twelve, but she should be talking about games and TV shows, school, clothes...anything but boys." Taking a throw pillow, Caleb collapsed back on the sofa and put it over his face, muffling his groan. Then he lowered the pillow. "How does she know any boys?"

"The Internet."

"That does it. The computer goes. I need her to keep the phone, but that goes to show nothing good can come from a girl her age having a computer."

"Do you have parental controls?"

"Yes, but that doesn't matter now, does it?"

"Well, I hate to tell you, Caleb, but she could probably make the contacts she wanted on her phone. Short of keeping her prisoner, you can't watch everything she does."

He was silent for a moment and then seemed to relax a bit. "You're right. I know you are. I guess I need to get a grip and realize she's getting older and is eventually going to grow up."

"I think she already is."

Caleb's gaze settled on her. "This is why I need you in my life, Caty. You keep me sane. You're very wise for a woman who's..."

"Never had children?"

Reaching for her hand, he caressed the side of her hand like he'd done at the Japanese restaurant. "Sorry. I didn't mean that the way it might have come across. I meant it as a compliment.

"No offense taken," she assured him. "I've worked with a lot of children, but mainly in a church or mission trip setting. At heart, kids are all the same. They see things at face value with a beautiful honesty."

He seemed to relax a bit, and Caty's heart melted a bit more. "I admire that you want to be such an involved parent, Caleb. I know it's not just because of...what's happening. You'd be a hands-on dad no matter the circumstances."

Tossing aside the pillow, he rose to his feet.

Caty lifted his left hand, staring at it. "Your wedding ring is gone." She looked at him. "You took it off?"

He nodded. "Last night. It was long past time. Let's take a walk outside. I'd like to show you the garden." Offering his hand, Caleb helped her from the sofa and they walked into the kitchen.

"Won't you need shoes?"

He grinned. "I have a pair of loafers parked by the back door."

The expansive backyard was private with tall shade trees and an abundance of fragrant flowering bushes. As Caty walked beside him on a narrow brick walkway, she heard the trickle of water nearby.

"This is beautiful. So serene and peaceful," Caty said.

"Thanks. The first time I saw the house, I knew it was the one I wanted. A large part of the reason was this garden and the pool."

That would explain the sounds of water. Caty breathed in deeply, smiling at the headiness of the fragrant roses and other flowers planted in abundance on either side of the walkway.

"The former owner of the house found solace in tending this garden after her husband died," he told her. "I picked the roses on the table tonight from this garden. Ollie does a terrific job of maintaining it for me." Caleb moved over to a rose bush and plucked a red rose. He removed the thorns while she watched. Returning to her, he bowed. "For you."

"Thank you." Caty inhaled the sweet scent of the fragrant bloom, touched by his romantic gesture. "Caleb, tell me if this is too personal, but what was *your* solace after Helena died?"

"Work. I poured myself into the corporation. As you know, I closeted myself behind closed doors. Some days, I worked almost twenty-four hours straight. Time, day and night, lost continuity. It's what I knew more than anything else, so it was comfortable, familiar. And safe."

Caty resumed walking, and he fell into place beside her. "Did you lean on your faith during that time?"

"Not like I should have. Frankly, I felt lost, and I floundered. Caty, my marriage wasn't what you might expect."

She glanced up at him sharply. "I don't hold any assumptions."

"Helena and I were young when we married. I loved her, but she was a pampered wild child who liked being social and going to parties whereas I was more quiet and focused. She never could understand the long hours I put into building the business. I regret the times I should have put everything aside and taken her off for a weekend or to a romantic dinner. I did those things fairly regularly, but it never seemed to be enough. We were both to blame when the marriage started falling apart at the seams. I never felt like I was enough for her. In some ways, I failed her."

"No one person can be everything for someone else. And the higher our expectations, I think the harder it is to accept when they crumble," Caty said quietly.

"I'd hoped having Lauren might strengthen the bond between us. I wanted more children, but Helena never did," he said. "She was content with one child, and although she was a good mother, my wife was a kid herself in many ways. I'm thankful Lauren has a few happy memories of her mother. At one point, Helena ran off to Paris. I'm not sure if she was alone, and I'll probably never know. I chose to forgive her. Divorce wasn't an option for me. When I pledged to honor her, I meant those vows."

"How did she die?" Caty assumed cancer, but she couldn't be sure.

"Breast cancer. She was first diagnosed at twenty-eight. Then she went into remission, but the cancer returned in full force four years later. She fought a brave fight, but in the end, the doctors couldn't save her. Only a miracle from God could have cured her of the cancer. She wrote a beautiful letter to Lauren that she asked me to give to her when I felt she was ready. I'm beginning to wonder if she's reached that point." When he glanced up at her, the dampness on her lashes tugged on her heart. "My question is, how will I know when the time is right?"

"That's something between you, Lauren, and the Lord," Caty said. "I take it you know the contents of the letter?"

"Yes. Helena shared it with me. She wanted me to know what she'd written. Since it's more about her hopes for Lauren's family, I've assumed it's best to wait until she finds the man she wants to marry."

"Pray about it, and I'm sure He'll reveal to you when the time is right."

Caleb nodded. "It's that old impatience streak in me again, I suppose. After Helena died, I established a cancer center in a Dallas hospital in Helena's honor. A substantial percentage of my personal profits from the sales of cigarettes and tobacco products in the Reidco stores have been donated to the center. I've had conflicting emotions about the irony of that, but it is what it is. I may have a battle on my hands when I make the announcement on Thursday morning at the quarterly board meeting, but I feel the Lord will honor my stance."

"I've always admired your strong stand," Caty said. "I have every reason to believe He'll continue to guide and bless your efforts. I saw Helena's photo in the living room, by the way. She was beautiful."

"Yes, she was." Caleb's voice was quiet. "She was a complicated woman who never seemed to find her own place. She'd gone from being Daddy's little girl—her father was a wealthy cattle rancher—to being my wife and then Lauren's mother. Although she was involved in a number of charitable and civic-minded groups in Dallas, she never took the time to figure out who Helena was, if that makes sense."

"I'm sorry, Caleb. That's sad. I think some people never find their place, unfortunately."

They stopped walking as they reached the pool.

"Oh, Caleb. What a perfect place to unwind at the end of the day." Stepping close to the waterfall, Caty dipped her hand beneath it and laughed as the water flowed over her fingers. The water was warm, and she could only imagine how relaxing it must be to take a swim at the end of the evening.

Caleb smiled at her enthusiasm. "You're not wearing a swimsuit under your clothes, are you?"

"Not today. Or I'd be seriously tempted."

He lifted his brows. "You don't need—"

"Don't even go there." She waved a finger in his face.

"The water's heated in the pool, and the Jacuzzi's right over there." Caty followed the walkway a few more feet and found the Jacuzzi hidden in a cozy alcove along with a brick oven and a large grill.

"You're welcome to come anytime." Sitting on the side wall of the pool, Caleb kicked off his shoes. When she moved to sit down beside him, he stopped her. "Allow me." He helped her remove one boot and then the other, his eyes never leaving hers. Finally, he lowered them on the pavement beside his shoes. Who knew something so simple could be so…sensual?

She dipped her feet into the water, and they splashed a little.

Caleb turned to face her. "I've had a few dates here and there in the past five years, but I haven't actively sought out female companionship. I won't lie. I've had opportunities, but nothing I wanted to pursue. Until *you* walked into my life."

He wrapped both of his hands around hers, his eyes earnest, his expression serious. "I value you as a friend. I need a woman who wants to share everything with me. Someone I can go to when I need advice. A woman who cares about me as a person instead of the man behind the corporation. Someone who likes me for who and what I am, flaws, warts, and all—the man who wants to be an honorable father and a man worthy of respect. A woman who understands my desire to help others and to better themselves. A woman who can love a man…"—his eyes searched hers and his words slowed—"who understands he doesn't want to journey through the rest of his life alone."

Caty's breath caught. What was he saying?

With one hand, Caleb skimmed his thumb over her cheek. "My question for you would be if that's the kind of man you could love?"

"I already do. I'm looking at him now."

"Very, very good answer." He leaned closer. So did she.

"Wait." She put one hand on his chest and felt his strong heartbeat beneath her hand. "You don't really have any warts, do you?"

"No. It was just an expression." His voice was low, teasing. "We have much more important things to discuss." Caleb's smile etched itself on her heart. Dipping his head, he brushed his lips over hers. "I've fallen in love with you, Caty, and I want to do this right. I want to court you. Give you flowers, take you to dinner, get to know your family, and have you beside me as I try to navigate the many moods of Lauren. And that's only the beginning."

Caty glanced up at the back of the house. "Do you think Lauren's watching us from her window now?"

"This area's well-hidden by the trees." He came closer and moved his arms around her. "At the moment, I don't want to think about anything but kissing you."

"Just keep holding onto me so we don't both fall into the pool."

"Now that's a thought." Caleb's lips captured hers.

Caty's heart soared, and she was lost in the pure *joy* of the moment.

Chapter 38

Caty glanced at the time on Thursday morning. Bowing her head, she said a prayer for Caleb's board meeting. *Lord, be with him as he presents his idea to the board this morning regarding the ban on tobacco products sold in the Reidco convenience stores. Give Caleb the right words and your confidence. If the response isn't positive, help him to accept the comments and be able to give a fair and calm answer.*

She'd made sure he'd gone into his meeting armed with all the stats he'd requested. He had the sales figures for the Reidco division broken down by store and category. He might have a fight on his hands, but if anyone could prove his point and convince the board, it was Caleb.

His flight back from Dallas had been delayed, and he'd arrived in the office only fifteen minutes before the start of the board meeting.

Caty returned to her reports. A half hour later, after checking and rechecking the latest sales ledgers, she'd found yet another discrepancy—a nearly twelve thousand dollar difference in the daily spreadsheets from the report for the previous week. Her heart dropped. *Oh, no.* What now?

Grabbing her corporate directory, she used her cell phone to dial the number for the Reidco station in Lubbock, one of three, and a different one than had reported the previous loss.

"Hi, yes. This is Catherine Lewis, Belac's chief accountant for the Reidco division. Who am I speaking with, please? Larry, great. Is Frank still the station manager?" She recorded a couple of notes. "Great. Would he happen to be around this morning? There's an important business matter I need to discuss with him."

After being told Frank didn't have a cell phone, she asked Larry to have Frank return the call as soon as he returned from his business in town. Drumming her fingers on her desk, she hoped Larry's estimate of thirty minutes or less for a return call would prove accurate. She'd met Frank a few times when she'd worked in the Lubbock office. She'd made the rounds of all the Reidco stations and convenience stores in Texas since the beginning of her employment. They'd numbered around fifty when she'd started five years ago, and now had expanded to more than seventy. New stations with stores were opening soon or scheduled to be built in the states surrounding Texas—namely in southern Oklahoma, eastern New Mexico, western Louisiana, and southwest Arkansas.

Caleb should be in the meeting now. Caty felt sure he'd have his phone off, but she felt the pressing need to send him a text. He did say he wanted to be advised of any further discrepancies immediately.

CALEB, DISCREPANCY FOUND IN LUBBOCK REIDCO REPORT. OIL STATION. ALMOST $12K. CALLED FRANK THE STATION MANAGER. WAITING ON REPLY.

In less than a minute, Caty's phone buzzed.

ONCE YOU FIND OUT DETAILS, I'LL ASK YOU TO COME AND JOIN THE MEETING. WE'RE IN CONFERENCE ROOM A. ARE YOU PREPARED TO EXPLAIN THE DISCREPANCIES TO THE BOARD? I THINK IT'S TIME.

Caty inhaled air and coughed. Explain this to the board? Steve Robison would be in attendance, boring holes in her. On the other hand, Caleb was her boss, and he'd be fully supportive. "I can do all things through Him who strengthens me," she said under her breath. She might need to repeat that a few times, as needed, in the next couple of hours.

YES, I CAN DO THAT, she texted back.

GOOD. LET ME KNOW AND I'LL HAVE YOU JOIN THE MEETING. THANKS.

Sitting back in her chair, Caty breathed slowly, in and out, in and out. She reasoned through why Caleb would want to make the discrepancies known. To make the guilty parties aware they were being watched? That the discrepancies had been noticed and were being investigated? That made sense.

Caty's phone buzzed, startling her. The number was unfamiliar but the area code was right for Lubbock. "This is Catherine Lewis." The man confirmed he was Frank, the manager of the Reidco gas station. She quickly asked her questions, couching them in vague terms, to try and find out if there was a damaged item, theft, a loss of some sort, damage due to rain or other natural disaster, or anything otherwise out of the ordinary.

As she expected, Frank reported nothing amiss. From his tone, Caty felt reasonably sure the man was stating the truth.

After thanking him, she disconnected the call and texted Caleb.

FRANK REPORTS NO DAMAGES, NO LOSSES, NOTHING OUT OF THE ORDINARY.

Within five minutes, she had a response. COME TO THE CONFERENCE ROOM NOW. BRING YOUR REPORTS.

Rising to her feet, Caty drew in a deep breath to try and calm her nerves.

Here we go. Lord, be with me.

Caleb motioned for Cordelia to open the conference room door. When Caty entered, he gave her a nod he hoped would encourage her. He hadn't meant to put her on the spot but no time like the present. Someone was stealing from the corporation, and most likely, it was an insider job.

"Ladies and gentleman," he said to the assembled group of eighteen individuals seated around the large, oval table. "May I introduce Catherine Lewis. She's worked for Belac in the Reidco division for the past five years as our chief accountant. I've invited her to join us today." He invited Caty to take a seat at the table. Unfortunately, that put her beside Steve. A quick glance at Steve revealed the older man's distaste at this latest development.

"We've had a number of accounting discrepancies on the books for Reidco in the past few months, and each amount is an increasingly larger amount," Caleb explained. "When Caty informed me this morning of the latest one, totaling nearly twelve thousand dollars, I decided it's time to make the board aware. Since you're all here, it makes more sense to tell you verbally than to send out an email concerning such a sensitive and confidential matter. I believe this is an inside job, and we have an embezzler in our midst. I intend to get to the bottom of this situation using every available means."

Cordelia visibly stiffened even as she continued to make notes. He'd probably hear about it later if she didn't approve, but her tense manner was probably more indicative of her unease on his behalf. Steve's face was impassive. The man was very good at masking his emotions and always had been. Several of the other men and women in attendance sat up straighter in their chairs with concerned expressions on their faces, as well they should. Not worried, exactly, but understandably surprised.

"Miss Lewis, if you would please share with the group the nature of the discrepancies, including the latest one you discovered just today." Caleb returned to his seat and sipped his water. He was proud of Caty as she relayed the facts and numbers, explaining to the board members in clear, concise terms. Then she told them of the latest loss and that she'd contacted the station manager in Lubbock, and he reported nothing amiss.

"I'll be watching carefully to see how this difference is recorded and find out the source."

"Who prepares the reports and sends them to you?" one of the ladies inquired.

"The station managers," Caty told her. "There are several other accountants in the Belac division who see these reports, and..." She took a deep breath and darted a glance his way.

"It's our contention that one of the other Belac employees with access to the accounting reports is the person responsible," Caleb answered for her. He hoped he hadn't stepped over his bounds, but Caty's expression was one of relief. Better that statement came from him. "We have a list of those employees, and we will be monitoring their actions carefully over the next few weeks. We can easily trace those who've worked on the previous reports, but the problem is, they've gone through a number of hands at all levels of the accounting department. They've all signed confidentiality statements, of course, subject to immediate termination if it's discovered they've shared financial information with anyone outside of Belac."

"Perhaps you should make the reports restricted," one of the men suggested. "Limit the employees who have access."

Caleb nodded. "I'm aware of the need to do that very thing, Barry. Perhaps I've been too trusting up until this point, but we'll be more watchful in the future. We'll also be installing security and safeguards on the computers and require stringent passwords for the database. Do any of you have any questions for Miss Lewis?"

No one did. Caleb thanked Caty, and she gathered her folder and departed the room. He wished he could go with her. He eyed them all. "I'm sure I don't need to remind anyone here in this room that any and all discussions within the confines of this conference room are to stay among us only."

Steve shot him a glare which he ignored. If Steve dared to bring up his suspicions of Caty before the board, he might very well fire him on the spot. He was nearing sixty-two, and the idea of offering him an attractive early retirement package sounded more appealing every day.

As some of the others began another discussion, Caleb braced himself for his big announcement about discontinuing the tobacco sales. He'd save that for last. That way they could clear other important matters first before any fireworks began. Hopefully, there would be none.

Moving his phone to his lap, he texted Caty.

YOU DID GREAT. WAIT FOR ME IN YOUR OFFICE. I'LL TAKE YOU TO LUNCH. PRAY FOR ME AS I FINISH THIS MEETING.

Caleb didn't expect a reply from her, but within a minute, he had one.

PRAYING. GO GET 'EM, SCRAPPY!

Chapter 39

An hour later, Caleb strolled into Caty's office and closed the door behind him. She couldn't tell from his expression how the remainder of the meeting had gone.

"Should I ask?"

Shaking his head, he laughed. "You know, the funniest thing was when one of them asked, 'What's next? Hot dogs?'" He slumped into one of the chairs across from her desk.

"I'm trying to get the connection here, but you'd better explain." Caty closed out the file on her screen and then logged off her computer.

"They're wondering if I'm going to ban hot dogs from the convenience stores. Because of nitrates and other questionable ingredients. And soda because it causes cancer in white Canadian mice or something." Resting his elbow on the arm of the chair, Caleb ran his hand over his hair and released a deep sigh. "All I can say is, I'm thankful the meeting's over."

"For your sake, I am, too. Other than the hot dog and soda remarks, how did they take the news about eliminating the tobacco sales?"

"Some think I've lost my marbles, and others are supportive. I'd say it's pretty much split fifty-fifty among the board members. I've told them that I've instructed the ad agency to put out a press release early next week announcing the plan." Leaning forward, elbows on his knees, Caleb groaned. "I know I'm doing the right thing, but sometimes it's difficult when you feel like David facing Goliath."

"Caleb, you've accomplished so much by being gutsy and a trailblazer in the oil industry. You know what?" Rising from her chair, Caty walked around the desk to where he sat.

He looked up at her and grinned. "Should I ask?"

"Stand up, please. I think you're going to like what I have to say."

"Sounds promising." He quickly rose to his feet. Facing her, he moved his arms around her waist.

"I find your self-confidence and intelligence extremely attractive."

"You do?" He tilted his head to one side. "A trailblazer, eh?"

"Very much so." She gave him a quick kiss. Then she grabbed her purse and locked her desk. "Where are you taking me to lunch?"

"Anywhere but Japanese," he said over his shoulder as he opened her office door and followed her into the hallway.

She laughed. "Or anywhere you need to teach me how to use the utensils."

Anneta's Bakery & Deli was packed with the noontime lunch crowd when they stepped inside. With one hand on her lower back, Caleb navigated them among the busy tables to a small table near the back of the busy eatery.

"You sure you wouldn't rather go somewhere more private?" He glanced around the place. "Nice décor, though." She knew he'd appreciate all the sports memorabilia from Texas sports teams.

"They have the best soup and sandwiches around if you can stand the noise," she said. "Here's a thought. You order for us today. Order what you think I'll like, and I'll do the same for you next time around."

He grinned. "That sounds promising. Or dangerous, depending on how you look at it."

After waiting in line for a few minutes, Caleb returned to their table with a pager. "They said it shouldn't be too long."

"Caleb, about the Belac project with TeamWork, I spoke with Miles yesterday. There's an annual Picnic in the Park event coming up the weekend after the dance at Lauren's school. I think that might be a perfect event to start."

"You had to remind me about the dance, didn't you? And no, as far as I know, Lauren hasn't asked the boy to the dance…yet. We're negotiating." He grinned to let her know he was teasing. "Okay, so tell me why you think this particular outing might be good for the corporation."

"You don't want to overwhelm any of your employees who haven't done a service project before. Basically, anyone who wants or needs a free meal is welcome to come to this event—homeless, neighborhood residents, low-income families, students, you name it across the board of all income levels and walks of life. Speaking of hot dogs, they're on the menu, so be forewarned."

She laughed when Caleb crossed his eyes. "The focus is on providing the meal, and there's music by some local Christian bands. Then there'll be a couple of speakers, some singing, and a small fireworks display as the sun sets. People come and go throughout the day, and there's no obligation for anything. We have a table with flyers, Christian materials, and a free Bible is available for anyone who wants one."

Caleb nodded. "I think you're right. It'd be a good way to ease my employees into the idea of a service project while also getting to know each other better on a more personal level. We need to promote the idea of our employees circulating, though. I don't want them standing in little huddles and especially not segregated by departments."

"This is your chance to lead by example. The new Caleb Reid emerging from his cocoon," she said quietly.

"I'm trying. Talk with Miles and get all the details. Can you arrange it with Sam? Find out what volunteers he'll need. If you would, start a sign-up sheet and a list of supplies to provide."

"I'm sure I can manage to do all that." She smiled.

"Once everything's in place, I'll ask Cordelia to send out an email next week to announce it to everyone."

"Order up for Caty! Come and get it."

With wide eyes, Caleb turned to look at the man behind the counter. "Wow. That guy's good. Does he announce for the Texans or the Astros? He should."

Caty grinned. "Not that I know of, but I've thought the exact same thing."

"I'll get our food and be right back." He quickly returned with their orders—chicken noodle soup and half a turkey sandwich for her, a club sandwich and potato chips for him, and two bottles of water.

"How'd I do?" He unloaded the tray and then handed it off to a nearby deli employee.

"Extremely well. Thank you." Bowing her head, Caty said grace.

"Here's an idea," he said as they began to eat. "I need to take you to see the bluebonnets before the season is over. Lettie's coming back to town early next week, after all—she's insisting—and to be honest, I'm glad. I don't cook all that well, and we've missed having her home with us. How about after work one night next week, we go for dinner and a drive? Are you free on Tuesday night?"

"I'll check my schedule. That sounds like fun. I haven't gone to see the bluebonnets in years."

"And then the next thing is an Astros game. I'll check their home schedule, unless you have it memorized," he teased. "I've never met a woman who knows as much about baseball as you do. We can belt out the National Anthem, chow down on hot dogs if we dare, shell peanuts, yell at the umpire, dance in the stands, and act like a couple of crazy kids in love. Share a kiss during the seventh inning stretch. That's the best idea yet, don't you think?"

"Caleb…?"

He popped a chip in his mouth and leaned one elbow on the table. With his most flirtatious smile, he gave her a broad wink. "Yes, Caty?"

She laughed as he aimed the chip for her mouth, teasing her with it. Leaning forward, she dipped for it like a bird and then swiped a couple of chips from his plate.

"This sandwich is very good, by the way." He took another bite.

"Glad you like it. This has become one of my favorite places." Caty wiped her mouth with her napkin. "Caleb, I need to tell you something, but please promise you'll hear me out."

"As long as you don't say, 'I can't date you,' or 'I'm not sure I can handle a man with a preteen daughter,' then I'm listening."

"Maybe you should fire me."

Chapter 40

"*Fire* you?" Caleb sputtered and almost choked on his sandwich. "I can tell you right now the answer to that is a definite no. N-O. No."

Caty leaned close. "Well, not *really* fire me, of course."

Not that he needed to worry he'd be overheard in the noisy deli, but he lowered his voice. "Tell me why you're suggesting it. Help me understand."

"I'm just thinking it might speed up this whole thing and force the person trying to steal from you to crawl out of the proverbial woodwork. If the person thinks I'm fired, then he or she might make a move."

"Banish that thought," he said. "Not going to happen. What purpose would it serve to fire you? Not to mention I'd miss you in the office. Knowing you're right down the hall is a great comfort."

"Thank you. Good to know I'm being compared to grilled cheese." She took a sip of her soup.

"Not comfort *food*, you crazy woman." He shook his head. "Caty, if it weren't for you, I'd be dwelling on that latest note. You've helped me find the joy in living again to the point where I'm ready to face down whatever challenges come. You've reminded me to put my trust in the Lord's hands, where it belongs. Where it's always belonged."

"I'm glad, but I also know you're tired of the wondering and the waiting. I'm tired *for* you."

"I think that might change soon." He took another bite of his sandwich. In spite of his words, an uneasy stirring in the pit of his stomach had started recently and wouldn't let go of him. He'd popped antacids like candy in recent days, something he rarely did.

She met his gaze. "Do you believe we'll have answers soon?"

Caleb nodded. "I can't say why, but yes, I do. Call it a gut feeling. I'm not usually wrong about these things."

"For the accounting issue…or the other?" Her beautiful blue eyes grew wider.

"Both. I'm beginning to believe they might somehow be connected." He gave her hand a reassuring squeeze. "Let's enjoy our lunch. Give me a chance to woo my gorgeous Reidco accountant."

"Caleb, when we first met, you mentioned bringing in the authorities to deal with the discrepancies. Do you think now might be that time?"

"I spoke with a police lieutenant recently. I proposed the situation hypothetically. Short of filing subpoenas, seizing computers, examining phone and email records, I'm not sure how we could pinpoint any one or more persons. At this point, I'm not sure I should expose Belac to lawsuits or a trial. When I mentioned the authorities, I meant when we know who's actually behind them."

Caty frowned. "That's frustrating. But you *will* eventually need to prosecute whoever's responsible."

"I understand that, but I'm waiting for them to make a false move. As I said, I honestly believe something will happen soon." He could only pray everything would come to a peaceful ending without anyone getting hurt.

Chapter 41

Monday Evening, the Following Week

"Caty, can you come over to Sam and Lexa's?"

In the middle of unpacking and sorting through another box of personal items, Caty checked her watch. Almost seven-thirty p.m. "What's up, Marta?"

"I'm hoping to solve that second clue. Lexa and Sam are out, but she told me she'd leave the garage door unlocked. I find it interesting that she didn't ask any questions when I told her Eliot had this game planned for me with clues. Something tells me she and your brother are in on the whole thing."

Caty laughed. "Why am I not surprised? Can you give me a half hour?"

"Sure. An hour if you need it."

"I didn't get a chance to tell Lauren about this clue. Can we try and include her in the next one?"

"Sure," Marta said. "This one seems to be more of a TeamWork-related thing, anyway. I'm surprised Eliot would make it this easy."

"Maybe it's not as easy as you think." Caty closed the box and darted a glance in the mirror. She was in her jeans and a T-shirt, but that would have to do for last-minute notice. "I'll call you when I'm almost there."

"Thanks, friend. I'd just feel better having you there with me, so I don't feel like I'm breaking and entering."

"Don't be silly. Nothing could be further from the truth."

Nearly forty-five minutes later, Marta leaned against the white Volvo station wagon and breathed out a dramatic sigh. "I thought for sure the bomb was the answer."

"Let me see that clue again." Caty held out her hand.

"I know it by heart," Marta said. "It's not ticking, but it's precious to the TeamWork crew." A moment later, she lifted away from the car. "We haven't checked beneath the hood yet. That's got to be it." Walking over to the driver's door, she opened it. "Where, oh where, is the hood release?" A moment later, Caty heard the latch unlock. "Found it."

After lifting the hood and securing it with the metal rod to keep it in place, Caty snapped her fingers. "What makes a car tick?" She didn't know a lot about cars, but she knew basic engine components.

"The battery?" Marta came around beside her and they both leaned over the engine.

"Right. Check all around it," Caty suggested. "If the next clue's not there, I'm fresh out of ideas."

Stretching, Marta felt around the sides of the battery. "Bingo! You are a genius." She held up a yellow Post-It note. "See, this is why I needed you here with me tonight."

"What's the next clue say?"

Marta read from the paper. "Clue #3: Her welcoming smile melts hearts but not her sweets. Is it just me, or does that sound either borderline sexist or really intriguing?"

Caty smiled. "Let's go with the really intriguing option."

"Speaking of which, what's happening with your handsome cowboy?" Marta said as they both walked outside and Caty lowered the garage door. "I gather by your mutual presence in church again yesterday that things are going well?"

The thought of her day spent with Caleb and Lauren made her smile. After the service, they'd enjoyed a leisurely lunch. His daughter did a majority of the talking while she and Caleb made eyes at one another like teenagers. Then she'd followed him back to the house where they'd made popcorn, curled up on the sofa, and watched a marathon of movies on a Christian channel, some decent and others unbelievably cheesy but clean.

"Do you have time for a cup of coffee?" Caty offered. "I'll fill you in. Admit it. That was your ulterior motive all along in luring me out here, wasn't it?"

Marta waved her hand. "Like it was such a hardship for you. I have to be at the studio by nine, as per the usual these days, but I have time for a quick cup." They agreed to drive separately and meet at a local coffee and pie kitchen.

"Well, blow me down and call it a night," Marta said after Caty caught her up-to-speed on what was happening. "Caty, you're practically married to the man! You've left me in the dark too long, my friend."

Caty didn't know whether Eliot had divulged anything to Marta about Caleb hiring him. Like with Sam, she hated not being free to tell her best friend so she could pray, but in case her loose lips might put Caleb or Lauren in danger, it was best to keep quiet. And pray. She'd ramped up her prayers for them lately, especially after Caleb had confided his suspicion that something would happen soon. That statement had made her uneasy, but she tried to follow her own advice not to worry and to put her trust in the Lord.

"In some ways, I can't believe everything that's happened in such a short time," Caty confided to her friend as she sipped her iced caramel macchiato. "*This* is sinful. See what you made me do?"

"I always knew when you met the right guy of God's choosing, you'd fall madly in love lickety-split," Marta said. "I had an idea it would be the handsome cowboy the moment you told me about him. Of course, I didn't know at the time he was your boss."

"Well, neither did I," Caty said. "I'm just thankful I haven't had any more pratfalls to make the man think I'm uncoordinated and clumsy." Laughing, she shook her head. "That day will go down as one of the strangest—and one of the *best*—days in the history of my life."

"Don't forget dinner with two of your best friends that same evening. I'd like to believe that the dinner sped your relationship along."

"Of course," Caty readily agreed. "Not to forget the separate invitations to join you and Eliot for church. You sure you two didn't coordinate that?"

"Completely in God's plan. I couldn't be happier for you. Caleb's a great guy. Not your average millionaire, I have to say."

"Stop that," Caty snapped, but she smiled as she took another sip of her drink.

"I'm only stating the obvious. Why, the man seems so down-to-earth I can actually believe he *does* put one leg in his pants at a time."

Caty shook her head. "Funny girl. He's worked hard for his success."

"I'm sure he has. I'm not discounting that. For one thing, if you marry Caleb, you won't have to keep working unless you want to." Marta arched her brows. "Until the cute little cowboys or cowgirls start coming along. Imagine what cute kids you two will have." She hesitated. "Have you and Caleb discussed children?"

"Whoa. Now you're *really* getting ahead of yourself," Caty protested. "From what I know *you* can stop working if you want, but I also know you love being the weather person extraordinaire."

The idea of marriage and children sounded more appealing whenever she spent time with Caleb, but until things were resolved... "That'll happen for you and Eliot before me, no matter what happens."

Stirring her iced caffè latte, Marta dipped her gaze but not before Caty caught her smile. "We're talking about it. 'It' meaning having a baby sometime in the next year or two."

Patting her friend's hand, Caty leaned close. "A little tip? It takes more than talking."

Marta laughed. "First, we need to move to a bigger place. Eliot's been so busy, and so have I, that we haven't taken the time to even compare notes much less go see any homes. Seriously, we need to plan another dinner together, the four of us. As soon as Eliot gets home, let's arrange something."

"Agreed." Caty touched her glass to Marta's. "Here's to friendship among good friends."

"To friendship and the handsome men we love." With a wink, Marta sipped her drink.

As she prepared for bed later that evening, Caty's cell phone rang. She smiled when she checked the display and saw that it was Caleb.

"How was your day?"

Snuggling under the sheets, Caty smiled at the sound of his voice. He'd called her once before in the late evening, and they'd enjoyed a long phone chat. She hoped this might become a wonderful evening tradition.

"Good," she said. "You must have been busy. I only caught fly-by glimpses of you."

"I'm sorry I didn't get the opportunity to stop in." After Caleb filled her in on his activities of the day, she heard his sigh.

"Is something wrong?" Propping against the headboard, Caty wrapped her arms around her knees, keeping the phone pinned between her ear and right shoulder.

"Nothing's wrong. I was just thinking about something I wanted to share with you. I hoped it wasn't too late since I know you told me you're usually up until eleven or so."

"I think I can make time to talk with you," she teased. "What's on your mind?"

"I've been making a concentrated effort to read my Bible lately. Lauren came to me over the weekend and wanted my explanation of the passage in Matthew where it talks about how it's easier for a camel to go through the eye of a needle than for a rich man to enter the kingdom of God."

"It's good that she's asking questions," Caty said. "Is she reading her Bible, too?" She knew Caleb had bought a new Bible for himself as well as one for Lauren. He'd admitted it'd been so long since they'd used them that he wasn't sure he could find their Bibles among the packing boxes in the garage.

"She is, although I believe she's picking and choosing verses. That's okay for now. At least she's reading parts of it. Anyway, we had an enlightening discussion. A good one, I think. Lauren told me not that long ago that she wished we weren't rich, and that if I didn't have money, we wouldn't be faced with these kidnapping threats."

Caty nodded and then remembered Caleb couldn't see her. "To be fair, from a twelve-year-old's perspective, I suppose that makes sense."

"At the time, I explained there are different ways to be rich. She knows how hard I've worked to provide nice things for us. She's been to countries most people never have the chance to see. Anyway, I studied a bit and told her how people originally used silver or gold coins, but that as life grew more complex, the need for a monetary system developed. And then, like so many things, money was abused. I shared the verse and told her that if we seek the kingdom of God first, everything we need will be provided."

"All very valid points," Caty said.

"I think the upcoming TeamWork project will be good to open Lauren's eyes to those out there who don't enjoy the privileges she does on a daily basis," he said. "Let's face it, most kids her age don't think about others as much as themselves. I explained how God tested Job but then blessed him with wealth. God blessed King Solomon with wealth and wisdom, and how Solomon is considered the wealthiest person who's ever lived. Abraham, Jacob, and many others were also considered wealthy. I think, in the end, Lauren understood that God doesn't look at having money as being sinful. If He did, He wouldn't have blessed so many faithful people with money."

"Exactly." Caty loved discussing things of the Lord with Caleb, and how it strengthened the growing bond between them. "Money itself isn't evil, but the worship of money is. Or falling into temptation and sinning in order to get more money."

"I told Lauren how the oil industry could crash, like it did not long before I entered the business, and we could lose everything. I don't expect that to happen, but it *could*."

"Caleb, along those same lines, from your perspective, what made you choose the end of Luke 6:38 for your theme verse for Belac?" She recited the Scripture in her mind: *For by your standard of measure it will be measured to you in return.*

"I'm glad you brought that up. That's something else I'd like to share with Lauren," he said. "I see it as God's promise. It's the idea of pouring blessings into our lap. That imagery comes from Christ and the ancient Middle Eastern grain market. People would go into the grain market to purchase *alap*-full—that's what it was called—of grain. The loose material of their garments went all the way down to the ground and was belted at the waist with a sash. When they went to the market, they pulled up the bottom of the garment and looped it through the sash to make a pocket. Then the grain was dumped into the makeshift pouch to fill their laps."

"I love that!" Caty said. "I've never heard that before. So, it's like it was a relatable, everyday experience for the crowd listening to Jesus."

"Right." She could hear Caleb's smile which in turn made Caty smile. "It's the idea that the Lord wants to overflow our lives with His blessings, and those blessings correspond to our own generosity, and in fact, are triggered by it. When I first started Belac, I was a wet-behind-the-ears kid, but my mom had ingrained it in me to always give back to the church. So, I did without thinking about it. It was like brushing my teeth or getting dressed to go out each morning. I remember she said something that I'll never forget."

"What's that?"

"'You can't outgive the Lord. When you give, He's always faithful to give back more.'"

"I think I'd like your mother," she said.

"I'll take you to Dallas sometime soon so you two can meet. I'm sure she'd love you."

As Caty said good night and turned off her light, she wondered how well Helena had gotten along with Caleb's mother. Perhaps the comparisons to his late wife were inevitable. From everything he'd told her, Caleb's relationship with Helena was complicated yet loving in many ways. At least he didn't say things like, *That's not the way my wife used to do it.* Caty shook her head, laughing at her silly thoughts.

He'd explained that Helena claimed to be a Christian, but her faith wasn't strong until near the end of her life, when she'd accepted the fact that she wasn't going to win her cancer battle. Caty's heart hurt for the pain Helena must have experienced as well as knowing she wouldn't live to see Lauren grow up, go to college, marry, and have children one day.

Her thoughts strayed to Suma. The pretty young receptionist had come to her office twice—the first time when Caleb had interrupted them, albeit for a good cause, and the second a longer visit during their lunch hour. They'd shared a sandwich Caty brought from home. The other girl hadn't said much, but Suma had asked Caty questions. Questions which clued her in that Suma was searching for meaning in her life. She'd told her she'd been eating more, eating healthy. Caty hadn't prayed with her, but Suma knew the offer was there. Through the years, she'd learned to be gentle with people. Forcing "religion" down their throats, or cramming their heads full of Scripture, could ultimately do more harm than good if it didn't somehow relate to their lives on a personal level.

"Making it personal," she mused. When her cell phone rang, Caty picked it up from the nightstand, half-expecting it to be Caleb again. Not that she'd mind.

Sam & Sarah Lewis.

"Hi, Mom? Or is this Dad? Everything okay?"

"Everything's fine," her father said. "I thought I'd call and see how my girl's doing tonight. Hope I didn't wake you."

Caty smiled. Dad sometimes called her at this hour to wish her good night. Her father could get nostalgic at times, and she knew he missed their late-night chats. During the time she'd stayed with them before moving into the townhome, they'd shared great, deep conversations about life, the Lord's plan for her life, her hopes, her dreams.

"Not at all. I just hung up from speaking with Caleb." That had slipped out naturally, without forethought. She hadn't even told her parents about him yet. An arrow of guilt pierced her.

A short silence ensued on the line. "Maybe it's a good thing I followed that nudge to give you a call." True to his character, her dad didn't sound chastising, and he was never demanding. "If you want to talk, I'm here."

Her eyes filled. "I hope you know I didn't purposely keep you out of the loop. This is all still so new for me. I'm trying to adjust to the idea myself."

"Is Caleb someone you work with?"

"You could say that." She inhaled a quick breath. She'd gone this far, so she might as tell him everything. "He's my...boss."

"I see."

"Are you shocked? Disappointed?"

"He's not married, is he? Not a scoundrel?"

She smiled. No one but her father would use a word like *scoundrel*. "Caleb's been widowed for five years, and he has a twelve-year-old daughter named Lauren. Dad, I never expected to fall in love with him, but I have. I'm as surprised as you probably are. I always thought I'd have the kind of love story like you have with Mom where you'd known each other for years. But, let's face it, I'm almost thirty, and no childhood boyfriends are knocking down my door. That doesn't matter, anyway. Caleb is a wonderful man, and he's a Christ-follower."

In the next few minutes, Caty told him how she'd gotten to know Caleb and Lauren. No doubt, her parents would get a kick out of the preteen. She couldn't tell her father about the kidnapping threats, of course. If she did, while he wouldn't forbid her to see Caleb, he'd be understandably concerned. With good reason.

"Caleb sounds like a wonderful man. If you love him, then I'm sure your mother and I will love him, too. I have to ask, though. Do you think you might marry this man?"

"It's still very early in the relationship, but if Caleb asks me, I'll tell him yes." She hadn't even needed to think about her answer. Was she crazy?

No, you're in love, Caty Bug. Gloriously, wonderfully, head-over-heels in love with Abernathy Caleb Reid. Maybe she'd doodle her name on a notepad like she used to do in high school. Catherine Lewis Reid. Or Catherine Grace Reid. Or Catherine Grace Lewis Reid. Any way she thought about it, the name was strong, solid, right. Now she was being silly.

You're not in high school anymore.

"Then that's good enough for us," her father said, breaking into her thoughts. "Your mother's putting together a party for Sam's birthday in a couple of weeks. I heard her talking with Lexa about going to that new country western place owned by a couple from our church. Maybe you can bring Caleb and Lauren along. I'll have Sarah call you about it in the next few days."

"That sounds terrific. Thanks for being so understanding. Thanks for being...my dad." Her voice caught on that last sentiment, but she meant it from the core of her soul. If only every kid were so blessed to have a father like hers, the world would be such a better place.

"Say your prayers and ask God to direct your path, Catherine. Like I told you that day we moved you into the townhome, trust in Him and He won't lead you astray."

"I know. Thanks, Dad. I love you."

"Always and forever."

Chapter 42

Caleb was nothing if not prompt. The Porsche came to a halt in front of her townhome precisely at six p.m. on Tuesday evening. Not that she'd peeked. Not that she hadn't left the office an hour early to make sure she'd be home on time for his arrival. They could have gone straight from the office, but Caleb had been in meetings outside the office all day. She hoped he wouldn't be too tired to see the bluebonnets tonight.

When the doorbell rang, Caty opened her front door with a bright smile. "Welcome to my humble abode, kind sir."

He wore his jeans and what she'd come to know was his favorite clothing—a tucked-in, white button-down shirt, and those fabulous cowboy boots. Pushing the door closed behind him, he stood in front of her with an almost shy, schoolboy smile. She wouldn't quite go *that* far, but for all of the man's confidence, she found this side of Caleb refreshingly sweet.

His appraising glance took in her jeans, pink cotton top and matching lightweight sweater, and then moved down to her red boots. "Hello, gorgeous."

"I could say the same. You always look handsome. I'm sure you roll out of bed handsome." Her cheeks colored. "I mean…"

From behind his back, he brought out a small bouquet of yellow roses and planted a light kiss on the cheek. "From my heart to yours, courtesy of my garden." Thank goodness he'd bypassed her leading comment, sparing her further embarrassment.

"They're exquisite! Thank you." She leaned into his kiss and then tweaked the cleft in his chin. "Come inside while I get a vase to put them in. Did you give your Stetson the night off?"

"Of course not. The hat's in the back of the car."

Caty went into the kitchen with the flowers while he waited in the living room. "Remind me to tell you the story of Sam and Lexa sometime. Yellow roses figure prominently into their love story. Not to mention The Alamo."

"That sounds like an intriguing story. Looks like you're settling in here nicely. Your place is great. I like the way you've decorated it. Maybe you could help me add some colorful touches to my house."

"Thank you. In many ways, you could say this is the home that Belac built." She heard his chuckle. "As far as your house, I think some colorful throw pillows would be good for the living room. You might be surprised what a little touch of color can do. Have you talked with Lauren about painting her bedroom?"

"We're going to the paint store on Thursday after school."

"Excellent." She was thrilled to hear it. "Lavender?"

"Yep. That's the compromise. She might change her mind before then, but we can negotiate."

Caty smiled as she pulled out a vase from beneath the sink and filled it with water. "I saw the press release about discontinuing the Reidco tobacco sales next month. Have you had any response yet?" She hoped there hadn't been any backlash. She felt sure there'd be plenty of discussion in certain circles, however.

"Let the games begin," he said. "I'm sure my competitors love me. I guess time will tell with the customers."

"You're doing the right thing, Caleb."

"I know, but I appreciate the vote of confidence."

When she glanced over her shoulder through the pass-through window, Caty saw him checking out the books on her bookcase. She'd seen the bookcases in his living room with primarily mysteries, thrillers, and biographies. He also had a large collection of coffee table picture books.

"Do you mind if I take a peek at Sam's book?" he called. "The one about the seven rules of marriage?"

His questions got her heart pumping faster as she snipped the ends of the rose stems and placed them in a vase she'd filled with water. "Not at all. Feel free to take it home with you. I can always get another copy. I think that one might be autographed to me, though, now that I think of it."

"I might borrow it and then buy my own copy. I'm sure I'll meet Sam, and I can ask him to autograph it then."

"You might get that opportunity soon." After putting the vase of roses on her dining room table, she joined him in the living room. "I understand my mom and Sam's wife, Lexa, are putting together a party for his birthday in a couple of weeks. They want to go to some new country western place. Do you two-step, Mr. Reid?"

"I can do more than that." He demonstrated the Cha Cha Slide and then lifted his hands out to the side. "So, you tell me. How'd I do?"

"You do just fine," she said, laughing. "Ready to go see some fields of bluebonnets?"

"I thought you'd never ask." He followed her outside and waited while she locked the front door. "Bluebonnets in the sunset with a beautiful woman in my arms? What more could a man want?"

Hand-in-hand, they walked down the walkway to where he'd parked his car. Caty loved how he spontaneously took her hand, how well hers fit inside his.

"I've never been in a Porsche before." She waited as he clicked the key fob. "It's very low to the ground, isn't it?"

"There's a definite art to getting in one gracefully. But you, too, can do it with finesse and charm."

"You sound like you're a teacher in a charm school. Or one of those smarmy infomercial guys."

Caleb laughed. "Banish the thought. Do they still have those? Charm schools? Maybe I should send Lauren."

"Your daughter's got plenty of charm. And spunk."

"Spunk is one thing, but she could stand to temper her outrageous remarks."

"Shock value," Caty said. "If you don't make a big deal of them, hopefully she'll give up."

"You are a wise woman, Catherine, and a great influence on my daughter."

"I'm not sure how wise I am, but you'd better show me how this is done if we're going to get to those bluebonnets tonight."

"Right," he said. "There are four main steps to getting in the car without any mishaps—turn, sit, swing, and duck. That last one is important, especially for a woman of your height."

"Turn, sit, swing, and duck," she repeated slowly.

"It'll make more sense when I show you. This is the turn part." He turned with his back to the car. "Then you have the sit part." He took small backward steps and then seated himself in the car. "Then you swing your legs around like so. And then, since you're tall, you'll probably need to duck your head to make sure you don't hit..." He

315

patted his head with his hand and gave her a sheepish grin. "Make sense now?"

"I'll let you know in a second. My turn," she said. "The part that worries me is the sitting part with my back turned away from the car. I don't want to miss the seat and land on the pavement or anything." She rolled her eyes, hoping that didn't sound ridiculous. "I'm completely serious," she insisted when he laughed.

"The easiest way to do it is to back up until you feel the bottom runner of the car against the backs of your legs."

"I don't know. That sounds a little complicated."

"Don't worry," he said. "After you do it a few times, it gets much easier. The other key is having an escort to assist you."

"Well, why didn't you say so? Promise you won't let me fall?"

"Promise. If you do, I'll pick you up." Pausing with one hand on the door, Caleb looked into her eyes. "The first day we met, I wanted to pick you up and carry you inside the building."

"You did?" The warmth invaded her cheeks. "That's a heroic sentiment, but should I ask why?"

"I was afraid you might hurt yourself since you'd obviously suffered those other mishaps."

Caty laughed. "I was a walking mess that day! It's a miracle I managed to have a coherent conversation with you. Hopefully, I've proven to you since that I'm not nearly as clumsy as your first impression of me."

"You're beautiful, Caty. Clumsy or not, any way you come. Don't even get me started on the Japanese restaurant. You were so cute in not knowing what to do."

"We need to get one thing straight," she said. "Don't call me cute. I don't want to be cute."

He dipped his head and brushed his lips over hers. "What do you want me to call you?"

Oh, my. "I, um, think beautiful will be just fine, thank you so much. Let's do this, shall we?" With Caleb's assistance, she settled into the car easily enough. As they headed out onto the highway, headed on the 74-mile trip to Brenham, Caty sighed. "I'm not sure I'll know how to act without our little chaperone along. I take it she's home with Lettie tonight?"

"She is. Max, too. Life as usual, or at least our version of normal. By the way, Lauren and I had a talk, and I gave my permission for her to ask that boy to the dance."

"I think that's wonderful. She'll go with you, right? It's not like a date."

"Good grief, I sure hope not. I don't look forward to talking with Lauren about the birds and the bees. I think she probably knows as much as I do, anyway. Or she can guess." Caleb shifted something on the console and then reached for her hand. Caty hadn't a clue about this car except that it was loud, sleek, and powerful.

"Lauren's growing up, but I doubt she knows as much as she thinks she does. Have you thought about being a chaperone for the dance?"

"I've already volunteered. After first making sure she could go and that it doesn't violate her probation period." Turning his head, Caleb gave her a wide grin. "I volunteered you, too. As *my* date. You don't think I'm going to stand by and watch my daughter dance with a boy if you're not there to hold *my* hand, do you?"

"Maybe you could take some pointers from my dad when you meet him. Does Lauren have a dress to wear?"

"I'm sure she doesn't. If you're willing, I foresee another shopping trip in your future." Caleb shifted again and the car surged forward as they hit the open road.

"Watch your speed there, Roadrunner."

"I need to show you what this car can do."

"And I suppose I'll be the one to bail you out of jail later?"

He grinned. "I'll keep it respectable."

"You'd better."

"I hear the bluebonnets are all over the area, as usual," he said. "I hear the bluebonnets in Brenham are plentiful this year, even more than usual."

"Perfection. This is such a great idea, Caleb. Romantic, too."

"Who knew I had it in me?" They shared a smile. "I want to dance with you in a field of bluebonnets and then take you to this great little barbecue place a couple of miles outside of Brenham," he said. "A friend of mine from high school moved down here a decade ago and started it up. You won't find better ribs and corn on the cob."

"I'll be starving by then," she said. "Now you've got my mouth watering and my stomach growling. Not many things I love in life more than great barbecue."

"I know."

She laughed. "Marta told you?"

"No. You mentioned it during our conversation on the phone the other night. When you told me that, I knew it was a given I needed to take you there."

"I did? Hmm. You listen well. Not that I didn't already know that."

"I listen to what's important."

Caty did a double take on that statement.

"What? Did I say something wrong?"

"Not at all. It's just that my dad said almost the identical thing."

"Is it a good thing…or a bad thing that I remind you of your father?"

"Good thing. No worries."

An hour later, Caleb pulled the car to the side of the road. The bluebonnets were in abundance and stretched in every direction as far as Caty could see. "Oh, Caleb! Isn't this marvelous?" She didn't wait for him to come around. In her enthusiasm, she pushed it open and stepped outside. Stretching her arms wide, Caty ran into the nearby field, spun in a circle, and raised her face to the sky. And then she felt a sneeze coming on.

Oh, no. This wouldn't be good. "A…a…a…." She clamped one hand over her nose, but try as she might, that sneeze was coming on fast and furious. "Achoo!" Her entire body shook with the force of her sneeze. Moving her hands over her face, Caty slowly spread her fingers apart and then dared to peek at Caleb.

Shaking his head, he leaned against the Porsche. Then he slowly began to clap. "Congratulations. That was the most impressive sneeze I've ever heard from a woman."

"The most disgusting display, you mean." She frowned. "I can't help it. I don't sneeze pretty."

"You're not allergic to the bluebonnets, are you?"

"I've never been allergic to them before, and for your sake, I certainly hope not. I wouldn't want to subject you to a big sneeze attack. Now you know my deepest, darkest secret."

"If anything, that sneeze makes me adore you even more," he said, lifting away from the car and walking toward her. Goodness, the man could walk. And talk. Say things that made her melt. "If that's your biggest, darkest secret, we have nothing to worry about."

Catching up to her, Caleb pulled her into his arms.

She laughed and pushed against his chest. Turning away from him, she ran farther into the field of flowers.

"We have to stay somewhat close to the car," he said.

Glancing around him, Caty noted the passenger door stood open. "Why is that?"

Pulling his keys out of the pocket of his jeans, he clicked something on the key fob. Country music began to play, a love ballad she recognized.

"That's like a magical key fob. It controls all sorts of things, doesn't it?"

Caleb bowed low. "May I have the honor of this dance?"

Touched, Caty bit her lower lip. Now *she* felt like a shy schoolgirl, and the cutest boy in school had just asked her to dance. She nodded and, without speaking, moved into his arms. They danced through that song and the next one. Caleb moved his warm lips to her cheek and then down to her lips until they were moving in a slow circle, their arms around one another.

"I love you, Caty." He'd whispered it in her ear, and her heart jumped when she felt a slight tremble in his touch.

She pulled back enough to meet his tender gaze. "I love you, too." She lovingly fingered the cleft in his chin. "And I especially love this cleft in your chin."

"Glad it's good for something," he said, rubbing his fingers over it in a self-conscious gesture. "I never liked it much."

"I've never seen a man with a cleft who was anything less than…" Caty stopped. Maybe that wasn't the best thing to say. "You're the most gorgeous guy I've ever known that has a cleft."

He laughed. "Good save." Pulling a small camera from his pocket, he aimed it in her direction. "Smile for the camera. Tradition and all that. The number one thing to do when you come see the bluebonnets."

Acting silly, Caty pranced around as Caleb snapped photos— close-ups and long shots. After she insisted, he handed the camera to her, and she returned the favor. When they finished, he walked to the car and returned the camera to the glove compartment.

Walking back to where she stood, Caleb leaned down and checked the ground, moving aside some bluebonnets. "I'm checking for fire ants," he said before she could ask. "So you won't get…"

"Ants in my pants?" She laughed as he rolled his eyes.

"Now who's being corny?" he said, giving her a quick kiss. "Legend has it you're not supposed to sit directly on a bluebonnet. No crushing. But you can pick them if you want."

"I'd rather leave them here, anyway. Besides, I have my gorgeous yellow roses."

Taking her by the hand, Caleb lowered to the ground, tugging her down beside him. "You're not worried about getting…bluebonnet stain…are you?"

"Not at all. Although…everything's better…" She'd started the little sing-song.

"With bluebonnet on it," he finished. Groaning, Caleb shook his head. "What have I created? You're as bad as I am." He laughed. "Come here."

Caty nestled in the curve of his arms, and he sat directly behind her. "I remember hearing some of the Indian folk tales about bluebonnets in Texas history classes," she said.

Caleb pressed his lips to her hair and then rested his chin on her shoulder. "Me, too. I remember digging a little further so I could tell Lauren about them. Helena and I used to take her every year to Ennis to see the bluebonnets. We'd take a train ride, and Lauren loved it. We all did. There were stories that the priests gathered the seeds and grew the bluebonnets around the missions, and that practice supported the myth that the padres brought the plant from Spain."

"Ah, but that can't be true since the two predominant types of bluebonnets are found only in Texas and no other location in the world."

"You are correct. And your hair smells great."

"Thanks." She smiled as he tightened his hold on her and slightly rocked them.

"I've heard the bluebonnets are as well known to outsiders as cowboy boots and Stetson hats," Caleb said. "The bluebonnet is to Texas what the shamrock is to Ireland, the cherry blossom is to

Japan, the rose is to England, the tulip is to Holland, and…there's one more I can't think of."

Caty thought for a long moment. "The lily is to France?"

"I think you're right. You get the prize. Like I said, you are a wise woman." Reaching for one of the flowers, Caleb ran his hand over it but didn't pick it. "Did you know Texas actually has five state flowers and they're *all* bluebonnets?"

"No, I didn't know that," Caty said. "We Texans sure do love them, that's for sure. 'You may be on the plains or the mountains, or down where the sea breezes blow, but bluebonnets are one of the prime factors that make the state the most beautiful land that we know.'"

Caleb chuckled. "Where did you hear that? I know that quote didn't come from Babe Ruth."

"It's from the ballad of our singing governor. And he would be…?" Caty waited, wondering if he'd know the answer.

"Texas has a reputation for singing governors," he said. "I'd guess…W. Lee 'Pappy' O'Daniel?"

"Ding ding ding. And now I pass the prize torch on to you," she said. "You are correct."

"The only person ever to defeat Lyndon B. Johnson in an election. Originally formed a band called the Light Crust Doughboys."

"You so made that up!"

"I so did *not*," Caleb insisted. "Look it up, and you'll see for yourself. After that, he formed his Hillbilly Boys band. He hosted a noontime radio show and became a household name in the mid-1930s. The show extolled the virtues of Pappy's Hillbilly brand flour, the Ten Commandments, and the Bible."

"I suppose you couldn't make up all that stuff and spout it out with a straight face. Doesn't get much better than that." Caty waved her hand. "The Ten Commandments and the Bible part."

"Nope, it doesn't," Caleb agreed.

Bending at the waist, she leaned close to one of the bluebonnets and sniffed. "I love the smell of them. Like freshly laundered towels."

"Maybe you should suggest a fabric softener scent—Texas Bluebonnet." Caleb snapped his fingers. "Guaranteed bestselling product. What do you think?"

"You know, you might be onto something there. Seriously. *I'd* buy it, and I'm pretty sure a lot of my friends would, too. And people are always intrigued by the whole Texas thing, so it'd sell across the country."

"Whoa. Back up there. The whole Texas thing?"

"You know," Caty said, grinning, winking at him over one shoulder. "For one thing, all the manly men we have right here in the Lone Star State. Like the one I'm looking at right now."

"You sure know how to flatter a man, don't you?"

"I try my best." She wrinkled her nose. "We got off track there, but it was a fun detour." She leaned back to kiss his cheek. "I love those paintings of bluebonnets in the Belac lobby. Did you pick those out or did you have a decorator?"

"No decorator. That's all my doing. I've had them for a few years. I always intended to put them up in the Dallas lobby, but I never did for some unknown reason. Helena loved them, and she was with me when I bought them."

Caty averted her gaze. "I understand. They bring back bittersweet memories."

"Yes, but like other things in my life, it's time to bring them out of hiding to face the world, so to speak. Most of the paintings are reproductions by an artist named Julian Onderdonk. He was a San Antonio-born impressionist who studied under William Merritt Chase in New York in the early 1900s. Then he returned to Texas where he produced some of his best work. The most famous of the paintings in the Belac lobby is called *A Cloudy Day, Bluebonnets near San Antonio, Texas*. The original was painted in 1918."

Caty nodded as Caleb described the painting in more detail. "I'm pretty sure I know which painting you mean, but point it out to me next time we're in the lobby."

"Will do," Caleb said. "The Dallas Museum of Art has several rooms dedicated to Onderdonk's work. George W. Bush had three of his paintings hanging in the Oval Office at the White House."

"See? I'm learning all sorts of things today. Onderdonk," she said. "That's quite a name. Try saying that three times in a row. Who knew coming to see the bluebonnets would be such an educational experience? You remind me of Sam. He's a history nut. Whenever we used to go anywhere as kids, he would spout all these facts, some good to know, but others totally random. Somehow, he always managed to make them fun."

Releasing her, Caleb fell back on the ground, half-groaning, half-laughing.

Caty stared at him. "Are you laughing or groaning? I honestly can't tell."

Stretching out on the ground, Caleb crossed his arms behind his head. "First, I remind you of your dad. Now I remind you of your oldest brother."

"Yes, but like I said about Dad, that's a *good* thing. They're both strong, solid, godly men. And so are you. Would you rather I compare you to a man of ill repute?"

Caleb sat up again. "I have a confession."

She lifted her brows. "A good confession or a bad one? If it's the latter, I'm not sure I want to hear it at the moment. This is too special of an evening."

"You decide," he said. "Here goes. I'm sure you know me well enough to know not much intimidates me. Not many people make me doubt myself. But your dad and your brother? Let's just say…well, they intimidate me. I want to meet them, of course, but they're a lot to live up to from what you've told me. Don't even get me started on your astronaut brother. He's in an entirely different league."

"Live up to?" Caty sat cross-legged, facing him. "Why would you even think you need to *live up to* either one of them? They have their faults, too. We all do."

"Not you." Reaching for her hand, he laced his fingers with hers.

"Excuse me, do you know *me* at all?" Incredulous, Caty laughed. "I'm stubborn, a little crazy, feisty at times, I'm not nearly the cook my mother is, I get mad when I can't get something the way I want it, I get emotional for no reason sometimes, I can be downright snarky in my thought life, I'm not always charitable—"

"Caty, you are perfect…for *me*. That's all I care about."

"You know how to flatter a girl, that's for sure, and I'm thankful you think so highly of me, misguided though you might be. Seriously, Caleb"—she strengthened her hold on his hand—"the two Sams in my family wouldn't want you to feel intimidated by them. I feel safe in saying they'll want to get to know you. Tell you one thing. After you meet them, invite them up to see the sports memorabilia in your office. Guaranteed, you'll be friends for life."

"Think they'd like to go to an Astros game with us?"

She nodded. "Now you're talking. *That* sounds like a very good idea."

Rising to his feet, Caleb held out his hand to her. "Dance with me in the sunset?" The beautiful deep blue sky was a collage of yellow, bright orange, and pink streaks, a glorious representation of God's masterful artwork.

Her hand in his, Caty rose to stand beside Caleb. "I can't think of anything I'd like more."

Chapter 43

"You're right. This is some of the best barbecue I've ever tasted." Caty beamed at Caleb from behind the rib smothered in honey barbecue sauce she held in both hands. She was adorably messy. For the last five minutes, he'd wondered if he could get away with kissing away the sauce smudged on her left cheek.

"You have to learn to trust me when I say things like that." Caleb ate another row of his sweet, grilled corn on the cob. He made a conscious effort not to smack his lips. Good stuff.

"Oh, it's not that I don't trust you. I just needed to experience it for myself," she said. "It's like going to the Grand Canyon, for instance. Pretend you've never been." She hesitated. "Have you?"

"Yes, but I'll pretend that I haven't."

"Okay, then. If you hadn't, I could *tell* you what a phenomenal view it is from the top. But until you go and actually see it for yourself—in person—to fully understand the incredible beauty of God's handiwork there, you can't possibly have the same appreciation for it." She took another bite of her meat.

Caleb shook his head, unable to contain his smile.

She lowered the rib. "What now? Did I say something wrong?"

"Not at all. I'm just admiring you and thinking what a creative imagination you have for an accountant."

She wiped her mouth. "Are you saying accountants are boring?"

"Are we back at that again? You have to stop putting words in my mouth."

Caty broke apart her square of cornbread and held out a chunk to him. "Peace offering?"

He took it from her. "You are so going to get kissed on your doorstep tonight."

"Well, I certainly hope so. I was counting on it." With a cute smile, Caty dug into her coleslaw.

"You two lovebirds enjoyin' your dinner?"

At the sound of the man's voice, Caleb rose to his feet. "Brian Harman, how are you, buddy?"

"Doin' great, thanks." The heavyset, jovial man gave Caleb a bright smile. "Business is good, especially durin' bluebonnet season."

"That's why we're here. Brian, I'd like to introduce you to Caty Lewis."

The other man nodded. "Don't worry about shakin' hands, darlin'. I can tell you've been enjoyin' my food. That's all the *nice to meet you* I need."

"It's been absolutely delicious," Caty told him. "One of the best meals I've had in a long time. Please don't tell my mother I said that if you ever meet her."

Brian laughed good-naturedly before turning back to Caleb. "How's the oil business treatin' you? I heard about the ban on tobacco products in your stores."

"I can't complain, and it sounds like you're up-to-speed on the latest Belac information."

The other man slapped him on the shoulder. "You didn't get to be a zillionaire by makin' bad decisions. I think you'll be fine. If you lose money, knowin' you, you'll figure out somethin' else to make up the deficit."

"I appreciate that, Brian."

Brian glanced back over at Caty. "I think you need to put a ring on this young lady's finger. Glad to see you happy again, buddy. You deserve it."

"We haven't known each other all that long," Caty said, appearing awkward. A pretty pink flush spread across her cheeks.

"Caty's worked for me for five years." Caleb locked gazes with Caty. "In some ways, I feel like I've known her much longer."

Tucking long strands of her dark hair behind one ear, Caty gave him an enchanting, sweet smile.

"Take it from me," Brian said. "When you know it's right, go for it. You know how fragile life can be, and so do I. Not that you asked for my advice, but I'm goin' to give it to you, anyway."

Brian rested one hand on Caleb's shoulder. "Don't wait for life to come to you. Things happen—some good, some bad—but you've got to rise to the challenges. Learn what you can from them, strip away the bad, and focus on the good. God gave each of us a purpose in life, and it's up to us to take the equipment He gives us to work with and try to figure out what He wants us to do. You're doin' a good job of it, my friend. Keep it up."

Caleb shook the other man's hand. "Good to see you again, Brian."

"Come see me again." Brian gave his shoulder a squeeze. "Your meal's on me tonight."

"Thanks, but I can't let you do that—"

The other man winked and angled his head at Caty. "Put the money toward a ring."

"Well, that was...something." Caleb dropped back into his chair. "Nothing like being obvious."

Caty didn't have one of her quick comebacks and concentrated on finishing her meal. She offered the last rib to him, saying, "Here, Adam."

"Thanks, Eve, but I think we have it backwards." Laughing, he ate it, and then she offered him the last bite of her cornbread. He leaned across the table and she fed it to him, which he enjoyed immensely. Sharing food with this woman was something he hoped to do a lot more of in the future, among other things.

The clear night sky surrounded the car as Caleb drove them back toward Houston. Still quiet, Caty curled into her seat, but he knew she wasn't asleep.

"Brian's comment about life being fragile," she said after a while. After starting to say something else, she closed her mouth and looked out the side window.

"Brian and his wife lost a child to leukemia. Happened a year or two before Helena died."

Caty gasped and moved one hand over her chest. "Oh, I'm so sorry to hear that," she said.

"Should we talk about it? You got pretty quiet after Brian stopped by our table. I thought we were having a great time." She'd been perfectly fine until then. Surely she wasn't upset by Brian's hints and teasing?

"I had a great time, Caleb."

"Then talk to me, Caty. Are you mad? Did I say something wrong?" He moved his hand over hers, thankful when she readily accepted the gesture. Lifting her hand to his lips, he gave it a quick kiss.

"You didn't say anything wrong. I just…got emotional. I warned you."

"*This* is emotional? You're not saying a word. I thought women usually cry or spout accusations, throw stuff, freeze me out." In some ways, that kind of behavior might be better to get things out in the open than this…quiet. Somehow he must have hurt her, and Caleb needed to know how and why so he could fix it.

"Maybe that's what Helena did, but I tend to get quiet and withdraw." Caty slipped down into the seat and wrapped her arms over her middle. "I can't be 'up' all the time. That's not…normal. Don't mind me. I'll get over it."

He stiffened at her mention of Helena. Surely she wasn't jealous? That didn't ring true to Caty's character. Unfortunately, she was right. Those actions *were* the kinds of things Helena would do.

When he came to the next exit, Caleb pulled off in a gas station parking lot and stopped the car.

"Caty, listen to me." He tilted her chin and made sure he had her eye contact. "*You* are the woman I love. Helena is in my past. I loved her, but our marriage was far from perfect. She's been gone for five years. I've had sufficient time to grieve, and now it's time to move on with my life. God knew who I needed, and when, and He brought *you* into my life at exactly the right time."

Leaning across the console, he kissed her lightly. Something was still bothering her even though she kissed him back. A little more enthusiasm might be nice, but he'd take it. "Are you mad about Brian's comments about putting a ring on your finger?"

"Indirectly."

Now he was getting somewhere. The irrational thought popped into his mind that Lauren could probably tell him what was happening in Caty's mind. She might only be twelve, but his daughter understood the way the female brain operated a whole lot better than he did. Clearly he was being an oblivious, clueless male.

"I can't help you if you don't share what you're feeling with me." His cell phone made a sound. Reaching for it, he stared at the display and groaned. "Oh, no."

Caty struggled to sit up straighter in the passenger seat. "What is it?"

He released her hand, fired up the engine, and zoomed out of the parking lot.

"Caleb, you're scaring me. Why are you going so fast?"

He eased up on the accelerator slightly. "That was a call from the house. It's an alarm that's triggered by the security system."

"Hopefully it's nothing." He appreciated the soothing tone of her voice, but he knew in his gut this *was* something.

"Do me a favor," he said, handing her his phone. "Call the house. See if Lettie or Lauren picks up."

"Sure." Doing as he asked, Caty dialed the number immediately.

"Hi, Lettie? This is Caty Lewis. I'm with Caleb, and he got a call he says was triggered by the home security system. Hang on a second. I'm going to put him on the phone with you." She handed the cell phone to him.

"Thanks." He took the phone and checked his speed, slowing down a bit.

"Lettie, I got an alert through the security system. Everything okay?"

"I'm not sure," she said. "A car with dark, tinted windows has been sitting outside the house, parked across the street, for the past few hours. It could be nothing, but I don't know why you got an alert. The house alarm didn't go off. Max did go crazy barking for a while, though."

Max barked? The breeder told him Bullmastiffs rarely bark. One of the reasons would be when he sensed danger.

Caleb needed to make a split-second decision. He couldn't take the risk that something would happen to them otherwise, especially since he was a good hour away from home. "Call the police. Get them over to the house. Tell them you suspect the security system's either been compromised or tripped and have them check all the entrances. I'll be there as soon as I can."

"I'll do that. Don't worry about Lauren. She'll be fine."

"Does she know about any of this?"

"Not yet, but I feel safe in saying she will soon enough."

Couldn't be helped. "Sorry, but explain to her what you know, and keep her as calm as you can. You're very good at that. Tell her I'm on my way back home. I have Caty with me. We should be there in less than an hour."

"Okay. We'll see you when you get here," Lettie said. "If there's anything else to report in the meantime, I'll give you a call."

"Sounds good." Caleb disconnected the call. He glanced over at Caty although he didn't dare take his eyes off the road for more than a few seconds considering he was pushing eighty mph.

"Father, be with us as we head back to the house," she prayed. "We pray nothing's amiss, and that the security system hasn't been compromised. We put this situation into your hands and ask you for your watch care over Lettie and Lauren right now. And pray Caleb gets us there without an accident. We ask these things in the name of your Son, Jesus. Amen."

"Amen." He briefly told her what Lettie had said about the car sitting on the street for hours.

"Prayer is always the best answer," she said.

Lord, let them be okay. At least Lettie had answered the phone and things sounded fine.

Next he punched in Eliot's number. "I have no idea where in the world Eliot is, but even if this turns out to be nothing, he needs to know."

Caty nodded. "Never hurts to have Eliot Marchand on the case."

Chapter 44

Caleb drove the Porsche past the front gates and navigated around three HPD squad cars in the circular driveway. "We're having a party now." Within a minute, he'd parked the car in the garage. Slamming his door, he started around the back of the car.

"I've got it." Caty pushed open the passenger door and started to climb out of the car, whacking her head in the process. "Ow, ow ow." She put a hand to her forehead. "You go on in. I'm sure they're waiting for you."

For a split-second, her *ow ow ow* reminded him of Lauren. Reaching around her, Caleb closed her car door and then took her hand. "I'll have Lettie get you something. Let me take a look." Brushing aside strands of her hair with his free hand, he checked her forehead.

"I think I'll live, Caleb. Come on. Let's go inside and see what they have to say."

After punching in the security code, he ushered Caty inside. Together they quickly walked through the kitchen and then into the living room. Lettie sat with four uniformed police officers. She appeared calm and in control, a good sign.

One of the officers stood from where he'd been sitting in an armchair.

"I'm Caleb Reid." Wrapping his arm around Caty's waist, he strode forward and offered his hand. "Thanks for your quick response in coming out to the house. This is Catherine Lewis." He'd never liked the term "girlfriend" for anyone older than a teenager. From the corner of his eye, he noted Lettie's quirked brow. He'd need to catch her up-to-speed although he felt sure she could connect the dots quite well on her own. Lauren hadn't stopped raving about Caty the entire time they'd visited Lettie in Dallas.

The officer nodded. "Miss Lewis." He told them he was Lieutenant Taylor and introduced the other three officers. The other men rose to their feet and stepped a short distance away to make room for them on the sofa.

"Please sit down," Lieutenant Taylor said.

Caleb took a seat on the sofa beside Caty. He glanced at Lettie. "Is Lauren upstairs?"

Lettie nodded. "She's fine." He'd go upstairs as soon as the officers departed. If Lauren was awake, he'd talk with her and make sure she was okay.

"We've taken Oliver Portman's statement as well as"—Lieutenant Taylor nodded to Lettie—"Mrs. Huffman's statement." He sat in the armchair again. "We checked the perimeter of the house and found signs of forced entry on the outside door leading into the garage. The security system is fully operational, and we found no evidence of tampering. It's our contention that your dog's barking stopped them. We've dusted for prints on the outside latch and the door. We also found two sets of footprints to the far side of the garage."

Caleb's pulse raced. "You believe that more than one person was involved?"

"Yes, that's the most likely scenario. The footprints would appear to be from male suspects although we can't be positive without further investigation."

"You're suggesting they either scaled the front gates or the walls, miraculously dodged the security system, and managed to get as far as the garage before Max stopped them?" His stomach felt queasy, and Caleb scrubbed a hand over his face. "So much for the best security system money can buy."

"Unfortunately, there's virtually no home security system that can't eventually be breached," Lieutenant Taylor said. Not reassuring.

"Where there's a will, there's a way? Please spare me the platitudes and clichés." Caleb rose to his feet and began to pace the floor.

"Mrs. Huffman told us Max is a new addition to the household. It was a wise one. Now that it's known you have a guard dog on the premises, it might discourage future attempts."

Stopping his pacing, moving his hands to his hips, Caleb looked at the officer and returned to his seat. "I hope you're right."

After Caleb answered a few routine questions, Lieutenant Taylor closed his notebook and rose to his feet. The silent brigade of officers followed suit. "You should know the department is aware of the kidnapping threats you've received in the past."

Caleb glanced at Lettie, but she gave a slight shake of her head. He'd wait and see exactly *what* they knew.

"The Dallas Police Department passed on the information from a previous report filed after the incident at your daughter's school," Lieutenant Taylor said, answering his unasked question. "I also understand you've hired a private security firm here in Houston to follow-up."

How did they know all this? Perhaps it was for the best. The more people working to help find the persons responsible, the better. The officer's statement hadn't sounded defensive.

"That's correct. I felt it the best course of action," Caleb said slowly. "I'm sure your department has a lot of cases to deal with. Without any substantial evidence or suspects, there's not much any of us can do."

"That might be true, but feel free to call us if you see anything, hear anything, or anything else comes up," Lieutenant Taylor said.

"I'll do that. Thank you again." Caleb walked the officers to the door, shaking each of their hands. As he closed the door behind them, he turned to Lettie. "Thank you for calling them and taking care of Lauren tonight."

"That's why I'm here."

Crossing the room, he pulled Lettie out of her chair and encompassed her in a hug. "You sure you're okay?"

"Perfectly fine, dear heart." She gave his cheek a kiss and stepped back after he released her. "Caty, I'm sorry we had to meet under these circumstances, but I certainly hope I'll see you again. Lauren and Caleb have spoken very highly of you."

Caty gave her a warm smile. "Great to meet you too, Lettie. I'm sure we'll see one another again."

"I'll say good night then." Lettie departed the room and headed for her quarters off the kitchen.

"Caty, will you come upstairs with me to talk with Lauren?"

She rested her hand on the side of his face. "Cast all your anxiety on Him, for He cares for you," she whispered. "And so do I." Her eyes searched his. "So very much."

Pulling her into his arms, Caleb held her close. "I'm grateful you're here. Thank you. Not that I gave you much choice since you were my passenger."

"Caleb, there's no place I'd rather be. I hope you know that." She touched the cleft in his chin and then started up the stairs. "Let's go speak with Lauren."

They walked up the stairs, hand-in-hand, and an image popped into his mind of coming up the staircase with Caty beside him as his wife. And that's when it hit him. Caty hadn't been perturbed by Brian's words, she'd been irritated with *him*. He'd been flippant and sarcastic by brushing off the other man's words about a ring. What a dunce. Hopefully, he'd get the chance to talk with Caty about it on the drive back to her townhome.

Lauren's bedroom door stood slightly ajar. Pushing it open, Caleb peeked inside the dark room, illuminated by the moonlight streaming through the open curtains. With her headphones on, eyes closed, she bobbed her head back and forth to the beat of music.

Seeing him, Lauren started and then jerked the headphones away from her ears. "Hey, Dad."

"Sorry if I scared you, baby."

"That's okay. I'm glad you came." She scrambled to sit up as he dropped onto the side of the bed. Wrapping her arms around him, she noticed Caty standing a few feet away. "Caty, you're here, too! Did you guys have a good time in Brenham?"

"We had a great time." Caty's quick response made him smile. She didn't seem upset now. The sobering events of the evening had a way of putting everything in its proper perspective.

"Come sit with us." Lauren gestured to Caty and patted the mattress on the opposite side of the bed from where he sat.

"We wanted to make sure you were okay," he said. "I hope you weren't scared by anything that happened tonight. Anything you'd like to ask me? Do we need to talk?"

"Not really." She scrunched her features in a frown. "I just want all this craziness to stop so we can get back to our lives and not worry."

"I know, and I'm sorry." He smoothed her tousled dark hair and pressed a kiss to her forehead. "Hopefully, it'll be over soon."

"I know you're doing what you can. Max was the best guard dog ever! You should have seen him." When Caleb heard a noise in the room—one he knew didn't come from the three of them—he spied Max, fast asleep, in a far corner of the bedroom.

"I didn't think you'd mind if he stayed with me tonight." Lauren shrugged. "Notice he's not *on* the bed."

Caleb chuckled. "I think I'll get Max a special treat or a huge dog bone tomorrow to thank him for a job well done. Lauren, did you talk to the police officers?"

Lauren shook her head. "Lettie told me to come upstairs. She said she'd come and get me if they wanted to talk with me. Lettie was cool. She didn't crack under pressure or anything. She said she hoped her sister didn't catch wind of any of this or she'd probably march all the way here and haul her back to Dallas. I guess her sister's pretty bossy."

Caleb resisted his chuckle and put one finger over his lips. "Mum's the word unless Lettie decides *she* wants to leave. If she decides to do that, we have to let her go." He prayed it wouldn't come to that.

Lauren turned to Caty. "You're being quiet tonight. Everything okay?"

Caty's smile turned Caleb inside out. "I'm enjoying this sweet father-daughter moment," she said. "I love watching you two together."

If possible, Caleb fell more in love with this woman. How was it possible to fall so quickly and know in his heart it was *right*? He definitely needed to marry her.

"What is that noise?" Caty glanced around the bedroom.

"What's it sound like?" Lauren shot him a grin. She knew as well as he did that it came from the sleeping canine in the corner. Make that the *hero* of the evening.

"I don't know," Caty said. "Maybe like a light scraping noise of some kind?" When she tried to replicate the sound, Lauren and Caleb both laughed quietly.

"That's Max, too." Caleb angled his head to the dog. "He makes some very strange noises in his sleep."

"He also likes broccoli," Lauren said.

He scoffed. "No table food, remember?"

"I couldn't help it. I dropped a piece on the floor by accident at dinner, and he scarfed it down before I could stop him. At least broccoli has vitamins in it, right?"

Lauren gave him a grin—calculated but cute.

Caty reached for their hands, joining them together. "My dad used to pray with me every night. Is it okay if we do that now?"

"*Every* night?" Lauren said.

"Pretty much, unless he was away on a business trip. Mom was there a lot, too, but it was always a special time I shared with Dad. I think after what happened here tonight, there's no better way to battle the forces working against us than to stand firmly on the word of God." She glanced at him. "Are you okay if I go first?"

"Go right ahead." He was glad she'd taken the initiative.

As they bowed their heads, Caty prayed first, and he went next. When he began to wrap up their prayer, Lauren jumped in to add a few words. Caleb's heart swelled with pride.

"I think we've started our own tradition tonight," he said as they concluded.

Lauren nodded. "Caty, will you stay here with me tonight?"

"I need to work tomorrow, sweetheart." Caty darted an uncertain glance his way. What to do? He wasn't good at making decisions like this. He'd love for Caty to stay at the house, but for several reasons, it wasn't the wisest idea.

"Not tonight, Lauren. You have Max here, and Caty's right about having to work tomorrow. I'll see you in the morning, baby." He gave her a quick kiss on the cheek and smiled when Caty gave his daughter a hug.

"You know, this family prayer time makes it seem like you're my Mom."

This time, Caleb darted a glance at Caty. Thankfully, she didn't appear blindsided.

"Maybe one day, Lauren."

"Really?" He noted Caty had lowered her gaze, but he sensed she agreed.

Turning to go, Caleb shook his head when Lauren reached for the headphones. "No more tonight. You have school in the morning. It's time for bed."

"Okay. You would not, could not, dare be late." After pulling her sheets higher, Lauren rolled onto her right side.

"Is Lauren a Dr. Seuss fan?" Caty asked as they descended the front staircase together.

"She used to love the books, and she started saying that recently. Out of the blue. Kind of like someone else I know. Uncanny, in some ways." He turned to face her as they reached the bottom landing. Reaching for Caty's hand, Caleb tangled his fingers with hers. "I know it's late, but do you have time to talk for a few minutes before I take you home?"

Her smile was weary. "Let's talk tomorrow. To be honest, I'm beat."

"You're right. My impatience is showing." He didn't like leaving things unsaid, but they'd had an eventful last few hours. Their date had turned into something a whole lot more complicated. Story of his life these days. In some ways, it didn't seem fair to drag Caty into the mess of his life. On the other hand, she'd made it clear she wasn't going anywhere.

Thank you, Lord, for this strong woman beside me.

The ride to the townhome was another quiet drive. Based on her soft, regular breathing, Caty had fallen asleep. He didn't have the heart to wake her and could only hope *he* wouldn't be up half the night.

As Caleb pulled the car to a stop outside her front door, he shut down the engine and watched her sleep. He brushed his fingers over her cheek, but she didn't stir. So lovely. He allowed his gaze to roam over her features, so serene and peaceful in her slumber, and then he touched a strand of her silky dark hair. Should he kiss her awake? Tempting.

Pushing open his door, Caleb climbed out of the car. When she still didn't stir after he opened her door, he scooped her into his arms and then carried her to the front door.

"Hmm," she murmured, groggy with sleep. Snuggling into him, Caty moved one hand over his heart. Although he understood it was an unconscious move, Caleb sighed. When she moved her fingers on his chest, stirring everything male inside him, he knew he needed to keep moving.

"Do you have your keys?" he whispered, his voice husky.

"In the pocket of my sweater. It's only the house key." He was surprised she hadn't brought along her purse. At least for tonight, she'd traveled light.

Shifting her in his arms, he felt awkward while reaching into her pocket. He quickly retrieved the key and inserted it in the front door.

She must not have a security system. Maybe he should check into having one installed for her.

No, you can't run her life. You don't have the right.

With Caty still in his arms, Caleb stood in the middle of the living room, debating what to do. After all the decisions he'd made, he found this decision an especially difficult one. Go figure. With a quiet chuckle, he gently lowered her to the sofa. Then he gently eased off one red boot, putting it on the floor, followed by the other. Spying an afghan over a nearby chair, he grabbed it and draped it over her.

"I love you, Catherine." Leaning close, he dropped a light kiss on her lips.

"Love you, too, Caleb."

"See you tomorrow." As he departed, he double-checked the front door a few times. Satisfied it was locked, he climbed into the car and departed.

~~❤~~

"Eliot? It's Caleb."

"You're up late, buddy."

Sitting on the edge of his bed in shorts and a tank, Caleb glanced at the clock. Almost one in the morning. "I know. Can't sleep. Did you get my message and have time to talk?"

"Let me call you back in five."

"Sure." He heard the muffled sounds of a woman's voice in the background.

"Hey there, Oil Man." Marta's upbeat greeting made him smile.

"Hi, Marta. Listen, I'm sorry to call so late. I didn't realize Eliot was home. I figured I was calling him across the globe somewhere." His cheeks burned. His call might have interrupted their reunion. His timing could have been better.

"No worries," Marta assured him. "With my International Man of Mystery—that's Caty's name for him—you never know where you might find my husband at any given moment. I actually just got home from the studio a few minutes ago. Eliot's going into his office if you can hang on a second."

He heard a click on the line. "I've got it, babe. Thanks."

"See you soon, Caleb," she said. "Before I go, can you, Caty, and Lauren have lunch with us on Sunday? I'm sure Kevin and Rebekah would like to come if that's all right."

"Sounds terrific. I'll check with Caty and you two can work out the details. I'll be happy to treat if you'd like to go out somewhere. You pick the place." Caleb leaned back against the headboard. How long had it been since he'd been at a gathering with friends? Not since a few years before Helena's death. *Too* long.

"Great. It's a plan." Caleb heard the line click as Marta signed off.

"Hey, Caleb. I got your message in-transit or I would have called you back earlier. Tell me what you found out."

He filled Eliot in on the latest, including the observations from Lieutenant Taylor. "Eliot, am I putting Caty in potential danger? She doesn't have any kind of security system in her townhome."

"My gut feeling is that she's not, but if you'd feel better, I can schedule protection for her. If it helps, Sam insists that his TeamWork ladies take a self-defense course. I feel safe in saying Caty probably took one, too, either in Dallas or Lubbock."

"Good to know. I love her, Eliot."

He heard his friend's soft chuckle. "I know, buddy."

"That obvious, huh? If I had my way, I'd marry her to keep her by my side. Then again, until this is resolved, that's probably not the best idea. Then I think that this may *never* get resolved—"

"Don't get yourself worked up over the *what ifs*," Eliot advised. "You could suggest to Caty that she move back in with her parents, or Sam and Lexa, until we can figure out who's behind the threats. However, knowing Caty, she'd shoot down that idea."

"I think we're close, Eliot. I also have a strong suspicion they're connected to the accounting issues." Caleb told him about the latest unexplained withdrawal and his ban on all tobacco products in the Reidco stations and convenience stores.

"Before I left the office today, I made it known via an email to all Reidco employees that there have been financial discrepancies. I put all personnel on alert that their files, records, emails, and computers could be subject to review and inspection." Caleb blew out a weary sigh. "I didn't want to do it, but if they *are* connected, this action could force these jokers into action."

"I think it was a good decision," Eliot said. "It's a proactive move. I think you're right. It could very well flush them out so they make a move. If it's an inside job, they've been purposely stringing you along these last few years. Trying to break you down, drive you crazy, make you realize your limitations."

"Don't remind me," Caleb muttered, massaging his fingers over his brow. He felt a headache coming on and swallowed a rare curse threatening to escape his lips. That wasn't his way, and he wouldn't start now.

"We'll get them, Caleb. We'll figure it out, turn them over to the authorities, and then let the justice system take over. Josh Grant has friends in high places. He'll take care of us."

"I appreciate your positivity, my friend. Sounds like TeamWork has friends around the globe in all walks of life."

"That's one of the best things about it," Eliot said. "The slogan for TeamWork is 'Rebuilding Lives Worldwide and Binding Souls for Christ.'"

"I would expect nothing less. Did you get the list of Reidco employees from Cordelia?"

"I did, yes. I'll start working on it tomorrow. If I need any personnel records, I'll call you on your cell and let you know."

"Thanks. I neglected to tell you one of the most important things about the events here at the house tonight."

"What's that?"

"Lieutenant Taylor gave Max full credit for thwarting the break-in here at the house. I owe you one for that recommendation."

"Glad he's working out."

"Me, too. He's quickly become a member of the family."

Chapter 45

Standing in front of the kitchen window the next morning, praying as he ate his oatmeal—his version of multitasking—Caleb scowled as an image of his late father popped into his mind.

"Go away," he muttered, tapping his spoon against the ceramic bowl. He'd made a conscious effort not to think about his father, but lately, the man kept pushing into the forefront of his mind.

Why now, Lord? He didn't want to think about him. He had more important things to consider. Because his father had rarely been there for him, Caleb had always placed a higher value on loyalty and family ties. He'd been raised by a mother who'd taught him right from wrong. He might have strayed from her teaching at times, but he'd always managed to find his way back.

His mother was the one who'd also taught him lessons in forgiveness he'd never forgotten. "Letting go of the anger and the bitterness is the first step," she'd told him. "God doesn't want your leftovers, Caleb. He wants it all, the good *and* the bad. Surrender your father to God and let *Him* deal with your feelings. If you don't, you'll be eaten up alive with bitterness, and it'll render you incapable of moving on to find the joy that God wants for you."

Wise words from someone who'd been rejected by someone she loved. He knew the feeling. Caleb would not, subject another human being to that same kind of pain.

"Okay, I get it," he said finally, finishing his last bite of oatmeal and lowering the bowl into the sink. After running water over it, he lowered his head.

Father, I surrendered Helena to you. Now it seems it's time to surrender my leftover anger about my dad to you. Forgive me for my unkind thoughts. He no longer has any power over me, and I'm sorry he's gone. Sorry for the things left unsaid, sorry for what we could have meant to one another. I ask you to help me because without you, I am nothing. With you, I am everything. Be with me as I try to figure out the source of these kidnapping threats, try to figure out what's happening with the Reidco account, and talk with Caty today to see if everything's okay between us. I love her, Father. Thank you for bringing her into my life, and Lauren's life. I don't deserve her, but I hope to spend the rest of my days thanking you for the blessing of Caty. I ask these things in the name of your precious Son, Jesus. Amen.

Oliver had already left for Greenbriar-Browne with Lauren, and the house was quiet. Lettie was elsewhere in the house. Grabbing his briefcase, he prepared to depart through the side door to the garage. Something caught his eye from the corner of the kitchen. More like an odd sound.

"Max," he said on a sigh, chuckling. Resting his briefcase on a chair at the kitchen table, he crouched beside the forlorn-looking dog. "Are you lonely, buddy? Come on. Let's go take a walk outside." Opening the door to the backyard, he stepped outside and inhaled the fresh scent of the roses. He was so thankful for this garden, and he knew how much Oliver enjoyed tending to the blooms. Max darted ahead of him, bounding around the yard.

He stopped on the walkway, enjoying Max's antics. Picking up a stray branch from one of the trees, he tossed it to the dog. For a few minutes, he laughed as he threw it to Max. The dog would catch it and then dutifully bring it to him, dropping it at Caleb's feet.

"Caleb?"

Startled, he turned and smiled. "Hi, Lettie. I didn't hear you." The look on her face alerted him that something wasn't right. She held a piece of paper.

"What do you have there?"

Dear Lord, not another threat.

"I was cleaning through some more boxes upstairs, and I found something I believe you should see. I would never have opened the letter if I'd known of the personal nature of its contents. I'm not sure why no one found it before now. It was in a box from the bedroom in the Dallas house, sandwiched among some of Helena's other personal mementos."

He arched his brows, his curiosity piqued. "May I see the letter?"

She held out what he recognized as one of Helena's signature notecards, and her hand shook from nerves as he took it from her.

"It was written by Helena a month before she died before she...rapidly declined." Lettie lowered her gaze and cleared her throat. "Once I started reading, I couldn't seem to stop, Caleb. I hope you can find it in your heart to forgive me."

"Of course, Lettie." His smile disappeared, and his pulse raced.

"I'll be in the kitchen if you need to talk." Lettie turned to go.

"Thank you." Caleb strolled into the alcove and sat heavily in one of the chairs. The only sounds were from the birds chirping and rustling through the trees, and the soothing water cascading in the waterfall.

Max bounded over to him and sat at his feet. Caleb reached for the dog and rubbed his head. Fingering the pale blue stationery, he smiled at the *H* embossed in silver on the front before opening the notecard. Until recently, he wouldn't have been able to smile in looking at her notecards.

Inhaling a deep breath, he began to read.

Dearest Caleb,

This hideous disease is going to claim me soon, and with that knowledge comes a certain amount of soul-searching. I'm sorry for the way I've treated you at times, sorry for the hurt and pain I've caused you. That was never my intention. You always have been, and you will always be a wonderful man, and the best husband a woman could want. I'm honored to have been blessed by your love. Your faith is a large part of who you are, and I regret not sharing in that part of your life the way I should have for too many years, even though Jesus is my Savior, and I have the security of knowing I'll spend eternity with Him in heaven.

A large part of me is ashamed of my childish behavior through our years together. We were both kids when we met and married. I've let you down, and I've let myself down. Please know how much I love you and our daughter. How much I've always loved you both. When I'm gone, I know you'll be the best father Lauren could ever have.

When we fought that awful night, before I ran off to Paris, I said horrible, despicable things to you. Things I didn't mean, things that were incredibly painful for you. Words you didn't deserve. If I could take them back, I would. Please know that. I should have told you this before, but I didn't know how to admit my shame and the horrible damage I'd done to you, and to our marriage. I'll be forever sorry for hurting you. Even now, I can't seem to find the courage to tell you these things in person. I am so weak.

Caleb, nothing happened in Paris. I know you've wondered. I did meet a man there, and at the time, I was confused about us. I had drinks and danced with him, but I went back to my room alone, not that it makes my actions any less of a betrayal. And then you called me, and we talked, and I knew I wanted to come back home. Same thing with those nights I disappeared. You were working hard to secure our future, and my doubts led me to act irresponsibly.

With all that said, please know that—in spite of appearances, at times—I remained faithful to you always. You are the only man I have ever loved. I deeply regret making you ever doubt whether or not Lauren is your child. You are her father in every way, Caleb—flesh, blood, heart, and soul. All the proof you need is to look at her. She's you in her physical features, but Lauren also has your fierce determination, stubbornness, intelligence, and fighting spirit. She is the best part of me and the best of who we were together. Lauren is the legacy I entrust to you.

I only wish I could have been more for you, my darling. You're much too good a man to remain single. I pray you'll eventually find the woman of God's choosing who will complete you and love Lauren like her own.

With my love always,
Helena

Tears streaked down Caleb's cheeks. The words that pierced his heart were at the end of her letter. *I only wish I could have been more for you.* For so long, he'd wished he could have been more for *her.*

Max crept closer to him. Looking up at him with those big soulful eyes, the dog rested a large paw on his knee. Through his tears, Caleb stroked one hand over his head. He did love this big old dog. A hummingbird flitted by, making him smile. Helena had always loved them.

"Oh, Helena. We were quite the dysfunctional pair, weren't we?" Why couldn't she have shared these things with him when they'd still had time to talk about them? Before it was too late? Their marriage had increasingly become a series of miscommunications and fights over inconsequential, trivial things. A roller coaster of emotional highs and lows. Everyone had their own decisions to make in life, and Helena had made hers in choosing not to tell him before her death. Knowing the contents of this letter five years ago, three years ago, at *any* point before now, would have been good.

"Your timing is perfect, Lord." It wasn't his place to try and figure out why he hadn't seen the letter before now. His job was to carry on with his life in the here and now and to invest as much of himself in Lauren as he could. That's what he'd been doing, and that's what he'd always continue to do.

I'm thankful you're at peace, Helena. The kind of peace you never had here.

He'd never regret loving Helena. She was right about one thing. The *best* part of their marriage had kissed him good-bye this morning and looked at him with the kind of respect Caleb believed had slipped beyond his grasp.

Thank you, Jesus. Great is thy faithfulness.

Another tear slipped down his cheek. "We did well, Helena," he whispered.

After sitting for another few minutes, alternately praying and lost in his memories, Caleb rose to his feet. His tears had fallen, his soul had been cleansed. The lingering sadness could finally be replaced with hope and optimism. At last, he had final closure on those years and could move forward.

And then he knew, as surely as though the Lord whispered her name straight into his heart.

Caty.

The reason he hadn't seen this letter until now was because he'd found the woman who completed him. A woman who loved him and Lauren unconditionally. Caty accepted them as they were, demanding nothing, expecting nothing in return.

Caleb's gaze settled on Max. "I know you're wondering what kind of nutty family you've gotten yourself into. We're not so bad once you get used to us. Thanks for protecting us, buddy. When I get home later, I'll have a special treat for you."

At the word *treat*, Max sat at attention. Hearing a noise, Caleb walked around the corner, past a row of tall hedges. Oliver worked near the back of the house, humming as he pruned some kind of bush. If it wasn't a rose bush, Caleb had no clue what it was. He checked his watch. He'd been sitting in the alcove longer than he'd realized.

Tucking the notecard in his hand, Caleb strolled down the walkway with Max beside him. "Morning again, Oliver."

The other man stopped his work and glanced at him over one shoulder, his surprise obvious. "Well, hello there, Mr. Reid. Taking some time off work this morning?"

Caleb glanced into the distance. "Not on purpose. Something important came up."

"Everything all right, sir?"

He nodded. "It will be. What's that tune you were humming?"

"'Younger Than Springtime' from *South Pacific*. Funny thing about that. I was humming that same song when I drove Caty over here the other night. Lovely girl, Miss Lewis. She's got fire in her. You don't find a rare combination of beauty and spirit like that often."

Caleb nodded. "I couldn't agree more."

Oliver continued with his work. "You know, there are lyrics in that song that make a lot of sense."

Caleb allowed a small smile. "I'm sure you'll share them with me."

Oliver began to sing. He paused at one point and gave him a pointed glance. "Once you have found her, never let her go."

"Nice lyrics," Caleb said when he finished. "Do you mind if I leave Max out here with you for a while?"

"Not at all. I'd love his company. I've always enjoyed dogs, and I'm sure Lettie won't put up a fuss. Max has a habit of stretching out in front of the laundry room door."

Caleb chuckled. "Oh, and Oliver?"

He stopped his pruning again. "Yes, sir?"

"I don't intend to ever let her go."

"Very well. Carry on then. Good to hear it." With a wide smile, Oliver continued his work.

Caleb sat in the driveway a couple of minutes later and dialed Cordelia. "I'm leaving the house now. Do me a favor. Find the phone number for Samuel Lewis, Sr. in Houston. It's probably in Caty's personnel file. I need to call him as soon as I get to the office."

"Right away, sir."

The smile in Cordelia's voice made *him* smile as he headed downtown.

Chapter 46

Sitting at her desk, Caty suppressed her yawn. If she dared to close her door and try and catch a power nap, she'd probably snore. It wouldn't be advisable to be caught snoozing on the job. She forced herself to sit straighter in the chair.

"Focus, Caty." Blinking hard, she stared at her computer. If this was indicative of how the rest of the day would go, she was in serious trouble.

A knock sounded on her door, and Caleb stepped inside. "Good morning."

"Good morning to you, too." Caty's pulse took a flying leap at the mere sight of him, this man she loved. No man in history had ever looked better in jeans, a button-down oxford shirt, and boots. She'd enjoyed a couple of brief glimpses of him in a suit when he'd gone to important meetings, but this was—hands down—her favorite look.

In his hand, Caleb held a single, long-stemmed red rose. "For you from Ollie. And me. I removed the thorns."

"Thank you." Rising to her feet, Caty accepted the flower he handed to her. She smiled and touched one of the petals. "It's beautiful."

He slid his hands into the pockets of his jeans. "Sleep well?"

"I did until I woke up at three," she said. "After that, I had a hard time getting back to sleep. Forgive me if I yawn at some point during our conversation. It's not a reflection on you. Any updates?"

"No. That's not why I'm here."

She twirled the rose. "Care to share?"

"Can you come with me?"

"Now? Where?"

"Yes, and it's a surprise."

"Sounds promising. I love surprises."

"I know." His gorgeous smile surfaced.

She inhaled the sweet scent of the blossoming rose. "Marta?"

"Not this time. Just shut down, lock up everything, and come with me, please."

"What a romantic sentiment." Caty laughed when he gave her a look.

Suma watched, unsmiling, as they passed by the front desk. As soon as they reached the outer lobby, Caleb covered her hand in his. When they entered the elevator, he moved his arm around her waist.

"Better be good," she whispered. "The Elevator People might be watching."

He chuckled. "I suppose you're right. They might wonder about their new building tenant if he's seen smooching one of his employees in the elevator." Caleb's gaze locked with hers and he kissed the corner of her mouth. "I'll take my chances. I'm sure the security guards have nicknames for the building tenants. They'll call us the Elevator Smoochers."

Soon enough, the elevator doors slid open on the ground floor. Keeping hold of her hand, Caleb led her in the direction of the front curb.

"Oh no, you don't." Tugging on his hand, Caty pulled him back. "Not my arch enemy, the curb."

He grinned and acted like he was falling off the edge to certain doom. Laughing, he planted himself on the edge. "It hasn't rained today, and there's no drainage issue. See? Dry as anything. In other words, there's no water to splash you from a speeding maniac driving a black Porsche."

Pretending to ponder his words, she glanced up at the sky and touched one finger to her cheek. When she looked back at Caleb, she gasped. What was the man doing? He'd dropped down on one knee. *Oh, my.* Her own knees went weak. Only one reason he'd do that, right?

As she watched, wide-eyed, Caleb took her left hand in his. "Catherine Grace Lewis, I've loved you from the first moment I saw you here on this sidewalk. How could I *not* fall in love with the beautiful girl who had a broken heel on her shoe, tissue hanging from her scraped palm, and a ripped seam? The girl who has the biggest sneeze I've ever heard and knows more about baseball than most men? You've captured my heart, and my life will be forever changed for the better. I love you, and my daughter loves you. You have become a part of our family, and you complete me as a person, and as a man. Nothing would bless me more than having you walk beside me as my wife and for you to help me raise Lauren."

Moving one hand over her chest, Caty ignored the gathering crowd of spectators.

"Look, Jane! That young cowboy is proposin' to his lady love. Isn't that the sweetest thing you've ever seen?"

"Get a room already!" an old man muttered as he ambled by them.

"Mommy! Look! It's the belly button lady."

That comment made Caleb glance over at the little girl. Then he looked back at her with lifted brows.

Laughing, Caty waved to the child and her mother. "Long story," she told him.

"I'm sure. I'm also aging rapidly here." After she offered her hand, Caleb rose to his feet and then circled his arms around her, tugging her close. "My heart is yours, Catherine. Marry me?"

"Yes, I will marry you, Caleb," she breathed. "I love you, too." He lowered his lips to hers, and Caty was blissfully, gloriously lost in the moment as she melted into him. The late morning was beautiful, sunny, overflowing with God's grace.

"Is this really happening?" she whispered when they finally ended the kiss.

Caleb leaned his forehead on hers. "It's really happening. The field of bluebonnets would have been better, but I'm afraid my timing isn't always the best. Might as well get used to it now."

She shook her head. "I don't need sunsets and fields of bluebonnets. This is the place where we first met, so it's the *best* place. In my heart, I feel as though I've known you forever." Stroking one finger over the cleft in his chin, she kissed him. "Those things are wonderful, but as long as you're with me, I have all I'll ever need."

"After spending time with Lauren last night, praying together...*that* felt like family," he said. "*You* feel like family. I want you there in the morning when I stand in front of the kitchen window and thank God for a new day. I want you curled beside me on the couch, watching movies or reading together in the evening. I want to cook with you, do dishes with you. Play in the pool and relax in the Jacuzzi with you."

Leaning his cheek against hers, he whispered in her ear. "I don't want to drive you home and leave you on your sofa, covered with an afghan. I want you in *our* home, in my arms when I go to sleep each night, and when I wake up each morning." Tightening his hold on her, Caleb's smile found its way into Caty's soul.

"I knew I loved you when you sent me Scrappy. You are a man of surprises, but the very *best* kind. That's a very promising quality, you know."

He chuckled. "I intend to give you much better gifts from here on out."

"They showed ingenuity and creativity. Besides, I don't need *things*."

"I know, but I can do it, so humor me, please." His smile sobered somewhat. "I can't put my life on hold for something that may never transpire. But, even it does, we can face it better *together* than I ever could on my own. Before I left the house today, something Oliver said gave me the idea to propose this morning. I knew I couldn't wait any longer. Well, it was the second thing. Lettie found a note written by Helena a month before she died. It was addressed to me, and it was a very personal note where she expressed thoughts I wish she could have shared with me before she died."

Compassion flowed through her for this man. "Are you okay?"

"I am now. At first, I wondered why no one had ever found the note before, but then I realized—like everything else—it was all in God's perfect timing."

"I'm sorry, Caleb."

"Don't be. The note was bittersweet, but it gave me final closure. I didn't have the opportunity to tell Lauren I planned to propose, but I'm pretty sure she'll be ecstatic with this news."

"I believe she will." Caty's eyes filled. "And what was it that Ollie said this morning?"

"Actually, it was something he *sang*."

She laughed. Dear Oliver. "Yes, I know about your singing driver."

"I asked him what he was singing, and he told me it was a song from *South Pacific*. Something about holding her and never letting her go. You've already gained a huge fan in Oliver. I also called your father and asked his permission to marry you."

"You did? How'd that go?"

"I introduced myself and then basically said, 'Sir, I'm Abernathy Caleb Reid. I love your daughter and, if she'll have me, I want to marry her.' He was understandably surprised, but apparently you must have talked with him about me."

She smiled. "I did, as a matter of fact."

"Your mother joined our conversation, and the three of us shared a great conversation. The most important thing to know is that they trust your judgment, and they gave us their blessing."

Mom must be going crazy about now, and Dad might be trying to keep her calm. She'd need to call them soon.

"Thank you for being sensitive enough to call my dad, Caleb. I'll need to meet your mother."

"We'll take care of that soon," he said. "Which brings me to the second part of my surprise. If we hurry, we can still make the appointment I set up with a ring designer. Then I'll take you to lunch."

"And then you expect me to go back and work?" She laughed. "I might need to take the rest of the day off. Something I rarely do, I hope you know."

"I do know." He winked. "In addition to everything else, you're also one of my most loyal employees." He glanced at her feet. "Do you mind walking four blocks to the jeweler or do you want me to go get the car?"

Caty gave him her hand. "It's a beautiful day. Let's walk."

Chapter 47

Tuesday, April 24, 2007

"Caleb, I'd like you to meet my parents, Sam and Sarah Lewis."

Feeling uncharacteristically nervous, Caleb stepped forward and offered his hand to Sam Sr. and then kissed Sarah's cheek. "It's an honor to meet you." He turned to Lauren. "I'd like you to meet my daughter, Lauren."

"Lauren, I can't tell you how wonderful it is to meet you and your dad," Sarah said. "We've heard so much about you both from Caty."

When Caleb squeezed Lauren's hand, she squeezed back.

As they waited in the lobby for the rest of the family, Sam and Sarah asked questions about Belac and then asked Lauren about Greenbriar-Browne. Caleb prayed she wouldn't say anything inappropriate, and they'd had a talk before leaving to pick up Caty earlier in the evening.

Lauren understood how important this evening was for all of them, and she'd promised to be on her best behavior. No reason to believe otherwise. Max was a good leverage point, he'd learned. If she misbehaved or said anything untoward, she'd lose privileges, and the dog wouldn't be allowed to stay in her room overnight.

With a sweet smile, Caty watched them interacting with Sam and Sarah. Her parents were an attractive couple, tall, well-spoken, and distinguished. With her hair and eye color, Caty took more after her father, but she had her mother's smile, sense of humor, and ready wit.

A former military man, Sam's dark hair was peppered with silver strands. Caty's father struck him as being a quiet man, certainly not as outgoing as his wife. When he did speak, he chose his words well. Caleb noted he wore a hearing aid and recalled Caty telling him about the inner ear disorder that had grounded him as a pilot back in the early 60s.

"Today is not only our Sam's birthday, but it's also the anniversary of the day when my Sam returned home to Rockbridge after serving overseas in the Air Force," Sarah told them. She winked at Lauren. "Back in the Stone Ages."

Lauren giggled. A real *giggle*. That alone was refreshing. "How long have you been married?"

Sarah slipped her hand into her husband's. "We married on Christmas Eve in 1962."

"That's like..." Caleb held his breath as Lauren did the calculation and prayed she wouldn't say anything offensive. "Forty-five years!"

Sam moved his arm around his wife. "I married the feisty, beautiful girl who couldn't wait to leave Rockbridge and become a nurse. She stole my heart then, and she reminds me every day why I married her. She worked in the local diner, championed the cause of its citizens, and loved *To Kill A Mockingbird*." He kissed Sarah's forehead. "She told me I reminded her of Atticus Finch."

"Still my all-time *fictional* hero."

"I love that book!" Clearly pleased by Lauren's enthusiasm, Sarah launched into a discussion with his daughter about the Pulitzer Prize-winning novel, telling them her husband had given her a signed first edition of the novel as a wedding gift.

"Cool," Lauren said. "Do you still have it?"

Sam grinned and high-fived her. "Would you like to see it sometime?"

Lauren moved her hand to her hip and gave him a saucy grin. "You *know* it." Any lingering doubts in Caleb's mind vanished. They were getting along famously. Better than he could have hoped.

"Should we wait for everyone else to get here?" Caty asked her mom after a server came to ask if they'd like to be seated.

"I'm sure they won't mind if we go ahead," Sarah said. She offered her hand to Lauren. "Shall we lead the way?"

Caleb leaned close as he walked with Caty to their table. "No wonder you turned out so great. Your parents are the best. Is this party a surprise for Sam?" He double-checked the inner pocket of his jacket to make sure he had the envelope with Sam's birthday gift.

"No. The big surprise bash for Sam was last year on his fortieth."

Shortly after taking their seats at a table, hearing a commotion, Caleb looked up to see a tall, dark-haired man with a petite, blonde woman approaching the table. No doubt about it, this had to be the birthday boy. He recognized him from the book he'd borrowed from Caty. The younger Sam's resemblance to his father was also remarkably strong. Three children bounced around them.

Walking close on their heels was Carson and...wow. The man with Carson had to be Commander Lewis. If it weren't for Sam's deep smile lines and the slight tinge of silver at his temples, Will could pass for his twin.

"I didn't know I'd meet Will tonight," he whispered to Caty. "I think I'm a little nervous."

"He still wasn't sure whether he could come when I spoke with him yesterday."

"I feel like I should stand at attention or salute or something."

Caty ducked her head and smiled. "He gets enough of that at work. Don't indulge him. Around us, he's just Will."

"Right." Caleb chuckled. "Like you're just Caty." He kissed her temple. "The most remarkable woman I know."

After the introductions were made and everyone was seated around the long table, Sam Sr. welcomed them all. "We're not only here tonight to celebrate Sam's birthday, we're also celebrating another momentous occasion." He nodded to Caty and Caleb. "Caty and Caleb's engagement."

Carson whooped it up, and Lauren joined him. Will came around the table to shake his hand, and they talked for a few moments. Caleb was pleased to find the commander surprisingly warm although much more reserved than his brothers. Lauren was having a ball chatting with everyone, and he hid his smile at her puppy love for Commander Will when he said something to Carson. Those two brothers seemed pretty close. A quick glance around the room confirmed half the females in the place were stargazing at the astronaut.

Retrieving the envelope from his pocket, Caleb handed it across the table. "Happy birthday, Sam."

"What's this?" Sam took the envelope from him. As he opened it, a grin spread across his face. "Thank you, Caleb. I'm sure we'll be happy to accept your hospitality."

"What is it, Daddy?" The little blonde scampered out of her chair and went over to her father, peeking over his shoulder.

"Mr. Reid has given us box seats to an Astros game with the Milwaukee Brewers at Minute Maid Park this coming Saturday."

"How nice of you, Caleb." Lexa gave him a bright smile. "Nothing could be more perfect for Sam." Caty had checked ahead of time with Lexa to ensure Sam would be in town and available to attend.

"Everyone is invited," Caleb said. "The more the merrier. Hunter Pence is making his MLB debut as the Astros center fielder. He's from Arlington High School near Dallas, and I've been watching him for a few years. Before the game, if you'd like, I'll be happy to give you a tour of the baseball memorabilia in my office."

Sam Sr. chuckled. "Caty didn't tell us about that. We'll look forward to seeing it."

Caleb held up one hand. "She's only being a loyal Belac employee. That has something to with a confidentiality clause which I can assure you I'll be reevaluating in the near future."

"You're going to love his collection." Caty squeezed his hand.

"That's so cool!" Joe said. "Uncle Will, are you going on Saturday, too?"

Will shot him a grin. "I'll do my best, Joe."

"Even though you were probably joking when you told Rebekah about having promotional baseballs made with Belac emblazoned on them, have you thought any more about that idea?" Caty asked as they ordered their dinners.

"Not yet, but I've come up with something I think you'll like. I'm going to be sneaky and make you wait until Saturday." He'd made a sizable donation as a new corporate sponsor for the Astros, and the league owners had promised their new banner would be added to the stadium by the weekend game. His loyalty to the Rangers would remain firmly in place, and he was also a part-owner in that franchise. As long as he kept it in Texas, no reason he couldn't support both teams.

Taking Caty's hand, he admired the engagement ring she'd chosen—a 2.02-carat, Blue Nile Signature Round Diamond on a platinum band. The facets sparkled in the light. He would have bought Caty whatever she wanted, but this one suited them both. Knowing they most likely wouldn't wait long to be married, they'd gone ahead and ordered a matching band for her as well as a simple platinum wedding band for him. Both his bands and Caty's would be engraved with the Scripture reference for John 15:4 as well as the word *Abide*.

After everyone had ordered, Sarah called for their attention. "Sam didn't want us to make a big deal about his birthday, so instead of celebrating his birthday, tonight we're celebrating Caty and Caleb's engagement."

Carson grinned. "Surprise!"

Beside him, Caty gasped, clearly as surprised as he was.

Sam Sr. rose beside his wife and lifted his water glass. "To Caleb and Lauren. Welcome to the family. Caty, thank you for bringing them into our lives." They all raised their glasses in a rousing toast.

"We have gifts," Lexa told them. She asked the kids to take everything to them.

Sam gifted him with an autographed copy of his *Seven Rules of Marriage* book, and her parents gave them a gift card to one dinner each at four different fine restaurants in the area. Carson gave him a subscription to *Kindred Spirit* and, together with Will, gave them a gift card to the local Christian bookstore. Will also offered a tour of NASA and Mission Control, an idea Lauren pounced on immediately, as well as Joe.

Lexa handed Caty an envelope from Doyle-Clarke Catering containing a gift certificate for a private catered dinner for up to eight persons in his home with the menu of their choice. "There's no expiration date," Lexa told them. Caty had told him that her father was especially close to his daughter-in-law, something to do with the fact that her mother died when Lexa was a young girl—close in age to Lauren when they'd lost Helena—and her father had more or less neglected her.

"We have something for you, too!" Prancing around the table, Leah and Hannah presented them with a rather sizable package wrapped in festive paper with brightly colored hearts.

"Go ahead. You can open it now," Leah said.

"Thank you, girls." Caty kissed each of their cheeks. "Caleb, I wonder what this could be?"

"It's from Joe and Chloe, too." Hannah giggled when Caty pretended to shake and rattle the box.

"Chloe is Josh and Winnie's oldest daughter," Caty explained as she carefully removed the wrapping paper.

"Just rip it off already. Why do girls always take so long?" Joe's comment made Caleb smile.

"My sentiments exactly, Joe," Carson said. This guy was fun.

Caty moved aside layers of tissue paper. "What have we here?" She held up two crowns made from gold poster board, decorated with fake jewels, and decorated with white fur trim around the bottom.

"You're the princess and prince!" Hannah said, clapping.

Leah beamed. "You have to wear your crowns all night!"

Sam laughed. "Don't let it go to your heads."

"Sam, I think we're going to get along just fine," Caleb said.

Lauren helped Caleb position his crown while the twins served as Caty's eager ladies-in-waiting. He'd wear that crown all night and dance up a storm to keep Lauren smiling.

Thank you, Jesus.

He'd never felt so much a part of a family as he did with Caty's family, and he'd only just met them. God always knows. The verse from Jeremiah 29:11 came to mind about the Lord's plans to give him a future filled with hope. A promise he would claim.

The threats were never far from his mind, but tonight—as much as any other time since they'd begun—Caleb felt at peace. No matter what happened, he could face the future with confidence.

Yes, he would *abide.*

They would be all right.

After their delicious meal filled with lively, ongoing conversation, the dishes were cleared. Caty smiled as Sam rose to his feet and announced, "Let's get to it. Time for some dancing."

Caleb pushed back his chair. "Shall we, Miss Lewis?"

"Dance with Lauren first, and then we'll dance," she said.

"And that's why I love you, my princess." Before he could act on the suggestion, her father approached and asked to dance with Lauren. Watching her dad move toward the dance floor with Caleb's daughter, Caty gave her mother a nod. Sarah gestured for her to dance with Caleb.

"Everything okay?" he asked as tears sprang into her eyes as they walked to the dance floor together.

"Fine. I'm afraid you caught me in another emotional moment."

He nodded to Lauren, standing between Carson and Sam Sr., laughing and spinning as they line danced. "Look at her. They've made her feel so welcome. I can't remember seeing her smile that big in a long time."

Who knew an oil man had such rhythm? Caty was in awe. Tucking his thumbs in his belt, Caleb moved like a natural dancer as they performed a few more line dances together. They boot-scooted, two-stepped, and then joined in the West Coast Swing beside Sam and Lexa. Caty smiled and gave Will and Carson a thumbs-up as they danced with their nieces. On occasion, Will swept one of the girls into his arms while Carson did the same with the other. Lauren even danced with Joe, and she found that incredibly sweet. She was more surprised to see Joe dancing. If Commander Will could dance, that must have given him inspiration.

A few times, Caty nearly dislodged her crown. Caleb's landed on the floor on numerous occasions, sending the twins into a fit of giggles as they scrambled after it, seeing which one could grab it first and plop it back on his head.

"Line dancing is good for the soul," Caleb said, breaking into her reverie. "At least, a *Texas* soul." His face was flushed from his efforts.

"You know it." A slow waltz began, giving Caty an opportunity to catch her breath. "Where'd you learn to dance so well?"

"My mom loves to dance Texas-style, and she made sure I learned. Those skills made me a novelty at Princeton until I taught them the East Coast Swing. That convinced a few of them we know how to do certain things right down here in Texas." He stressed his drawl on that last part and then stole a quick kiss.

A short time later, after a few more line dances, Caleb danced with her mother while Caty danced with Dad.

"Caleb is a good man, sweetheart." He kissed her cheek. "Your mother and I are thrilled for all of you."

"Thank you, Dad. Your opinion means everything to me. I know Caleb might not be what—"

"Not as tall as we expected?" His blue eyes smiled when Caty looked up at him. "Honey, we can't predict who the Lord will bring into our lives. Your mother and I have prayed for your husband since before you were born, same as we've done for all our children. There are no prerequisites or limitations on that person. All we've asked is that your husband be an honorable man who loves the Lord and loves you with all his heart. Our prayers in that regard have been answered. And Caleb has a lovely daughter to boot."

Caty's heart swelled with love. "You're the best. Say, would you mind going with Caleb to fly model airplanes sometime?"

He smiled. "Not at all if that's something he enjoys. That's one kind of airplane I've never flown before."

"From what I gather, that's the one happy memory Caleb has from when his dad was around. He left the family when Caleb was ten to drive a truck on the open road, and he died a few years ago without ever contacting them again."

"I'm sorry to hear that. Then all the more reason to fly a model airplane with him. I can see if Sam and Joe can join us. Maybe Carson."

"Not the first time. Make it just the two of you. If you go again, then invite the others."

Her father leaned his head on hers. "Sounds like Caleb's risen above adversity. His story reminds me somewhat of Sam's friend, Marc Thompson, in Boston. Marc's dad was a famous basketball player who played for the Celtics in the NBA."

"I did hear that somewhere along the way." Caty pulled back to look at her father as they continued to dance. "Marc played for the Red Sox farm team in Pawtucket, right?"

Her father nodded. "That's correct. His dad developed a brain tumor and pushed everyone out of his life. He died alone without reconciling with his family. As a result, Marc stepped up to become the male figure for his mother and sister. Then, as you know, he went on to become a highly successful business owner of a sports agency in Boston."

"I guess having their fathers leave like that *can* make a man stronger," Caty said. "I'll tell you one thing." The unspoken sentiment was that it could also have had the opposite effect.

"What's that?" Her dad's grin surfaced.

"I can't wait to meet who the Lord has waiting for Will and Carson." Leaning her head on his chest, Caty heard the low rumble of her father's chuckle.

"That makes two of us. It could be that Will is destined to remain single, but I doubt it."

"I hope not. We both know Carson will get married once he settles down."

"Yes, Carson needs to find his place first," her father agreed. "Will's found his place, and that needs to be his sole focus for now. Rightly so." Sam Sr. shook his head. "Sometimes I still can't believe your mother's dream from all those years ago is coming true in a few months."

Caty smiled. "That pleases you as much as anything else, doesn't it, Dad? That it was Mom's dream?"

A smile creased his handsome face. "Every bit as much as Sam leading his TeamWork crew." He kissed her cheek. "And the work you're doing with the Montford Mission. Not to forget your sisters in raising their wonderful families and working on their own ministry projects. I realize how many families have children who stray from the faith, but your mother and I are blessed that all of you have stayed close to the Lord. I don't know of many families who can say the same."

"You and Mom have created a true legacy of faith, Dad. Thank you for that. Have I told you lately how much I love you?"

"You just did. Love you, too, Catherine." He moved his hand over his heart as the song ended and Caleb came to claim her once more. With a nod, her father took her hand and joined it with Caleb's and then quietly departed.

She caught Sam's eye as he danced with Lexa, and he winked.

And then Caty made one more turn on the dance floor with Caleb, the princess and her prince for the evening.

Chapter 48

Saturday, May 12, 2007

Caty wasn't sure what was more fun. Watching Lauren with Justin or watching Caleb watching the two young people.

He grunted. "I never thought I'd be sitting here, eating ice cream after the Greenbriar-Browne dance, while my daughter and her first crush are sitting across the room making eyes at each other."

Caty smiled. "Kind of like I'm making at you right now?"

"I'll never get tired of it with you, Caty. I also refuse to call this her first date."

"That's because it's really not. I keep telling you that." Why wouldn't he listen? "I had a little chat with her before the dance started, Caleb. Lauren understands you won't allow her to date 'for real' for another few years."

She grinned as she scooped another bite of her ice cream. "I'll never forget the look on your face as you saw your young lady come down the stairs tonight in her pretty pink dress."

"Look at them. Were we ever that young?"

"I don't know about you, but I was...once upon a time," she said. "But I'm thankful everything in my past led me to being here with you right now. Slurping ice cream and wondering how I ever got so blessed."

Caleb swung his gaze back to hers. "You say things like that and I have to ask...Caty, will you run away with me tonight? If the plane's free, I'll have the pilot fly us to Reno, and we can be married by morning."

"Hmm. Tempting. You *do* like your surprises, don't you?" With a small smile, Caty spooned another bite of her praline ice cream from the cup. In her midnight blue gown, she didn't want to take the chance she'd spill any of the sweet treat on her dress.

"You think I'm joking? Sam told me about marrying Lexa in San Antonio. It's not like surprise weddings are unheard of in your family."

"Yes, but although their wedding was a surprise, it wasn't really a shock."

He tilted his head. "How so?"

"I'm sure Sam told you he'd been gone for a year on a trip to Africa. That mission ended up being pretty dangerous, as it turns out. During that year, Mom mentored Lexa. She was still young in her faith, and she took Lexa under her wing. I feel safe in saying the entire family fell in love with her. Sam let us know he planned to meet her in San Antonio but swore us all to secrecy. Hardest secret I've ever had to keep other than not telling people I work for Belac," she admitted. "Did he tell you about the yellow roses and asking the children to run over to Lexa and give her flowers?"

"He did. Sounds like a movie considering it took place in the front of The Alamo."

"I suppose it does." Caty grinned and took another bite of her ice cream. "I was proud of you tonight, Caleb. The highlight of the evening was seeing you dance with the headmistress."

He grinned as he took another bite of his butter pecan ice cream in a waffle cone. Clearly, he wasn't as concerned about any drops of ice cream falling on his black tuxedo or black necktie. The man was a dream all his own in that tux, a close second to his casual look. Who was she kidding? Caleb looked good in everything he wore, and then some.

"Winthorpe was a good dancer once she settled down and allowed me to lead." After another bite, Caleb gave her a rather sly smile. "Want to know the highlight for me? Seeing the look on your face when you saw that guy you knew from years ago. The one *you* had a crush on. Grant something or other."

Caty laughed. "Grant Sims. I can't believe he showed up, especially since I'd just told Lauren I'd gone to my first boy-girl dance with him. Of course, Lauren was more interested in whether or not I kissed Grant."

"And…did you?"

"I'll never kiss and tell. No," she added quickly. "Besides, he only wanted me for my English tutoring skills."

"Good thing for me." Caleb waggled his brows and kissed her hand.

"Why, Caty Lewis, I heard you were here. Give me a big hug, precious girl." Bea Richardson, owner of the ice cream shop, hurried over to her with open arms.

Caty rose to her feet. "Bea, it's been too long. How are you?" She gathered the kindly woman in a warm bear hug.

The older woman kissed her cheek and then released her. "As well as can be expected. I finally hoodwinked one of my grandkids into taking over the shop, so I'm indulging in some leisure time and doing some traveling now."

"You deserve it," Caty said. "Enjoy every moment."

"That doesn't mean I won't be coming in here often to see my favorite customers. I live pretty close." With a wide smile, Bea turned to Caleb. "Time to introduce me to your devastatingly handsome escort. Honey, where have you been all of Caty's life?"

"Bea Richardson, this is Caleb Reid." Unsure what more Caleb would want her to say, she'd leave it at that.

"Nice to meet you, Caleb."

"The honor's all mine, Bea."

"Sam and Lexa live not far from here, and sooner or later, all the members of Caty's wonderful family started coming to my shop. Not to mention Sam's crew, especially Kevin and Rebekah and those adorable twins. So, tell me. What do you do for a living, Mr. Reid?"

"I'm in the oil business."

"Are you now?" Bea lifted Caty's left hand. "Judging by this ring, I'd say you do mighty well for yourself. Congratulations, Caleb. You couldn't have picked a nicer family to marry into." Bea patted Caty's cheek and happy tears glistened in her eyes. "I couldn't be happier for the two of you. How's Marta these days? I don't see her much since she started doing the weather every night." Bea winked. "You might tell her to stop in sometime and see me."

"Marta's great. Caleb went to Princeton, as a matter of fact," Caty said. "Same as Eliot."

"Well, is that a fact?" She waved her hand. "Mighty fancy."

"On scholarship," Caleb said. Caty loved how humble he was. Even at the Astros game when he'd been introduced as the newest sponsor of the baseball team, he'd kept everything low-key. And then hollered as loud as anyone when the Astros had gone on to stomp the Brewers by a score of ten to one. Caty had lost her voice with all her whooping and hollering. She'd laughed when Caleb made a point of chowing down on three hot dogs and making sure he was photographed for the corporate newsletter. From now on, the Belac CEO would be in full view for anyone to see. He was encouraging meetings with his employees, and that was only the beginning.

A new era indeed for Belac and Reidco, in particular. The sales for Reidco had taken a hit initially after the tobacco sales were pulled. Caleb had expected that, but they were steady otherwise, a good thing. The Lord would bless that decision.

After chatting with them another few moments, Bea excused herself. But not before giving Caleb a warm hug and telling him she hoped to see him again soon. "Now that Caty's back in town, I expect you to be regulars."

"We will," Caleb answered for them both, making Caty smile.

"Why is it that cereal tastes so much better after midnight?" Caleb sat across from her in Caty's kitchen.

"Beats me. I can't believe you're eating again."

Caleb had removed his jacket and tie, and his tuxedo shirt was unbuttoned a few buttons. She'd been babbling the past twenty minutes since he'd brought her home in an effort to keep the conversation flowing so she wouldn't drool over him. Her attraction was at a peak, and the man was driving her to utter distraction.

"Lauren had a really good time tonight," she said. "This is one of those special moments in her life she'll never forget."

"I hope you're right. I know I won't forget it." Caleb released a sigh. "It seems like only yesterday I held her as a baby and now look at her. In a few short years, I'll be dancing at *her* wedding."

She smiled. "You'll have lots of opportunities for making memories with Lauren. There's a whole lot of living to be done in the meantime."

"Caty, every single moment I spend with you is showing me how much of life I've missed in the past, and how I need to claim the *joy*." The only sound in the kitchen was the ticking of the large wall clock, reminding her of the clock in his office.

His smoldering gaze met hers. She hadn't bothered to turn on the light in the kitchen, and the room was quiet and dim. Incredibly romantic.

"Would you please finish that bite?" Slowly, Caty rose to her feet, needing his kiss more than her next breath

"Done." He lowered the spoon into the bowl, his cereal forgotten. Moving quickly around the table, Caleb pulled her into his arms.

She lowered her lids as he pressed his lips to hers, gently at first and then with a hunger and need that stole her breath. Her heart pounded, and she was close to losing control. Caleb's hands were in her hair, and the way he held her, the way he kissed her, empowered her and made her feel undeniably feminine. More than ever before in her life. She couldn't wait to become this man's wife. His hand moved to her neck, supporting her when she felt so weak she almost couldn't stand.

Finally, Caleb broke the kiss. Still holding her, he drew her tight against his chest, so close she felt his strong, steady heartbeat. "I should probably go now."

Caty nodded and tried to catch her breath. "It's probably best."

"I'm sorry, Caty. I hope I didn't offend you."

"Oh, you didn't offend me," she said, laughing a little. "I was right there with you." She smoothed one hand over her hair, knowing it was a lost cause. Not that it mattered since it was the end of the evening. "Thank you for that."

He chuckled, low and deep in his throat. "I hope I didn't scare you."

"Do I *look* scared?"

"No," he said quietly. "The look on your face makes me feel like the most blessed man on the planet. By the time of the Picnic in the Park next Saturday, I'm hoping we can announce our wedding date." He caressed her ring finger and planted a soft kiss on her open palm. She loved when he did that. Loved all his romantic overtures. Loved *him*.

"How about setting one now?"

His smile soared into her heart. "Name it."

"You know I'd like to be married before Will's mission in October. September?"

"Much too far away."

"August?"

He shook his head again. If the man had his way, they'd marry in the next few weeks.

"How about June?" Close enough.

"Sounds perfect. Pick a Saturday." Reaching into the inside pocket of his tuxedo jacket, Caleb pulled out his phone and showed her the June calendar."

"How about the 16th? In the middle of the month?"

He noted it on the calendar. "Done. Can't wait. We'll discuss details this week."

"Perfect. I'll get Lauren involved. We'll have fun together."

"And I'll schedule the plane and fly you to dinner in Dallas sometime next week so you can meet my mom."

Her eyes filled. "I will love that."

Caleb draped his jacket over one shoulder and silently led her into the living room. They stood facing one another beside her front door. "Have I told you tonight how beautiful you are?"

He didn't give her the opportunity to respond as he tipped her chin and kissed her so thoroughly Caty felt all resistance melting away like a snowflake hitting the warm ground, dissipating on contact.

She shuddered and pushed him away with what little strength remained. "Caleb, go please. Now."

"Good night. See you in the morning. I love you, Caty."

"I love you, too." Church. Yes, they definitely needed to be in church. She stood in the doorway and waved as he started the car and headed out into the night.

As she closed her front door, she paused. What was jogging her mind? Something about Richardson's. *Sweet treats.* Bea's comment about Marta and encouraging Caty to have her friend come into Richardson's...

Caty snapped her fingers. Yes, that *had* to be the answer to the third clue! What was that clue again? She'd written it down upstairs.

Lifting the skirt of her evening gown, Caty went up the stairs to her bedroom and checked her notebook. "Her welcoming smile melts hearts but not her sweets." She darted a glance at the clock on the nightstand. Being the weekend, Marta was off from the station. It was too late to call tonight, but she'd see her at church in the morning.

Driving down his street as he approached the house, Caleb eased up on the accelerator and leaned close to the windshield when he spied a dark sedan with tinted windows sitting across from his front entrance. He muttered under his breath, debating whether to call the police.

"Enough," he muttered. He roared down the street and slammed the Porsche to a halt behind the car. There was a slim possibility this wasn't the same car as before, but he knew in his gut whomever sat behind the wheel was no friend. He felt like ramming into the car, but the driver would probably haul out of there, and he doubted anyone would ever show their face.

Call the police. Don't act rashly, an inner voice warned. What good would it do Lauren if he were the one kidnapped?

"They won't do that because I'm the one with the money they want." Jumping out of the car, Caleb ran to the driver's side of the parked car, waving his arms like a crazy man. Maybe he was. He didn't care anymore. He wanted this over and done with now. He needed to claim his life back. Lauren's life. Move forward with Caty without this cloud hanging over their heads.

"I'm here!" He opened his arms and planted his feet apart. "Come out, you cowards, and talk to me. Tell me what you want. You want my blood? Take it. Want my money? Tell me what you want, but you sure as anything won't get my daughter!"

The car's engine started, and it pulled away from the curb. Running behind the car for at least a block as it gained speed, Caleb continued to yell. His neighbors would probably report him. Again, he didn't care.

Finally, he stopped. *Enough.* Spent, he doubled over, breathing heavily. He thought he was in shape, but his emotions were involved, and that made it tougher.

Dragging himself back to the car, Caleb climbed inside and waited for the entrance gates to open.

"Lord, I trust you with everything in me," he said as he waited. "But when does it end? I'm asking you to please give us resolution for my peace of mind."

Standing in the shower a short time later, Caleb scrubbed his hair with such force his scalp would be raw if he didn't stop. He was full of anger, questions, resentment. His heart attitude wasn't right, but what could he do? Perhaps he should schedule a meeting with Pastor Baldwin. Or Sam.

Wait. That thought stopped him cold. Unless Caty had told him, Sam probably didn't know about the threats. He groaned. If Caty's wonderful family knew about them, how would they react? How could he expect her not to tell them? They'd given him no indication they were aware.

They'd love you, Caleb. They'd pray for you, and pray with you for a resolution. He knew that. Telling them would serve no purpose other than to worry them. Could he marry Caty without her family knowing about them?

No.

That truth hit him as sure as a hard kick to the stomach. Doubling over, Caleb leaned one hand on the wall of the shower for support, feeling sick. Her father thought he was honorable. What kind of man married a woman and kept something so vital from her family? They'd forgive him, but under those circumstances, he doubted they'd trust him for a very long time. He couldn't blame them. In their shoes, he'd feel the same.

He couldn't do that to them. More importantly, he couldn't do that to Caty. He loved her with everything in him. Loved her enough to postpone the wedding if needed. His hormones had taken over earlier in the evening, and he never should have pushed her for a wedding date. He only had himself to blame.

"See what you've done?" he said, accusing the unseen forces behind the threats. "You've reduced me to being the kind of man I never wanted to be. Show yourselves." He'd given them every opportunity to take him, do what they wanted with him. Perhaps he'd been foolish. But what had they done? Driven away and left him standing in the middle of a deserted street.

Stopping the water, Caleb dried off in short order. He dressed quickly, pulling on his sleep pants, not bothering with his shirt. Heading back into the bedroom, he grabbed his Bible and dropped onto the king-sized bed. He checked the concordance in the back, searching anything he could think of for dealing with one's enemies. He found several.

Exodus 14:14: The LORD will fight for you while you keep silent.
Lord, I have a hard time keeping silent.

Proverbs 29:11: A fool always loses his temper, but a wise man holds it back.

Caleb blew out a sigh. *Lord, I'm a fool, and I've lost my temper over this situation over and over again.*

Isaiah 48:22: "There is no peace for the wicked," says the LORD.

Lord, I surrender my enemies to you, but I need your help to do that.

Romans 12:19: Never take your own revenge, beloved, but leave room for the wrath of God, for it is written, "Vengeance is mine, I will repay," says the LORD.

That one was tough. *Vengeance is yours, Lord.*

Putting the Bible on the pillow beside him, Caleb stretched out on the bed and closed his eyes. "Lord, take this bitterness away from me. I know it's wrong, but I have a hard time. You know my heart, you know my deepest desires. I'm a weak man, but with you, I am strong. If it's not wrong to pray this way, please make my enemies known and keep everyone safe. Then you can have at them and dole out your vengeance freely."

He heard his cell phone. Who would be calling him now other than Caty?

He pulled himself up and grabbed his cell phone on the nightstand next to the bed.

"It's Eliot. Sorry to call so late, Caleb, but I knew you'd want to know this."

"Lay it on me."

"I've checked the surveillance tapes of the lobby on the day the last envelope was delivered." Between the time you, Caty, and Lauren went to lunch that day and returned to the office, no one from outside of Belac entered the office lobby. There were a few comings and goings by employees, but they used the key entry system."

Caleb beat the heel of his hand against his head. "You're saying it's an inside job?"

"Looks like it."

His jaw tightened. "Do me a favor. Check further into two of my employees—Martin Hillyard and Steve Robison. Get back to me if you find anything suspicious. If you look on Belac's website, you'll find their photos if you need them. Let me know if either of them show up anywhere on that surveillance tape."

"You've got it buddy. Talk with you later."

Groaning, Caleb plopped back on the bed. "Well, Lord, I guess in its own way, this is an answer to prayer." He lifted his arms. "Bring. It. On."

Chapter 49

Saturday, May 19, 2007

Caty kept one eye on Lauren as she helped set out the supplies beside where Caleb manned one of the grills at the Project in the Park. Now and again, she overheard snippets of what Lauren was telling Suma. She knew she'd told her about the game Eliot had devised for Marta although Caty had warned Lauren not to reveal their names to anyone because that would be an invasion of their privacy.

For whatever reason, Lauren seemed drawn to Suma, but the other woman had acted aloof and standoffish with Caty in recent weeks. One day soon, she'd invite her to lunch so they could talk. She'd left a couple of notes and a card on Suma's desk which had gone unacknowledged. As always, Caty would continue to pray for her.

"So, the next clue is this," she heard Lauren tell Suma. "It may seem minor, but it's incredibly major. What do you think that could mean?" If Lauren didn't get back to helping Ollie soon, she'd have to remind her.

Caty's attention was drawn back to the task-at-hand. Caleb was the grill master extraordinaire while she loaded the hamburgers and hot dogs into buns. Several other Belac employees worked nearby. Cordelia and Lettie worked together to help with the children's games. Even Ollie had come, and he was like the Pied Piper as he fashioned balloon animals. Miles waved to her and smiled from another grill.

The turnout of Belac employees wasn't as great as they'd hoped, but they'd keep adding events in the hope that the number of volunteers would grow. With Belac as a corporate sponsor of the Astros, Caleb planned a number of group outings.

Marta and Eliot, as well as Rebekah and Kevin, worked nearby, assisting wherever they were needed. Winnie and Josh Grant worked alongside their two younger children to hand out bags of chips, and Sam and Lexa and their kids manned the dessert table.

"You look awfully cute in an apron, Mr. Reid." Caty tossed him a grin.

"Why, thank you." He winked. "You're gorgeous as always."

His flirtatious manner was encouraging. Caleb had been subdued since Saturday night. She knew the phone call from Eliot weighed heavily on his mind with the information about the threats being an inside job. He'd shared with her his frustrations in seeing the car on his street. How he'd challenged them and even chased the car down the street. While thankful he shared everything with her, she felt almost as helpless as he did when no answers were forthcoming.

What's the answer, Lord?

Squinting in the sun, Caty spied Martin Hillyard in conversation with Steve Robison under a nearby tree. Martin was in his mid-40s, and never married. She didn't know much about him even though she'd attempted to be friendly when they worked together in Lubbock.

"Wonder what discussion's about over there." Caleb angled his head toward the two men.

"I wondered the same thing," she said, trying not to worry. "Okay, I'll tell you that Martin is the primary Reidco officer I thought might possibly be connected with the accounting discrepancies. I caught a few errors in his reports in the past and called him on it. He didn't seem pleased, but he corrected them."

"How recently?" Caleb tossed more hamburger patties onto the grill. They sizzled, and he pressed down on the meat and then proceeded to flip others. The man could multitask with the best of them.

"When we both worked in the Lubbock office in the past two years. To be honest, I felt like his work was sloppy at times, and I had to double-check him."

"Accounting records?" He glanced around the area. So did she. They couldn't risk being overheard.

"Not in those instances, but perhaps they were indirectly connected. This is my opinion only, and I have no concrete evidence, but a few times I felt as though he'd exaggerated the projected revenue figures for the stations in his reports. From what I was seeing, his numbers were grossly misrepresented. When I first discussed it with him, he flat-out told me I was mistaken. Then I showed him the audits, comparisons, and latest monthly reports. Basically, I called him out on it."

Caleb looked over at her. "Are you suggesting he falsified records?"

"I'm saying he did until I called him on it."

"And why do you think he would do that? Simply because he was sloppy or for any other purpose?"

"Martin's a smart man, I know that much." She hesitated.

"Caty, this could be significant. Why didn't you say anything before?" He frowned. "I find it a little odd we're talking about it now. At a park. With me standing at a grill. Wearing an apron. On the other hand, if my office is bugged, maybe an open park is actually the *best* place to have this conversation."

She lowered her gaze. "I'm sorry. Maybe I should have told you, but that's a serious accusation. He's an executive vice president of Belac's largest division, and I'm the chief accountant. He's worked for you for ten years, and I've only worked for Reidco for five. Besides, Martin revised and corrected his reports because I made sure he did. I've kept an eye on his reports ever since. Not that it's even my job, and that's another reason why I felt uncomfortable. I felt if he knew I was watching him so closely every month, he would have had me fired for being Catherine Lewis, the Reidco Whistleblower."

"You're also now my fiancée."

"So?" Caty resisted moving one hand to her hip. "That has no bearing on the matter."

Caleb's forehead creased. "Eliot hasn't been able to find anything on them. The next step is to get a court order and subpoena the records. We can't do it without going through the proper legal channels according to Josh Grant. Eliot asked him under the cover of anonymity."

"If Martin's behind it, he's careful and covering his tracks well," Caty said.

They interrupted their conversation as they greeted picnic goers who'd come to load their plates. For the next few minutes, they were kept busy. Eliot and Marta kept an eye on Lauren, and for that, Caty was grateful.

Caleb leaned close when they were alone again. "I guess my bottom line question is whether or not you believe Martin's capable of purposely altering the records, falsifying entries on the accounting ledgers, and then somehow funneling the funds out of Reidco? In other words, do you think he's embezzling from my corporation?"

He watched her with the fierce intensity of a man fighting for what was his. Rightfully so.

Caty nodded slowly. "That's more than one question. Yes, he's more than capable. I think he could have, but I can't possibly say whether or not I think he's the culprit. Up until these last two discrepancies, the amounts weren't nearly as alarming. As you know, financial losses aren't exactly uncommon, but losses that were later discovered to be falsified isn't anything I've dealt with before. You know that. And you'd better turn those patties and dogs."

"You're right. We have a few more well done hamburgers and hot dogs if anyone asks. Eliot did tell me that his review of the surveillance tapes showed a number of employees coming and going during the time we were at lunch the day the envelope was delivered. A few of them went behind the desk for something or other, including Cordelia. He's going to see if he can blow up the images and study them."

"Maybe I can ask Suma," she said. "On second thought, that wouldn't be good. It's like she's erected an invisible wall where I'm concerned. I think we need to wait and see what else Eliot finds first. The fewer people we involve, the better, at least for now."

"You're right. Now more than ever, I'm convinced this is all connected. Why are they doing this, Caty? Why do they hate me that much?"

"You know why. Because you have what they want, or what they think they want. It's not personal no matter what you might think now."

"How can it *not* be personal?" he snapped.

She checked her watch. "I'm going to take Lauren to get something to eat. I'll send Kevin to relieve you at the grill in a few minutes. Come and join us." She pointed to a tree across the way. "We'll be sitting over there."

"Sure. Sorry." He reached for her hand. Taking it, she squeezed and gave him what she hoped was a reassuring smile.

"It'll be okay, Caleb."

"I know. Keep praying for me, please."

"Excuse me, are you Caty Lewis?"

"That's me." Caty glanced up at a young man standing nearby. She'd never seen him before.

"I was asked to give this to you." He handed her a piece of paper and then quickly departed.

"Thanks." She shrugged and put her plate of food on the ground.

Lauren sat beside her. "What is it? A love note from Dad at the grill saying how much he loves you and already misses you?"

Wiping her hands on her napkin, Caty unfolded the note. "It's from Marta although it doesn't really look like her writing. I've only seen her cursive."

"Is it another clue? Maybe she figured out the latest one," Lauren said, taking a drink of soda.

"Well, it says to meet her over by the ice cream truck in five minutes. She wants to show us both something." She glanced around the area. "Have you seen an ice cream truck?"

"No, but I haven't looked for one either," Lauren said. "Are you finished? I am."

Caty nodded. "Why don't you gather up the plates, and I'll grab the soda cans. We can toss them in the recycling bin and then go in search of an ice cream truck."

"I see it! There it is." Lauren pointed to the truck on the far end of the park. "Race you!"

"You're going to make me run after that meal?" Laughing, Caty started after her.

The closer they came to the ice cream truck, the more Caty felt a sense of foreboding.

"Lauren, stop!" Something didn't seem right. No one else was around. Caleb might be upset that she'd brought Lauren to such a remote area without telling him. The man was already snappish.

She felt something cold and hard push into her back. "Don't move. Don't scream. Don't do anything except walk forward." Ahead of her, Caty spied the same young man who'd brought the fake note to them as he approached Lauren from behind. When she started to scream, a hand clamped over her mouth, stifling her cry.

"I warned you," the man's voice growled close to her ear. "Don't make me hurt you. You and the girl come with us quietly, and no one gets hurt. Walk. *Now.*"

Frantically glancing around the area as she moved toward the ice cream truck, Caty saw Miles within shouting distance. He stood beneath a tree talking with a pretty blonde girl. What could she do? She couldn't endanger Miles, and he seemed oblivious to her.

Lord, help us. Please.

Caty began to limp.

"What's wrong with you?" the man snarled, shoving whatever he held in his hand against her spine. She didn't want to speculate what it was, but it was either the barrel of a pistol or some type of sheathed knife. She shuddered and crossed her arms over her stomach.

"I have a pebble in my boot. It's cutting into my foot."

"Whiny woman. Take it off."

"What?" That's exactly what she intended to do. When she started to turn and look at him, he jerked her arm.

"Take the boots off and leave them. Keep walking." Seeing that Lauren was a good thousand yards ahead of her now, Caty made a big deal about the pebble. The man grumbled, and she said whatever she could think of to distract him. She whined, she fussed, and she acted as if her life depended on it. Maybe it did.

It was a blessing in disguise that he wanted her back turned to him. As she continued her antics, Caty managed to slip her cell phone out of her pocket. Pushing a button to engage the tracking device Caleb had installed on her phone only a few days ago, she did a little dance—gyrating and acting like a fruitcake—while she tugged off her right boot. All the while, she prayed that cell phone on the fast track down her arm. By God's great mercy, her idiocy distracted the guy long enough that he didn't notice as the cell phone dropped into the boot. Seconds later, the left boot fell on the ground.

The man wrenched her arm. "About time. Get a move on. We can't dawdle."

Caty began to run in her bare feet. Panicked, she couldn't see Lauren. Pushing ahead, she caught sight of her again within seconds. Lauren still had her cell phone although they'd probably confiscate it first thing. She almost screamed but then thought better of it.

Jesus, please let them find my boots. And my phone. May it somehow lead them to us.

Within minutes, she and Lauren were pushed into a black van with tinted windows parked behind the unmanned ice cream truck. No one was around this remote area of the park. Lauren looked up at her with wide eyes. Caty nodded. *Trust Jesus*, she mouthed.

The man who'd brought her to the van climbed in, but the younger man who'd had Lauren slid the door closed. The van's bench seats had been removed.

"Now, we're going to blindfold you, and we're going to take a little ride, ladies." He picked up a dark bandana from the floor of the van and proceeded to wrap it around Lauren's head. Then he did the same with her. No one said anything.

Not long after, Caty felt a prick of something on her arm. "What are you doing?"

"Giving you a little something to help you enjoy the ride, princess. Relax now. Just sleep."

Chapter 50

"Eliot!" Caleb ran toward him.

The other man turned. He'd been in conversation with Sam. Good. Well, maybe not. Sam might very well kill him once he found out what was going on.

"I can't find Caty or Lauren. Neither one of them are answering their cell phones. How could this happen? *How?*"

"I'm sure they're not far away," Sam said.

"Sam, you don't understand." Gasping, Caleb had never felt more desperate. "I should never have let them out of my sight."

"Where did you last see them?" Eliot jumped into emergency mode.

"Someone want to explain?"

Eliot turned to Sam. "There's no time. Sam, we don't want to spoil the picnic and alarm everyone. This is personal with Caleb. Caty and Lauren might be in danger, but I assure you, we'll find them as soon as possible."

Sam appeared wary and shot Caleb a look he couldn't define. He trusted Eliot implicitly, and that worked in his favor. He really didn't want to have to deck Caty's brother. He'd need to do some explaining later.

"I'll do whatever's necessary," Sam said. He tossed his half-eaten plate of food in the nearest trash can. "We can talk another time. Let's find them. What do you need me to do?"

"As hard as it is, we need you and the other TeamWork members to stay here and carry on as usual," Eliot said. "You're their leader, and I need you to be calm."

"I can do that. Call me and keep me posted on what's happening as soon as you can." Sam's piercing stare zeroed in on Caleb. "Can you promise me that much?"

He nodded. "Promise. I'm sorry, Sam. Eliot's the best man to have around in circumstances like this. You know that better than I do. We'll bring them back safe and sound. I don't know when, but we will. You have my word."

Sam closed his eyes and put one hand on Caleb's shoulder, the other on Eliot's. "Father, go with these men now. Keep them safe. Keep Caty and Lauren calm, and we ask you to wrap your tall and wide hedge of protection around them until they can come home safely to us again. We claim power and strength in your mighty name, and we ask that the forces of evil against them will fall in defeat. We ask these things in faith, and in the precious name of your Son, Jesus. Amen."

"Amen." Caleb nodded to Sam, and the other man departed. What a godly man.

Eliot turned to Caleb. "What was the last thing Caty said to you?"

Think. His brain was numb. "The tree." He pointed to the tree where Caty indicated she'd be sitting with Lauren. "She told me that she and Lauren would get food and be eating beneath that tree."

Caleb took off at a run after Eliot. Why hadn't he brought Max? Lauren had begged him, but he'd decided he didn't want to have to deal with getting him into the SUV. They could find nothing near the tree, and Caleb waited while Eliot figured out his next strategy.

Miles came running toward them. "Mr. Reid, sir, I found Caty's red boots over there on the ground. At least I think they belong to her. She had on red boots, right?"

His heart took a flying leap, and Caleb grabbed the boots. "Yes. These are Caty's." He looked at Eliot. "She loves these boots. Caty wouldn't willingly leave them behind without good reason."

"Do you know where she is, Miles?" When the young man stared at him, Caleb said it again. "Where's Caty?"

The confused young man lifted his hands. "I don't know. I guess I thought she was with you."

"Did you see Lauren?" Caleb barked.

"No, sir. What's wrong?"

"They're missing," Eliot told Miles. "Where did you find the boots? Show us exactly where you found them."

"Over here. Follow me." Miles ran, and they both followed.

"They were right here." They stood in a remote, deserted area of the park. No one was around, and an out-of-service ice cream truck sat nearby.

Eliot took the left boot from him. "Check the boot."

"What are we looking for?"

"A sign from God, most likely."

Eliot turned his boot upside down, shaking it. Caleb did the same, and his eyes widened as Caty's cell phone slid out into his hand. He turned on the phone, staring at it with wide eyes. "Look."

"What is it?" Eliot and Miles both looked over his shoulder.

"Caty had this tracking device installed just this past week. Like you suggested, Eliot. Looks like she somehow managed to activate it and get the phone down into her boot."

"Smart woman." Eliot took the phone. "It's only got a fifty-mile radius, and they got a head start. We have no idea where they're taking them. Let's move!"

"Whoa," Miles said as Caleb took off with Eliot beside him. "God bless!"

"The Hummer or the Porsche?" Caleb called to Eliot as they raced across the large park together. Of course, their vehicles were parked on the opposite end.

"Depends on whether you go for scrappy or overpriced talent."

"Give me a break," Caleb muttered. Funny man. Caty must have told Marta. Oh well, women talk about things like that. He knew that. Didn't matter. The only thing that *did* matter was finding Lauren and Caty. At least Eliot had a sense of humor. He'd left his somewhere unknown about a month ago.

"We're taking the Hummer. I know Houston. You don't," Eliot hollered over one shoulder, already several lengths ahead of him. The guy was ex-military, powerful, and fast. What did he expect? He wasn't exactly a wimp, and he was keeping pace close behind Eliot, so he had no reason to be ashamed.

"I can pretty much guarantee you'll be getting a phone call any minute with instructions on what they want and where to meet them. Where to make the drop."

"Make the drop?" Caleb said, incredulous. "Are you serious? People actually say stuff like that outside of some cheesy action movie?"

"Yep. They do. Get in, Caleb." Eliot unlocked the doors to the Hummer.

He couldn't easily just *get* in a tank. He needed to hoist himself up and climb inside the thing, and that's precisely what he did. "I'm sure glad I work out regularly." Caleb slammed the door and roared back against the seat as Eliot tore out of the parking lot, tires squealing. He managed to get the seat belt on. He glanced at Eliot, and he had his belt strapped across his body. When had he even done that?

"Here. Take the phone and guide me. I hope you can navigate."

"I thought that's what this tracking thing did." Caleb tried not to gasp for air, but he did. Couldn't help it.

"Just give me the cross streets and keep me posted where they're at."

"Got it." Caleb read the current coordinates to him and prayed under his breath. "You've done this before, I take it." He cringed and ramped up the silent prayers as Eliot careened around a corner and floored the accelerator. Caleb clutched the armrest and held on to the bar near the Hummer's ceiling as Eliot made a sharp right at the next corner. "Do you have some kind of police immunity? If you don't, I get the feeling we might be stopped." He had to be going at least seventy.

"No offense, buddy, but please shut up, and let me drive."

"Right. Sorry."

"It stopped!" Caleb shouted fifteen minutes later. They had to be somewhere down near the docks. He could smell water, and he heard the call of seagulls as they sailed overhead.

"Pull over." Caleb started to open the door but stopped when Eliot put a hand on his arm.

"Stay in the Hummer for now. You're not going anywhere. Not yet. Give me the cross streets."

After Caleb read them to him, Eliot slowed the Hummer and pulled to a halt beside a curb. He took the phone and studied it. "No call yet?"

"No. It's a private number, and I don't give it out freely."

"Is this the same phone you got some of the messages on?"

"Yes," Caleb said.

"Then it's not as private as you think. Technology is invented every day to outsmart what was created the day before."

"That's real encouraging."

"Give me Lauren's cell phone number. I'll put a trace on it."

Caleb leaned back against the seat and recited the numbers by heart.

"They'll be calling you soon. What they don't know is that we're nearby." Eliot pulled out his cell phone. "As soon as we find out their demands, I'll call Lieutenant Taylor. You can trust him. Be prepared to hand over some financial information unless you want to leave and go get the money yourself."

"Good to know. No bank is open right now. If you think I'm going to be this close to where my girls are and leave them, then you're nuts."

"That's what I knew you'd say." Eliot shot him a look. "I'd feel the same way. They don't want cash, Caleb. They're going to ask you to wire the funds to an offshore account. Do you have any idea how much money you have access to?"

"Depends on what they ask for."

"This isn't a time to negotiate, Caleb."

"I know that. I can get them whatever they want. My funds are available at the touch of a fingertip, as frightening as that really is."

Eliot looked over at him again. "It's going to be okay. We're going to give them what they want, but you'll get it back. I've dealt with this kind of situation before."

"Not that I doubt you, but how can you be sure, Eliot?"

"You have to trust me. I have connections everywhere. I'll arrange it so it looks like the funds are in their account, but they'll be funneled into another fund. Once we get them in custody, it'll be rerouted back to you."

"Glad you know these things." Caleb glanced out the window. "Where are we, anyway?"

"Somewhere along the 25-mile stretch of the Port of Houston." Eliot had been studying the phone map.

Dear God, please give Lauren and Caty safe. Keep them strong. Thank you for Eliot.

Caleb's cell phone rang.

Chapter 51

"Ow ow ow."

Caty's eyes fluttered open. Who said that? Where was she?

She was lying on a hard concrete floor. Propping up on her elbows, she surveyed her surroundings. Seemed to be a large but empty boat storage facility. She heard the *keow* and *ha-ha-ha-ha* sounds from the seagulls. Hopefully, she was still in Houston somewhere.

Hearing a soft moaning sound, she blinked hard and sat up straighter. *Lauren!* Everything started to come back to her.

"Caty?"

"Sweetie, I'm here. We're going to be fine." Glancing around, Caty saw no one. Heard nothing.

"I know that, but where's Dad?"

"I'm sure he's doing everything he can to find us. Eliot's beside him." That had to be true. She prayed they'd found the boots and her cell phone with the tracking device. "Do you have your cell phone?"

Lauren rubbed her head. "No. That'd be too easy. That mean kid took it from me. He's probably texting all my friends now and sending them perverted messages."

"Let's hope not."

"Well, look who's decided to join the party."

Caty turned. "Suma?"

"In the flesh. Guess your little plan to convert me didn't work, Caty. Sorry." She shrugged and gave her a withering look. In her stylish designer jeans and silk blouse, Suma looked more ready to hit the Houston night scene than carry out a kidnapping and extortion attempt.

That's all it will be. An attempt.

"What do you want?" Caty stared at the other woman, holding her gaze steady. She was fighting for Lauren and her future with Caleb. She didn't think they intended any harm to come to her or Lauren, but she couldn't take chances.

"What do most people want?"

Caty gasped as Martin Hillyard strolled into view. He'd been dressed in jeans and a polo at the picnic. Now he wore shorts, a T-shirt, and sandals.

"You couldn't let it alone could you, Caty? You had to stick your nose where it didn't belong. Then, to top it off, you had to start sleeping with the boss."

"She's not—"

"Shut up, you little..." Caty cringed as Martin spewed a profanity. She shot a look at Lauren, silently warning her not to provoke these people. Lauren gave her a slight nod. Good.

Was Steve lurking somewhere nearby, too? Caty glanced around the warehouse.

"If you're looking for Steve, he's not part of this."

Caty stared at Suma. "Thanks for the info."

Suma snorted. "He's a pathetic old weasel who sends jewelry to women in interoffice mail because his wife won't..." Caty tuned out the last part of her words. She darted a glance at Lauren and saw the girl with her hands over her ears.

A sense of relief flooded her that Steve wasn't involved. He might be pathetic in some respects, and he might be ready to go on forced early retirement, but he hadn't betrayed Caleb. For that, she could be grateful.

"We're waiting for Reid to wire the money, and then we're out of here. But first we'll make sure you're tied up nice and tight," Martin said.

Suma strolled forward, her high heels clacking on the concrete floor. "An abandoned warehouse like this? It could be days, weeks even, before anyone discovers your dead bodies."

"Cut the dramatics, Suma."

"Shut up, you little do-gooder!"

Caty jutted her chin. "You know what? No matter what you say, no matter what you do to me, I'll still pray for you. Christ is in me, and I know where I'm spending eternity."

"Go Team Caty!" Lauren ducked her head when Suma shot her a glare.

Martin strolled closer. "She asked you to be quiet. I'd suggest you do it. In case you haven't noticed, Suma's not a very nice person."

Suma's dark eyes flashed, and she spouted a vile, derogatory name at Martin.

"Well, that's quite a filthy sailor mouth you have," Martin shot back.

"You two are a comedy of errors." Caty rolled her eyes. She deserved an award for her performance. If she survived the evening.

I'm trusting in you, Lord. Please let them find the boots and not some homeless person, as awful as that sounds. That thought hadn't occurred to her until now.

"Spill it. As long as you intend to leave us here to rot and die, what's the plan? Might as well share it with us." Caty looked from Suma to Martin and back, wondering which one would squeal on the other first. They were already clearly at odds. No doubt all this waiting around and masterminding business was exhausting.

"As soon as Daddy Reid puts the money in our account, we're out of here." Suma scraped a metal chair along the floor and sat on it, crossing her legs, swinging one foot back and forth. Martin followed suit. Why did they have to scrape those chairs instead of picking them up? The sound was obnoxious and grating.

"How do you know he'll do it?" Caty challenged.

Suma laughed. "You must be stupid. He'll do it because we've got what he wants most in life right here." She nodded to Lauren. "His little princess." She moved her slow, angry gaze to Caty. "And his—"

"Don't you call Caty another word or I swear I'll deck you!" Lauren scrambled to her feet and then swayed. She put a hand on her forehead. "Whoa. I'm a little dizzy. I shouldn't have done that."

Caty moved over to her. Lauren sat down on the ground and Caty positioned herself behind her, cradling her between her propped knees, holding her upright in the process. She wrapped her arms around the girl.

"Thanks for defending me, sweetie." She squeezed Lauren's hand and held on tight. "Love you."

"You, too." Caty didn't know Lauren was crying until a warm tear landed on her hand. "Shhh." She rocked her gently. Thank the Lord these two weren't monsters. If they were, they'd probably hurt them physically in some way. "We're going to be fine."

"So, what's your plan?" Caty asked next. "Are you jetting off in a private plane somewhere that can be shot down by a police helicopter? Are you going to make a dramatic exit by speedboat that someone could have booby trapped?"

"Yeah. It could explode and blast you into tiny little scraps of humanity that no one will ever trace." Lauren shook her head and clucked her tongue. "What a pity. Reduced to fish food."

"You don't know when to shut up, do you?" Suma rose to her feet.

"Shut up, Suma." Martin scowled. "In spite of the fact she's severely annoying, this kid is entertaining me, which is more than I can say for you."

Caty laughed at the absurdity of it all. She couldn't help it. Best kidnapping she'd ever attended.

Martin's cell phone buzzed. He retrieved it from the pocket of his shorts and stared at it. "The money's there. We need to move," he told Suma. "You get the rope and tie them up, and I'll get everything else ready."

"Let Lauren go. Keep me here," Caty said. "Kill me if you need to, but she's a defenseless, twelve-year-old child."

Lauren raised her hands. "Why does everyone keep harping on that? Kids have feelings, too. And we're not exactly stupid, you know."

"Quiet, Lauren." Caty kept her voice firm that time.

"No deal," Martin said after first looking at Suma for confirmation. "We're sticking to the original plan, and there'll be no screw-ups."

Suma looked at him for a long moment. She hiked her sleeve and glanced at her watch. "We have forty minutes to get to the plane. We've only got clearance for another ten minutes after that or we're stuck here in Houston until tomorrow."

"Seriously?" Caty balked. "You're going to South America or somewhere?" She shook her head. "You couldn't be more original than that?" She looked at Martin. "You look like you're ready for Club Med."

These two didn't scare her. They were playing into every ridiculous C-movie action flick she'd ever had the misfortune to watch. She blamed that on Carson although Will sometimes liked them, too. She put one hand on her forehead. Maybe Lauren wasn't the only one feeling light-headed. Could be the effects of whatever drug they'd injected in both of them.

"You know the saddest thing of all?" Lauren scooted away, and Caty rose to her feet. A little shaky, but she could do this. "The fact that you..." She stopped and looked at Lauren. She wouldn't say anything about Caleb. They'd made him doubt himself, made him go nearly mad with worry, but for what? To steal from him? The entire thing made her sick to her stomach. To think what they'd put the poor man through for years. What they'd subjected Lauren to as a result?

"Did you hear that?" Suma looked over at Martin. "What's the plan now, big man?"

Caty listened, and so did Lauren. There it was again.

Please, Lord, let it be Caleb and Eliot. Sam. Lieutenant Taylor. Anyone. Someone.

Chapter 52

Eliot burst into the building in a blaze of glory, and Caleb was right behind him.

Martin pulled out a pistol. "Stop right now." Moving over to Lauren, he put his arm around her neck.

"Stop bluffing, Hillyard." Caleb walked forward slowly, hands in the air. "Let her go, and let's end this madness right here. Right now."

"I swear I'll shoot her brains out. Or would you rather I splatter Caty all over this floor right in front of you? Try living with that the rest of your days, rich man."

The hurt in Caleb's eyes was almost unbearable, and Caty's heart reached out to him. Sure, she didn't want her brains splattered all over the concrete floor of an abandoned Houston storage facility. That'd be a pretty pathetic way to die, but still, Caleb was the best man she'd ever known. Where was that gun when she was mouthing off?

She moved her gaze heavenward. *Thank you.*

"Who are you talking to now?" Martin demanded.

Suma laughed. "Who do you think? Jesus, you fool. Might as well kill her now and put us all out of misery." Caty's eyes widened when Suma took the gun from Martin. He kept his forearm wrapped around Lauren's neck. Thankfully, Lauren remained immobile. Seemed she finally understood it was time to be quiet and not say a word. Not move a muscle. All those clichés that people always say in movies. Things like they're going to blow someone's brains out.

A lone shot rang out, and Caty jumped. Suma yelped and started cursing worse than she'd ever heard from anyone. Suma glared at Eliot. "You actually shot me? Seriously?"

He shrugged. "Sorry about the designer shoe."

"Look out!" Lauren yelled. "Incoming!" She put her hands over her ears and cringed, prepared for the next expected onslaught of profane words.

Martin grabbed the gun from where it had fallen at Suma's feet. The woman had removed her shoe. *Good shot, Eliot!* Great aim to the big toe on her left foot. That bullet tore clean through that fancy shoe. Caty started toward Suma.

Suma put one hand in front of her. "Don't even come near me, Jesus girl."

"You need help. Let me do that for you."

"I'll wrap it up and limp out of here."

Martin started waving the gun around like a crazy man. When he raised it and aimed the gun at Lauren, Caty took a flying leap as another shot rang out. She landed on the floor, on top of Lauren. They both groaned. Caty moved her hands over her body. She seemed intact. Lauren was fine, too.

Caleb! Within seconds, he was on the ground beside them both, hugging and holding them close. As though he'd never let go.

Martin was writhing on the floor. Grimacing in pain, he grabbed for his right knee as he stretched and reached for the small pistol.

Eliot moved forward and straddled the man. "I've never killed a man yet. I don't think you want to break my record."

"Great line, Eliot!" Lauren applauded. "You should sell that one to Clint Eastwood."

Eliot made quick work of getting Suma and Martin cuffed. Within another minute, police officers swarmed the building.

"Whoa. Those are SWAT guys." Lauren's blue eyes grew wide.

After giving the police their statements, Lauren and Caty were allowed to leave.

"Do you need to go to the hospital to get checked out?" Caleb said to Caty as he walked outside with her.

"I think we're both fine. As crazy as it sounds, it was probably the most anti-climactic ending for a kidnapping and extortion attempt in the history of the world."

"Thank the Lord," Caleb said, drawing her close with one arm and Lauren with the other.

"It's okay to cry if you want, Dad."

"Caty, if you hadn't left those boots and somehow managed to toss your cell phone in there, I'm not sure what we would have done."

"Eliot would have figured out something. He's like James Bond," Caty said. "Do you have my boots, by the way?"

"They're in the Hummer."

"I think I'm going to donate a bunch of pairs to the missions. Every girl in Texas needs a pair of red cowgirl boots."

As they climbed into the vehicle, Lauren sat up front with Eliot and Caty curled up in the warmth and security of Caleb's arms. "They did give us some kind of drug."

"Eliot, let's make a stop at the nearest ER," Caleb said, kissing Caty's forehead. "I can't take a chance."

"Then you'd better call Sam first. He's been ringing my cell phone like crazy the past hour."

"I'm probably already in the doghouse with your brother," Caleb told her.

"What's that mean?" Lauren asked.

Caty gaped. She knew a lot of things but hadn't heard that old cliché?

"It means Sam's ticked off at me. I can't blame him."

"He won't care," Caty said. "All he wants to know is that we're all safe."

Caleb nodded. "That I can do. And that's what I intend to do the rest of my life." He took his phone in hand and called her brother. Then handed her the phone.

"We're fine, Sam. Just tired. We'll talk tomorrow. If you don't mind, don't say anything to Mom and Dad. Caleb and I will share everything with them." She darted a glance at Caleb, and he nodded. "Now that we can."

A tear slipped down Caty's cheek. In spite of the weirdness of the evening, things could have turned out so much worse. Blessings abounded. She leaned into Caleb, clinging to his shirt, loving the feel of him, the scent of him. "I can't believe all they put you through for all these years," she whispered.

Caleb's chest rose and fell with the force of his heavy sigh. "Like you said, the only thing that matters is that you and Lauren are safe. In a strange way, the events of the past few years have forced me to stare down my fears and acknowledge that God is the One in control." He shifted and held her closer, pressing a kiss to the top of her head. "Always."

"When you think about it, if those accounting discrepancies hadn't happened, it might have taken a lot longer for us to meet," Caty said.

"Oh, I think that would have happened anyway." They were quiet as Eliot started up the Hummer

"Wait, can you get your money back?"

"Not a problem." Caleb dropped a light kiss on her lips.

Lauren twisted around in the seat. "Yeah. How much are we worth, Dad?"

Laughing, he settled back into the seat, keeping his hold on Caty. "Every last cent I have. And then some. Besides, it all belongs to the Lord, anyway."

"What's going to happen to Suma and Martin now?" Lauren asked Eliot.

"Justice will prevail. They're going to be taken to the hospital, and from there the police will take over." He glanced back at Caleb. "They paid for a bunch of no-name thugs to do their dirty work…the notes, the phone calls, the car outside the house…all of it."

Shaking his head, Caleb blew out a sigh. "I asked the Lord for it to be over, and He answered that prayer." He tightened his hold on Caty's shoulders. "I'll be forever grateful."

"And we keep praying for them," Caty said. "I really thought I was getting through to Suma, but her love of money consumed her, I suppose. I'll need to visit her. Or at least try."

"You'll really go see her in jail or prison or wherever she is?" Lauren's eyes were side. "Can I come?"

"We'll see," Caleb said.

"I love you, Caleb." Caty surrendered to the overwhelming urge to sleep.

"Rest, my love."

She was safe. Lauren was safe. That and their love for one another was *all* that mattered.

Thank you, Jesus.

Chapter 53

Saturday, June 16, 2007
The Wedding

Caty peeked outside from where she stood by the kitchen door of Sam and Lexa's home. Finally, it was her wedding day. In the next thirty minutes, at seven o'clock, the ceremony would begin. She'd marry the man of God's choosing, and her dreams, beneath the towering sugarberry trees. The evening temperature was comfortable, and a slight breeze ruffled the branches of the trees.

Thank you, Lord, for this beautiful day.

If it had rained, they'd move indoors. The wedding was small and intimate, limited to family members and their closest friends, the way she and Caleb both wanted.

They'd have a larger reception in another month after they returned from their honeymoon in Hawaii. After the events of the last few weeks, especially, Caty wanted nothing more than to relax on a beach with her husband beside her. They planned to fly between the islands for the first week, and then Caleb's mother, Jennifer, and Lauren would fly to meet them in Kauai, the Garden Island, where they planned to explore the waterfalls and scenic drives together. Jennifer and Lauren would have their own suite, of course. That made Caty smile.

She spied Josh escorting Chloe, Luke, and Emily to the white chairs on the large lawn. Pretty as a picture, Chloe was turning into quite the young lady. Holding hands, Luke and Emily walked beside their daddy while Chloe walked ahead of them. Emily and Rachel were already seated with their husbands and families, and she'd visited with them the night before when they'd all gone to dinner. Caty smiled again when she spied Aunt Tess, Uncle Charlie, and her cousin Clarissa taking their seats.

She felt a hand on her back, and Lexa appeared by her side. "Ready, sweetie?"

Caty breathed out slowly and smiled. "My whole life. Where's Dad?"

"He's with Caleb, Sam, Carson, and Eliot. They're praying together. They'll be going out the front door and around to the backyard in about five minutes. Winnie's giving everyone their cues."

Caty glanced at the clock on the wall. Ten minutes until seven. "Thank you."

Her mother floated into the room. In her tea-length, pale pink dress and wrist corsage of pink rosebuds and orchids, she was breathtaking. Sarah enfolded Caty in her arms.

"Honey, I need to take my place in just a moment, but I needed one more hug from my darling girl. I know I've already told you ten times today, and I've hugged you twice as many times, but I love you. Caleb's a wonderful man, and we know he's the man of God's choosing for our lovely Catherine Grace. You're a beautiful couple, and we love Lauren and any future children you may have. You'll have a blessed life together."

"Thank you, Mom. For everything. My entire life." Resisting the urge to bite her lower lip, Caty blinked back tears. "Somehow, even that doesn't seem adequate."

Sarah touched her cheek against hers. "Remember, my love. That's what mothers do. I think you already know a little something about that."

"Yes, I do. Love you."

Marta hurried into the kitchen and gave Mom a quick side hug. "Mrs. Lewis, you're looking fabulous as always." As Sarah departed, her matron of honor scooted over beside Caty. "I just got a peek at Caleb. Your groom is gorgeous in his gray tuxedo, my friend. The best man's not bad, either. I don't see Eliot in a tux nearly enough, so it's a real thrill."

Lightly pressing her fingers on her lips, Marta touched them to Caty's cheek. "Eliot and I couldn't be happier for you. You're just"— she sniffled and waved away Lexa's offer of a tissue—"the most glowing bride ever. I love that you're wearing your mother's wedding gown and veil, Caty. It's vintage but so classically elegant. Isn't she simply beautiful, Lexa?"

Lexa smiled. "Absolutely, but dry those tears. Whatever you do, please don't make Caty cry."

Marta took her hand and held on tight. "You okay, girlfriend? This is it."

Caty breathed out slowly. "I'm nervous, but it's the *best* kind of nervous. I need you all to pray that I don't stumble and fall flat on my face at Caleb's feet."

Marta smiled. "If you do, Caleb will sweep you into his arms and not relinquish you until that ring is on your finger."

"Speaking of prayer, let's do that now." Lexa gathered them together by taking their hands and drawing them into a small circle.

"Don't start without me. I'm here!" Lauren flew around the corner and into the kitchen.

"We're going to pray now. Come and join us." Lexa stepped aside so Lauren could stand on the other side of Caty.

"Father, we ask your blessing on the marriage of Caty and Caleb today," Lexa began. "You are the creator of love. We thank you for Caty's sweet spirit and her heart for you. We thank you for bringing Caleb into her life and for his strong commitment and faithfulness to you. We ask for your continued blessing on their lives together with Lauren as they continue to serve you."

Quiet footsteps alerted Caty that someone else had entered the kitchen. She opened one eye as her father walked behind her. Planting both large hands on her shoulders, he rested his head gently on hers. She reached for his hand.

Marta squeezed Caty's other hand. "Lord, I pray you'll bless our friends Caleb and Caty with a long and happy life together. Give them babies to share their love. When the inevitable storms of life come, please help them to always remember to look to you for answers to those things that seem impossible. To lean on you for the strength to carry on when the odds seem insurmountable, and to never forget the greatest love of all that has brought them together."

"Dear Jesus, thank you for Caty," Lauren prayed. "She makes my dad happy, and we love her very much. I hope they have a great honeymoon, and I look forward to Nana and me going to Hawaii to meet them. Maybe they'll give me a baby brother or sister soon."

"We ask all these things in the name of Jesus," Lexa finished. "And all God's people said…"

A chorus of *Amen!* rang all around Caty.

Lauren hugged her father. I love you, Grandpa Sam." The sight of those two brought Caty close to tears.

"Always and forever, Lauren."

Lexa was beside her in a heartbeat and handed Caty her bouquet. Dipping her head, Caty inhaled the sweet fragrance of the pink roses grown in her mother's garden as well as in the garden from Caleb's home, symbolic of the two households of faith joining together on this beautiful day.

"Lauren, here's your bouquet." Lexa handed it to her. "You look lovely, and so grown-up."

"Thank you, Mrs. Lewis." Rebekah had styled Lauren's hair, and she'd added dainty fresh flowers. Lauren's gaze rested on Caty. "I love your dress. You're beautiful. Can I call you Mom now?"

Caty nodded and opened her arms. "If that's what you'd like, but I'm okay with Caty, too." As Lauren wrapped her arms around her waist, Caty closed her eyes. *These* were the moments of life. The moments she'd treasure forever. The moments of overflowing joy.

Lauren understood she wasn't a replacement for her mother. But the Lord entrusted the care of this precious girl to her, and Caty would do her best with that awesome responsibility.

"I like calling you Mom. I love you, Caty." Pulling back, Lauren giggled and then sniffled. "I guess I can call you both now, huh?"

"Yes, but if I were you, I'd still call your father Dad, not Caleb." She tapped Lauren's nose. "I hope you realize I'm not just marrying your father today. You're the biggest part of him, Lauren. He's entrusting his heart to me, but he's also giving me the honor of helping to raise you."

"I'm already halfway raised, so I think you got yourself a bargain."

Caty gave her another hug and kissed the top of her head. "I'd say so, young lady."

Winnie poked her head inside the door. "The men are in place, and Kevin's just started playing. Everyone ready?"

Lexa nodded. "They're ready." *Love you,* she mouthed to Caty as she slipped out the door ahead of Marta to scoot to her seat.

Kevin began playing Pachelbel's "Canon in D" on his classic guitar as Marta began her slow walk up the white-draped aisle. Lauren waited for her cue from Winnie, who stood beside the back door.

Dad stepped into place beside her.

Caty admired her father's strong, handsome profile. "This is it, Dad."

"This is the day the Lord has made," he said, his voice a bit husky. He gazed at her with all the love in the world in his blue eyes. "Let us rejoice and be glad in it." Gathering her in his arms, he kissed her cheek. "My baby girl, you've made your mother and me so proud." He eyed her dress. "I haven't seen that dress in a long time. You're beautiful."

Thank you, Dad, she mouthed, not trusting herself to speak.

With her oldest brother officiating, and her youngest brother assisting, Catherine Grace Lewis married Abernathy Caleb Reid. In so doing, she also gained a daughter of her heart. Sam's charge to them as a couple stressed that marriage wasn't easy. He acknowledged they'd already survived strenuous challenges most long-time married couples had never faced—and hopefully never would. Together, they'd clung to the Lord's promises, and they'd refused to live in fear, and would continue to do so throughout their married life.

God's will always prevails. Onward and forward from this day forward.

Closing his Bible, Sam smiled at the end of the ceremony. "And now, by the power invested in me by the great State of Texas, and by the Lord Almighty, I now pronounce you husband and wife. Caleb, you may kiss your bride."

Caleb drew her close. "Abide," he whispered.

"Abide, my love," she whispered back before his lips met hers in their first kiss as a married couple.

Their families and closest friends tossed rose petals as they made their way back down the aisle. They didn't plan to stay long, but their guests would continue to party on as long as they wished.

An hour later, Caty prepared to leave with her husband. They'd changed their clothes and stood outside Sam and Lexa's home saying their good-byes...for now. They both laughed when they spied the Porsche with JUST MARRIED written on the back window and tin cans attached to the bumper.

Marta rushed over to her. "I figured out that last clue," she said. "Eliot's taking piano lessons, and he just played a song for me on Sam and Lexa's piano."

"Eliot's taking piano lessons?" Caleb raised a brow.

"Don't say a word," Eliot warned, pulling his wife close.

Caleb shook his friend's hand. "I wasn't going to say a word. If anything, I think it's awesome. I would have thought that clue had something to do with baseball."

"Me too," Caty said.

"You would." Marta looked up at Eliot and they both beamed.

Caty laughed and clapped her hands. "Wait! You're having a baby?"

"Yes!"

Caty's smile broke out, and she hugged Marta close. "Congratulations, my friend. What a great day this is. We'll have so much to talk about when Caleb and I get back from Hawaii."

"That's not all," Marta said. "He teases me because I've told him that I don't care where we live. In other words, it's a *minor* detail for me. With my new job as the full-time weather person, thank you very much, we'll be house hunting in the near future."

"Making it *major*," Eliot said. "I never claimed to be the best at these kinds of games. Cut me some slack people."

"You're invaluable with what counts, buddy." Caleb embraced him. "You are the best man to call, and I can't begin to thank you enough for what you've done for my family."

Eliot grinned. "That's what friends are for."

"Don't forget to toss your bouquet," Marta reminded her. "Everyone's ready."

"Oh, I'm glad you said something." Lauren handed her the bouquet. Saying a quick prayer, Caty tossed it high over her head, hoping for the best. Then turned around to see where it landed.

As if the thing had a mind of its own, the bouquet bonked her second eldest brother on the head. Will stared at her, wide-eyed, as it bounced off his head and fell straight into his hands.

Then Will aimed and flung the bouquet at Carson.

"Oh no, you don't." Laughing, Carson dodged it.

"Let the games begin," Caleb said beside her. They laughed and shared a sweet kiss.

"Sometimes prayers really do come true. You're up next, Commander Lewis." Caty saluted him and then blew kisses to her family and closest friends. Climbing into the car while Caleb waited, she bumped her head. "Ow ow ow."

"Caty? Are you okay?"

"Just embarrassed to have an audience for my clumsiness," she muttered. "Oh well, I was Clumsy Caty when you met me, and it seems Clumsy Caty is back."

"Only until we reach the honeymoon suite, and then you're my forever Catherine Reid."

Oh my, if those words didn't send shivers of anticipation…well, pretty much everywhere.

Caleb kissed her forehead. "We're going to need to review the method to get in the car," he told her as he slid into the driver's seat.

"Maybe you need a bigger car." She snapped her seat belt and gave him a cheeky grin.

"We shall see." Caleb laughed as he started the engine and moved his hand over hers.

Lowering the window, Caty waved to their guests. "See you soon! We love you all." Turning to face him, she smiled. "I'll spend the rest of my life loving you, Mr. Reid."

"That sounds promising." At the end of the street, Caleb stopped the car beside the curb and pulled her into his arms.

She pulled back. "You seem to like curbs. Everything all right?"

"Yes," he whispered, nuzzling her neck and feathering kisses all the way up to her waiting lips. "I just need to kiss my wife properly."

And so he did.

The End

The Lewis Legacy Continues!

Stay tuned for Will's story in
Pursuit
Coming in late Fall 2016

About the Author

~~♥~~

In addition to *Abide*, JoAnn Durgin is the author of the prior novels in the beloved Lewis Legacy Series: *Awakening*, *Second Time Around*, *Twin Hearts*, *Daydreams*, *Moonbeams*, and *Enchantment*, as well as *Prelude*, the prequel to the series. Her other works include *Catching Serenity*, *Heart's Design* and its sequel, *Gentle Like the Rain*, *Love So Amazing* and *Love So Divine* (The Wondrous Love Series, Books 1 and 2), *Echoes of Edinburgh*, *Perchance to Dream*, and the popular Starlight Christmas Series.

A former estate administration paralegal, JoAnn now writes contemporary Christian romance full-time and lives with her family in her native southern Indiana.

JoAnn loves to hear from her readers! Please feel free to contact her:

WEBSITE: www.joanndurgin.com

FACEBOOK: www.facebook.com/authorjoanndurgin

TWITTER: JoAnn Durgin@Gr8tReads

Awakening
The Lewis Legacy Series, Book 1

A God-fearing man. A God-seeking woman. For Sam Lewis and Lexa Clarke, it proves a combustible combination.

Lexa Clarke signs up for a TeamWork Missions summer assignment expecting adventure in a far-off, exotic country. Instead, she's sent to sweltering San Antonio to help rebuild homes destroyed by sudden flooding. She survives the four-hour bus trip from Houston, dust in the lungs, a flat tire, a tool-throwing incident and a spitting goat—not to mention an inquisition from a distractingly handsome cowboy—all before reaching the work camp.

TeamWork director Sam Lewis isn't sure what to think of his newest volunteer. She's feisty, witty, and incredibly pretty, but looks more prepared to board a cruise ship than build houses. Burned by a past betrayal, he's got a job to do, a reputation to uphold. Sam can't afford to be distracted by a woman who attracts animals, defies his rules, finds trouble at every turn and questions God's purpose. But when she tumbles from the top beam of one of the houses into his arms, Sam suspects his life will never be the same. During their weeks together in the TeamWork camp, Sam and Lexa learn the power of forgiveness and healing.

Enduring a chain of incidents which challenge their faith, trust and growing relationship, they look to the Lord for guidance as together they discover a love greater than either could ever imagine. At the end of the eight-week work camp, Sam is committed to a year-long, dangerous overseas mission for TeamWork. Can Lexa trust the Lord enough to let him go? Will Sam safely return and keep his promise to meet her at the Alamo? You'll keep turning the pages of this sweeping romantic adventure.

With great characters, plenty of humor, enough emotion to make you shed a tear or two, and an ending that'll have you cheering, Awakening will leave you breathless. Hold on tight. The adventures of Lewis and Clarke have only just begun!

Second Time Around
The Lewis Legacy Series, Book 2

Marc Thompson is on top of the world—a newlywed with a beautiful wife, the owner of a thriving Boston sports advertising agency, and a century-old home they're renovating in the suburbs. Then the unthinkable happens. Two months after the wedding, Marc sits in a hospital emergency waiting room after Natalie suffers a horrible fall. One shock follows another. Not only does his wife remember nothing of their life together, but now he has a personal timeline to reconnect with her—seven months.

Marc's gold wedding band mocks him, a glaring reminder of a promise broken by a rotting basement stair and his own negligence. His renowned psychologist advises him to court his wife again—a daunting task the first time around. Then Marc's pastor suggests he call Sam and Lexa Lewis of TeamWork Missions, a ministry dear to Natalie's heart. Determined to help her reclaim her life, the young groom makes great strides until a ghost from the past surfaces, opening fresh wounds and threatening to destroy it all.

With Natalie's trust shattered and Marc's faith wavering, they head to Milestone Ranch outside Helena, Montana, with TeamWork for a two-week work camp. But instead of romancing his wife in the freezing November temperatures with warm fires and shared sweet moments, he's out in the cold and back at square one. Even if Natalie recovers her lost memories, will she forgive him? If not, can Marc come to terms with his deepest fear—the failure of his marriage?

You'll root for Marc and Natalie as they fight against the odds and discover that surrendering all at the throne of grace doesn't mean failure. It's simply called faith. And it might be the only way to finding their way back to one another…the second time around.

Twin Hearts
The Lewis Legacy Series, Book 3

Joshua Grant is a man redeemed. He's worked hard to put the past behind him. A mergers and acquisitions attorney in a prestigious Baton Rouge law firm, he pours his energies into his career, hurricane relief efforts, and numerous civic and charitable causes. A near-fatal event in the life of a fellow TeamWork Missions volunteer prompts him to make some apologies, starting with his friend and mentor, Sam Lewis, Domestic Missions Director for TeamWork in Houston. It's been more than four years since the fateful events in San Antonio when Sam threw him out of the missions camp, and he's still haunted by the bittersweet memory of his final meeting with another TeamWork volunteer. When he also seeks her forgiveness, Josh gets the shock of his life. Could turning his deepest sin into his greatest blessing be God's answer for his hurting heart?

Rebekah Grant, Josh's twin sister, is torn between two men. Adam, a dashing British aristocrat, offers her a world of exotic travel, socializing with royalty, fabulous couture and the life of leisure. Then there's sweet Kevin, the strong, intelligent, faithful TeamWork member. Will the shy Louisiana lumber man ever take the step of faith to move their relationship to the next level? What Kevin lacks in terms of Adam's style and panache, he more than makes up for with heart-stirring kisses and soul-searching conversation. When Rebekah suspects Adam is planning to propose a second time, she knows it's time to make her decision. Juggling both suitors is wrong for so many reasons, but what's a girl to do if she wants to marry and have children in her lifetime?

When family tragedy strikes, Josh and Rebekah learn the true meaning and value of love, loyalty and what's most important in life. Leaning on the encouragement and support from Sam and Lexa Lewis and their TeamWork friends, both twins look to the Lord for His divine guidance. It's up to them to stake their claim on love before it slips beyond their reach, which means it's also time for a road trip from Louisiana to the peace to be found in seeking and finding the sweetest desires of the heart.

Daydreams
The Lewis Legacy Series, Book 4

It's early December 2002, and Amy Jacobsen is living the dream: a job she loves with a trendy New York City magazine, a Manhattan walk-up inherited from her grandfather, and a busy social life *without* the unwanted complication of a steady boyfriend. During dinner one evening with her Wall Street financier brother, Mitch, she spies Landon Warnick at the next table. He's one of the most influential, successful and youngest magazine publishers in the country—not to mention one of New York's most eligible bachelors.

After Mitch wrangles a meeting between the two, Landon wastes little time asking her to dinner. Usually wary of smooth men and romantic entanglements, Amy questions her sanity when they share a cozy carriage ride in Central Park and she comes *this* close to kissing him. Is it the joy and wonder of the Christmas season that's put stars in her eyes or the enigmatic, intelligent, challenging and incredibly handsome man?

The following weekend, she travels to Louisiana to be a bridesmaid in a wedding and a reunion with Sam and Lexa Lewis and some of her dearest friends and fellow volunteers in TeamWork Missions. Headed down the aisle at the wedding, Amy's steps falter. Standing at the front is a groomsman who flew into town only an hour before . . . She does a double take. What's Landon Warnick doing in *her* world, with *her* friends? Perhaps more important, why does he suddenly have a Texas drawl and a crescent-shaped scar on his forehead? Sharing a romantic dance at the wedding reception, she casts aside her better judgment and kisses him. She's lost her mind, and her heart might not be far behind, it seems.

Let the adventure begin! Is the Lord showing her the right man for her heart or is Amy in *way* over her head?

Moonbeams
The Lewis Legacy Series, Book 5

Mitch Jacobsen's younger sister, Amy Warnick, has tried to pair him off with her fellow TeamWork Missions volunteer, Cassie, for over a year. Why can't Amy understand that the harder she pushes, the faster he'll run? Dating a woman who lives 1,600 miles away—no matter how gorgeous and compassionate—isn't on his radar.

Cassandra Thorenson wants nothing to do with a man who works with money and contributes to corporate greed. Dating a Wall Street broker—no matter how handsome and funny—is the last thing she needs.

Surely, the Almighty must have a better plan.

When these two meet during a TeamWork mini-reunion in Houston over Valentine's Day weekend, Mitch and Cassie discover they have a lot more in common than they'd ever imagined. Their plan to resist one another quickly derails and then an unexpected event sends them all reeling.

Let the sparks and the tempers fly!

Enchantment
The Lewis Legacy Series, Book 6

Sam and Lexa Lewis and their TeamWork Missions volunteers are together again! A two-week mission brings them to New Mexico—the Land of Enchantment—as they work on a church building alongside their new friends in the One Nation under God congregation of Native American Christians. Outside forces, both unseen and overt, impede and threaten their efforts. But with faith to guide them, and the strong bonds of friendship to sustain them, the crew faces the challenges together as they persevere for the Lord's glory.

Eliot Marchand hopes the mission in Albuquerque will finally give him the opportunity to pursue a relationship with the beautiful Marta Holcomb. With his dangerous assignments around the globe, and little time to spend with her, is a relationship worth the risk to both their hearts?

Successful business owner Dean Costas wants to get to know the lovely Sheila Morris better, but his court-appointed charge, Felipe Hernandez, might cause trouble after he takes a liking to Sheila's pretty 14-year-old daughter, Angelina. Will Dean have time to romance the shy widow or will they need to focus their energies on chaperoning the teenagers?

Bringing together every couple and familiar characters from the previous books in The Lewis Legacy Series—including the TeamWork children—*Enchantment* will sweep you away! Love is in the air, so join the fun with the crew for Albuquerque's International Hot Air Balloon Fiesta, a one-of-a-kind TeamWork Talent Show, revelations and updates in the lives of the close-knit crew, the introduction of one new TeamWork volunteer, and even a surprise visit from two beloved characters.

Enchantment. Visit with old friends, make new ones, and fall in love all over again!

Prelude
Prequel, The Lewis Legacy Series

The Beginning of the Lewis Family Legacy

What's a guy to do when he comes home to stay and the girl he wants can't wait to leave town?

On April 24, 1962, U.S. Air Force Captain Samuel J. Lewis returns home to small Rockbridge, Texas. Six years older, Sam is the boy who moved four houses down when Sarah Jordan was ten. A teenager who nicknamed her Tomboy and teased her like an older brother. That boy is now a handsome military man who makes her heart race, but what does she know of love or life?

After his years away, Sam finds himself drawn to Sarah. The sassy, funny girl he used to tease has grown up into a beautiful charmer with wit and intelligence who challenges him like no other woman. Sarah's frequent reminders that she's leaving Rockbridge to attend nursing school, along with her encouragement to date other girls in town, unsettle him.

During the eventful summer of 1962, their friendship grows deeper and blossoms into love. Sam knows he can't hold Sarah back from achieving her dreams. When an unexpected financial gift gives her the needed funds to enter nursing school, they face saying good-bye earlier than expected. Are Sam and Sarah destined to be together or go their separate ways?

The exciting prequel to the popular contemporary Christian romance series, The Lewis Legacy Series, Prelude is the love story of Samuel J. Lewis and Sarah Jordan, parents to the core character of the series. Prelude lends insights into the Lewis family history in this heartfelt story of family, friendship, and love. A story of never letting go of our dreams, and how faith, sacrifice, and trusting our lives to the Lord's guidance will always triumph over our human fears and temptations.